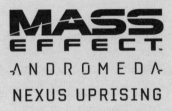

MASS EFFECT

ANDROMEDA

NEXUS UPRISING

FORTHCOMING FROM TITAN BOOKS

MASS EFFECT ANDROMEDA

Annihilation
by Catherynne M. Valente

Initiation
by N. K. Jemisin

NEXUS UPRISING

JASON M. HOUGH AND K. C. ALEXANDER

TITAN BOOKS

MASS EFFECT ANDROMEDA: NEXUS UPRISING
Print edition ISBN: 9781785651564
E-book edition ISBN: 9781785651571

Published by Titan Books
A division of Titan Publishing Group Ltd
144 Southwark Street, London SE1 0UP

First edition: March 2017
10 9 8 7 6 5 4 3 2 1

Editorial Consultants: Chris Bain, Mac Walters, John Dombrow

A CIP catalogue record for this title is available
from the British Library.

Printed and bound in the United States.

Did you enjoy this book?
We love to hear from our readers.
Please email us at readerfeedback@titanemail.com or write
to us at Reader Feedback at the above address.

TITANBOOKS.COM

NEXUS UPRISING

PROLOGUE

Even the worst hangover of her life couldn't keep the smile from Sloane Kelly's face.

She stood, hands clasped behind her back in a posture expected of a security director, on a ceremonial platform erected inside one of the Nexus's many docking bays.

Up until yesterday, the bay had been full of ships, each bustling with people and equipment, workers and staff. As the last-minute preparations were made, Sloane held one last briefing with her security officers, drilling down the procedures they'd all prepped for until she was confident they could enact them in their sleep.

An unnecessary test, Sloane knew. She'd worked damn hard to ensure her people were up to the ironclad standards of the Initiative, and they didn't disappoint. By the time the last box had been ticked and the massive space station had been declared ready for launch, her teams were as rock solid as she'd ever hoped for.

Years of planning. Hours upon months upon years of work. Hundreds of thousands of applications, and the manpower needed to sort them all. Sloane had never seen the like, and all that focus and drive had been poured into one thing—the Nexus. Smaller than the Citadel, but more advanced and streamlined than anyone had ever thought possible. Even half-built, its corridors and wards folded down and locked in for launch, the gleaming station drew every eye. Once they arrived in Andromeda, construction would begin again, turning all the stripped-down parts of the Nexus into flourishing districts and functional docks.

But before all that, the Andromeda Initiative had to get underway. So here she was, standing on this platform with a smile she couldn't shake—and a hangover throbbing behind her forehead. The pain of that indulgence was real enough. This wasn't some kind of dream.

This was a goddamn miracle.

And she was its Security Director. Standing here with only one ship in the bay. The cavernous interior caused an enormous feedback echo she wasn't used to, turning whispers into shouts and words into a distorted wave. As soon as everyone had said their goodbyes, the *Hyperion* would leave, carrying with it the human Pathfinder and his crew.

Jien Garson, founder of the Andromeda Initiative and awe-inspiring in her own right, stood a step in front of Sloane. She hugged Alec Ryder as if they were old friends, as she had with the other Pathfinders just before their ships had gone. Side by side with Ryder, Garson looked laughably diminutive, with the top of her head just barely reaching the man's shoulder. Even Sloane stood taller—though that did nothing to alter Garson's larger-than-life presence.

The two separated slightly, still clasping each other's arms, and exchanged final good wishes.

Sloane couldn't hear them clearly over the echoes, but she could read their faces. Garson, all hope and excitement. Ryder less so, but that was just his way. She'd never taken his aloofness to heart.

Funny to see them now, acting so professional and

diplomatic. All business, unlike the previous night's farewell party. Thousands of pioneers, plus twice as many more of their friends and family, had all gathered for one final hurrah before the mission began. The last night of 2185 AD. For those joining the Andromeda Initiative, it was the last night they would spend in the Milky Way.

By the time the Nexus arrived at its destination, all this—these people, their families, and all the problems in this galaxy—would be six hundred years in the past. Millions of light years in their wake.

Wild, when she really thought of it. Jarring, and a little frightening. Not that Sloane was *scared*. She shifted her weight foot to foot, caught herself and firmed her stance. Not scared, more like…

Anxious.

A new galaxy. A new start, for them and for her. And as Security Director, Sloane would have far more influence than the grunt she used to be. Born too late to solve anything, strung out too far by old men in uniforms slinging around old grudges. And that was just the human side of it.

This time, she thought, *things will be different.* Decisions would be made *better*.

No more battle lines drawn between species. No more old vendettas, greedy piracy, no more Skyllian Blitzes. This time, they had a chance to do things right, starting with a station full of handpicked pioneers eager for the same dream.

Sloane wasn't alone. All of the pioneers had signed up with a hope for something different. Something better. Everybody locked it down behind a veneer of pride, dedication to work, or just raw enthusiasm, but Sloane knew.

Leave it to a farewell celebration to crack that shit wide open.

Everyone had wanted a party that would never be forgotten. They got that much. Well, except for those euphoric moments that this party, like all great parties, had claimed as tribute. Sloane resisted the urge to rub her pounding temples. It wasn't very professional to be nursing a hangover the day of the launch.

Not that I'm the only one.

Jien Garson put up a good front, but if she wasn't hiding a pounding headache and burning gut, Sloane would eat her badge. Still, the woman was hard to read. She finally released Ryder's arms and took her place beside him, not a shred of green around her proverbial gills. As she looked at the gathered leadership of the Nexus, all standing in a line beside Sloane, the overhead lights gilded her high cheekbones and tawny skin in shades of sheer glee. No sign of headache or exhaustion, not even a nauseous damper to the sharp gleam of intelligence in her straightforward gaze.

There was so much more to the woman than met the eye. More than Sloane had initially credited her for. Boy, was that a mistake. Whatever else the Council said, whatever else the private investors said, the Andromeda Initiative was *her* mission more than anyone else's. Garson had proposed the idea and rammed it through mountains of resistance and red tape by sheer force of will. She'd even managed to convince Alec Ryder to join as the humans' Pathfinder—no small feat, given his widely known obsessions to his own array of mysterious projects. By all accounts, Ryder had been a damn good asset before he'd lost his wife, leaving him on his own to raise two kids and whatever demons he carried over it.

Sloane had overheard committee members taking bets on whether he'd sign up or not. His N7 designation carried a hell of a lot of weight, but so did he. A few meetings with him told Sloane he wasn't a man to be taken lightly. Given that Ryder now stood beside Garson—with something resembling eagerness, even—Sloane figured a few people were starting the journey a bit less rich than when it all started. Then again, she'd also heard his kids had joined the program. That had probably been enough to goad the man into the role. Or maybe the kids had. Who knew?

Kids or not, she had a suspicion Ryder wasn't going to be as easy to work with as maybe the committees hoped. She didn't have to be a mind reader to know he was impatient. All this ceremony probably grated. "Let's get this over with," he was often heard to say. "So the real work can start."

Always more real work.

"Well," he said, dusting off his hands and *right* on cue, "it's time to go. So the real work can start."

Sloane's smirk earned her a quizzical stare—she wasn't even sure he registered her as anything more than another body, to be honest—and a nod. She nodded back.

As if remembering the same courtesy, he gave the rest of the staff the same nod. "Godspeed to us all."

Garson's grin was full and unfettered. "See you on the other side."

To Sloane's surprise, Ryder's impatience made room for a brief chuckle.

Whatever he found funny, they didn't dwell. Another few minutes of farewells and then it was over. Ryder boarded the last shuttle, which quickly departed without further fanfare. He had his own job in the Initiative, and the *Hyperion* would depart soon after the Nexus.

The plan was as simple as they could all make it: The Nexus arrives in Andromeda first and completes its final stages of construction, unfolding like an origami surprise from its compact travel form. The Pathfinders would arrive soon after, guiding their arks to dock with the central station. Once up and running, it would serve as a central hub of logistics and government in the colonization of the new galaxy—the Citadel, as it were, of Andromeda.

Only better.

Garson didn't like it when people called the Nexus that. Sloane understood why. The Citadel carried a lot of baggage for a lot of people, humans or otherwise. Between the politics, the Council's efforts at out-maneuvering each other—or, collectively, the krogan—and all the bullshit about humans being "too young for the responsibility"…

Sloane shook her head, as if she could shake the irritation out. The list was long, and the death toll attributed to the backlog was even longer.

The Nexus would be everything the Citadel had failed in.

She watched as the hangar doors clanged shut behind Ryder's shuttle, and a thrill of excitement coursed through her, leaving goosebumps in its wake.

This was it. The final gateway outside the Nexus, at least for a long, long time. Sloane couldn't look away. They all stood in place, watched as the narrow beam of light from the shuttle's thrusters got thinner and thinner. Until the doors sealed shut with a final, poignant *clang*.

Sloane blinked. Looked around furtively, unwilling to be the one to break the silence left behind.

Garson had no such compunction. "Now we rest," she declared, cheerfully brisk and deliberately nonchalant. As if she knew what Sloane was feeling. What they all felt. "I'm actually looking forward to this part."

"You are?"

"Why not?" She stretched. "A little sleep, and then we're there. I don't know about you," she added, laughing, "but I think we've earned a nap."

Several of her staff chuckled politely. The others gave knowing, happy nods. They were really going. Really getting it done. "The Nexus," an announcer trilled over the system-wide comms, "is prepared for final inspection. All personnel to your designated stasis pods."

Garson held up a finger, pointing up at nothing as the echoes rebounded. Most came from the sudden rise of chatter, of giddy laughter and nervous exhales. "Hear that?" Her dark brown eyes sparkled. "Let's get to where we need to be!"

Sloane took a deep, steadying breath.

"Repeat," came the voice, "all personnel to your designated stasis chambers. Launch will commence shortly."

"To a new world," Sloane muttered. To herself, really, but Garson slid her a sideways glance full of amusement.

"To a better galaxy," the woman corrected.

Yeah. Okay. Sloane liked that one, too.

‌‍‎‏

Sloane walked with the party of the core leadership as they finished one last ceremonial review of the vessel. Everything was as it should be, and she felt enormous pride at this culmination of all the hard work they'd already done.

She'd known it going in, but every time she paced the ship, she thought it again. The Nexus was a freaking marvel. Part ark ship, part space station, the construct was second only to the Citadel in scope and ambition. Yet unlike its spiritual progenitor, this place had been built by *them*. For them.

For a new future.

Humans, salarians, asari, turians. The only non-Council species on board the Nexus were the krogan, and the Nakmor clan had signed on under the contract of working for it. Even so, equals or not, they'd all come together, driven by Jien Garson's vision. And they'd done it. The Nexus was almost ready to go.

Sloane stood back as the leadership made their way to the designated cryostasis pods. Of them all, she only had more than a passing relationship with two: Garson herself, and Matriarch Nuara, who served as one hell of an advisor on the team. Whatever else the asari did, Sloane appreciated having the long-lived Matriarch on board.

If they were going to make a successful run at this, they'd need the asari's wisdom. And, Sloane noted with an inward laugh, her biotics. Only a fraction of the Nexus's passengers and personnel possessed the ability, and much of that came from the asari themselves. Having Nuara made a lot of them feel better, too. Remnants of speciesism the Nexus's journey was designed to quell.

They were all in this together, now. Nuara and Garson clasped hands, friendship clear between them, and parted with encouraging farewells.

Sloane watched them carefully, mindful of the

launching procedure. Their pods had to seal correctly, with no abnormalities in final readings. They and the other first-tier leaders would be first to wake in Andromeda. The hierarchy was set, and it began with top-tier staff—a trained and prepared doctor among them. Top medical would follow, then Sloane would wake soon after. Then the colonization effort would begin in earnest.

A short nap, huh? Sloane shook her head, bemused by the brevity of the concept. Six hundred years was a bit more than a nap. Not that they'd feel it.

She waited while the others, personally escorted to their stasis pods, exchanged farewells and encouragement. She'd oversee the sealing of this chamber before returning to hers, where part of her team was already fast asleep.

Soon enough, Sloane found herself alone with Garson. As if the woman felt like she had to, she waited and watched with Sloane until every pod was sealed and blinking all the right colors for successful stasis.

Sloane wasn't sure what to say.

Garson had no such problem. "Did you enjoy my speech last night?" she asked brightly.

"Er…" When the woman's smile turned wry, Sloane grinned sheepishly. "I didn't hear it. I was…" She trailed off, trying to frame an excuse that was honest, but didn't make herself out to be a total asshole. *Not my thing* probably wasn't it.

"It's alright, Director Kelly." She tapped her nose with a knowing finger, dark eyes openly laughing up at Sloane. "It was a very busy night."

"Busy," Sloane repeated. And if Garson believed that, Sloane was a naked quarian. "Yes, exactly. Lots to prep. Briefings and things."

"Well." She stepped into her own waiting pod, her tone amused. "If you want to listen to it, there is a recording in the core. Just in case people needed some last-minute inspiration."

Sloane shrugged, but knew she would. "Everyone *did* say they really liked it," she admitted. "I guess I should know what my team's been raving about."

"Good. Do that." Another smile, this one more her signature power move. Clean, bright, and not a thing weak about it. Or her. Garson hadn't gotten this far by being a pushover.

Sloane respected that.

Garson lay back, adjusting the folds of her uniform. Like maybe she'd get uncomfortable? Sloane wasn't sure how it'd all work, but she figured a centuries-old wedgie would be among the worst of their problems.

She may have dodged most of the science meetings, but she'd seen Garson's meticulously noted plans, cleverly rewritten so even the laymen among the Nexus crews could get it. The data had long since come back. There were habitable planets, welcoming space, lots to explore, to settle, to grow.

They were pioneers, the first to travel to another galaxy, and by whatever gods among them, they'd get it done.

Every last one of them believed that. Sloane did, too.

A wrinkled stasis uniform wasn't really on her list of priorities. But hey, whatever floated Garson's pre-launch freighter was fine with Sloane.

Garson folded her arms over her chest, drawing Sloane's attention back to the woman nestled inside the comfortably detailed interior. "The other side," she murmured, as if more to herself than to Sloane.

"Andromeda." Then, meeting Sloane's gaze, she asked, "What do you hope to find there, Director?"

She blinked. "Hmm... I haven't much thought of it." An outright lie, and at Garson's crestfallen look, Sloane added wryly, "How about a cure for the common hangover?"

That earned another bout of laughter, bright and genuine. "We can only hope," Garson said, still chuckling, and gave Sloane the nod. *That* nod. The one that said the time for talk was over.

Sloane oversaw the closure of the pod. She smiled at the leader of the Initiative through the small porthole, patted the pod twice in old habit, and waited until the indicators all showed cryogenic success and stability.

"The other side," Sloane echoed—and the advent of *her* real work.

Rubbing the lingering effects of the previous evening from her temples, she began her own final inspection. For whatever reason known to whoever designed the procedure, Director Kelly had wound up with the strange honor of being the last awake.

It was up to her to declare the station safe to fly. *A ceremonial gesture*, she reminded herself, but that little excited portion of her brain also reminded her that she wielded the power to stop it all. If anything at all was amiss, she could put the whole thing on lockdown.

That meant something, didn't it?

"Not that anything *could* go wrong," she said aloud as she walked the long, echoing corridors. The place was built by the top minds in the whole galaxy. Everything down to the last wire was the end product of countless hours of genius. If something went wrong now, it'd have to be an act of some pissed-off god.

Sloane didn't believe in gods. Or in dodging

procedure. Not when it was this big, the stakes this high. The final walk was one of the few items on the departure checklist at which she hadn't rolled her eyes.

In truth she'd been looking forward to this ever since the plan had been made. A few hours of blissful silence and solitude to roam the halls of the station—*her* station. The place she'd sworn to protect and shepherd on its great mission. The place for which she'd given up her life in the Milky Way.

Granted she hadn't left much behind. Not really. No family, no responsibilities beyond that which she'd earned with the Alliance. There were pioneers who had given up much, much more. When it really came down to it, Sloane was only really leaving behind baggage.

A galaxy's worth of it. Old scars. Enemies made across old battle lines, and subsequent grudges lobbed diplomatically across political tables. Idiot officers far more concerned about the shine on the medals earned on the back of dead soldiers…

The old, familiar anger welled in the back of Sloane's mind. She gritted her teeth and shook her head again, which mostly served to set her hangover back into swing.

Enough was enough. She'd landed the best job in the entire galaxy—soon to be two galaxies. She had the chance to make it right, and right *now*. Though even that was jumping ahead. First, the journey. Then the time for change. Which sounded a hell of a lot better to her than the poor suckers left tangled in the Milky Way's red tape.

Sloane went through her checklist with unwavering attention to detail. She didn't care if it took her six hours or six days, she would make damn sure every last door was closed and locked, every supply crate was properly stowed, and no nefarious "rogue elements" were hiding in the air vents.

Mostly, this meant a lot of walking. Which meant the perfect time to pull up Garson's speech on her omni-tool. The speech, much like the woman herself, had zero preamble.

"Tomorrow we make the greatest sacrifice we have ever—or will ever—make," Garson began. Bold words, and confident as hell. "At the same time, we also begin the greatest adventure of our lives."

Sloane agreed with that. The lure of the unknown wasn't her drug of choice, but she appreciated the excitement.

"Many have weighed in. The gossip, the media coverage, even threats, have had more than enough to say." She spread her hands, as if she could hold the weight of all the thousands of hours of committees she'd attended. "Some claim this plan is nothing more than an attempt to flee the galaxy we helped shape, taking our *very* expensive toys—" Her eyebrows lifted.

Sloane chuckled.

"—and going somewhere else to play. Others decry our mission as the most expensive insurance policy known to any sentient species."

Sloane would've been happy to punch out this metaphorical *they*. Instead, she had to settle for muttering a terse epithet, and continued on her path. At least there was no one to hear her talking to her omni-tool.

"The message I left with the *Hyperion* is similar to the one I'm saying to you now. You are about to embark on a journey unlike anything ever attempted before. And make no mistake…"

The holographic Garson paused, looked into the

camera for a long moment. Sloane's step faltered as she watched. She felt a chill run up her spine, crawl across her scalp. In that deliberate pause it felt as if Jien Garson stared right at her.

Focused on her. *Really* saw her.

Her and the thousands of pioneers like her.

"This *is* a one-way trip. What all those politicians, naysayers and threats don't understand is that we are here, together, because we believe in something they don't. We put our effort and our faith into something those people can't imagine, can't even begin to understand. In other words, *they*," Garson said flatly, "are wrong."

Sloane nodded. Firmly. *Hell to the yes.*

"The circumstances that have led to the creation of this magnificent station are vast and varied, that much is true. We all know some of these reasons." But with this, Garson smiled faintly. Reassuring or rueful, Sloane couldn't tell. "None of us can know them all, not even me. Yet they are only part of the equation. You and I," she said, gesturing to Sloane—to the audience, "are the other part."

Sloane found herself nodding again. Silently shouting another *hell yes*! She was another part. A big part. Sloane had plans. Ideas. And Garson had already made it clear she liked that. A new way for a new hope, right?

"Each and every one of us has our own reasons for volunteering to go," she continued, "and those too are legion. Some of us feel a sense of duty. Some of us do indeed fear what the future has in store for the Milky Way. We flee our past, we seek a future. We wish to begin anew. We crave the unexplored wonders that no doubt will reshape all that we know." Garson smiled, encouraging. Warm. "All equally valid, in my estimation—but that's not important here. What *is* important as we depart, what I want to be sure you all know as you prepare to cross this ocean of time and space, is this…" She held her breath a moment.

Sloane couldn't help but admire the woman's skill, especially compared to her own. Sloane's speeches tended to be short and to the point. Things like *get it done* or *put them down*. Things you could say fast and on the ground.

But the camera loved Jien Garson. Her force of will, her *trust*, radiated out through every pore. "None of those reasons," Garson said plainly, direct and without so much as a shred of humility, "matter anymore. *Not for us.* What matters now, for you and me, is what we do when we arrive. Who we become, and how we carry ourselves in Andromeda."

Sloane halted as she stared at the image. Yes. *Yes!* Garson got it. More than she'd ever hoped, the Initiative leader *got it.*

"We journey in one of the most incredible marvels our species have ever created," the founder reminded them, "built in a spirit of a cooperation that is without precedence in our galactic history. We carry with us, collectively, centuries of culture, millennia of government, beliefs, of languages and art, incredible knowledge, and incredible sciences. Hard-won things, the result of endless work, unfathomable suffering and, most importantly, the efforts of countless billions of sentient beings over millennia and across dozens of worlds.

"We carry all these things like the honed tools of an artist, to our great empty canvas. To Andromeda." Garson's hands came together. "We go," she said intently, "to paint our masterpiece."

Sloane leaned against the wall, staggered by the power of the woman's words. Just *words*, and yet Sloane knew without a shred of doubt that if Garson commanded her to stride into hell, Sloane would. In a heartbeat. Because that was Garson's strength, she thought.

People. Knowing them. What moved them.

What they hoped for.

Garson allowed a moment, then once again fixed her deep, knowing gaze straight ahead. "So I say to you now what Pathfinder Alec Ryder just said to me." Her smile, Sloane thought, could power Ilium. Another oratory skill Sloane had never bothered with. Why should she, when people like Garson had that on lockdown?

"I will see you all on the other side." A pause, and the light caught the high shape of her cheekbones as her grin deepened. "When the real work can begin."

The recording ended. Silence descended in its wake, heavy as fog and still as ice. It was cold in the halls, and would be for another six hundred years. But Sloane? She didn't feel the cold.

She'd been a soldier for a long time—her whole life, really. She'd witnessed speeches made to celebrate victories, others intoned to condemn atrocities. War had been her path for so long, the life of a soldier her only way, that she'd forgotten what a speech about hope could do to the brain. A new start, huh?

Sloane shook her head, laughed aloud. It rolled back at her from a thousand echoes in the barren corridor. "Andromeda," she said aloud, trying the word out. *Andromeda*, the echoes whispered back.

The other side.

She stood there, leaning against one bulkhead out of a million, not even really sure exactly where she was, and took that moment to *feel* the ship. Listened to it breathe in its own mechanical way. The whirr of systems engaged and ready, the constant dry whisper of circulated air. That one would stop soon enough—there was no need to waste the power when nobody needed the air.

Next, Sloane would sleep. For hundreds of years. Across that eternity of cold nothingness, the Nexus would reach its destination guided by meticulous programming.

Sloane pushed away from the bulkhead and continued her rounds. She passed through the hydroponics farm, the machine shops and the archives, the sterile places that would become the great plazas once the station unfolded into place. Over there would be the cultural offices, and her own security headquarters—the best, she thought with fierce determination, there ever was.

She made sure everything was where it should be, and as it turned out, everything was. It was perfect.

The Nexus was perfect.

Sloane checked a box, and the station lit its engines and set off. Simple as that. So smooth, she barely felt anything. She grinned, pleased with the ease of it all, and returned to crew storage to shed her omni-tool, stow her gear, and prep for her own cryo. Soon enough, she returned to cryostasis chamber 441. The small room was one among countless others on the Nexus, each identical to the last. Eight pods, a surgical couch for post-revival certification, terminals, and little else.

This was it. The final step.

Sloane lowered herself into her stasis pod, and

found herself adjusting her uniform. The same way Garson had. With a sudden snort, she gave up and pulled the hatch closed.

"Cryostasis procedures logged," a mechanized voice said. "Rest well, pioneer."

Naptime, huh? Smiling, Sloane closed her eyes.

Within minutes, she—and everyone aboard—slept.

CHAPTER ONE

Thawing from stasis was meant to take time. A gentle process. Warmth gradually applied to cells dormant for centuries, neurons carefully coaxed back into firing.

Synthetic fluids mixed with precise amounts of the sleeper's blood, a ratio changing by the smallest of fractions over several days until, finally, the body crossed a threshold, becoming whole again. Vitals checked, and then, only then, would the final mixture of drugs be injected under expert supervision.

Or something like that. Sloane Kelly didn't really remember the specifics. How much time, when the process was supposed to begin—these were things left up to the techs who built the stasis pods. They knew better.

At least they were supposed to.

Whatever the instructions had been, Sloane was damn sure that abruptly launching from deep stasis into six shades of hell wasn't how it was supposed to work.

Alarms.

Lights.

Everything heaved. A deafening noise, an aggressive shriek like rending metal, assaulted her ears, physically squeezed her entire body.

She opened her eyes.

Disjointed wires cast sparks over the pod's viewport, forcing her eyelids closed again as her spinning brain popped aftershocks across them. Everything crashed together in a disjointed cacophony of light and thunder and motion and *adrenaline*. The small pod whirled around her, momentum shifted side to nauseating side as she flattened both hands on the pane, elbowed out in reflex and hit solid metal.

Pain ricocheted up her arm and helped jerk her foggy brain back into alignment. *Out.* She needed *out.* Her pod was failing. Torn free of its moorings maybe, rolling around in the chamber. Had to be. The air stung her nose and lungs, the wrong mixture and far too warm. It stank of chemicals and old sweat.

She slammed a tingling foot against the front of the stasis pod.

"Failsafe," she shouted into the cramped space, as if the word might crawl back in time and remind the engineers of this stupid metal coffin to include an eject latch.

As if on cue, a calm mechanized tone sounded, at odds with the world into which she'd awoken. The pane sealing her within protective transport unlocked with a hiss of air almost as loud as the klaxons that shrieked through the open seam. She felt the breath being sucked from her lungs, replaced by the cold bite and stale taste of the outside.

Then a new smell. *Ash.*

Double vision slowly gelled into horrifying truth: *smoke.* That was smoke pouring in from the outside. Fire flickered somewhere to her left.

Shit. It's not just me. Which means—

Slam-dropped out of stasis meant the rest of her body needed time to remember how to function. Her brain couldn't process it all. Every cell screamed to fight, to respond to the skull-rattling alarms of the Nexus under fire, but the adrenaline surge to her limbs only made her twitch violently as feeling came back into them.

Sloane gasped for breath, pounded at the viewport. Red lights flashed.

The Nexus *is under attack.* No other explanation made sense. The thought finally pushed through her overwhelmed mind. Served to focus her.

That was the only reason she'd be woken up in this manner from the centuries-spanning sleep the Nexus had been programmed to take. Or maybe it had only been a few years. Hell, it could have been hours. No way to know, not yet.

As head of security for thousands of pioneers, Security Director of the goddamn Nexus itself, she needed to pull herself together and *find out*.

Her body got the message. It just didn't react very well to the command. Sloane fell out of the stasis pod before it had completely opened, her limbs a twitching mass of hypersensitive pins and needles. Her lungs expanded, took in air laced with sparks and smoke.

It seared all the way down.

Sloane coughed. Her eyes burned, streaming already from ash and the acrid sting of burning chemicals, but she didn't have the time to waste choking on it. She staggered to her feet, forced her leaden body to move.

It may have felt claustrophobic in the small pod, but it was a thousand times worse out here. Half of the room remained hidden in shadow, dimly lit up by emergency lights that winked and flickered. *Emergency lights aren't supposed to do that.*

Fire and smoke roiled amid shattered debris.

Sloane cursed, half staggering toward and half falling against the stasis chamber beside hers. The interior was miraculously clear, which left plenty of room for a hardened turian fist to pound against it in mirrored panic. Kandros, one of her best officers.

"Hang on!" Sloane shouted, her voice guttural from smoke. She slapped the viewing pane twice, and furious pounding from inside ceased. A muted voice barely broke through the barrier, but she got enough to catch the drift.

Hurry up.

Possibly with more profanity.

These pods were supposed to be opened by timer, not manually. At least not by her. Sloane didn't have the first clue about how to operate this tech, but she didn't have much choice here. The closest terminal lay somewhere beyond the shower of sparks, and based on the backlit wreckage, she didn't think it'd be much help, anyhow.

She didn't have her omni-tool, either. She'd stored it, as per procedure. Personal belongings weren't supposed to be returned to their owners until revival had been certified and they'd been briefed by their supervisors.

"Damn it," she hissed through clenched teeth. She pushed herself fully upright, casting around her for something, *anything* that would get this oversized coffin open.

The fires painted the chamber in hellish orange, black, and gold. Through the stinging smoke, silhouettes struggled—personnel caught inside pods and trying frantically to get out. Some of the pods had already cracked, but whether their occupants had survived, Sloane couldn't tell.

Every second mattered.

Which meant screw the soft touch.

Sloane sprinted to a pile of bent metal bars and shattered bits of things she didn't recognize. Soot and oily residue coated most of it, but some had been torn free by pure shearing force. Something big had hit them.

As sweat poured in rivulets down her face, she grabbed a heavy girder and dragged it back to the lifepod.

"Hang on," she croaked again, jamming the shattered, sheared end under the opening seam. Somewhere behind her, someone screamed. Raw. Brutal. She flinched, even as she threw her weight against the improvised pry bar.

The metal groaned.

Hairline fissures spread like frost across the viewport, but it didn't budge.

"Damn it, *come on*," she snarled, curling her bare hands around the scarred metal and shoving with everything she had.

From inside the pod, three-fingered claw-tipped hands splayed against the dusted pane. Another unintelligible shout, but Sloane got the idea. *Amazing*, she reflected in a grimly amused little corner of her mind, *what an emergency can do for language barriers.*

"Now," she shouted, for her own sake if nothing else. She threw everything against the bar just as the turian forced his weight up against the lid.

When the seal cracked, it did so suddenly, sending Sloane to her knees amid the debris and forcing the lid to crack in half. The broken end whirled out into the chaos as Kandros all but fell out of the pod and landed beside her in a clatter of narrow limbs. He gasped for breath, looking rattled but no worse than she felt, at least.

No real improvement, she'd bet.

"No time for celebration," she said to him, her

voice barely more than a croak. Sloane grabbed the edge of the broken pod and gestured with the bar. "Save who you can." It was an order, flat and simple. Tenderness wasn't her way. The security team knew that, were used to it.

Smoke whirled as Kandros managed, "Yes, ma'am," and staggered to his feet. Like Sloane, all he had going for him was the Nexus uniform. Protective and comfortable for a centuries-long nap, but not much good against serious threats.

By unspoken agreement they took opposite sides.

Every step filled Sloane with more and more concern. Had they been attacked? Boarded? Had they even made it out of the galaxy?

Had Cerberus attacked them? Pirates?

And if so, what had happened to their Milky Way escort?

Desperate as that thought was, she had to put it aside for now.

She took her impromptu can-opener to every pod in sight, working them over with furious intensity. Metal groaned, accompanied by the gasps of surprise, of effort, the swearing and questions she couldn't take the time to answer.

"Get 'em out first," she told Talini, one of her more experienced officers. The asari stumbled away, swaying wildly on still-numb feet.

Save who you can.

It became a silent mantra, a thing Sloane said to herself with every face pulled from crackling wreckage. Beyond the small chamber, a larger one held civilians and other random staff. Whether or not it was safe, she couldn't tell. Everything was chaos. Across the way, sparks rained down on the asari as she helped a hobbling human away from the worst, two personnel following. One nursed an arm bent at an unnatural angle.

Sloane couldn't keep track of it all. Trusting her team, she focused on the pods she could reach. Fourteen stasis pods gave way under her efforts in as many minutes.

Only eight occupants crawled out.

She let the lid close on the mangled remains of Cillian, one of her own unit. Whatever had taken out the Nexus like this, it'd thrown a massive energy surge back into the systems. Burst wires and smoking, charred power converters were everywhere. Many of the stasis pods had fried the poor souls inside of them.

Fury jammed a pounding tic in Sloane's jaw. Soot-smeared, hands blistered from searing metal; none of it even came close to the horror and rage welling inside her. She clambered over Cillian's grim coffin to reach whoever else she could, choking on the unfairness— the fucking tragedy of it all.

There weren't many left. Kandros passed her with a slumped human braced against his shoulder. A grim-faced salarian she didn't recognize shepherded two terrified teenagers away from the chaos.

A group of frightened civilians huddled away from the billowing smoke, covering their mouths, noses and breathing orifices with whatever they could. Hands, arms. Strips of their uniforms.

Enough. She shifted focus, eyes scanning ruined walls obscured by smoke, looking for the switch she needed. Manual fire-suppression switch. She saw it, saw the occasional burst of sparks trickling out like water from behind the panel, but below it, in a cabinet she'd forgotten they'd put here, a fire extinguisher sat gleaming behind tinted glass.

Sloane rushed to it, kicked the glass hard only to remember, the hard way, that her usual protective boots weren't part of the cryostasis uniform. Her toe exploded in pain even as the quick-shatter covering broke into a clattering mess on the floor.

Broken toes? *At least one. Great. Just great.* Sloane ignored the pain, wrenched the extinguisher free, and set to work.

A short blast to each flame. The compressed mixture roiled out and over the fires and sparks, and the room dimmed more and more each time, but that was okay. She could live with that. All around her people coughed, cried out. Someone screamed. Another crashed to hands and knees, vomiting.

Yet with each blast from the extinguisher, Sloane heard less pain. The sounds became those of worry, of people who could assist the ones who'd taken the worst of it. Each little shift in tone gave her that much more resolve.

Somehow, amid the groaning chaos of straining metal and crackling fire, they all convened in roughly the same place. Sloane tossed her spent extinguisher aside.

"Everybody stay together," she ordered. She forced the malfunctioning doors open, shoving her shoulder against the creaking panel until it slid wide enough to let everyone through. When the last staggering survivor passed, she let the door slam closed behind her.

Sweat plastered her hair and uniform to her skin, soot made her eyes sting. Body aching, she slumped against the door. A quick catalog confirmed her injuries—broken, throbbing toe, minor burns, bruises and scrapes—but nothing that would impede her progress. Good. She shoved herself off and surveyed the antechamber. It was quieter, as if the hell on the other side of the door had been just a bad dream.

Beyond the next door lay the way out. And likely more danger.

As she took in the char-smeared, horrified faces around her, she realized less than half had made it. So many pods.

But there was nothing they could do about it. Nothing Sloane could do except get the survivors somewhere safe and lock this shit down.

They'd have to mourn later.

Kandros dragged the torn sleeve of his uniform under his chin, leaning on his improvised lifepod hacker. The metal bar had seen better days. So had the turian. "So," he said, pitching his voice over the shrill alarms. "What happened?"

The group looked at each other, then at Sloane.

She wished she had answers.

"Don't know," she said, but that wouldn't fix anything, so she jerked a thumb toward the exit. "Let's find the hell out."

"Yeah." The turian pulled the bar up onto his shoulder. "I figured you'd say that."

CHAPTER TWO

The hall outside had fared worse.

A bundle of severed wires hung from a bent ceiling panel, the tips spitting blue-white sparks that left black pockmarks on the floor. Smoke flowed along the ceiling, growing thicker, pushing downward. As far as Sloane could see, the damage ran the length of the corridor.

"Ventilation's offline," Sloane noted. She struggled for matter-of-fact, barely managed curt. "Fire suppression, too. My guess is comms took a hit."

"Thorough," Kandros noted.

They exchanged a look. She could see her own assessment reflected in her officer's eyes. The damage extended well beyond their sleep chamber, which meant one of two things: either a very bad accident, or an attack. Perhaps even from within.

The sheer panic *that* would cause…

"Here's what we're going to do," Sloane said, pitching it louder so they could all hear. "Kandros, take these people with you. Somewhere safe."

"Like where?"

Sloane considered it, then lowered her voice. "Colonial Affairs. Not their offices, but the hangar where they keep the shuttles. At least you'll be ready to bug out if it comes to that, and if not, the life-support systems on those ships might be more stable."

"Good call. Where will you be?"

Sloane glanced to their right, in the direction of Operations. "I'll be trying to figure out what happened. Whatever's going on here, it's big. Stay safe, hear me?" She eyed his hands, where a pistol should have been. Not that she had anything better to offer. They both claimed bent, battered pipes and metal beams. *Just great*.

He narrowed his eyes, well aware of her thoughts, and nodded briefly.

She liked that about him. Her time with turians, her friendship with one in particular, had given her a hell of a lot of insight into turian tics. Kandros appreciated that insight, and Sloane appreciated his trust.

It made for a solid team.

"I'll head for Operations," she added. "Find and stay near a comm. I'll get in touch with you somehow once I know what's going on."

"Ma'am."

One of the good ones. She knew better than most how invaluable that kind of dedication was. Sloane clapped him on the narrow width of his carapace, and was off.

She kept to the wall, ignoring the doors she passed. Each remained closed, and for the moment that was fine. It would keep any fires from spreading. She checked the status panels next to each, though. They all said the same thing. A single glowing red word: *offline*.

That bothered her as much as anything. The Nexus, engineering marvel that it was, had been designed by more committees than Sloane had thought possible. And fuck did they love *redundancy*. Each one of these panels should have three, maybe even four, links into the station-wide systems array. To be offline served only to confirm her growing fear—something either very bad or very surgical had happened here.

She needed information, and she needed it fast.

Sloane loped along the hallway to the next intersection. An emergency bulkhead door had attempted to seal it off, only to get blocked half-open, rotaries spitting sparks. A glance confirmed the blockage: a corpse, caught in between the doors as they opened, closed, caught on brutalized flesh, opened again. Closed. Repeat.

The body was burned beyond recognition, laying under a pile of debris—bits of machinery and cabling that had fallen from the ceiling. The smell made Sloane want to retch. Sweet and disgusting all at once, rancid flesh and charred bone.

But she'd done this before. Swallowing her bile, she knelt and checked the uniform, rolling the body slightly to see. Fire or maybe some chemical reaction had rendered the name tag illegible. A salarian, from the shape of the head. Hell of a way to go. Sloane let the body gently down. She stepped over it as best she could and squeezed herself through the gap.

She had to leave the poor bastard there. The door would seal without it, trapping her on this side—and who the hell knew what with her.

Heat warmed her cheek and forced her to squint. Opposite her, an open flame erupted from a pipe that had punched right through the wall tiles and been ignited by a sparking cable. The air reeked of gases her lungs weren't meant to breathe.

But flames meant oxygen, and that meant this hallway had been pressurized. It wouldn't have been that way for the long, cold flight between galaxies. So they either hadn't made it out of the Milky Way, or they had arrived in Andromeda.

There was small comfort to be found in either of

those options. At least they weren't stranded in the vast emptiness between the two.

A figure pushed through the thickening smoky haze. Sloane, weaponless, automatically dropped into a fighter's stance. Not that it would do much good against armed intruders—

The uniform pronounced him one of the station's own. The man staggered forward, sweeping one arm back and forth in front of his downcast face, trying in vain to wave away the choking fumes.

But a uniform, tattered as it was, didn't mean jack right now.

"That's far enough," Sloane barked. "Name and rank, *now*."

He stopped, shaking hands held up in instant surrender. The paler skin of his palms oozed angry fluid, raised burns criss-crossing both hands. She sympathized. But then, anything could have caused those wounds—opening searing-hot cryopods, or a little sabotage gone wrong. She needed to know which one.

That was her job. The man visibly trembled. "What's happened? Are we under attack?"

"That's what I'm trying to find out," she replied flatly. "Now who the hell are you?"

"Chen. I'm... I'm just a junior regulator," he added, but coughed violently on the heels of it.

Sloane didn't recognize the name. "What department? Medical? Please say medical."

"Sanitation."

"Perfect. Just fucking perfect." She shook her head. "Look, it's not safe out here. Go back to your stasis pod."

"N-No!" His recoil was as physical as it was visceral. "I can't!" Visible tremors coursed through the man's narrow build. "It's awful. Everyone's dead. I think. I just ran. There was fire, and—pods were just… just—"

Yeah. She got it. She reached out, caught his shoulder and ignored the crackling pain it caused her hand. "Listen," she said, steadying him. "I'm Security Director Sloane Kelly."

"Security?" His eyes, streaming in the smoke, crinkled with effort. "We're under attack, then. We must be!"

Because the alternative was so much worse.

Sloane made a face. Her mouth tasted like ash. Her throat stung. She felt like she hadn't eaten or drank anything in centuries, which might be the case. But he wasn't any better off than she was, and given the look of him, he was no saboteur. Not unless he'd cherry-bombed the operation restrooms for a laugh.

She wanted to sigh. She didn't. "I don't know what's going on, okay? I'm trying to figure it out. Show me where your stasis pod—"

"I'm not going back there. I can't." He gestured back the way he'd come. "If you want to go stare at it, be my guest, but you won't…" A sob thickened his voice. He ducked his head, swiped the back of his hands against his face. "The whole thing sealed off. I barely made it out. I don't know… I still can't…" The shoulder under her hand shook violently.

Sloane sized him up. Sanitation, huh? Her gut said he'd fold at anything uglier than a backed-up drain. "Okay. Okay. Listen, you need to make your way to the CA hangar, understand?"

"Can't I stay with you?" Pleading. Scared.

She barely held back a grim smile. He wouldn't like it. "Sure, Chen. I'm going to check your stasis room."

He reversed stance so fast, she found herself holding

air as he slipped by her. "Actually, the hangar sounds pretty good," he said quickly. "You said it's clear?"

Thought so. "Watch out for stray wires," she said instead. "Now get going. Others are gathering there, you'll be safe."

"Thanks. Thank you." A pause. He swung back her way, then back the way she'd come. Then, with a manic kind of helpless smile, added, "You be careful. Director. Ma'am." A final, wobbly gesture, then Chen stumbled off. Vaguely in the right direction.

Sloane watched him go. He'd make it. Probably. The damage looked worse her way, not his. "Careful doesn't get the work done," she muttered.

IIIIIIIIIIIIIIIIII

The janitor had not exaggerated.

She found the door first, across the hall from where it should've been attached, laying on one side. The room itself looked like a war zone. Stasis pods lay jumbled like so much garbage, and many were open. Sloane had seen a lot of death in her life, but could not keep her own hand from covering her mouth at this sight.

The bodies lay everywhere. Dozens of them. Many were burned, others had just been heaved from sleep and lay crumpled against the walls and furniture. One lay splayed under an overturned pod, only the hand and foot visible from underneath.

Everything was still, silent but for the hiss and crackle of busted tech and sparking wires.

"Anyone in here?" she called out. Not because she had any hope there would be, but because she'd never forgive herself if she didn't. But there were no replies. Not even a desperate cough.

Bodies splayed out, casualties of some big stupid

mistake or somebody else's pride... Yeah, these were images she thought she'd left behind.

Sloane turned away, battling down a growing sense of gut-wrenching dread. Adjacent to the pod chamber was a reception room. Her recollection of the Nexus's layout gradually came back to her. Cryostasis chambers were sprinkled throughout the vast ship, and bundles of them were connected to special rooms where newly awakened crew members could relax and acclimate while they waited for their superior officers to come and welcome them to wondrous Andromeda.

Meanwhile someone from medical would evaluate their health, psych would make sure they hadn't lost their marbles while asleep. A representative from Sloane's team would be on hand in case they *had* lost their marbles and, as a result, their cooperative spirit.

That was how it was supposed to go, anyway.

They'd all drilled for disaster scenarios, yet no one had imagined a total failure of... *everything*.

The room would've been nice, if not for the large support beam that had fallen right down the middle of it, smashing couches and tables beneath its weight. Sloane could picture this place, crowded with personnel milling about and talking excitedly, all buzzing with the ambitions Garson had fanned. It was a small mercy, Sloane figured, that this calamity had happened while the vast rooms, halls, plazas, and parks were still empty.

A long, shuddering groan echoed through the entire ship. Sloane frowned.

"That can't be good."

On the wall across the room, a rectangular panel caught her eye. A terminal, exposed by an open panel. The screen was on, displaying the Initiative's logo.

Sloane vaulted an upended couch and wove her way between a mess of overturned tables and chairs. Halfway there, a loud *pop* triggered the survival instinct that had seen her through too many battles to count. She dove for cover.

A shower of sparks rained from the ceiling. The room went dark, save for emergency lights along the bases of the walls, and that single glowing screen behind the open panel on the far wall.

A body lay beneath the display. An asari, sprawled and lifeless under the weight of a light fixture shaken loose in the calamity.

When nothing else exploded, Sloane eased from her precarious niche and studied the body. The asari didn't move as she approached. Didn't breathe. Nothing.

Sloane Kelly shifted her focus to the screen, telling herself now was the time to gain a sit-rep. Except the logo was gone now, replaced with that damned red word again: *offline*. Sloane wanted to scream in frustration.

Instead, she checked the body, already aware of what she'd find doing it. The woman had become *the body* in Sloane's mind.

The chaos another battlefield.

Fire. Ash. Destruction.

All of it caught up to her when she touched that still neck. This woman had sacrificed everything to come here. They all had. And for what?

Loss. Disappointment. Death.

Sloane clenched her jaw. This stranger was a friend for the simple reason that they'd shared the same goal, given up the same things.

What had the asari's final thoughts been? Fear, Sloane supposed. Anger, maybe.

Mission failed.

The other side didn't seem to be at all what they'd expected.

A single, wet cough broke the silence. Sloane's focus slammed back to the asari as her body heaved, and a trickle of fresh blood scored rivulets down her chin. Some semblance of life returned to her pale violet eyes. "M-Mayday…"

Sloane wrapped an arm under her shoulders, kept her from thrashing. "You're going to be okay. We may be under attack, so save your energy and—"

"I'm not," the woman wheezed, pink foam frothing at her lips, "dead… soon e-enough." Her faded eyes rolled toward the offline terminal. "Initial…" Sloane held her as still as possible as the asari's filling lungs ground her words to rattling coughs. Gritting her teeth, the alien gripped Sloane's tunic in a bloodied fist and managed, "Not attack." Every word bubbled. "Damage is compre… hensive…."

Sloane sat hard on the floor. Tried her best to keep the woman steady. But it wasn't easy. Her mind struggled to wrap around the situation. "We hit something, then."

"No." Bloody teeth bared as the asari fought another wracking fit. "Too even. Too… *ugh*…"

"Easy," Sloane cut in, covering her hand and gripping it tight. "Stay with me. I need your intel. Sabotage?"

Somewhere in the depths of the asari's pain and struggle, humor found its way out in a graveled, burbling laugh. "You… didn't—" Blood and flecks of foam sprayed in an uneven pattern. Her eyes closed, a tear sliding down one bruised cheek. Even as she still smiled. Sloane frowned. "Physics," the woman managed. "Sensors. D-data…"

Sloane considered what to do next. She needed

answers. And leadership. "My priority now is the safety of Jien Garson. The council."

"Chamber 00," the asari said, confirming what Sloane already knew. It was a choking whisper.

This was it. Soldiers without a doctor present didn't make it off the field with symptoms like hers, and Sloane wasn't that. Her frown twisted. "Your name?"

The fist in her uniform weakened.

Nobody left forgotten. "Your name," she demanded, bending over the asari. Her uniform said only T'vaan.

It was all Sloane would get. The gurgling rasp of the asari's last breath ended in nothing—silence, stillness. The hand dropped, and didn't so much as twitch again. Sloane bowed her head for a moment, all she could afford as the station shuddered around her. Gently, she set T'vaan's—no, *the body* back onto the floor, her fist hard against the surface as she pushed herself back up to her feet.

It was a mistake to think of everyone here as friends. There were thousands of crew in those stasis pods, and some of them, a great many of them perhaps, had to have gladly left their pasts behind. Garson had said it herself: a one-way ticket.

They'd all been naïve to assume it'd be one without loss.

"Stasis chamber 00," Sloane repeated, drawing strength from the words. "Thank you."

Her injuries cracked and throbbed, burned and—in the case of that broken toe—screamed at her as she jogged across the debris-strewn chamber. But it was all nothing to the thought that drove her: what was the status of the council?

All else considered, they—*Garson*—had to have made it through alive.

Please, Sloane chanted silently, each syllable in time with her aching steps. *Please*.

||||||||||||||||||||

The halls blurred together. One darkened, damaged tunnel after another. Every stasis chamber she passed was still sealed, the state of the inhabitants unknown. She had no choice to leave them that way. Saving one room of Nexus crew members mattered little if the entire ship was at risk, and the more she saw, the more she came to believe it.

In one narrow hall a change in the light gave her pause. Power coming back on? No, she realized. In her rush Sloane hadn't even noticed the floor-to-ceiling window beside her.

Only then did the view beyond truly register.

For a moment she just stood there, speechless. Bits of the scene spattered her spinning mind, coalescing fitfully into a whirl of light and dark and pinpricks of color. The viewing pane looked out onto a plaza, one of the larger installations that left room for wards to fold into for traveling. A place people were meant to stroll and discuss the important details of colonizing a new galaxy.

It was a ruin.

The window offered an unimpeded view all the way down the length of one of the Nexus's great arms. Several kilometers of meticulously designed and constructed habitat. Factories, hydroponic farms, hospitals—everything they would need. Everything that would sustain them.

All she could see was the flames, the gouts of venting gas, the walls sheared in jagged lines, the exposed girders. Devastation on a massive scale, and beyond it all, an unfamiliar sea of motionless stars.

It wasn't the Milky Way. Sloane would know. Spending a lot of time staring out ship windows made for a strange sort of familiarity. Palaven, Thessia, hell, she'd have been happy to be looking out at Omega's starscape.

This was disorienting, with its glittering net of blue, red, and white stars and trailing web of eerily colored threads of gas and stardust. They were definitely not home.

But what about their *new* home?

Impossible to tell.

Sloane Kelly ran now. Feet pounding in an all-out sprint despite the fresh howls of agony from her broken toe, the fog of her stasis hangover pushed to a distant corner of her being. She knew she'd pay for this later—if there *was* a later.

She hoped to hell there was a later. One she and the council could talk about, maybe over drinks. Lots and lots of drinks.

Hallways flew by in a blur, until finally she reached the door she'd been looking for, marked by a simple '00'.

It was wide open.

Sloane pulled to a stop just before the threshold, caught her breath. A moment, just one to steel her resolve, and then she slipped inside.

The stasis chamber resembled any other chamber. A perfect clone of the one Sloane herself had struggled to secure and exit. The only difference was the scope of damage. The tragedy of bodies.

There was neither.

Every pod here was wide open. No sign of death, of damage, of fire or physical malfunctions.

One glance and she determined that the room was empty. Utterly silent. At least there weren't any corpses. She'd take any victory she could at this point, no matter how small. But relief stubbornly waited. She needed to find Garson, to hear her orders. To bring good news to the survivors.

At least that would be normal.

She turned on her heel, her mind already shifting to a backup plan, when a weak cough broke the silence.

Sloane paused, scanned the room again. "Hello?" Nothing.

Then another cough, and a wan, "Hello? Someone there?"

"I'm here," she confirmed, taking swift steps into the room and scanning its darkened pods. "Where are you?"

"Here." A raised hand, just visible beyond a metal table. Sloane slid across the table and dropped into a kneel beside the woman lying flat on her back. Blood from a gash on her forehead ran down her nose and cheek, and her eyes weren't quite focusing in the same direction.

"How bad is it?" Sloane asked, her eyes snapping from the injury to the name printed across the left breast of her bloodied suit. *Addison.* Foster Addison, another senior-level crew member, like Sloane. Colonial Affairs, if memory served.

Addison brought up one hand and tentatively probed the cut. The blood had already started to dry around the edges, though a fresh line welled from the middle when she touched it.

The woman grimaced. "I'll manage. A bit dazed."

A bit? *Yeah, right.*

Sloane detoured to the first-aid panel, mercifully

intact in this oddly untouched chamber, and found a kit with packets of medi-gel safely tucked inside. Once back at Addison's side, she popped the seal and slathered the cool gel on Addison's forehead. "This should help."

Addison grimaced, eyes clenched shut again. "Not one for bedside manners, I take it."

"No bed," Sloane pointed out as she sat back and removed her own boot. "No doctors, no point." She dabbed the gunk on her throbbing, swollen toe, then packed the gel all around it for extra cushion.

"Ugh."

Sloane ignored the woman, waited several seconds for the pain-dampening effects to kick in. It still hurt to pull her boot back on, but not nearly as bad as before. "Okay. Niceties over." When she looked up, Addison had managed to stand upright, though braced against a pod.

She surveyed the room, then frowned shakily at Sloane. "Should you be in here?"

That, Sloane decided, was probably concussion talking. It was too inane to be anything else. She ignored that, too. "Where are the others? Garson?" Sloane glanced around a second time just to be sure. Every stasis pod in the room stood empty. Contrary to her thin hopes.

Addison squeezed her eyes shut. When she opened them, her gaze seemed a little less cloudy. The gel on her forehead was already turning matte, sealing the wound. "We were all up in Operations. For…" She shook her head a fraction, like she had to shake the thought loose. "For the arrival."

The arrival. Awakened for the *arrival.*

The news felt unreal against the chaos surrounding it. "So…" Sloane stared at her. "We made it?"

The injured woman nodded, opened her eyes. "We did."

"What the hell happened, then? Attack?"

Addison went still. Then, as if suddenly putting two and two together, fixed a concerned stare on Sloane. "Who are you? You look familiar."

Two and two, Sloane thought in irritation, clearly added to five. "Security Director Sloane Kelly," she said patiently. "We've met."

"Ah. Security. Of course you'd jump to that conclusion, then." She coughed, closed her eyes once more. Two fingers pressed around the swollen flesh of her wound. The gel was probably already kicking in to numb the area. Sloane's toe had settled to a whimper. As had her hands. "Let's not assume an attack," the woman continued. "We didn't come here to war with whomever we find here."

"Yeah, yeah, peaceful and friendly, I know the speech. Doesn't mean the locals heard it." T'vaan hadn't agreed, though. She'd died believing there was no attack, died in Sloane's arms talking about some kind of sensor issue. Sloane frowned. "So what *did* happen?"

This time, Addison's voice cracked. "No idea. But," she continued more forcefully, "we should go check."

Sloane debated leaving her behind, but decided against it. If Operations had fared as badly as cryostasis, she'd need all the help she could get. She offered the woman a supporting hand. "Can you walk?"

Addison gave a shaky nod, and ignored Sloane's proffered hand to take the first unsteady steps away from her support.

She didn't fall over, so Sloane let her offer drop. She did, however, make sure she matched the Director's pace within steadying distance. Just in case.

They walked in relative silence for a moment. As Sloane eyed the woman's straight back, a thought occurred to her. "Why weren't you in Ops?"

Addison shot her a glance. "I'd just left it to find Jien."

"Find Jien?" By sheer reflex, she grabbed the woman's arm. "She's alive?"

"At last check," she replied, but frowned in bemusement at Sloane's hand. "Before official launch of arrival protocols, the science team wanted to nail down final readings. Jien had just stepped out, so when we were ready, I went to get her."

"No comms?"

She shook her head. "I didn't see the need."

Sloane jerked a thumb back the way they'd come. "You thought she'd be in there?"

This time, her fellow director looked away, pulling her arm from Sloane's grasp. "Uh, no. I stopped in there for a sec."

"Why?"

"I had to use the... restroom."

Sloane frowned. "What, they didn't set up facilities near Ops?"

The woman stared straight ahead, though Sloane saw the tic in her suddenly set jaw. "Don't be rude about it, Director," she said tightly.

Defensive, much? "Sorry, *Director*, are my questions bothering you?"

Addison shot her another glance, this one cool. "Unless they're leading to an epiphany or an accusation involving malevolent biological functions, maybe focus on what's important?"

Ugh. *That's right.* Sloane remembered exactly why she hadn't bothered making an effort with the Colonial

Director. Attitude for days.

Sloane smiled tightly. "Sure." Her gaze turned instead to the corridors they strode through. They were much neater. Much less, well, torn apart than the ones she'd left. "So, did you find Garson?"

Addison shook her head, though grudgingly. "I was heading back to see if she'd returned when the whole ship lurched. It was like hitting turbulence in an atmospheric flight, only far worse. The floor actually fell away from me and I think I hit my head on the way up… or maybe down. I don't really remember."

The asari had said something about physics. Sloane had been in spacedrops that felt like that. Maybe that's what she meant?

She filed that away, too. Right now, she had too many puzzle pieces and no final image. "While in Operations, did you see anything that might explain it?"

"You mean like, what, alien soldiers rappelling in through the windows?"

"I'd assume you'd see that much," Sloane replied thinly. "If you were at your post."

That turned Addison's shoulders rigid. "There was nothing of the sort. No ships, no attack fleet, nothing you can shoot, Security Director Kelly. I'm sorry to disappoint you."

Sloane turned on her, irritation spiked. "We're in a lot of trouble here, in case you hadn't noticed. I'd appreciate straight answers, delivered instantly, and less judgment about my role on this ship." Her tone, icy as it was, earned her a widened stare. "So what I mean by anything," she finished curtly, "is *anything*. Sensor data. Unexpected debris in our path. Giant fucking *space monsters*. Anything."

Foster Addison did not tell her to fuck off. The

woman held her ground, but Sloane could see that the rebuke stung.

Good.

Almost good. She lifted her blood-streaked chin. "No need for sarcasm, Director." Punching her, Sloane reasoned, wouldn't help anything. And would be a total overreaction.

Lucky for her.

Addison forged on. "We were in the right place. The stellar neighborhood matched our nav charts. There was… concern, perhaps, among the science advisors about some of their readings. They figured six hundred years might have worn down the tech a bit. Wanted some time to untangle the array and parse the data. That's when I left to—"

"To take a leak."

"To find Jien," she corrected frostily.

"Without the readings?"

Addison threw up her hands. "For pity's sake, nobody needs outward sensors to use internal facilities. Now, how about we do less interrogation of perfectly natural events, *if you please*, try to get some *actual* answers." She gestured for Sloane to lead the way to the door, and beyond.

Fine. It beat speculating with a concussed social worker, anyway.

Silently venting all the things she *wanted* to say, Sloane made it only a few steps into the anteroom when the Nexus began to tremble.

CHAPTER THREE

"What the hell is that?"

Sloane didn't have an answer. The ship trembled and quaked all around them, heaving as if stretched in too many directions. They swayed, colliding into each other before both women found their feet. The awesome shriek of metal tearing apart echoed through the corridors. Addison half-ducked, throwing an arm over her head.

Sloane had only just locked her stance down, preparing for a deeper roll, when the shifting stopped. Again, metal strained and groaned, rolling hollowly through the otherwise eerily hushed chamber. When it faded to nothing, they stared at each other in grim silence.

For a long moment, nothing moved.

Not them.

Not the ship.

Sloane let out a breath she hadn't realized she was holding. "No follow up," she said. "That's good—or at least it isn't bad."

"Another explosion?"

"Doubtful."

"How can you be sure?"

Sloane braced a hand against a tilted column and studied the bulkhead above them, half expecting it to suddenly crack and fall. What a way to go. "Because it didn't feel like one," she said flatly. "Whatever this is, it's affecting the whole ship, like… like an earthquake."

"An earthquake in space?"

"Now who's being sarcastic?" Sloane retorted.

"I figured I'd meet you at your level," Addison muttered, more than a little superiority in the curt jibe. That earned her a hard glare.

"All I'm saying," Sloane said, dredging up her failing reserve of patience, "is that none of my 'under attack' bones are twitching. And that jives with what a technician postulated on my way here." Much to Sloane's dismay. In some ways, an attack was easier to handle. Protect the station, kill the intruders.

"Who?"

"T'vaan, I think. Asari."

Addison's eyes widened. "She's all right?" The hope in that sentence, the fact it ended on a question, was enough to kick an ache in Sloane's conscience.

Wordlessly, she shook her head.

Crestfallen, Addison seemed to deflate, withdrawing a little more from Sloane. "She was one of the science team."

Yeah. Sloane figured. She nodded, focused her attention again on the empty chamber. The ceiling held. "Well, she echoed what you said. Something weird on the sensors. So which way to Ops from here? Let's figure this out."

"Past the Cultural Exchange and along the spoke arm." Then, in a somber tone, "Unless the path is blocked."

"Then let's move," Sloane said, "before anything else collapses."

On that, they could both agree. Even so, she eased her pace. Her toe ached mightily, and she didn't like the way Addison's wound had already begun to purple under the medi-gel. Concussion, definitely. She kept a wary eye on her, trying to figure her out. Leaving the bridge? And to find Garson, no less. She'd failed in one, but maybe that was just coincidental. Maybe she'd gone looking just as Garson returned to the bridge.

If she'd stayed, would Addison now have the answers to this mess?

Maybe.

If what she said checked out, Sloane wouldn't want to be in those shoes when that report hit somebody's desk. Leaving one's station when shit hit the fan? Looked bad. Even for a director.

No, not just somebody's desk. Jien Garson's. Addison reported directly to her, just as Sloane did. Although knowing the Initiative's ideals, they'd figure out a way to have a committee review Addison's misstep.

Despite her personal aversion to bureaucracy, and her own occasional run-ins with disciplinary boards, she had faith in the Nexus leadership. Garson would do the right thing, however committee-happy she and her team might be.

Assuming, the suspicious little voice in Sloane's investigative nature piped up, the woman was telling the truth.

A fact she'd let sit for now. All things considered, she'd suspected just about everyone of potential sabotage at this point. Evidence first, conjecture later.

A sudden clatter tore through her reverie, made Sloane jump back, her pulse racing. She'd never missed her weapons so badly as now. Ahead, a panel split from the wrong side and spilled its guts all over the corridor. Tubes hissed and writhed, releasing a hot blast of steam.

So much for less destruction. Beyond the thrashing mass of tubing, more sparks lit the dark. The devastations that flickered in shadow looked so damn odd compared to the section of clean corridor they stood in now.

At least *she* hadn't yelped.

Sloane made Addison wait, leaving the other director fighting to steady her breath. Sloane sniffed the air gingerly. No noxious fumes, at least. *Small favors.* No flames, either. Just broken ship. Broken wires.

Broken plans.

"Shit," Addison breathed. "Hope that was nothing important."

"One more busted pipe," Sloane observed, "out of thousands. Let's keep focused." She wiped steam and adrenaline-induced sweat from her brow. Later, maybe, when the worst of this was behind them, she could worry about a single broken pipe. Or thousands.

Stepping gingerly over the writhing tentacles, she winced when a few jumped and sputtered. Droplets of cooling fluid arced up onto the wall.

"Not too hot," she said over her shoulder. "Just stay away from the active ones."

Addison wrinkled her nose as she followed. She was starting to look a little bit glassy around the edges, despite her attitude. "It's like something rolled through and just..." She flailed with a grimy hand. "Ripped out bits here and there."

"Stay focused," Sloane repeated hastily. "It'll get sorted, eventually."

"Forgive me if I don't share your optimism, but eventually isn't going to cut it. We had enough to do already to begin our mission. But this..." A silence descended, broken only by the hiss and sway of the cords as they left them behind.

A tinge of guilt poked Sloane's conscience. "Garson will have a plan," she said without looking back. "We're in Andromeda, after all. The other side. We made it."

Maybe that surprised her reluctant companion. Maybe she just needed to hear it. "Yeah." A slow agreement. But at least it was that.

For a time neither spoke. Even when Sloane had to step around four more bodies, Addison remained quiet. Numb, more like. It was a hell of a lot to take in.

"Let me know if you need to rest," Sloane tried.

"We're about two sections away," Addison said instead. She pressed the heel of her hand against her forehead. "Jien had intended to hold a briefing before…" Again, a wave of vibration, though mild compared to before, rippled around them. She winced, held her stance and waited it out. When it died, she smiled a grim little slash. "Before all this."

Sloane set her jaw and proceeded at a pace too quick to be strictly safe, but at this rate, they'd at least get answers faster. The whiplash of hope to fear to nerves would get her before anything else did.

She hoped they would be answers they wanted.

Damn. There was that word again. *Hope.*

It was what fueled them all. Every last one of the people still in stasis, every man, woman and child who had registered with the Andromeda Initiative—every species, human to turian to salarian to asari. Hell, even the krogan had signed on looking for a way off their wasteland homeworld, all because of *hope*.

Now on the brink of going up in flames with every step closer to Operations, every push past destroyed paneling and hanging tubes and wires. The debris scattered around the corridor had flaked off the paneling that had been so warm and gleaming when Sloane had first walked it.

Now all she could see and smell was char. Ruin.

We go to paint our masterpiece.

If anyone could get things back on track, it was Garson.

"Oh, no…" Addison's voice. Breathless from strain—or concussion—and shattered down to a whisper. She froze mid-step, a hand to her mouth.

Sloane tore her thoughts away from the ephemeral threads of the future, automatically reaching out an arm to steady the woman. But it wasn't needed. Addison stood on her own fine, but her eyes bulged, shock or horror or something worse.

"The door…"

Two tiny words, and somehow, Sloane just *knew*.

Hope wouldn't cut it.

The reinforced door Addison stared at hung ajar from its mooring, which should have been impossible, given the mechanics of it. As if something had sheared right through it, pushing the metal paneling outward in a jagged bloom.

By habit, Sloane reached for her weapon—a firearm she didn't have. *Damn.* Old habits didn't help when everything else had gone to hell.

Squaring her shoulders, Sloane approached the door—what was left of it, anyway. Addison followed close behind her, and as darkness gave way to eerie light, they both sucked in a ragged breath.

Sloane's came out on a low, "Holy mother of—"

This time, Addison did sway.

Sloane's instinct was to jerk back, to hold her breath, every last bit of her exposed skin prickling in bone-deep fear. Part of Operation's vast front wall, and the hull plating beyond, had sheared away, replaced at some point with a translucent inflatable bulkhead by automatic emergency systems. It looked, at first glance, as if there was no wall at all, but worse was what lay beyond. Outside.

Against the cold spray of stars, twisting tendrils of black and ash-gray splayed wide, curled and drifting threads flecked with orange and yellow light. A bizarre anti-nebula that unfurled like a frayed ribbon stretching into the distance, like synaptic pathways spreading in eerily visceral threads.

"What is that?" Addison whispered.

Sloane had to force her brain into gear, to unfreeze her limbs. They weren't going to float off into space. They wouldn't suffocate.

Even better, perhaps, was the fact that the Nexus's emergency protocols had worked. The barrier had saved Operations.

Or… tried.

"I… don't know," was all Sloane could say. She'd never seen anything like it. Beyond the bulkhead, the ephemeral strands of *whatever* seemed to float in the void of space like something separate from it. There, but not *in it*. Like… Her mind flailed for the right thought.

"Like tangled hair in a swimming pool," she said aloud.

"Gross," Addison murmured.

Sloane agreed. But even so, she visually traced a long tendril, captivated in some small way by the points of orange and yellow winking within it.

Until it ended, lost in the blank canvas of space.

Or hidden by the sudden rotation of a hunk of metal, drifting into view.

Sloane's eyes widened. "Is that...?"

"Part of the Nexus," Addison confirmed, breathless. She raised a hand to her mouth. "But how?"

Question of a lifetime.

If she'd meant to say more, it died on an abrupt sound of distress. "Oh. Oh, *no*." Addison took a step forward, limbs stiff. "No, no..." She wasn't looking at the same incredible view anymore. Sloane's focus shifted from the dark, nebulous ribbons, the hunk of pocked and cold metal, and instead to the room.

Bodies.

A half-dozen, at least, just inside the room. More amid the overturned desks and furniture that littered the space beyond.

The Nexus's senior leadership.

"Oh, fuck," Sloane whispered. She scanned those nearby, hoping against hope that none was Jien Garson. But they were too far away to recognize. Too battered to readily find out.

The closest had an asari's fringe. Nuara. The last time Sloane had seen her, she'd hugged Garson in farewell. Laid in her pod like it really was just a nap and they'd all be happy and free and get to work upon waking.

Not even close.

She'd crumpled against the shorn edge of the outer hull, just this side of the emergency bulkhead, but it wasn't enough. Based on placement, on the fact there were no bodies floating just beyond the seal, Sloane could guess what had happened.

The Matriarch had shielded the room as best she could until the emergency bulkhead could deploy. It wouldn't seal in the air, and in the end, it hadn't worked. But she'd tried to hold it off, to keep the staff on the right side of the bulkhead.

The bloody damage told Sloane a torn hull had not been the worst problem on the bridge.

Fires. Chaos. Emergency efforts. Nothing had saved them.

"Shit," Sloane whispered.

Addison took a deep breath. Visually *forcing* herself into gear. "There's nothing we can do for them." She turned from the view and moved to search the room, gingerly stepping over debris. Outstretched hands. People, *shipmates*, charred and broken.

Sloane knew, grudgingly, that she had the right idea. If there were survivors, they'd be deeper inside.

She turned her attention to the part of the huge room that hadn't been torn away, her heart already sinking. The spacious chamber, perhaps the grandest of all those inside the station, was barely recognizable.

A giant viewscreen suspended from the ceiling had split in half, falling on a series of control consoles that ringed the forward-facing portion of the chamber. The consoles, smashed and dark, were beyond repair, but it was the chairs on which Sloane focused. They were crushed. Utterly flattened. Debris littered the floor. A grand, sweeping stairwell that led up to an observation deck above them had collapsed. Or maybe it had been smashed by something falling. No way to tell. All of it had been jumbled, shaken, and thrown about many times.

It was too much to process. Sloane moved without thinking, to the nearest hunk of debris. A section of railing from the deck above, twisted and splayed across a bench. She lifted the broken mass and heaved it aside, then dropped to her hands and knees and looked under the bench. Dead eyes stared back at her. A dark-skinned man, mouth hanging open in a silenced scream. Marnell Phelps, senior bridge technician, Sloane recalled. A good man. Dried blood traced a line from the corner of his mouth to a small pool on the floor. His eyes were glassy and still.

"Jien?" Addison called out. She began walking around the room, repeating her call, a little more fear in her voice with each cry. "Jien!"

Sloane threw a smashed chair aside. Pushed a desk upright, ignoring the pain as a broken viewscreen fell and landed on the toes of her uninjured foot. At least the pain, she noted as she swore, wasn't nearly so bad as breaking it. "Just fucking great," she hissed on the end of her diatribe, making a note to find more medi-gel.

But when she peered over the desk, another body lay behind it, dampening all else.

"Found someone," she called. "A human." Unrecognizable at first glance. The body had been brutally crushed. Sloane checked the name on the left breast of the uniform. Bloodstained, but legible. "Parker," she added, looking up.

Addison had stopped her efforts, waiting. Now her eyes fell closed. "Miles Parker, Assistant Director of Hydroponics."

With care, Sloane laid aside the heavy desk that had crushed the poor man. Thinking about his terrible fate twisted her gut, but it was the mention of hydroponics that hit her like a mallet. If the seed vault had been breached…

Focus. Sloane couldn't allow herself to worry about that. Not now.

The search went on. Body after body, each a blow to Sloane's morale, but none were Garson. It felt like an hour before there was nothing left to search.

"She's not here," Addison said. Her voice seemed

steady, but a glance at her face proved otherwise. "Now what?"

A good question. Nobody had prepped for *this*.

CHAPTER FOUR

"Search party," Sloane said. "We need to find Garson and any other survivors."

Addison shook her head, though reluctantly. "Succession protocol. We have to assume the worst. If she's gone…" she trailed off, her eyes settling on the temporary seal around the front half of the room.

"She could have just gone to take a leak," Sloane said. "You did."

Addison did not take the bait. Not this time. But it did seem to gall her into squaring up. She leveled her gaze on Sloane. "She's missing. There are clear procedures—"

"Fuck that," Sloane snapped, "we aren't—" She caught herself. Checked her anger. "Look, I appreciate… Addison, no offense but we should—"

A harsh, grating sound caused Sloane's words to die in her mouth. The noise repeated, and her first thought was that the field holding in their air was beginning to fail. She stepped back, Addison matching her twice over.

The sound came again, this time louder. Not from the barrier, she realized with relief, but the far door.

Sloane's hand went to her hip again, grasping for that pistol that still wasn't there. She swore, crouched slightly and pivoted, ready to run or engage depending on who or what came through.

Two hands curled short, thick fingers around the

door, now half-open, and heaved it the rest of the way wide. A figure ducked through, reptilian, with broad head, bulky shoulders and wide-set eyes.

A krogan. A female krogan, with a frown so deep you could hide beneath it. A frown Sloane knew well.

She rose from her crouch, stepped forward and couldn't hide a half-grin of sheer relief.

"Kesh. Damn it's good to see you." And she meant it. The sight of the superintendent gave Sloane the second glimmer of hope she'd had since waking. Nakmor Kesh knew the guts of the Nexus better than anyone else aboard, having overseen its construction. If Jien Garson was the leader of the Nexus, Kesh was the steward.

The krogan strode forward, her head swooping from one side to the other. "Director Kelly, I'd say the feeling is mutual," she gestured to all the damage and dead, "but after all this, it's good to see anyone at all still breathing. Where's Jien Garson?"

"The question of the hour," Sloane admitted.

"One of many," Addison said, stepping forward. "Jien is missing."

Sloane gave the krogan engineer a recap of everything that had happened. As she spoke, several other lower-level crew members wandered into Ops in the krogan's wake. Dazed and nursing wounds, they looked like the walking dead. But they were able bodies, all of them, and Initiative pioneers. Sloane could see the glimmer in their eyes, despite everything. That spirit of wanting to help. The undying fire of survival. "We need to organize a search party," she added for the benefit of the newcomers.

"More importantly," Addison began, but Kesh was already nodding.

"Right now, we need to save whom we can," the krogan said, cutting off the other woman. Not rudely, Sloane noted. Not really. Just firm. That was Kesh, though. Rational, for her kind, and dedicated.

Addison took note. "I'll take this," she said, shaking her head. "See what we can do. Maybe the two of you can figure out what happened." She moved off without waiting for a reply.

Sloane watched her organize the stragglers into pairs. "She's kind of a people person, isn't she?"

"When allowed," Kesh said, turning away. "Might I ask what Addison felt was more important than a search?"

"Succession protocol."

"Ah." Kesh looked back again, that frown carving deeper lines in. The search pairs moved off into the dark corners of the room, picking through debris with trepidation. So much death, Sloane couldn't blame them.

"Hey, Addison?"

The woman looked up.

Sloane's frown, crooked and grim, telegraphed more than just words. "Keep a list of who—" She paused, then managed carefully, "of the names here."

Addison nodded, just as grim, and turned back to the grisly task.

Sloane shifted closer to the krogan woman. "We're in a lot of trouble here, aren't we?" Sloane asked, loud enough for only Kesh to hear.

She met Sloane's gaze with a directness only a krogan could levy. "Welcome to Andromeda," she muttered in graveled quiet. "The other side, indeed." Kesh dusted off her hands as if she'd just finished diagnosing a coolant overflow. "I'd rather know facts. Do any of these terminals work?"

"Not that I've seen," Sloane admitted, feeling suddenly useless. A security officer in the midst of an engineering nightmare.

"Fine." She rolled her wide shoulders. "Let's see if we can fix one."

She began to move through the room, a strange echo of Addison's search party's movements, ignoring the biological casualties as she poked and prodded at the mechanical ones. Sloane helped her for a time, but in truth was only slowing the krogan down. After a while, she left Kesh to it and joined Addison near the spot where the commander of the Nexus would normally sit, overseeing the vast station with a cup of tea in one hand.

The grand commander's chair was overturned, pushed back several meters from its dais, the corners of its fabric charred away.

"Any sign of Garson?" Sloane asked, though she could see the answer written plain across Addison's face. "Any survivors at all?"

The woman shook her head, too numb to even speak. She sniffed hard, ran the back of her hand across one eye, and blinked. Tears or dust, and Sloane would bet the woman would claim the latter. She didn't ask.

Addison held out a datapad for Sloane to view. Names had been hastily entered into its flickering screen. "That's everyone who woke for the arrival ceremony."

Sloane's mouth dropped open. It required a force of will to clap shut. She swallowed. Only two names were not crossed off: Addison's, and Jien Garson.

"I feel so damned useless," Addison said, voice far away. She wasn't looking at Sloane anymore. Or the bodies. Sloane couldn't tell for sure, but the woman had the thousand-light-year stare of somebody about to roll headlong into emotional shut-down.

Sloane clapped her on the shoulder, earning a jarred breath and snapped-back attention. "Don't sweat it. There's plenty to do. We need to find somewhere to store the bodies. Help me—"

"I mean *here*," Addison cut in, emphatic. She laughed, dry and ironic. "In Andromeda. Director of Colonial Affairs. What a joke. We'll be lucky if we can colonize the room next door."

"Hey," Sloane said, frowning. "That's enough."

"What, you're going to tell me everything will be okay? That this is just a setback? Look around you. There's no recovering from this. It's over. Without Jien, without our leaders—"

"This one," Kesh barked from across the room. She was kneeling in front of a terminal with a cracked screen and more than a few signs of charring, but otherwise the device looked intact. "I think." Another pause. She squinted. "Maybe."

Hell, Sloane would take a *maybe* at this point, gladly. She patted Addison on the same shoulder, the way she would any of her own. "We'll discuss it later, but I wasn't going to spew some bullshit happy-gas, okay? I was going to say that you can still help."

"How?"

"How were you planning to colonize the worlds around us?"

"That's the arks' job. But we have shuttles. We—"

"Ships, exactly, and if we need to evacuate the Nexus..." she trailed off as comprehension dawned in Addison's eyes. She knew those ships, their capabilities, their capacities, better than anyone.

"Come on, let's see what Kesh found."

The woman nodded, followed her back across the

room. At least she seemed more focused now.

With a series of impatient grunts and snarls of frustration, the krogan performed surgery on the innards of the one computer that wasn't totally destroyed. For all her bravado, Sloane stood aside and just watched. Numbness spread like ice through her core, overwhelmed by the extent of the disaster.

Yet if all she could do was keep the others on task, it was something, right?

There was a pop, a shower of sparks. Kesh swore. Another failure. Another thing to fix.

"Would it help if I punched it?" Sloane asked bitterly.

Kesh glanced at her, a flat stare that had even Addison flinching. Then, wordlessly, the krogan balled one large hand and popped the terminal sharp and hard.

The screen flickered to life. Information began to pour across the surface.

"The hell that worked," Sloane said doubtfully.

The krogan grinned, and smacked her on the shoulder. "Let's see what we can find out!" Everyone huddled around as Nakmor Kesh manipulated the screens, impatiently shoving obvious alerts aside. "Hmm."

"What is it?" Addison asked.

"Won't let me in."

"Do you know how to use it?"

Kesh made a deep, annoyed grunt. She did not turn from the screen. "Emergency protocols are in full effect." Now the krogan did swing her massive head around, turning to face Addison and Sloane. "That requires Garson to acknowledge and clear, and that has not happened."

"She's missing," Addison said, defensively.

"The system doesn't know that."

"What are you getting at, Kesh?" Sloane asked.

The krogan gestured at the display. When she spoke next it was as if she was quoting from the procedures manual, which Sloane guessed was exactly the case.

"In the event of station-wide emergency, if the commander does not acknowledge this state within a certain time period, a lockdown is initiated until the appropriate individual, as identified by pre-programmed succession protocols, can be summoned to stand in their place."

"Okay," Sloane said. "That's Addison then, isn't it? Let her do it."

"Possibly." Kesh studied the panel. "But the procedure is very specific. We need to go down the list, marking off those… incapable… of filling in until Garson is located."

Addison passed her datapad over, a bit reluctantly Sloane thought. They waited as Kesh manipulated the interface, striking six names in rapid succession from the chain-of-command list. Well before Addison's name was reached, however, the protocol produced a listing that wasn't on the datapad, or part of the arrival ceremony group.

Addison squinted at the display. "Wait." She pointed at the text. "Who the *hell* is Jarun Tann?"

iiiiiiiiiiiiiiiiiiii

"Jarun Tann," the salarian said. "Deputy director of revenue management."

"Perfect," Sloane muttered, shaking her head. "Just fucking perfect."

The chamber which housed his stasis pod had seen only minimal damage in the "event," as Addison had taken to calling the disaster. Tann, along with everyone else in here, had remained asleep, and woke now only because Kesh had the maintenance override in her repertoire of tech miracles. The only one, it turned out, who did. At least still alive and accounted for.

The salarian had sat right up, almost chipper, probably assuming this was the expected revival from the long sleep and that he could get to work counting beans or whatever the hell it was his job was supposed to entail.

At Sloane's tone his expression changed. He studied her, then Addison, and then Nakmor Kesh. The sight of the krogan looming over him made the salarian recoil involuntarily. "What's going on here? You're not the revival team."

"I'm Sloane Kelly, security director."

"We're under attack?"

She shook her head. "There's been a terrible accident. The station is in trouble. Which is why we've woken…" she could barely say the words without emitting a terrible bewildered laugh. *Deep breath, deep breath.* She steadied herself. "Which is why we woke you."

"An accident? Related to revenue?" His eyes drifted in Kesh's direction and then whipped back to Sloane. The tax wonk squirmed in his stasis pod. "If this is some kind of prank—"

"No prank," Sloane said. "I wish it was, believe me."

"I don't understand."

Addison let out a long sigh. "At the moment, you're the most senior crew member present and accounted for."

Silence descended among them. Tann stared at her.

Addison's smile was brittle. "According to emergency command protocol, the Nexus is yours."

That sunk in. *"What?!"*

The word hadn't even finished echoing before Kesh said slowly, "Until, that is, we locate Jien Garson."

A tricky situation made slippery. Jarun Tann was an unknown, a newcomer to the leadership gathered, and as acting director, they knew nothing about him. To have a salarian and a krogan in close proximity...

Sloane did not miss the thick note of menace in the krogan's voice.

Neither, she noted as Tann's already large eyes got larger, did he.

CHAPTER FIVE

Kesh followed the others back to Operations, then waited in silence as Jarun Tann studied the display listing him as the temporary commander of the Nexus.

Sloane stood beside him, arms folded across her chest. Addison sulked a short distance away. No, sulked wasn't quite right. The human fumed. She clearly had expected, though certainly not hoped, to be the next in line for command in this situation. Instead, for reasons none could fathom, this middle-management finance officer had been higher on the list.

The salarian stood there, scratching idly at the back of his neck, reading his name on the screen over and over as if it might provide some hidden explanation.

Kesh remained by the door, arms hanging at her sides. The fact of his ascension grated. Deeply. The salarian species had, after all, developed the genophage that neutered the krogan clans. Even now, centuries later, it was the salarian species who lorded it over the struggling krogan. Every last one seemed inclined to bring it up.

To look down their stubby noses at the krogan.

Kesh had hoped to step away from all that. To work with cooperative folk, species more inclined to respect what the krogan brought to this new table.

And maybe in part, the sting she felt was the lack of recognition. The tint of betrayal to her indignation. But she knew herself well enough to recognize that at heart, she was an engineer. The station's situation wasn't getting any better the longer he waited, and Kesh was already running a list of necessary repairs in her head.

Whatever else the salarian expected, Kesh knew her job.

As if aware of it, aware of the others, Tann, without ceremony, finally acknowledged the display. He stated his name and woefully unimpressive title to clear the security. The screen winked out, and then more information began to flow across its surface. Kesh couldn't help herself, crossing the room to stand behind the three others.

Emergency ECS (end of cryostasis) protocol, the screen read, above Tann's name.

Two more names were displayed, along with their status and, more importantly, their purpose: *Directors Foster Addison and Sloane Kelly, advisors to the temporary commander*.

Kesh was not listed. Nor any of the other two dozen or so known to be awake.

It shouldn't have surprised her. Shouldn't have stung. All this data did was confirm what Kesh had suspected. She had not been awoken for a sudden and absolute need for leadership. She wasn't among those designated for such responsibility.

A krogan wasn't meant for that. Not even here, where everyone had touted the words *fresh start* as if they knew what it meant.

They didn't. Not the way she and her clan did.

Nakmor Kesh, one of the greatest contributors to the very station now falling apart around them and who knew the Nexus better than most, had been woken to clean up the mess. She stared at the back of the salarian's head and tried to imagine why anyone would have put him in charge. Discounting her own contributions, Kesh figured at worst, Director Sloane Kelly should have been leading in this scenario.

But then, Kesh knew the reason. Politics. Council politics, anti-krogan politics, red tape. Call it what they would, it had to be the source.

A fresh start born out of old, destructive habits.

This truth bit deep. She'd hoped—indeed, based her decision to come on this mission in the first place— that they were leaving, *truly* leaving, the Milky Way behind. All the prejudices, all the old scores. A chance, in other words, for the krogan race to begin anew as equals to the peoples around them. Not just because they said so, but because they'd show those same peoples exactly *why* they were every bit as competent, industrious, and determined as they were.

At the departure celebration, she'd admitted as much to Nakmor Morda. The veteran warrior had roared with laughter, and drank deep to the folly of idealism. The memory left Kesh embarrassed... and angry. She had the right to hope for a better way of life. Stronger integration.

She was nobody's naïve youth. But Morda, she was a different entity entirely. Harder, brutal when necessary, and Clan Leader for a reason.

Kesh did not relish the day the leader would wake to this so-called new galaxy.

"Hold on," Sloane said, gesturing at the screen. "Everyone in my chamber was woken up, and the one adjacent. How do you know *I* was part of this... protocol or whatever?"

Kesh grunted something impatient. "The logs don't lie," she said flatly. Without being asked, she stepped forward—muscling the salarian out of the way simply by getting close enough—and brought up the screen now that terminal access had been unlocked. "The other pods were genuinely damaged, but not yours. See here? That group, and these three. Pod damage. Otherwise they would still be asleep now, or worse. But yours, that was protocol."

"But I remember it damaged."

"*After* protocols had begun." Kesh's thick finger stabbed the line.

Sloane opened her mouth, seemed to think better of it, and said nothing.

"It appears," Tann said to the two human women standing on either side of him, "that the three of us will be spending a lot of time together."

"Until Garson is found," Kesh added pointedly.

It was as if she were not even in the room. Part of her, the undiplomatic part—the krogan part, steeped in lifetimes of conflict—wanted to ram her fist in the salarian's flat, ugly face.

The security director saved her the effort.

Sloane shook her head, her features grim. "Yeah. Not happening."

"What?"

"Advisory, my ass. Until this situation is under control I'll be calling the shots." She forged right over Addison's breath for words, over Tann's blinking onslaught of speechlessness. "This is an emergency, a possibly deadly one, and until we're out of this damned mess, the last thing I want to do is argue costs with a revenue officer, no disrespect."

Kesh fought a vicious thread of humor.

The salarian met her gaze, mouth tightening, and then focused squarely on the Security Director. "I understand your concern, but the mission protocol—"

"Fuck protocol. Look around us, Tann. We're going to be lucky to survive the next hour. And you know what? Fuck the mission, too." Addison's eyes flared, surprise and anger. "I'll worry about the mission when the last fire has been stamped out."

The salarian drew back, but froze when Kesh lumbered to her feet. "Security Director Kelly is right." Simple words. Simple tone. She wasn't the placating kind.

The woman frowned. "Call me Sloane, will you? Titles give me a headache."

Kesh could respect that. "Sloane," she amended, "is right."

Tann's eyes narrowed. "Your opinion is noted."

She may as well have suggested they repaint the Nexus Tuchanka-gas pink for all the consideration he gave it.

It took more energy than Kesh had to keep the irritation from her voice.

"Fact. Not opinion." She gestured toward the screen. "Life support is failing. Everything from core power to ventilation is taxed beyond spec as the ship tries to compensate for all this damage."

They all stared at her. Various degrees of inquiry and bemusement. Or, in the salarian's case, outright impatience. There was no time for this.

She growled, raising her voice. *"The Nexus is dying."*

Sometimes only bluntness worked.

All three snapped to a different kind of attention. One that processed this new data with, in Kesh's opinion, not nearly enough fire.

Tann looked at Addison. Addison looked at

Sloane. Sloane just narrowed her eyes, staring at the lone functioning screen, lost in thought. Kesh could almost see the wheels turning in there.

The salarian dusted off his sleeve. "Well then. I suggest—"

Sloane cut him off with an upheld hand. She looked to Kesh. "Who's in charge of life support, and are they still alive?"

Kesh knew the name already. The turian reported to her directly. She poked and swiped at the screen.

"Calix Corvannis. Competent, if a bit... you know, turian." She noted Sloane's lips quirk, just enough. The human understood. Adding a turian's casual arrogance to this party would be a fascinating new thorn in Jarun Tann's side, to say nothing of the species' unique devotion to the meritocracy. One foolish move, and they'd all hear about it.

In various degrees of respect, depending on said turian.

Calix was a good officer, but he had a way of holding his cards close. Kesh had learned to respect his space, and he to respect her orders. How that would hold up in this new environment, only time would tell. "He is still in stasis," she observed. "Status... at-risk, but nominally. Like everyone else."

"Wake him."

Tann frowned. "What?"

"And his crew," Sloane added, ignoring him.

"Wait just a moment," Tann said, raising his voice. He held out his hands, though whether to get Sloane's attention or make Kesh belie the order, she didn't know. "That does not seem wise at this stage."

Sloane whirled on him. "Are you telling me that it's not *wise* to fix our failing life-support systems? Really?"

Give credit where it's due, Kesh thought grudgingly. The salarian held his ground.

"I am asking if it's wise to add more oxygen-consuming, waste-producing bodies to this situation," he replied stiffly. "Life support may be failing, but it's already struggling to provide us a breathable atmosphere, is it not, Nakmor Kesh?"

Kesh glanced at the display. "The air will become toxic to the humans first, in about... forty-three minutes."

"There," Tann declared, as if handed a victory. "You see? Wake this Calix Corvannis and whoever else, and it might cause the very system you wish them to fix to instead fail."

Sloane Kelly closed her eyes and pressed her fingers to her temples. "So what's the alternative?" she asked. "That we let life support fail *slowly* because trying to fix it might cause it to fail faster?"

Tann smiled. "I haven't suggested anything yet because you interrupted me."

Sloane's lips curled into a genuine snarl.

"Both of you relax, please," Foster Addison said, stepping between them. "Speak your mind, Tann. Just be quick."

The salarian gathered himself, straightening his sleeves. "Wake *only* this Calix fellow and let him decide if the situation calls for additional help. He is, presumably, an expert. Perhaps he can recruit some of us who are already awake to assist, instead of increasing the non-stasial population."

The red-haired woman didn't hesitate. "Agreed." She looked at Kesh, as if it were decided.

Sloane let her furious glare bore into Tann for a few more seconds, then turned to Kesh as well. "Wake Calix, then. You and I will meet him at his pod, appraise him of the situation and help, if needed." She infused more bile into the word "help" than Kesh would have thought possible of a human, but it was a petty gesture. Even Kesh could see that the salarian had a valid point.

She nodded to Sloane and marched toward the exit, stepping over smashed equipment and lifeless bodies as she went. Sloane followed, saying nothing else.

"What should we do while you're gone?" Addison called after them.

"Find Garson, before I go insane," the security director muttered.

Kesh said nothing.

Louder and over her shoulder, Sloane called out, "Try to keep the reactors from going critical. Barring that, if you can get communications working, that would make things a hell of a lot easier. Do you agree, Deputy Director of Revenue Management Tann?"

"It seems a prudent—"

"Good."

Kesh led Sloane Kelly out of the room and into the fractured hallways of the dying Nexus, glad that no one could see the gallows humor she could feel cramping her facial muscles. Every krogan liked a good fight, whether it be against the elements or some living being. Whatever lay ahead, it wouldn't be boring.

She accelerated to a full run, Sloane limping slightly but still right on her flank. They were at war against that old and tenacious enemy: the clock.

The clock, Kesh noted, was winning.

||||||||||||||||||

"Sure you know where you're going?" Sloane asked.

Kesh rolled under a support beam fallen diagonally across a hall. She came to her feet, leapt over a bed, and powered on. Some of their route was dark, and a small emergency light on her uniform provided just enough illumination.

The mess didn't faze her. Finding a bed all the way out here? Now that took some incredible physics.

"I all but built this place," Kesh said between strides. "I know the Nexus 'like the back of my hand,' as you humans say." She thought about that for a moment. "I've never met a human who really knew the back of his hand, though."

Sloane grunted, dodging the same obstacles. Impressively enough, she'd fallen back only a few meters. At a particular junction, Kesh skidded to a stop and darted off to the left.

"It's right up here."

"Hold on," Sloane called after her.

Kesh turned in time to see the human tapping away at a small keypad on the wall, one of the few still functioning. A panel beside it had the markings of security.

The panel slid open, revealing a small cache of emergency supplies. Sloane reached past a bank of medical kits and selected a pristine Kessler pistol. She checked the load-out and activated the weapon.

"You believe we will need it?"

"A precaution." Sloane shrugged. "Comfort."

"You can't shoot space, Sloane."

"I don't intend to," Sloane replied with a half-smile. She was remarkably less edgy away from the others. More focused. "But some civilians came out of stasis when I did. They were panicked and barely manageable. We don't have time for that kind of crap now. If this Calix wakes up and loses his shit, we're all dead."

"Point taken. Still, do me a favor?"

"No promises."

Kesh spread her hands. "Calix is the only person on board who really knows the life-support systems inside and out."

"You don't?"

She didn't rise to the bait. "I do, but I have my exceptionally skilled hands full. So if you need to shoot him," she continued mildly, "aim for the leg."

Sloane laughed, a full sound that told Kesh everything she needed to know about the human's sense of humor. Much more like a krogan's, or a turian's, than not. "Deal," she chuckled. "But I don't plan on shooting anyone. Call it an attention-getter." She pocketed a few clips of ammunition and a first-aid kit, then slung an emergency rebreather over one shoulder. Kesh grabbed one as well, and they were off once again.

Halfway along the next hall, a series of red emergency lights embedded between floor and wall flickered, then bloomed to dim life. Overhead, a useless alarm began to wail, only to be silenced a few seconds later.

Kesh rested her hand on one wall. The faintest of tremors rippled under the thick skin of her palm. "She's coming back from the brink."

This earned an amused snort from Sloane Kelly, and no more. Instead, she ran on, taking the lead.

"Left here," Kesh urged at the next junction. "Chamber D-14, on the right."

This corridor looked as if it had taken the brunt of the station's damage. An illusion, for Kesh knew other sections had fared worse, but she'd yet to traverse devastation like this. The floor had buckled upward, a bundle of wrapped conduits and pipes poking through the bent metal tiles. Like a broken bone through weak human skin.

Steaming orange liquid dribbled from the sheared pipes, spilling down the raised section like volcanic discharge. A bank of lights, still dark, swung from the cables that should have connected them to the ceiling.

"What a fucking mess," Sloane muttered. "You sure the terminal said Calix was in stasis?"

"As of ten minutes ago, yes."

They scaled the little mountain of floor tiles, stepping over the orange river of foul-smelling fluid.

Miraculously, the door to D-14 was undamaged. With emergency power holding, Sloane tapped in a code on the crooked panel beside it and stepped back as the door whisked open.

A silent, pristine chamber awaited, cast in dim red by lights around the perimeter of the floor. Like coffins in an ancient tomb, eight stasis pods faced in toward a central examination couch on a rotating dais. Frost still clung to the window of each pod.

Kesh's gaze swept across them all, finding a green light on each. Finally. Something going right. She shouldered her way past Sloane, bent over Calix's pod. A swift check over the control terminal brought even more relief.

"Integrity confirmed. He's okay."

"Finally," Sloane said, mirroring her own thoughts. "Wake him. And not the gentle way, there's no time for it."

While Kesh input the commands, Sloane wandered over to the terminal beside the examination couch, trying to activate it. Judging from her curse, it didn't respond.

"Try the comm," Kesh suggested. Sloane moved to the small device mounted beside the door. Slapped a button. Poked it. In her peripheral, Kesh watched her make a fist and punch it—more of a love-tap, really. Well, it wasn't the human's gift.

"Dead," Sloane announced.

"Well, best ready your weapon, the thaw is almost complete. Vitals look good."

The pair stood shoulder to shoulder, facing the stasis pod. A full minute passed with no indication that anything had changed, except for the frost on the porthole condensing into fine droplets.

Then a hand slapped against the glass, smearing the water. Kesh leaned in and used the manual override to open the pod. There was a hiss of stagnant, foul-smelling air from around the seal of the two sections. Kesh lifted the top, rotating it upward and out of the way.

The turian lay still, eyes closed, wet stasis suit clinging to his avian-like frame. After a few seconds and with eyes still closed, he spoke.

"Why is it so quiet?"

Turians had a way of speaking, a kind of flanging effect that made it sound like two tonal voices in one throat. Kesh found the result to be pleasing to the ear, though she knew human counterparts who did not.

Rugged from his ungentle wake-up, Corvannis's usual slow tones sounded thicker. Less confident.

Kesh glanced at Sloane. The security director studied the engineer. Whatever she saw, it seemed to reassure her. "We're in trouble. We need your help."

That earned the turian's attention.

"You don't say. What kind of trouble?" Calix blinked several times, his eyes a bit less bleary each time. Finally, he lifted his head a bit, winced, and laid it back, the bony crest pressing into the form-fit cushions. Somehow, he dredged up humor. "Given the method of wake-up, the warm weaponized welcome—" Sloane lowered her pistol a notch, but only just. "—and the lack of medical, I'm going to guess it's the critical variety."

"It is," Sloane said. "We'll explain on the way. You need to get up."

Calix groaned. He managed to get his arms free, and rubbed his eyes with two fists. When he reached out, Kesh wrapped one hand around his thin, lean arm and helped pull him from the grip of the cushions. He needed her help to stand. "Nakmor Kesh," he managed, once his joints unstuck. "Good to see you."

"And you," she replied. "Especially alive."

"That why she bring a gun?" he asked, tilting his head toward Sloane.

"A precaution," Sloane cut in. "In case you weren't in a cooperative mood."

"Expect that?"

"I've known a few turians," she replied, but lowered the weapon entirely. Kesh couldn't fault it. The species was known for many things, but blindly following just anybody wasn't one. Calix, he had never pushed for the things others of his ilk had—glory, renown, position.

What he had demanded, and what Kesh had eventually facilitated, was trust. He knew his work, and he knew his crew.

Now, he unfurled his two fingers and thumb from Kesh's supportive arm and gave Sloane a nod. "So I've heard," he said simply, earning himself a glower. "Perhaps, then, you could give me a minute to get my mood—"

"Negative. Life support is going to fail in thirty-two minutes. You're going to fix it, right now."

Kesh felt his arm stiffen in her grip, even as he fought a yawn. "No other viable sections?"

"Life support for the *entire* Nexus."

That did it. Calix finally seemed to focus. He fixed a quizzical gaze on the woman. "You're joking."

"Come and see for yourself," Kesh said, shaking her head. "If it is, it's the worst joke in the galaxy."

"Right." He couldn't seem to look away from Sloane. Knowing turians—knowing him—he was trying to figure out her angle.

If only there was one.

Kesh chalked his lack of concern up to a mind still clawing its way out of six centuries of sleep. She pulled his arm over her shoulder and helped him through the room, past the exam couch where—in a normal wake-up from stasis—a subject would receive several hours of muscle-atrophy treatment, along with hundreds of tests and rejuvenating injections.

In the hall, faced with the devastation, Calix gasped with a mixture of pain and awe. "Looks like a krogan wedding came through."

Kesh snorted. "We don't have weddings."

"I can see why," he shot back, clearly getting his wits together.

Sloane wasn't as amused. "This is no time for jokes," she snapped.

Calix held up his one free hand, a conciliatory gesture.

Sloane scowled, turned and leapt up onto a buckled section of flooring.

"Where are we going?"

"Operations."

Calix shook his head, causing Kesh to pause

instead of following. "Waste of time. If the rest of the Nexus has been hit like this, you need to take me to the workshop. Besides, it's closer."

Sloane looked over his head at Kesh.

When she nodded, the Security Director wasted no breath arguing. "Fine. Lead the way."

"Tell you what," Calix replied with a grimaced kind of amusement. "You lead the way, I'll shuffle along on Kesh's arm and we can all pretend I'm slightly better than a sack of dead vorcha right now."

It was like he couldn't help himself, Kesh noted thoughtfully. Sloane cracked a smile, even if it was a hard one, and replied simply, "Deal."

Maybe it was no time for jokes. But she couldn't ignore the fact that despite all that, the human seemed far more at ease in the company of krogan and turians than her own kind.

Or salarians, for that matter.

Which seemed obvious to Kesh.

Together, they moved as fast as they could. Calix told them which turns to take, and remained unfazed when they had to double back due to an obstacle—namely, a hallway rent open to the vacuum of space. A whole chunk, three meters in diameter, had been torn from the hull, temporarily sealed just as Operations had been.

Kesh had tried to keep a running tally of all the things that would need to be fixed. By the time she reached *shorn hull, lower corridor*, she just gave up.

Everything would need to be fixed. Even the things that appeared undamaged would require testing and recertification. Months of work. Maybe years, and without supplemental work teams and the warehouses and hangars full of spare parts.

"You haven't told me what actually happened here,"

Calix said, breaking the silence. "Were we attacked?"

"Sensors are still offline, along with just about everything else, but it appears we hit something."

"A ship? Or something natural?"

"Jury's out," Sloane replied curtly. "The sooner we can get this rolling, the sooner we can figure out what happened."

Kesh could offer no better.

The turian was not one to waste time with empty words. He fell silent once more, content to focus on warming up his sleep-heavy limbs. Kesh found herself carrying less and less of his weight and balance as he slowly regained control. Then, when she felt confident enough that he could at least walk on his own, he cleared his throat. "In here," Calix said, nodding toward a door. The signage on the wall read LIFE-SUPPORT CENTRAL MONITORING.

The panel didn't work, so Kesh stepped in and heaved the two doors apart, allowing Calix through. Sloane started to follow, but stopped at Calix's upheld hand. He wasn't looking at her, but at the room.

Like everything else, it was a mess inside.

"How much time do we have?" Calix asked.

"Twenty-four minutes," Sloane said instantly.

"I need to go wake the rest of my team."

Sloane stiffened. "There's not enough time—"

"I need them right now," he said. "Or do you have thousands of those rebreathers on hand?"

Sloane cast a glance at Kesh, who could only shrug. The security director's hesitation lasted only a second longer, and then Calix strode off the way they'd come. "Stay here," he said over one shoulder, then he disappeared around a corner.

The human stared after him for a moment. "Is he always like that?"

Kesh's snorted laughter echoed in the tumbled chamber. "Calix Corvannis is like many of his kind," she said. "Except it's for neither glory nor position that he seizes control of moments like this."

"Not big on the meritocracy, then?"

She shrugged. "I don't know his history, Director Sloane. Not entirely. I never saw the need to ask. What I can tell you is that he is an extremely talented engineer, slow to anger and protective of his own. A concept," she added, "that includes that which he oversees. Systems or staff."

Sloane raised an eyebrow. "And you let him just make decisions like that?"

Again, Kesh lifted her broad shoulders. "Unlike most, I don't feel the need to second-guess my crew. When Calix operates on his own terms, he does so for good reason. And to success," she finished pointedly.

"You trust him."

"Enough to let him implement the entire cryostasis system."

Sloane whistled, low and under her breath. "Will he need help collecting his crew?"

That, Kesh didn't know. "You have spent more than your fair share with turians," she said instead. "What do you think?"

Whatever she did think, Sloane wasn't about to share it with Kesh, that much was clear. Back in the Milky Way, rumor had placed the human in *very* close proximity to another turian. Kaetus, if memory served—and it usually did. Surprising no one, Kaetus had boarded the *Natanus*, the turian ark destined to dock with the Nexus soon enough.

Whether it was friendship that had him following Sloane into Andromeda or, as gossip suggested, something more, didn't concern Kesh. Nor did the existence of said turian. What mattered to her was that Sloane was familiar enough with turian ways that she'd be willing to let her engineer do what he did best.

Something she appeared to allow, for now.

Kesh would take what she could get. Calix and she would both earn the trust needed to operate unfettered in this failing system. The fact Sloane appeared to prefer their species would only help. "Now," Kesh said briskly, clapping her hands together hard. "We might as well keep busy."

"I guess so," the woman sighed. She stretched hard, rolled her shoulders, and bent to work.

With Sloane's help, fallen equipment was righted, debris cleared from a bank of control screens.

In record time, Calix Corvannis returned with a bleary-eyed group of seven engineers of junior rank. Junior, Kesh knew, only because they refused to surpass their supervisor in rank. They leapt right to work, as if they didn't need instructions. Not that Calix was silent. He barked the occasional order, using terms and abbreviations Kesh did not recognize.

He knew these people very well. They'd worked together for a long time. In fact, they'd all volunteered for the Nexus as a group, Kesh recalled. Something had happened on Calix's previous post, a labor dispute during which—the notes attached to the report she was given had explained—he had gone against orders for the well-being of his team.

She didn't know the details because he was too humble to talk about it.

Whatever the case, they were loyal after that, "to a fault," in his words.

"They said they'd follow me anywhere," Calix had said dryly, "so I thought I'd test them on that with Andromeda. Turns out they were serious."

She'd asked if he was satisfied with that.

"I don't hold anybody to anything they don't want to do," he'd told her, nodding in the direction of his team as they'd worked. "They want to leave, they can. But they saw the Initiative specs, heard the speeches, same as me. They're here because they want to be, Kesh. They'll work hard."

She had never been given any reason to doubt that.

And thank the stars for it. Now they needed every last one of them honed and ready.

At a tersely shouted order from the turian, two of his team raced off in unison to fix a stuck valve, one deck below and three over.

Kesh stood back, resisting the urge to check the clock. Not that there was any need. Sloane saw fit to call out the remaining time as each minute ticked away. Fifteen. Soon enough it was only ten. Then five. The engineers worked furiously, but with the kind of calm usually reserved for a drill.

"Two minutes," Sloane called, with less fervor than prior. Her voice sounded breathy, her tone weakened. The air now tasted of burned chemicals. It smelled even worse, and that was to a krogan. Kesh could only imagine what the humans were experiencing. Indeed, after uttering those words, the security director pulled her rebreather mask over her face and sat down.

Kesh didn't ask if she was okay. She wasn't, obviously. Only time could tell now.

And time was exactly what Calix called. "That should do it. Confirm?"

Sloane and Kesh waited as the engineering team verified the surgery they'd just performed.

"Oxygen levels stabilizing," one said.

"Filtration at eleven percent," another, an asari, said. "Now ten... nine. No, wait. Hovering between nine and ten percent." The tension drained from the room. They smiled at one another.

"Success?" Sloane asked, her voice muffled by the full-face mask.

Calix let out a breath, reaching his long arms up in a stretch. "Let's just say we've bought ourselves twenty-four hours. Maybe more."

Sloane let out something that might have been one of her profane phrases that were meant to suggest gratitude. Kesh couldn't hear her. She reached for the mask, only to pause when Calix waved at her.

"You'd better keep that mask handy. The air in here is still poisonous, and will be for a while."

Visibly short on breath, Sloane let her hand fall and said loudly, "We can't fix all this damage to the Nexus if no one can breathe."

"Sir?" the asari engineer said.

Calix turned to her. "Go ahead, Irida."

"If we returned unnecessary portions of the Nexus to a state of vacuum, and used the sorting membrane—"

"—we could create a pocket of custom atmosphere. Good thinking, engineer." The asari, Irida, grinned at the praise.

Sloane rubbed her temples again. "Explain that?"

"Bring the good air here, shift the bad elsewhere, and leave most of the Nexus with nothing at all."

"Sounds like a shell game," Sloane said. Calix

recognized the archaic reference.

"That's because it is." The turian raised a hand to stave off Sloane's next objection. "It leaves us with a section, maybe two, containing perfectly safe air. With some clever rerouting we can move that air wherever it's needed."

Kesh pulled Sloane aside. She leaned in and lowered her voice. "We still do not know where Jien Garson is. If she's wandered—"

"She can't have gone that far."

"It's a risk."

"We don't have much of a choice here, Kesh." Then, louder, to Calix. "Do it."

Kesh studied the human. "You don't want to run that by Tann, first?"

"Tann can bite—" She cut herself off. An improvement, Kesh noted. The narrow victory had settled the human some. "He'll understand. Besides, better to ask forgiveness, isn't it?"

CHAPTER SIX

Jarun Tann sat cross-legged on the floor of Jien Garson's office—technically his office now, at least for the time being. He held a glass of asari honey mead in both hands, throat still tingling from the first sip, a pleasant warmth spreading through his belly.

He stared out through the impressive floor-to-ceiling window, one of the long habitat arms of the Nexus stretching out several kilometers before him. Doing so, he could just about manage to convince himself that everything would be okay. Then he smirked, amused and annoyed that his mind would flirt with that very human way of thinking.

Their ability to filter and twist reality had always eluded his comprehension, and yet the more time he spent around them, the more it seemed to happen to him. Or it threatened to, anyway. He would have to analyze this when things calmed down.

If things calmed down, he corrected himself, not *when*. "When" implied certainty of success, a mere matter of time. When Garson was found, not if. He had his doubts, born of a sense of realism, but he'd yet to voice them. Let Sloane Kelly or Foster Addison speak of *whens*. A useful tool when rallying the crew. Garson herself had said it, too. "*When* we reach Andromeda…" He would presume nothing.

If was realistic. *If* allowed for the possibility of failure, and thus the ability to plan for that.

If we reach Andromeda.

If we can fix life support in time.

If Garson is—

"Life support has stabilized," Addison said. He glanced up at her. Hadn't even realized she'd returned to the room. She took the mead from his hands and allowed herself a rather generous gulp.

"They did it," she added, and gulped again.

Humans. "Well, that is wonderful news," Tann said aloud.

Addison went to the window and stood there. He watched her face as reflected in the glass, translucent over a mass of stars. And over that, that skein of black none of them could identify. The fear that chased them all remained, but greatly diminished. Determination had replaced doubt, success a barrier against whatever private worries she carried.

He wished he'd known this would happen, wished he'd any reason at all to research the Initiative's leading committee. Starting anything ignorant bothered him immensely.

Addison sipped one more time, nodding as if reaffirming something to herself. "Damn, that's good. Where did you find it?"

He pointed to an open panel to one side of Garson's desk. It had popped open during the calamity, revealing a rather impressive assortment of beverages. Some had toppled out, but none—wonder of wonders—had broken.

Addison smiled on seeing it. "Jien's going to be pissed that her supply was raided."

"Under the circumstances," he replied calmly, "I think she'll forgive me."

Addison drained the glass. As if possessed of too

much energy, she paced back to the large desk, rounding it. She seemed poised to sit in the large chair behind the massive marble slab, a tactic he wondered at, but instead simply set the empty cup down and faced Tann.

"Do you think we'll be able to salvage the mission?"

Tann smiled at her. "It is only a matter of *if*," he said, pleased at the wordplay.

Addison's brow furrowed. She opened her mouth to question him, but evidently thought better of it. "Any progress on comms?"

"The screen behind you," he replied, gesturing. "I started a routine to determine what connections, transmitters, and receivers are still available, with instructions to create a new mesh based on the results. Optimized for coverage, of course. Some, err... less critical wiring is being repurposed as needed."

"You did all that?" Her surprise galled him. "I thought you were revenue."

Let her think that. It served his purposes well enough, for the moment. "Well," he said demurely, "the routine already existed. I knew this because I approved the budget for it, and also recall with perfect clarity the moment it came back balanced."

Addison eyed him.

Had he lost her? Tann bit back a sigh. "I selected the program," he said patiently, "then pressed the big button marked 'GO'." He flexed his long fingers, like some kind of button-pressing champion.

Addison, it seemed, wasn't quite yet in the mood for humor. Even so, this earned a tick of amusement from one corner of her mouth. "Gold star," she murmured.

"Eh?"

"And by 'less critical wiring,'" she said, louder, "you refer to...?"

Tann turned to face her now. "Did you know that Medical—and I mean the entire section—was configured with a premium sound system?"

"Sound?"

He tilted his head. "Soothes the patients."

Her eyebrows lifted. "Nice."

"Yes." A beat. "State of the art, incredibly well-designed. The finest minds came together to incorporate the art of sound with the science of it. Never before had any station claimed the like." Her eyes were getting wider. Her skepticism, as well. Tann allowed himself a brief smile. "Well, it *was* state of the art. I'm afraid they'll have to find soothing somewhere else, now."

When Addison laughed, she did so bluntly. No coyness to her. "Nice," she said again, but dryly.

He shrugged. "I thought it better we have functioning comms in the area."

Her humor faded as he studied her, until it seemed she replayed something else in her head. Something he didn't understand, until she murmured, "We make the greatest sacrifice any of us have ever, or will ever, make."

The quote sobered him. After a moment of silence, he set his own glass down on the desk and offered, somewhat hesitantly, "Perhaps a fine sound system was not what she had in mind, but…"

But what? But at least they'd gotten a brief bit of amusement from it.

And semi-functional comms.

Addison seemed to understand, though she waved at him as if brushing away the moment.

The terminal chimed.

Saved from the painful effort of conversation, Tann stood and crossed to it. The director joined him. "Let's see what we've got."

The view wasn't pretty. Tann chewed on his lower lip as he analyzed the mess of lines and bubbles. Vast sections of the Nexus were not covered by the comms, and even the areas that were could barely be considered so. There were hallways where one end had a connection while the other, just a scant ten meters away, had nothing. Labs where the edges of the room were fine but, were one to be standing in the center, they'd find themselves totally cut off. Overall, the dark areas edged out those in the light.

"Hmm." Addison didn't seem impressed.

"I believe the phrase we're looking for is 'better than nothing,'" Tann suggested.

"Sums it up quite nicely."

"I motion that we initiate this configuration change." He gave her a sideways glance. "All in favor?" This earned a brief smile.

"You don't need my vote, acting director."

Tann shook his head. "I feel confident in achieving success together." He paused, and repeated, "All in favor?"

She shrugged. "Aye." But any victory she may have taken from the moment quickly and obviously faded to guilt. Her voice dropped to a whisper again. "I can't believe this happened. Suppose… suppose Jien is… What the hell are we going to do?"

"Survive."

A blunt answer for an obvious question.

It was her turn to glance at him. She searched his eyes. "It's not enough though, is it, Tann? The mission—"

"I *meant* the mission. The mission must survive. Above all else."

"If the Pathfinders arrive to find there is no Nexus—"

Awkwardly, he placed a hand on her shoulder. "One thing at a time. We both agree, the mission is the most important concern. Good. But to accomplish that we've got…" He turned her toward the expansive window, and its view of the broken ship, "a lot of work to do. Hard choices to make. Likely more death and pain to absorb. Bodies to jettison before disease—"

Foster Addison let out an involuntary laugh.

"What?" he asked her.

"Nothing," she said. "Just… maybe you should let me handle the motivational speeches."

"Another point," Tann allowed, "on which we most certainly can agree."

She stared out over the wreckage for a brief moment. Tann furiously worked various conversational gambits through his filters before deciding simply that he had nothing. Logic didn't suit her, entirely. He wasn't sure how to proceed with sympathy.

Instead, he waited until she shook off the shadows of her thoughts and turned. Her facial features, he was relieved to note, had settled into harder lines. Determination was back. Much preferred. He could channel that.

"Can we try the comms now?" She raised her arm, showing off her wrist. He didn't get it until she added, "Maybe Jien can be located by her omni."

A fine idea. The initial staff, as evidenced by Addison's own omni-tool on her forearm, would have geared up first thing.

He swept a spindly hand at the comm panel. "Delighted."

With ease, he programmed the computer to initiate the new connection matrix—a process that only took several seconds. Most went green, but a few immediately reverted back to red or, worse, remained dark. Wires to replace, antennas to reconnect. He ignored it for now. Long fingers swiping across the display, he brought up the map and pushed, pinched, and pulled it around.

"Hmm…" A common enough sound heard around here, he reflected wryly.

Addison peered at the digital mass. "Where is everyone?"

"Exactly my concern. Biometric location is offline, it seems. Database corruption maybe. Another thing to fix—but no matter," he said abruptly. "Let's see if anyone can hear us." He tapped and held the transmit option. "This is Jarun Tann. If you can hear me, please find the nearest comms panel and reply. If the nearest one doesn't work, well, I hope you're familiar with the process of elimination."

He could hear his own voice coming from the adjacent Operations room, as well as echoing through several nearby corridors. *A good sign.* He felt pleased.

Silence stretched. Tann waited. Beside him, Addison shifted on her feet.

Then, just as Tann considered whether he should try again, the comm flicked on.

"Sloane Kelly here." The familiar voice boomed through the room's speakers. "Nice work, you two."

"And you as well," Tann replied. "I cannot help but note that we have not suffocated in the vacuum of space."

Addison shot him a disbelieving eyebrow.

Well, whatever. They knew what he meant.

"Calix and his team deserve all the credit," the Security Director replied. Oddly humble, he thought, wasn't it? "They've already begun work on reversing the damage, but it's going to take some time."

And his team, eh? That only slightly worried him—as much for the extra breathers as the little bit of rebellion he saw in the act. Still, the ability to draw breath pleased him enough, for now. Tann decided not to question it.

Out loud.

Privately, he wondered if they'd even tried fixing the problem with only Calix involved. Sloane seemed like the consummate security officer—which in Tann's experience meant her default reaction to any problem would be immediate and overwhelming firepower. Figuratively speaking.

Something to keep an eye on. He filed this observation, aware too late that he very likely was meant to say something obligatory at this juncture.

Addison caught it. "Please thank them for their efforts."

"I will. Has Garson turned up?"

"Sadly, no," Tann replied. "And bio location isn't working."

"Of course it isn't. Hardly anything is." Sloane paused. "Damn. Well, I've been sending out search parties whenever someone has a spare minute. We've started moving bodies to a temporary morgue in one of the labs."

"Understood. Return to Operations." Within nanoseconds, he realized how much that had sounded like an order. Too soon, given Sloane's obvious misgivings about his temporary leadership status. "At your earliest convenience," he added. "We have much to discuss."

"It'll be a while." Sloane's voice bristled over the comm. "Life support was only the first of our problems.

We're not out of the woods yet."

"Addison and I understand that, but—"

"Out."

The link closed.

Well, he tried. Tann did not sigh. Not out loud, at least.

||||||||||||||||||

Sloane lifted her finger from the screen.

"Calix has things under control here," Kesh said. She had been standing just behind her while she spoke to Tann. "I'm going to check on the rest of the krogan, make sure their stasis pods weren't damaged."

Sloane sighed. She understood the desire. Wanted to do the same for her team, more than anything. "Power is still unstable. Sensors are hosed. Shields, too. Who knows how many fucking rads we're absorbing just standing here."

Nakmor Kesh inclined her head in agreement. "All true. And like life support, all things that will require trained teams to repair. That means krogan, in many cases. I need to make sure they're safe."

"There may be another way," she said, still working through the idea. "Hang on a second."

Kesh waited as Sloane identified herself to the comms panel. The system recognized her, but this failed to result in what she'd hoped for. The system that allowed her to locate crew, no matter where within the Nexus they were, was dark. Still, she could communicate. Open broadcasts only, but it was a start.

"Sloane Kelly to Kandros. Please respond." When no answer came, she repeated it.

This time, his reply came a few seconds later.

"Kandros here, along with Talini and six other

survivors." Aside from the obvious good news, his unasked for sit-rep told her that she had an audience and should guard her words. He wouldn't know that the comms weren't closed. Not yet.

She'd tell him later. "Report."

"We went looking for ships, but you're not going to like the result."

She winced. "Tell me."

"The explorers are destroyed. Or at least, most of them are destroyed. Something tore through docking like a thresher maw through sand. The Pathfinders' ships took the brunt."

"Shit." Sloane rubbed at her forehead. In the back of her thoughts, a free-floating bit of station floated across the memory of Operations. Kesh made a low, thoughtful sound. "You said 'most'?"

"Yeah. There's no trace of the others." A beat. "Just a damned big hole."

Just great.

Kandros followed up with, "But it's not all bleak. We took shelter inside one of the shuttles in hangar two. Situation cramped, but stable."

Kesh grunted in approval. "Smart thinking. Self-contained, provisioned, life support, even a medical bay. Very smart."

Sloane nodded agreement, but filed away the data for later use. She hadn't quite reached the point of ordering everyone to retreat to safe ground.

"Leave Talini in charge there," she said to Kandros. "I have a task for you."

"Name it."

Sloane grinned, bolstered by his attitude. "Make your way to stasis chambers..." She glanced at Kesh, an eyebrow raised.

The krogan rattled off a series of designators, assuredly where the bulk of the krogan population had been placed. Sloane repeated them, just in case he hadn't caught them all.

"Got it?"

"Copy that," he replied. "What's the mission?"

"I want a status report. How many made it, how many… well, you get the idea."

"Understood. Anything else?"

"Be safe."

She could practically hear his long-suffered smirk. "Always. Kandros out."

Sloane dropped her hand from the screen. "There, now I know the status of the other half of my team, and soon you'll have the info you're looking for. Everybody wins."

"Thank you, Sloane Kelly." A grave thing, given the seriousness of her tone.

Sloane waved the krogan's gratitude off. "We each got something we needed. No need for thanks."

Kesh regarded her. "But you need something else." Not a question. Observant, Sloane thought. By far.

And right. "I do," she confirmed.

"Which is?"

"Nothing much." She just couldn't help but yank the krogan's chain. Just a little. "Only a power core in the first stage of meltdown. Noticed the alert when we left Operations, decided it best not to panic everyone just yet."

Kesh growled, and if krogan could have hackles, Sloane had no doubt they'd be bristling. "And you wait until *now* to tell me?"

Sloane made no excuses. Darkly amusing as it was, her choices weren't great then. They were better now, thanks to Calix's team. "Now that I know we're not going to suffocate? Yeah."

The krogan stood there, immovable as a wall. Staring at her.

Goading krogan, Sloane understood, was the subject of a violent betting pool for a reason. "I'm hoping this is where you tell me how we're going to fix it," she suggested.

Kesh shook her head. "You can't fix a core in stage one of meltdown," she bit out. "You jettison it and move very far away."

Sloane opened her mouth. Paused. Cast her future to fate and said helpfully, "But engines aren't—"

"One thing at a time!" Kesh roared, hands thrown to the ceiling in frustration.

IIIIIIIIIIIIIIIII

Sloane worked side by side with Kesh for twenty-six hours.

Through sweat and blood and the power of multicultural profanity, the failed core was manually jettisoned and, in a moment of inspired genius on Addison's part, tugged out to a safe distance by a semi-functional cargo drone. Everyone now awake had to hunker as deep as possible in the bowels of the mangled space station in order to weather the resulting blast, but it worked.

Three times during the already insane day, she was contacted by Tann, or Addison, or both, each requesting that she find her way to Operations so they could have a meeting. A damn *meeting*, while the Nexus went up in flames all around them.

Not likely.

One emergency fixed only led to the next, and

all the while life support remained stuck at 10%. No capacity for waking additional help. Sloane and Kesh rushed from one section to another, until Sloane finally collapsed, exhausted, on a half-burned couch in the lobby of an embassy that now seemed so comically unnecessary that she snorted in laughter before drifting into restless sleep.

The fourth comm blast came just as sleep had fully embraced Sloane Kelly. She'd curled up, one folded arm serving as pillow, when the annoying chime yanked her back to consciousness. She bolted upright, ready to tell that salarian where he could stuff his "discussion."

Before she could, his words stopped her cold.

"You're needed in hydroponics," Tann said. "I'm afraid there's more bad news."

"Is it Garson? You've found her?"

"Would that we had," he said, a grim note to his voice. "This is something else. I'm sorry, Director. But you need to see this."

CHAPTER SEVEN

"Kesh and I will be there as soon as we can."

Jarun Tann glanced at his companion. Addison's features betrayed nothing. Well, then. "No need to pull Nakmor Kesh away from her tasks," Tann said. "It's not a, er, technical problem."

As expected, the Security Director did not take well to subtlety. "I'll take that under advisement." As usual when dealing with Sloane Kelly, the link abruptly ended.

Tann stood silently for a moment, shifting his weight from foot to foot. Then, thoughtfully, "I should have been more emphatic."

"It'll be fine," Addison said. She sat on a bench, knees together, hands clasped in her lap. The bench itself sat askew, the bolts that held it in place having been sheared in the disaster. It straddled the common area and the area of spongy, synthetic soil it was supposed to face. A fine patch of bright green grass should have been growing there by the time Tann awoke, had everything gone as planned.

"If Kesh is with her, we'll manage. It may even be a good thing. Her knowledge of this station is—"

"Unrivaled," Tann finished, locking the hint of acid welling up behind a determined smile. "Yes, I know. But the protocol was clear. You and Director Kelly are to advise—"

"The protocol." Addison sighed the words.

"*Really*. Take a look at this place, Tann. Protocol should be the least of our concerns."

Perhaps. In part. He began to pace. Rubble skipped away from his feet, clattering across the floor. The hydroponics section, like everything else, resembled some ancient abandoned place, a shadow of the idealized and perfectly engineered marvel it should have been. Quieter, maybe, but no less devastated.

That made this moment so important.

No. He was right about this. "I disagree," he said. "A lot of very intelligent people spent vast amounts of time working through every situation we might face, planning for every contingency. We'd be making a huge mistake if we threw all that out and started relying on snap decisions made by whomever happened to be standing around."

He reached the wall, turned.

"That is no way to govern," he added, before proceeding on another circuit of his route.

Addison remained silent.

So much so that he paused mid-circuit, stopped in front of her. "You agree, surely?"

"I suppose…"

It trailed off, leaving Tann humming. Not quite the fervor he'd been hoping for, but at least she was listening. He continued to pace. Each step brought a new line of thinking, another possibility to account for. Yet it all came back to the same thing.

Jien Garson, truly a brilliant mind, had overseen the protocol encoded into the Nexus's systems, which had led to his awakening. His presence here, his role, was essentially due to her direct order, and he intended to respect that by fulfilling that role to the best of his ability. Director Addison may feel bitterness that she was not chosen for the role, but that was not Tann's fault. Nor his responsibility. Only Jien Garson would be able to explain the reasoning there. *If* she turned up.

Another turn, more walking, more thought.

Jien Garson could never have guessed that a calamity on this kind of scale would befall her mission. In truth, the leadership protocol could have just as easily wound up with two human janitors and a krogan dental hygienist—easily the worst job in the known universe—as its new leadership, had they happened to be the three most senior surviving crew. More power to them, had that been the case!

Turn. Walk.

Think.

That worst-case scenario had not happened, of course. The protocol had whittled down the list and found him, a full seven rungs below Administrator Garson on the leadership ladder. Addison and Sloane would advise him just as they would have advised her. He hadn't asked for this. He'd staged no coup. Jarun Tann was here to do a job, whatever was required of him, and if this was it, then he would do his duty. The mission mattered, above all else.

Turn. Step.

Freeze.

Boots before him. How long had they been there? He glanced up, met the tired, bleary eyes of Sloane Kelly.

"Make this quick," she said, without even a courteous attempt at preamble. "I'm busy."

"And hello to you." Abruptly, he realized he'd walked right in front of the door and blocked her path. "Come in, come in." He swept an arm toward the innards of Hydroponics and followed the security director inside.

She greeted Foster Addison, then sat on one of the benches, looking on the verge of collapse. With the two women occupying the only two benches, Tann moved to stand nearby. He had nothing to lean on, so he clasped his hands behind his back and waited.

Addison said nothing, forcing Sloane to break the silence.

"What's the goddamn emergency?" she demanded. "There's nothing on fire here. No dead bodies. So... *what*?"

"No fires," Tann agreed. "No bodies, true. Notice anything else missing, Director Kelly?"

"I don't have the energy for puzzles, *Acting* Director Tann. Spit it out."

The impact of the revelation, he reasoned, would serve enough to take the spite from her use of title. "Very well." He pointed at the closest bay. "No crops," he explained, enunciating each syllable.

Sloane merely sat there, looking exhausted. Maybe he was being too obtuse?

Then, with a shrug, she said, "Okay. So? We just got here. Plants take time to grow."

"There should be buds," Addison volunteered. Ruining his grand reveal, of course. These humans. No respect for finesse. "Several weeks before our arrival the first seeds should have been placed by automated systems, so that a crop would already be started as the crew was revived."

Tann walked to one of the auto-gardeners, removing a bag he'd placed there thirty minutes earlier. He took it to Sloane and laid it at her feet. Inside were the remains of a few hundred small plants, shriveled and burned.

"Radiated," he said. "Every last one."

The security director studied the plants. She spread

her hands. "So we start another batch. Right? When necessary. We have supplies. I'm not a botanist but—"

"Exactly," Tann cut in, seizing the opportunity. "Not a botanist. Nor am I, nor is Director Addison. And a botanist, a whole team of them, is what we need."

"Tann," Sloane said, frowning, "we talked about this. You even argued against the concept. With everything going on, the last thing we need is more people running around. We've barely got things working as it is. More strain on the systems is a bad idea."

"More data," he said flatly, "means decisions must be revisited. In this case, I disagree with your assessment." He raised his hands in defense, staving off her no doubt profanity-laced retort. "Please, let me explain."

Perhaps it was the *please* that did it. Sloane deflated a bit. She glanced at Foster Addison, perhaps looking for support. The other woman simply waited in silence.

"Fine," she sighed. "What's the reasoning?"

Tann tipped his head. "Our situation is still critical," he said, "but the immediate threat is over."

"You can't know that," she said hastily. So much for that. "Hell, we don't even know what this threat is, and implying that you do is dangerous."

"All I mean," Tann said in slow emphasis, "is that the fires have been put out. The hull breaches are sealed. I agree there could still be aftershocks, or new attacks, whatever we want to call them, but there may not be, either. Can we at least agree on that?"

Addison gave a single nod.

Sloane shrugged.

"There. Progress. Given that assumption, I think it's time that we turn our attention to the mission."

"You've got to be kidding me." Sloane stared at his face, which Tann hoped projected calm confidence.

"Holy shit, you're *not*. You're actually serious. Save this shit for Garson, there's no need to be—"

Tann lifted his hands once again. "*Please*, Director, let me finish. I hope, as we all do, that our guiding visionary will be found alive and well, very soon. I remind you that I did not ask for this."

Sloane shook her head. She did not believe his sincerity or motivation, that was plain, but lacked some way to combat it. Or perhaps she couldn't decide on which vulgarity to use next. He pushed on before she could.

"We need to adjust our immediate goals. Change our focus. From survival to recovery. I believe our ultimate goal, to support the mission of the Pathfinders, is still possible. Indeed, not just possible, but *critical*. We can't have them arrive here only to find the Nexus…" he swept a hand across the devastated hydroponics bay, "like this."

"And you have a plan to accomplish this?"

He did, but he fully intended to fold it in under the guise of inclusion. "We all do, consciously or otherwise. Let us discuss the options, and decide."

"Decide," Sloane said with a sardonic laugh. "So that's why you wanted Kesh away."

"It's not as simple as that," he replied.

"Don't be so offended," she snorted. "It's exactly like that."

"Okay, yes," he replied, exasperated by the woman's distrust. And observations. "It is like that, but not for the reasons you no doubt are thinking."

Now Sloane really did laugh, loud and energetically. "We're in Andromeda now, Tann. Don't you remember Garson's words? Check all that old bullshit at the door."

"I don't recall her saying anything quite so vulgar."

"I'm paraphrasing. It's what she meant, though. None of our old scores, our stupid and unjustified prejudices, apply here."

"As I said, this is not the reason for my concern. I simply feel that the protocol—"

Sloane waved her hands in overdone acquiescence. "Right, right. The protocol that so neatly made you boss." She blew out a sigh that undercut any humor with sheer frustration. "Let's finish here. I've got a station teetering on the brink, and you've got a proposal in mind. I can see it all over your aerodynamic face."

Tann cocked his head. "Hydrodynamic. We are not a species suited to—"

"*Whatever.*"

He wondered if he would ever get on Sloane Kelly's good side. So far, it didn't seem possible. In the end, of course, it didn't matter. He had the power to make decisions. As long as he had a sympathetic ear with Foster Addison, such decisions could be ratified. Not unanimously, perhaps, but still a majority, and that was all they truly required.

"Very well. I suggest we wake a more significant part of the population," he explained. "Experts in all the various systems. Life support is already taken care of." No accusation here. "Hydroponics, power, medical, communications, sanitation, sensors, astronavigation, and a dozen other areas, however, are offline or at best critical, and will remain so unless we wake the people necessary to begin correcting the problems."

The problematic human was already shaking her head. "No can do," Sloane said. "Not enough air. Or food. Or water. You said you wanted to shift from survival to recovery, but your recovery team will make survival impossible."

It was an echo of the argument he'd fed her. He was savvy enough to recognize it—and also how to navigate it. That's where Addison would come in.

And on cue, she did. "Supplies can be augmented."

"How so?" Sloane asked.

"From nearby planets." She raised her eyebrows. "Which is what my people were cultivated for. I overheard your discussion with your officer," she added. "What was it, twenty-some-odd hours ago?"

"Twenty-six," Tann replied, but decided to round it when Sloane shot him an incredulous look. "And some minutes."

Thirty-seven minutes, to be precise. Not that he figured they'd appreciate a salarian's photographic memory.

"I know it's a blow that we don't have the Pathfinder scout ships," Addison continued, "but I've been thinking. We *can* send shuttles, scout the nearest worlds. They could return with air and water, even food. We might even find help. Chances of that are low, I'll admit, but non-zero."

"Shit, Addison, we can't do that either." Sloane scowled, locking her hands under her chin—a posture, Tann noted, that let her put her fatigued weight on her elbows, braced on her knees. She glowered at them both. "Saying no to you two puts me in the position of bad guy here, but fine. I'll be the bad guy. You heard Kandros. We're out of ships. If another event occurs, or life support takes a turn for the worse, we're going to need those shuttles to evacuate the Nexus."

"What are the odds?" Addison queried, her brow furrowed.

"Evacuation is still a very real possibility," Sloane replied. "Especially since we still don't know what caused the breach. If we should be talking about anything, it's how we're going to get thousands of stasis pods off this station in a hurry, and where we'd even send them if we could."

"We are aware of habitable planets—"

"We don't," Sloane cut in grimly, "have the manpower to fight hostile native species."

Addison's expression clouded. "We're *not* here to fight, Sloane. Negotiations can be—"

"Yeah, yeah, I remember the speech," she retorted. "But unless we have a copy to forward whatever life forms exist in this galaxy, I'm not willing to bank on a peaceful welcoming committee."

Addison's jaw set. Shoulders tight.

Tann saw fit to intercede before it culminated into something much… louder. Granted, he hadn't thought of the evacuation issue, but it wasn't an insurmountable obstacle. "You raise a valid concern," he began, only to pause pointedly when Sloane muttered something he thought sounded like, "Gee, thanks."

If sarcasm could be a weapon, the woman would be an assassin with no concept of collateral damage. Meanwhile, his validation of a legitimate concern seemed to have frayed Foster Addison's trust in him. At least enough that she was now glaring at him, rather than her temporary opponent. He bit back a sigh.

Mentally, he added at least one psychologist to the list of those who needed to be brought up from stasis. Perhaps a whole team, of diverse species, to help the crew deal with the shock. *Yes, a good idea.*

Tann clasped his hands behind his back. "If there is no room for compromise, then we are at an impasse."

He started to pace. "The dilemma is that we do not have the staff to make repairs to the Nexus in any reasonable time frame. Our current skeleton crew can, at best, keep the station limping along, however I think we can all agree that such a scenario does not present a very bright future for us or our mission?"

Addison nodded emphatically.

Grudgingly, Sloane did too.

Tann went on, still pacing. "Also, we cannot send our shuttles, because they are needed here in the event of station-wide system failure—a very real possibility, as Director Kelly—"

"Sloane."

"—Sloane," he amended, "has pointed out." More nods. This time, though, it was Addison who hesitated and Sloane the strong affirmative.

They all knew where they stood. Good.

"Then," he said firmly, "my original proposal is still best. We wake the crew needed to make repairs, instruct them to work quickly and efficiently within severe resource concerns. Addison's ships will remain ready to evacuate all personnel, awake or otherwise, at a moment's notice."

Sloane Kelly, to Tann's surprise, was no longer frowning. Something had caused her mouth to stretch into a broad smile.

He didn't know what to make of that. "What is it?" he asked cautiously. "Have I accidentally made a joke?"

"No," Sloane replied. "It's just that the crew we'll need to pull off all these repairs are mostly from the labor force." Her smile deepened. The bite, he realized too late, came with it. "Kesh's people." A beat. "You know. *Krogan*."

Tann stopped pacing.

"We should make a list," she continued, too brightly for the environment, "of all the krogan workers we're going to need."

"I—" Tann swallowed, his mind painting pictures of a Nexus full of krogan. He shuddered at the thought. Too late now. All he could do was try to keep it in check. "I have some ideas on who we will need. Perhaps some additional security staff would be wise…"

Sloane's grin only widened. Clearly the difficult human woman found joy in his discomfort.

"There's a few people I will need, too," Addison said. "My assistant, William Spender, for starters, plus a select few members of the colonial team to inspect the surviving shuttles. For all we know, they were also damaged in this calamity."

"Like I said, make a list. I'll review it for security concerns." Sloane glanced at each of them in turn, making sure they were paying attention. "What happens, by the way, if we wake a bunch of people and find we can't support them?"

"They return to their stasis pods," Tann said simply. The obvious answer, yet Sloane looked dubious. This time, though, she didn't press. Instead she stood and moved past him, headed for the door. As she went by she clapped him on the back.

Hard.

Tann swayed, wincing in mingled annoyance and surprise.

"We're all in agreement," she said briskly. "I'll let Kesh know. Meeting adjourned." Just like her arrival, she left at her own cognizance. His shoulder still stung when the doors closed behind her.

Even so, Tann felt a smile creep over his face, and it felt surprisingly good. He'd accomplished something here. Not much, granted, but it was a start.

An *if* was so much more likely to become a *when* with a start.

IIIIIIIIIIIIIIIIII

In the hall outside, Sloane went to the nearest comm panel and punched in her first officer's ID. Thank all hell they'd managed to lock down the comm systems while she'd worked her ass off with Kesh. She didn't want this one blared over every speaker. Then thrown in her face when the salarian wanted something later.

"Kandros here," his reply came, a minute later.

"It's Sloane," she said. "Can you talk?"

A shuffling sound, then the click of a door closing. "Yeah. Go ahead."

She considered her words carefully, and made doubly sure Tann and Addison had not joined her in the hall. Satisfied, she angled herself to the best possible surveillance vantage and kept her voice low. "Put together a team of officers, led by Talini. Trustworthy people."

"How many?"

"Enough to guard the supply rooms that are actually accessible." Supplies were cached all over the Nexus, but the bulk of the station remained cold and airless, inaccessible due to damage. Sloane saw no need to put soldiers in front of those doors. Not yet, at least.

"Have we got a problem?" Kandros asked.

"Negative," she said, "but it's only Tuesday, if you follow."

"Heh. Yeah. I follow."

"Good. Sloane, out." She killed the link, and went off in search of Nakmor Kesh.

Her path wound through one debris-strewn hall

after another. She passed a series of apartments that overlooked one of the great arms. Their doors, less robust than those on the cryostasis rooms, had all torn off and now lay in an oddly neat row on the opposite side of the hallway, as if a construction crew had placed them there in preparation for installation.

On a whim she paused at one room and stepped inside. One of the smaller layouts, barely more than a bed, table and chair. No personal belongings; those would all be in deep storage until whoever had been assigned this room came to get them.

If they were even still alive.

Hell, Sloane hadn't even seen *her* quarters since before they launched. All shiny and new. Who even knew if that section of the station had survived?

The thought left a wistful pang in her chest. So much for her own office, right? Much less bed.

Sloane sighed, turning her back on the lonely room, and left. She reached the end of the hall, turned, and pushed on, past the shuttered Transportation Office, then Immigrations.

The chances that either would ever be staffed and actually used seemed so remote that she wondered if they might be better off turning them into shelters.

A soft noise, behind. Sloane drew her sidearm, whirled, aimed.

"Just me, just me," Jarun Tann said hastily, hands up.

Sloane narrowed her eyes. "Are you following me?"

"Of course," he replied. Then appeared to think better of what he meant. "I mean, not in that sense."

"What other sense is there?"

He stepped out of the shadows. "In the awkward sense of two people who have finished a conversation but also need to travel in the same direction."

She eyed him, but she'd be damned if she'd ever taken to salarian expressions. Turian faces were one thing, but there wasn't enough... *I don't know*, she thought distantly. Not enough lines, not enough distinct *features* on the amphibious faces of the salarian species. The horns were easy enough to recognize, large oval eyes, sure. But they all had those.

Whatever the reason, she wasn't sure she believed him.

Tann took her silence as a lack of understanding.

"I was returning to Operations, and thought I'd let you get well ahead of me to avoid any... any of the aforementioned awkwardness. And then you stepped out of an apartment only meters in front of me. It felt odd to stand there and wait, so I—"

"It's okay, Tann. I get it."

"Then perhaps you could lower the weapon?"

Sloane did so, doing her best to hide a grin. She'd scared the hell out of him, she realized, and found she didn't mind so much. A little fear could be healthy.

"So, Ops, huh? What's on your agenda next? And get the hell over here, I don't bite."

The salarian did his best to look casual as he crossed the rest of the gap and fell in beside her. They walked in silence for a bit.

Not for lack of words, Sloane realized as the salarian hummed one of his thoughtful noises. He was a thinker, this revenue wonk. The kind that weighed every word.

Which didn't make him any more trustworthy, all things considered.

"It is so hard to prioritize," he finally said, "with so many problems facing us."

"Yep. No argument here."

He nodded. "I felt, after our meeting, that I finally had a free minute. I thought I might check on something that's been bothering me."

"Just one thing?"

The salarian paused, sliding Sloane a thoughtful, cautiously amused look. At least, she thought it was that. "No," he said, and that caution gave birth to a weak smile. "No, but let us focus on this one thing in particular."

"Which thing?"

"Specifically, the *thing*," he said, stressing the word as if pleased by the byplay that led to it, "that we ran into. Whatever it is, it is foreign to us, or the sensors would have noticed it and alerted someone."

"The sensor arrays had been damaged," she pointed out.

"Were they?" He laced his thin hands together, tucking them into the sleeves of his attire. "Or did the technicians believe they were, based on the inability to parse the data?"

Her eyebrows raised. "Okay, so? Doesn't change anything."

"No," he allowed. "But I am worried it was not a singular event."

"Ah." She'd thought about this, too, especially whenever she tried to sleep. With so many known problems, worrying about unknown ones seemed pointless. But now that he'd brought it up, she worked it over. "When we located Ops the first time," she said thoughtfully, "there was a violent quake. The whole ship lurched, and it sounded like the hull peeled back somewhere."

"Weakened structure failing, perhaps?" He cocked

his head. "Or another meeting of station and whatever we had run into?"

"If it was a run-in," she pointed out, "I saw no ships—" Her words went dead. So did her pace, frozen in the middle of the corridor.

Tann's brow moved in what she took for inquiry. "You saw something?"

"Maybe." She frowned, pinching the bridge of her nose between thumb and forefinger. "Everything was one large adrenaline rush."

"Ah." Tann patted her arm cautiously, in what passed for sympathy. "Understood. Human evolution is predicated on the rise of prey to predator, but it never truly evolved redundant systems to effective process—"

"Tann."

He stopped. Cleared his throat. "Adrenaline," he said, way more succinctly, "can play havoc with logical thought."

That she would buy. Sloane picked up her pace again, once more flanked by the salarian. "The clearest thing I remember is that nebula out there. Or some kind of energy wave? I saw it hovering near the part of the station that... I don't know, that ripped off." She was reaching, and she knew it. She raised her hands. "I'm not an astrophysicist, so take your pick. But I can't shake that there's something there. Something we haven't seen yet." *Or missed.*

Tann glanced at her. "Without sensors, it is impossible to find out. However, I thought perhaps if we studied the data gathered *before* we impacted this... You believe the unusual nebula to be the key?"

"It's the only thing I saw," she said, shrugging once more. "And given how close it is, I'd be *really* pissed off if we ignored it, only to run into it later."

"A fair assessment. We shall earmark that theory as among the first to investigate," Tann said, with so little argument Sloane found herself eyeing him sidelong as they walked. "In fact, I rather relish the idea of learning something new about our new galaxy."

"You?"

"Well, of course," he replied, gathering himself up. "Who else is available to decipher the logs? There can be a great deal of information buried in even partial records."

"I guess the devil's in the details."

To her surprise, he gave a little chuckle. "One of my favorite human idioms. Yes, exactly. Even if our systems did not recognize the coming assault as a threat, it may still have a record of it."

"And you'll be able to figure this out?" she asked. It seemed the least she could do to try for sincere. All things considered, sensor data tech seemed less intrusive than *acting director.* "I thought revenue was your area of expertise."

At this, his slender shoulders straightened. It was hard to tell, but she thought his skinny salarian chest may have even puffed up some. "Math is my expertise," he declared. "Sensor logs are not so different from cost-basis figures."

Heh. "If you say so." They walked a bit farther, passing one of the huge common areas. It should have been filled with excited pioneers holding flutes of champagne. Instead it resembled a dumping ground for unwanted furniture. A disaster, like everything else. "Still," she mused. "What happens if it's, you know... actually in our way? We can't move, we can't shoot at an invisible target."

"Hence my comment about priorities," he said.

"Do we fix hydroponics first, so that we can eat in the weeks or even months to come, or do we get the maneuvering engines back online so that we can avoid another collision? Plus, there is the possibility that this is widespread. We may need to alert the Pathfinders."

Of all the things weighing on her mind, preying on her sleep, the Pathfinders had been firmly shunted aside. At least until now.

If they, still in stasis, coasted into this mess…

She rubbed at the bridge of her nose with one finger. "Tann, you're giving me a headache."

"It is a difference between us, I think," Tann said. "Forgive my presumption, but you prefer narrowly defined problems. Whatever is pressing at the moment gets all of your attention, and when that is fixed, you turn to whatever waits just behind."

"And you're a big-picture kinda guy, is that what you mean?"

"Another lovely phrase."

She stopped. They were at the door to Operations, and he hadn't seemed to notice. "Where are you going with all this, Tann?"

"Just making conversation," he said, already large eyes wide.

"Right."

He sighed. "Okay, your sharp investigation skills have seen through my sinister plan."

Sloane's turn to laugh. Even for him, that was too patently false a surrender. She gestured for him to go on.

"What I'm trying to say, Secur—Sloane, is that if, for example, I *do* discover that we will need maneuvering capability straight away, and I suggest as much to you and Addison, I ask that you keep in mind my methodology. In other words, if I ask for engines, it's because the math says we need them more urgently than we need seeds."

"It's more than just math, though." Sloane frowned down the length of the empty corridor. "People are hurt. People are dead. Are you saying that if you come to me claiming we should fix engines instead of, I don't know, life support, I should just accept the goddamn math and not question you?"

"I'm asking for a little trust. If the data says that fixing life support now might save ten lives, but fixing engines would kill the ten, yet save thousands later, then we should fix the engines."

"Damn. That's cold. Even for a salarian, that's cold."

"So is the universe, on average. However," he continued, as if ordering some kind of extra, "I can promise you that while I am busily applying mathematical value to the immediacy of any situation, other parts of my vast intellect are experimenting with other options." He gave her what she imagined he thought a friendly grin was.

Maybe all salarians tended to look snide. Maybe it was just him.

Sloane shook her head, her goodwill fading. It left her as cold as his calculus. "So you're saying I should trust you twice over," she said slowly. Her incredulity mounted with every word. "Once that your math is rock solid, and the other that you'll come through with better options?" She barked a short laugh. "You're right, Tann. It is a difference between us. So let me give you another piece of data to analyze." She shoved a finger in his direction, only narrowly missing his bony chest. "Acting Director or not, if your math says to do X for some potential future benefit, and my gut says save someone's life right-fucking-now, my gut is going to win, every time. That clear?"

He studied her for a moment, once more tucking his hands into his sleeves. Then, with a slight nod, he murmured, "Abundantly."

The door to Operations hissed open, and Nakmor Kesh came lumbering out. Unprepared for the sudden company, Tann almost fell over his own feet leaping out of her way.

Sloane didn't even bother hiding her snort. At least until the krogan's gaze met hers. "Oh, shit. What now?"

Kesh's large head swung around to pin on Tann, who busily attempted to right his dignity. At the weight of her silence, however, he stopped fussing with his apparel and frowned. "What happened?"

The krogan's voice graveled low. "Jien Garson." Before either could leap to questions, she shook her head. "They found her."

||||||||||||||||||||

The temporary morgue had been set up in one of the Biology labs, several decks away. Kesh led the way, with Sloane beside her and a very silent Tann trailing behind.

"They're up to almost a hundred dead now," Kesh was saying. "With biometrics offline, and the bodies... well, you saw a lot of them. You know what it's like."

"They didn't know they'd found her," Sloane said anyway. A hollow explanation, an ugly one, but it made sense.

"Exactly."

Kesh pushed into the frigid room and went straight to a desk where two life-support techs were standing by. On the table was a sight Sloane had seen many times in her career: one body. One body bag.

She'd never thought, not ever, that Garson would ever be inside one.

"Where was she found?" Sloane asked Kesh.

"In one of the apartments near Operations," came the answer, but not from the krogan. The tech had answered. A gaunt man, with tired eyes. "We were doing a room to room, clearing bodies."

The other of the pair added, "Wounds are consistent with all the rest. Environmental damage. Significant burns. It's... not a pretty sight."

The door swung open and Foster Addison rushed into the room. One look at Sloane's face and the last glimmer of hope bled out from her eyes.

Sloane waited for the woman to join her at the table, and pulled back the bag. At first, Sloane couldn't piece together any evidence of identity. Much of her face hid under charred skin. The smell was terrible, burnt and swollen flesh left to rot for untold hours in open air, but Sloane forced herself to stand strong. *Don't gag.*

A somber silence fell over those gathered.

A million thoughts raced through Sloane's head. Too many to grasp. To shape. She covered the body back up.

Addison gripped the edge of the table with white-knuckled fingers. "We'll have to organize a burial," she said, voice ragged.

"Negative," Sloane replied, cutting the idea before it could grow into something bigger than they could handle. Too harsh, but nothing to be done about it.

"I agree with the security director," Tann volunteered.

"I didn't ask," Sloane snapped, but checked her anger. It wasn't really aimed at him, calculus or not.

Besides, his role as acting director just became a bit more solid. There would be no more avoiding him in hope that Garson would turn up and save the day. "Addison, no offense, but a burial is the least of our worries. We don't have the time or the manpower."

"Or," Kesh rumbled, "the facilities."

"We should keep her here," Sloane continued, grateful for the krogan's support, "along with everyone else, until—"

"Until we can do it right," Tann interjected, surprisingly firm. "She deserves as much."

"They all do," Sloane corrected. She couldn't help herself. There were nearly a hundred bodies in the room, and they all deserved the respect of a proper farewell.

Nobody argued. Nobody moved or spoke. Not for a while, save for Kesh who laid one huge hand on Garson's covered brow. A tender gesture, but not surprising. Garson had moved mountains to bring the Nakmor clan along on this journey.

It was Tann, in the end, who broke the silence. "We all wish to mourn, but there is a lot of work to do. If I may be so bold, our brilliant founder would have wanted us to do everything we could to save this mission before anything else."

It was the kind of thing you couldn't argue with, delivered with absolute perfect tone and understanding. Sloane gave him a nod of respect for that, which he returned in kind.

With nothing left to say, to do here at Jien Garson's side, she left.

There really was a lot of work to do. The mission depended on them, now.

And only them.

CHAPTER EIGHT

The trio stood in a half-circle, surrounding the oversized stasis pod. The room had a chill to it, and it wasn't from the air.

Couldn't be, Sloane thought. *The ventilation systems are barely working.* No, the frigid mood came from Nakmor Kesh, who stood facing the pod. She hadn't moved or said anything for several minutes.

Best to wait, Sloane decided. Let the krogan mull this over, for it was her decision to make. Sloane glanced at the third person in the room, Calix, who leaned against a table across from her, arms folded across his chest, chin lowered. The turian appeared to be asleep on his feet, and who could blame him? His team had been fighting against the life-support systems for days, and as of yet couldn't claim any kind of victory other than "it's not completely broken," which considering how much damage the station had suffered, was a hell of an accomplishment.

And then there was the news of Garson's death, weighing on everyone. The Nexus had a shadow cast across it now, and Sloane wondered if it would ever lift.

Finally, the krogan stirred, swinging her large body around to weigh the gathering. "Let her sleep," Kesh said.

Sloane studied her. "You sure?"

Kesh nodded, once. Decision made.

Clan leader Nakmor Morda would, for the time

being, remain asleep. Sloane had never met the krogan clan leader, but she'd heard plenty. Bar stories. War stories. Stories of the kind of surly brutality you'd expect from a krogan who'd reached her level of rank and fame. Though Morda led the clan, she had deferred authority to Kesh in matters of station maintenance and care. That left Kesh the de facto leader while Morda slept.

Morda, it seemed, preferred not to deal with other races unless it was a combat scenario.

Well, maybe that was an unfair assumption. But Sloane could read between the lines when she had to. Officially Morda had designated Kesh as the Nakmor Clan's ambassador to the rest of the Nexus. You didn't delegate that sort of thing unless you wanted to stay far away from it.

Yet matters within the clan, as Kesh had explained, remained Morda's to make.

As long as she was awake to do so.

"I am sure," Kesh replied, but on a heavy gust of air. "She would not want to be bothered with all this. Too much collaboration required."

Calix grunted a laugh, then tried unsuccessfully to turn it into a cough. Kesh didn't seem to notice.

"If it turns out we face some new enemy out there," she added, "well, that will be a different story. And one no doubt she will relish."

"Okay then," Sloane said, pushing up from the desk against which she'd been leaning. "I'm fine with it if you are. Let's wake the others."

The second chamber lay empty, its occupant already disgorged. The unit had failed due to a ruptured casing, resulting in the death of the krogan inside. One of several, and each one handled grimly by Kesh.

They all moved to the third, and Calix began the

revival process. Since the biometrics database was offline, a special maintenance code was required; one Sloane did not know. For the time being, at least, only Calix and his supervisor, Kesh, could initiate a manual waking.

She liked it that way.

Calix tapped in the last few characters. He stepped back. "It takes several minutes."

The pod began to warm as fluids pumped through the thousands of pipes and tubes hidden within its casing. Soon the crystals of frost on the inside of the window began to vibrate, then all at once they turned to water droplets.

More time passed.

"Vitals look good," Calix said. *Déjà vu.*

"I will proceed to the next one," Kesh said. She didn't wait for confirmation, simply went about it in the same grim manner.

Calix glanced at Sloane. "That smart?"

Sloane lifted her shoulders. "According to the list we've got hundreds of crew to wake. I don't know about you, but I've got better things I could be doing."

"Don't we all." He moved to the next pod and began to manipulate the controls. "At least they get a gentler waking. Comparatively."

Sloane glowered at the back of his spiky fringe. "Which reminds me, why the hell didn't any of you brainiacs put an emergency eject on the inside?"

"We did." He didn't spare her a glance, but his tone brimmed with humor as he carefully tweaked the controls he worked on. "You just didn't pay attention in class."

"That's—" She hesitated mid-protest. Thought about it. "Okay, that's fair," she admitted. She'd preferred training simulations and security logistics to what she'd figured would be a class on insignificant details for a device she'd only be sleeping in.

Showed what she knew.

Sloane refocused on the pod in front of her. The process neared completion. Inside, the krogan began to stir. Her hand went reflexively to the pistol at her hip.

Kesh's heavy step fell behind her. "Maybe I should handle this part," she said. "The krogan part, I mean."

"That smart?" Sloane asked. Her deliberate echo of Calix's words earned another amused grunt from the turian.

Kesh waved her off. "No offense, Sloane, but if any of my clan wake up in a foul mood, it would only be worse if a human were the one to subdue them."

Sloane affected wide eyes. "Oh. Then we should give Tann the code and let him do it."

"Very funny."

"I would pay good money to see that," Calix called out.

This time Kesh really did laugh. A deep rumbling that shook her whole body. Sloane grinned, stepping away at the same time. It was good, she figured, to find the moments of levity in the slog.

"Fair enough, Kesh. Just make sure you explain to them our situation before, during or after your whole krogan thing."

"Of course."

"If any of them are suffering from—"

"I can handle it," she said firmly. "Go wake your team, and get started on the rest."

The pod cracked its seal, foul-smelling steam hissing out in a line around the door. It flew open with a whoosh, and a very wet and angry-looking krogan all but surged out, muscles engaged. "Who dares—" the male began.

Kesh slammed her forehead into his face, sending the krogan sprawling back into his stasis pod.

Sloane blinked.

"I have this," Kesh said as the other krogan roared. Shock or pain or—

Sloane didn't even want to consider what else.

"Yeah," she said, backing up to the door. "Yeah, I guess you do." Calix joined her, having initiated the warming sequence on the other four designated pods in this chamber.

Roughly half of the list consisted of krogan workers, all members of the Nakmor clan. The rest, Sloane hoped, would be easier to manage. She led Calix through the labyrinth of corridors to their next group, and with each step she felt a bit more confident. Having a krogan force on the brink of up and running meant lots more work to get done.

Security came next. That had been non-negotiable, despite Tann's protests that the rest of the crew would be less likely to panic if they weren't waking up to the barrel of a gun.

"No guns," Sloane had assured him. "Just a reassurance that things are under control. Remember what these people sacrificed to join this mission, and what they went to sleep dreaming of finding when they arrived. We're going to crush those dreams, Tann, so we need to be ready for any reaction."

The salarian seemed utterly baffled by this, but Addison's agreement ultimately swung the argument in Sloane's favor.

She and Calix worked methodically. Eight veteran members of her team were woken. One's vitals were suspect, so his warming was paused until a doctor could assess. While the security team acclimated, Sloane and Calix moved on, preparing to wake another group from his staff. Life-support technicians, who doubled as field medical staff. This time there were no malfunctions. Sloane gathered both groups and explained the predicament they were in and the plan, with some technical backup from Calix.

After that, the process took on a life of its own. Calix became less the technical expert and more of a runner, moving from pod to pod and entering his maintenance override. Sloane debated asking for that ability when they'd started. Things would go a lot quicker if more people had it.

And another part of her didn't like the knowledge being held by just two people. It was risky, given the danger they were all in. Those concerns, however, lost out to the down side—if the override privs were disseminated, and people started waking whomever they wanted to without oversight, they could wind up with catastrophic overpopulation.

The list was already massive enough.

Eight teams followed Calix, a security officer and a life-support tech in each, to handle the health assessments and brief those who awakened. Doctors and nurses first, then the engineering teams responsible for all of the Nexus's complex machinery and technology, then various assistants and other random crew either Tann or Addison had insisted be part of the effort.

By the end of it all, the operation had become self-sustaining. At least until the end of the list.

Then it was time to put them all to work.

That evening, dead on her feet, Sloane left the security duty in Kandros's capable hands and found a couch to collapse on in one of the less-devastated common areas. Just as her eyes were sliding shut, Tann and Addison appeared.

Oh, come on…

"Ah, here she is," Tann said, approaching.

Sloane sat up and propped herself against the cushion. "Now what?"

"Nothing, we just wanted an update." Tann grinned. It was probably supposed to be sympathetic, perhaps even encouraging, but to Sloane he just looked smug. "But we can let you sleep."

And risk getting called out on that, too? "No, it's fine." Sloane ran a hand over her face and blinked. She was too tired to point out that they couldn't "let" her do anything. A cup of water appeared in her hand and she gulped it down. Only after did she realize Addison had handed it to her. Sloane muttered thanks.

Now, the summary. "Team leaders from every critical systems group are up, plus some of their crews," she said. "About a hundred and fifty in all. Sadly, fourteen from the list were dead in their pods, which had failed because of… well, you know. We left them that way, no need to add more to the morgue if they're already contained."

"How awful."

"Terrible," Tann agreed. "Still, it is a better ratio than I'd expected."

Sloane could only nod. With some sleep and a meal, she might rip into him for how callous he sounded, but right now she just wanted to get this over with and lay down. "Kesh woke a similar number of krogan, so we're about halfway through the list."

"Any casualties from their ranks?" Tann asked.

"A few. They fared a little better."

"That's... good," Addison said, but awkwardly.

"Yes," Tann agreed. "Excellent news, indeed. However, I thought you'd be through the entire list by now."

Right. Like he could do better. Sloane eyed him. "Each person we awaken needs some handling, diagnosis, and a briefing."

"Still, our capability to do that should multiply, yes?"

"Doesn't matter. Only Kesh and her chief life-support tech, Calix, have the maintenance override code needed to open the pods." She held up a hand. "And before you ask, we're not handing that code out, because we don't want mistakes, or more people up than we can handle. Even *I* don't have it."

He didn't seem impressed. By the lack of sharing or the numbers, she couldn't tell. "Fair enough," Tann said, though his tone carried a lot of skepticism.

She changed the subject, trading her successes for his. "Any news about what caused all this?"

Tann folded his hands, looked at Addison.

She shook her head, frustration evident. "We're still blind. Sensor logs are a mess of garbage and false alarms."

"The sensors were, in fact, damaged during flight, but not to the level the logs seem to indicate," Tann added. Sloane didn't fail to note that he left the admission of failure to someone else, while swooping in with his own version of silver lining.

Bureaucrats. They were all the same, weren't they?

Sloane barely even cared enough to nod, then yawned. "Okay. Let me know what you learn. Can I sleep now?"

"Of course," Tann said hurriedly, just as Addison patted her shoulder and said, "Rest while you can."

She fell onto the cushions, closed her eyes, and was asleep in seconds.

IIIIIIIIIIIIIIIIIIIII

Her dreams were of Elysium, horrors witnessed and committed during the Skyllian Blitz. Pirate assaults had never been a joyride, but the Blitz was something else entirely. The tiny contingent of Alliance uniforms in the far-flung outpost had no reason to assume they'd end up braced against a whole fleet, much less one with a *cause*.

The conflict had made some soldiers' careers. Made them heroes, earned them choice placement. Blooded men and women with the char of real battle in their eyes.

But it broke others.

Sloane didn't know where she'd fallen in— somewhere between blooded and broken—but she'd never forgotten those long days. The worst days of her life, no matter what battles she fought after, or what pirates came through the Traverse later.

It was the kind of thing she'd joined the Initiative to get away from.

But if nothing else, it was also something that left a permanent scar. An instinct, honed there and in a dozen other combat theaters. That instinct brought her instantly awake, pistol drawn and aimed at the intruder.

It took a few seconds for Sloane to remember where she was. The couch in the common area. Several dozen others were sleeping around her, wherever they could find space. Still others remained awake, tucking into rations or talking in hushed tones. A few were crying, or shell-shocked, or both.

On the couch opposite her, a human man she did not know sat, waiting. He stared at her wide-eyed, and slowly brought his hands up to signal surrender. Sloane realized then she had her pistol aimed right between his eyes. She lowered it.

"Who are you?"

"William Spender."

"I know that name," Sloane said, trying hard to shove the groggy fatigue from her head. "Why do I know that name?"

"Colonial Affairs. I'm Foster Addison's second-in-command." A beat. "Assistant Director Spender."

"Ah." Another wonk. Fantastic. She holstered the weapon and rubbed her eyes. The man, Spender, lifted a mug from the table and held it out to her. Steam rose from within.

Maybe not so much a wonk after all.

Sloane's mood brightened. "Coffee?"

He paused. Looked down into the mug. Winced. "Oatmeal," he admitted.

"I hate you." Mood souring just as fast, Sloane took it anyway. There was no spoon, so she gulped it. The warm sludge hadn't been sweetened, but even she could admit that it tasted surprisingly good.

Spender looked around. "I could try to find some coffee."

"Forget it," she said around a mouthful, "I don't hate you."

The man smiled. "You just love coffee?"

She didn't answer. Just shrugged amiably.

William Spender, Assistant Director, had the most punchable of faces—that of a politician's over eager intern. Brown hair he'd somehow found the time to comb, clean teeth, and big too-sincere-to-be-sincere eyes that all but telegraphed intent. *Please let me help you so that I may appear helpful.* Sloane held her amusement in check and finished the food.

By the end, he hadn't moved.

She raised an eyebrow at him. "You're still here. Which means the oatmeal comes with a price, I'm guessing?" she asked.

Spender shrugged. "A security matter, actually."

The fog of sleep vanished. "What's happened?"

"Oh, no, no!" He held out his hands, placating. "Nothing. I just… Foster has put me in charge of consolidating our supplies. Cataloging what survived the, er, incident. That sort of thing. We should collaborate on locations to store it all."

Sloane's other eyebrow joined the first. "Okay. Question: Why do I care?"

"Because," Spender replied patiently, "it needs to be somewhere secure."

"Ah." Sloane set her cup on the nearest stand. Paused, and frowned at him. "Wait. Addison's worried about theft?"

"Director Tann suggested some might not appreciate the need to conserve, given our circumstances." Again, that smile. "Foster and I agree."

Oh, hell, Sloane thought. She knew exactly what *some* Tann worried about, and she wanted to throttle him for holding on to such backward thinking. Still, in a roundabout way, he brought up a generally broader point. Weapons and life-saving necessities, to be safe, probably needed to be stored somewhere safe. "Doesn't the station have a warehousing district?"

"Several, actually. The only one nearby, however, is inaccessible."

Not surprising. "How about one of the hangars,

then? Only one has ships in it, the rest are all to be filled once there's traffic."

That had him brightening, like he hadn't thought of it. Maybe he hadn't. Sloane had no idea how he operated. But even the way he nodded, like one part encouraging and one part settled, made her feel like he overplayed his efforts. "That might work," he mused. "Yes, I think that would be perfect."

"Glad to help," she said wearily. "Talk to Sergeant Talini. She can make sure *everyone* appreciates the need to conserve."

Again Spender nodded, this time with a knowing half-smile. "I'll run it by the other directors, just to make sure everyone's on board with our plan."

"Yeah, whatever." *Suddenly it's "our" plan,* she thought, irritated. *What a weasel.* Sloane waved him off. "If you need me to tell them to be on board, let me know. In the meantime, I'll get a couple of my people to check out the auxiliary hangars and pick one that's suitable."

The man stood. At least he knew when a conversation was over. Sloane lay back on the couch and threw an arm over her eyes. Her body demanded more sleep. Or coffee. What it didn't want was another day of putting out fires.

She could guess just which of those she'd get.

But since he was here?

"If you find some coffee, Spender..." Sloane called out to the diminishing sound of Spender's footsteps. She let the sentence trail off, pointing a finger at her mouth instead.

From somewhere toward the door, she heard him chuckle. "Understood," he replied.

Just the idea of it seemed to quell her body's state of fatigue. And her mind wouldn't shut up. Every possible gap in her thoughts, those places where true rest lurked, was filled instead with concerns. How many were awake now? Had there been any problems? Did Kesh need help?

It was the idea that Tann might be guiding the priorities of the workforce that finally drove her to swing her legs off the couch and stand up with a groan. She felt stiff, thirsty, and she was hungry again. Her limbs felt like a drunk volus clung to each one, dragging her down.

Maybe there was no coffee. Yet. Sloane, out of options, defaulted to the only thing that could help.

Stretching her legs, she made her way out of the commons, through the larger weave of people beginning to fill it, and lurched off into a brisk morning jog.

It would do. Until coffee.

iiiiiiiiiiiiiiiii

An hour later, still desperate for that coffee, a sharp headache pressing at the back of her eyes, Sloane stood atop a desk and faced more than six hundred Nexus crew. The area wasn't meant for an assembly. It should have been a tranquil office space for the administration staff.

Woulda, shoulda. If wishes were packets of Earth-grown brew, they'd all have coffee for days.

Most of the assembly stood. Some were sitting on tables or in oversized chairs. Many were on the floor, still getting over the fog of a crash-awakening from stasis. "Cryo-funk," she'd heard a few of them calling it. The term seemed to be spreading as fast as news of the loss of their leadership.

Nervous chatter filled the room. Sloane picked out phrases here and there.

"What will happen to the mission?"

"Can we go back? Is that even possible?"

"The Pathfinders will save us."

"It has to have been an attack. What aren't they telling us?"

"So many krogan…"

She didn't even bother trying to ignore it all. Better to let it all wash over her, absorb it. Because this was better than mass panic, which at least for now remained comfortably below the surface.

"Let's get started," she said as loudly as she could. She had to force the words out of her mouth. Then she raised her arms above her head, willing quiet. Some noticed. Many more did not. Sloane laced her hands atop her head and looked up at the ceiling. "Don't make me yell," she said, more of a sigh than anything else.

She didn't have to. Kesh slammed one heavy fist into the nearest table. The *boom* tore through the vast space, and by the time it echoed back, Sloane had everyone's full attention.

"Thanks," she muttered.

The krogan shot her an unrepentant smile. Mimicked by each krogan around her.

"This isn't a speech," Sloane said to them. "It's not a pep talk. We don't have time for that shit. What this *is*, is a battle plan."

A murmur swept through the gathered crew. She let it settle, using the time to will a fresh spike of pain to retreat in her skull.

"Most of you are aware of what's happened," Jarun Tann said loudly, interrupting her.

Sloane glanced right, mouth twisting. She hadn't noticed that he'd stepped up onto the desk beside her. Great. *He* seemed to have *plenty* of time for this shit.

He went on, a bit louder. "Even so, let me explain it once so there is no confusion, or rumors." Even though what they mostly had was just that. Rumors, conjectured between the directors. Great. "As far as we can tell this was not an attack. Once the sensors are back and the science team can investigate, we'll know with absolute certainty, but what I can tell you is that upon arriving here the Nexus collided with what appears to be a natural phenomenon."

Wait a second. They'd only just speculated on this.

"Long tendrils of densely packed particles," he went on. "This… this *scourge*, whatever it is, has done a staggering amount of damage to the station."

Shit. It was too late to retract now. Even if their hunch was right, the only thing she could do was focus them inward, not outward. People didn't always need all the intel.

Fuming, she cut in. "Which is why you're all awake." Annoyance laced her tone, and she didn't really care if he knew it. "You're all experts in the Nexus's various systems. We need you to do what you do best—analyze, stabilize, repair. The goal right now is to keep the station functional enough to support us. Secondary to that is making sure we can evacuate if further damage occurs."

"Evacuate?" someone called out, and they sounded alarmed. "Are we still in danger?"

"Why not evac now?" another crew member near the back shouted.

"We're not evacuating," Sloane snapped. "Have you already forgotten why we came here?" Several of the crowd looked away. "Did you forget the risks? It was all fun and games when you signed up, a bright shiny dream, but now here we are. And the first sign of trouble, you want to call it quits?" The crowd stirred. She glared at them. "What the hell is the matter with you?"

Tann placed a calming hand on her arm, and interrupted again.

"What Security Director Kelly means is that we do not know if the Nexus is out of danger yet. Until we do, we must remain vigilant, and do everything we can to right our ship. The mission has not changed, and we all have a duty—"

"Who the hell are you?" someone shouted. Sloane couldn't see for sure, but she thought it was a turian near the center of the room, wearing the uniform of the hydroponics team.

The salarian flinched. Even through her irritation, Sloane felt that one.

Who the hell, indeed.

But Tann wasn't one to lose face in a crowd. "I recognize your confusion," he said, keeping his hand on Sloane's arm. Probably as some kind of solidarity act. "I am Acting Director Jarun Tann. Per emergency protocols, I've been—"

Sloane shook her head, cutting him off. "Wrong touch," she muttered, and faced the crowd directly. "We're in a world of shit here, and that means changes. Here's what you need to know: Tann's filling in for Garson. I'm handling security." She gestured for the third member of their little council to step up onto a third desk. "That is Foster Addison, Colonial Affairs—"

"And advising our acting director," Addison said for herself, more curtly than Sloane thought necessary.

All right. Fine. If everyone wanted to carve out a bit of the turf, they may as well do it here. Sloane inclined her head at Addison, and looked back to the crowd. "We're the three most senior people aboard.

You're awake because this station needs help. That's it. That's the situation. Now let's get to work, because I want to live. And like all of you, I want our mission to succeed."

Dead silence.

Sloane clenched her fists, waiting for Jarun Tann to once again lamely try to contribute his bullshit. For once his instincts were in line with hers, though. He said nothing. The turian who'd asked the question held Sloane's gaze for a moment, then started to nod, slowly.

With that, others began to murmur. Not the tone of argument, to Sloane's ears. One, multiple, of consideration. Things to do. Checkboxes to tick.

Good.

Addison surveyed them all. And of them all, maybe it's best the soft touch came from her. "We all remember Alec Ryder's words," she said, earning more nods. "Making our way here was one thing, but we all knew what came next."

With sudden widened eyes—the salarian version of a lightbulb moment, Sloane guessed—Tann snapped his longer fingers. "Now," he said with far more flourish than it required, "is where the real work starts."

This resulted in more than a few chuckles. A few snorts. A lot of more firm acknowledgement.

Even better. This? This worked out a lot better than she'd imagined.

"You all know your systems," Sloane said, raising her voice over the drone of collaborating voices. "Do whatever it takes, just get them stable. We're only focusing on this section of the station for now. The rest is unpopulated and unpressurized, anyway." Small knots of like-minded professionals began to gather together. Sloane had to speak even louder as the crowd began to naturally shift into gear. "If you need help, need a hallway cleared or a bent door removed, Nakmor Kesh has a few hundred of her construction team available to assist. Make use of them."

The few krogan flanking Kesh let loose a thunderous, and entirely unnecessary, rattle of graveled roars and cheers.

It did not, as Tann jerked in surprise and Sloane hid a grin, result in a stampede of panicked bipedals.

Enough was enough. They all knew their tasks. The supervisors among them would maintain order.

She stepped backward off the desk. The crowd immediately began to disperse, a thousand conversations erupting all across the room.

"Good luck to you all," Tann said, voice raised for all the good that did. He was a breeze against the storm. He turned then and stepped down.

Sloane offered a hand to Addison, who took it with thanks as she hopped down. "There," she muttered.

Sloane shot her a quizzical half-smile.

The woman shrugged. "Whatever comes of Colonial Affairs," she replied quietly, "I'm not going anywhere."

Pessimistic, maybe. Sloane couldn't blame her. Right now, settling colonies felt like light years away. And maybe that was what was eating Foster Addison. Her job. Her role.

Was she content with advisor to the acting director?

Sloane wouldn't be. But then, she had plenty to do in security. She gave Addison's arm a reassuring squeeze and let her go. They turned, Tann falling in beside them. "I think that was a fine moment," the salarian said, his tone as accomplished as if he'd planned the whole thing. "Now, if we can continue this momentous unification into the future, we shall all be just fine."

What little silver lining Sloane had gleaned soured.

Spender waited nearby, his omni-screen already up and notes made. "Well," he said brightly. "That went well."

Sloane brushed past him. "Find me coffee," she all but growled. "Then we'll talk about 'well.'"

He got out of her way.

CHAPTER NINE

With most of the private quarters under vacuum lock, Jarun Tann had taken up residence in a research lab. He doubted it would ever see any actual research. Not for a long time, at least.

The lab was adjacent to the outer hull, of which a giant section had been ripped away by "the Scourge." He had taken note of the term's popularity after his impromptu words during the briefing. A week of use and one unfortunate brush with a drifting tendril of the stuff had seemed, he was pleased to note, to cement its use among the populace.

Although he would have preferred that it did not scar its purpose so completely into the crippled station to do so. A term was all well and good, but the lingering effects this Scourge had left among the woken workforce lingered.

Another reason why Tann needed to take a moment, exist somewhere quiet and isolated. Away from what he thought of as the collective weight of the masses. Worry, focus, effort... frustration.

Here, in this abandoned lab, he had room. He had, if he'd pardon himself the pun, *space*. Most of the gear in this room had been sucked away at hull breach, leaving a long, narrow area devoid of furniture or really anything at all. As in Operations, the temporary barrier covering the gap offered an exceptional view. Of the stars. The ragged edges of the station.

The energetic tendrils of the Scourge, with its colorful, fiery array of pinprick lights.

A perfect place, in other words, for Jarun Tann to pace, and to think. It was quiet, far from the commons where much of the crew had taken to sleeping. They found solace in numbers, comfort in the presence of others. Quiet conversation, or even just the sounds proving that others existed.

In any normal situation, he'd feel the same, but this situation—this calamity—was very much in the abnormal category. It required focus. Careful, deliberate thought. Tann knew himself, his limitations. All his life he'd battled an inability to filter out distractions.

When he needed to think, *really* think, he required absolute silence. A lack of motion other than the steady footfalls of his own two feet, and perhaps a nice tiled floor beneath that glided under him at a steady, flawlessly maintained pace.

This was the primary reason he'd left his omni-tool in the antechamber. Its incessant communications were usually welcome—Tann preferred to be informed over the alternative—but not when he needed the space to think.

Much had happened in a week. The Nexus was stable now, and the Scourge seemed, after the last brush with whatever spreading tendril, to be a phenomenon they'd passed through and left in their wake. No one would really know until sensors were repaired; a project that had met with delays and a borderline farcical amount of calamity.

Sensors, sensors, Tann thought. They may all be floating blind, but the shuttles in the Colonial Affairs hangar surely should have some capability in this regard. Perhaps Addison was right. *Perhaps a few should be launched, if only to give us readings from our immediate vicinity.*

It might even be that they could make contact with the Pathfinders, and solicit help. *Yes,* he thought, about-facing to pace a new path. *The Pathfinders. Certainly they could—*

No, no, a terrible idea. He stopped that line of thought. Each and every one of those shuttles would be needed if another system failed, or worse, if the Nexus hit another vein of this mysterious Scourge. Evacuation would require every last square centimeter of space they offered, thanks to the large population now awake.

They represented less than a fifth of the overall total personnel, of course, but everyone remained confined to a fraction of the Nexus's total living space, too. Most of the station, like most of her crew, remained frozen.

Everything, in his view, hinged on the matter of *population.* Each crew member who woke became a "bag of needs," as he'd heard a turian describe them. Easy for them to say, of course, with their highly unique dependency on dextro-amino acids. Human, krogan, asari and salarian personnel had to worry about four times the emergency supplies.

Then again, he supposed the overall stock for turian biology was less, too.

A bag of needs, eh? Each member a mouth to feed, an air-breather, a mind that had opinions on the wisdom of their interim leader's decisions.

Weight. And a lot of it.

He'd known that this population surge would stabilize the Nexus. He also knew that, once awake, few if any of the crew would entertain the idea of returning to sleep. They saw revival from stasis as like being born again. A kind of metaphysical hatching.

Every possible outcome played out in his mind, save for the positive ones. If everything went well, he'd be right there with the others, raising a toast to all the hard work and team effort that had saved the mission. He doubted anyone would lift a glass and praise all the thought and planning, but that was an acceptable loss. He was used to that.

And yet there were the problem scenarios to consider. They were legion, to put it mildly. It all came back to supplies. Mouths to feed, thirsts to quench, waste products of which to dispose. Life was many things, but chief among its traits was its incredible efficiency at turning food into feces, and that simple process lay at the core of all his concerns.

Supplies. They would dwindle far too quickly for comfort.

He'd already predicted the first reports of theft. A simple question asked in a hallway about where a crate had been placed. "I thought I'd left it there," met with "I didn't see it, are you sure?"

Somewhere, out there, in this vast yet tiny corner of the Nexus, were the clever ones. Those who also saw the potential problems looming, and consciously or not, they'd begun to plan.

This wasn't necessarily malicious behavior, Tann understood, but merely a survival instinct. When one foresees trouble on the horizon, one prepares.

So what to do?

He paced and paced, aware dimly that his omni-tool languished beyond the lab, chirping away for his attention. Spender, no doubt, or perhaps Addison. They sought his opinions, and relayed news.

Sloane Kelly and Nakmor Kesh, on the other hand, had yet to fully admit to his position as director, even after the discovery of Garson's body. He always had to seek them out when the situation required. Always had to be the one to ask.

But he accepted this, as well. Early days, these were.

Kelly was slowly extracting herself from the emergency-responder mindset. Kesh, well. She was krogan, wasn't she? She would operate in ways ceded by her genetic predisposition for violence and aggression. This was what krogan did.

This was why he did not argue when Sloane Kelly demanded more of her security team be awakened.

More mouths to feed, certainly, but there were no krogan among them. When push came to shove—and it always did with the violent species—he could count on Sloane's security team to put down the trouble.

For that, he required Sloane Kelly's trust. Or at least her effort.

For better or worse, he viewed the leadership arrangement as a triumvirate. Him, Addison, Sloane. If he began to make unilateral decisions now, he had no doubt they would find a way to remove him from his place here and doubted anyone would argue. They would begin to make decisions based on their own myopic view of things. Problematic, and he felt sure Jien Garson understood that.

Almost certainly, this was why his name had come up. A level head, a broad perspective. They needed him, and yet he needed them.

So be it.

Addison often adopted the role, reluctantly, of tiebreaker. It was the "reluctantly" part of that equation that troubled Tann. She was taking this disaster worse than the others. She wandered, said the bare minimum, with a curtness that rivaled Sloane's on a good day.

In the rare cases where the leadership met to discuss something, she let the conversation be led, following whomever she felt was the closest to the right call, but with no enthusiasm.

There had been a spark, briefly, when she'd advocated for exploring the nearby worlds, perhaps finding an alternative location for the mission of the Nexus if the station itself could not support it. He could have done more to nurture that, he thought now, but instead he'd sided with Sloane.

The mission came first, and the shuttles were needed here.

But perhaps he'd failed to consider the full ramifications of that moment. He could have ceded that argument, and in return won a more reliable ally. Instead, the moment had left the erstwhile Colonial Affairs Director feeling as if her entire purpose for being on this ship had been relegated to "if we ever get around to it."

Problematic. Very problematic.

It seemed to have the unforeseen consequence of tapping Addison's motivation. Her deciding votes had become essentially random and that, in turn, made all of Tann's thoughtful deliberation rather a waste of time. Which meant—

A pause. A stop, mid-step, as the idea unfurled like a Sur'Kesh nightbloom. "Ah!"

Aborting his pacing path, he turned toward the door, strode for it. He knew exactly what to do.

In the hall he picked up his omni-tool from the floor and fixed it to his wrist. There were several messages from William Spender—status updates on various recovery efforts. Tann had not asked for them, but appreciated them all the same.

Spender, it seemed, had also failed to unravel Addison's sour mood. Instead of waiting for improvement, he'd taken it upon himself to find other ways to help. Initiative like that should not be discouraged. Tann would use what was made available to him.

Later. For now, he ignored the messages.

Grateful for the combined efforts of his prior genius and the systems technicians who had strengthened the signal, he took the opportunity to contact Sloane on single point-to-point communications.

She answered after a few seconds, audio-only, as seemed to be her custom.

"I'm busy," she said.

Also her custom.

Clanging, tools whirring all peppered the background of her comm signal. The focus today was on hydroponics, he knew. Not the growth of crops, which was still a dubious prospect given the state of the seeds, but the "less sexy," as Sloane put it, side of that department—the bacteria vats. These were crucial to normal station operations, not only for their ability to convert waste into fertilizer, but also to produce drinking water as a byproduct. Both were sorely needed.

"Fully appreciated, Security Director," he said. "I have a personal favor to ask, actually."

"No shit?"

"I imagine," he replied dryly, "that you have plenty of *that* around you now."

Tann walked as he spoke, heading for the primary junction corridor that linked this part of the Nexus with the warehousing district. Kesh and her work crew had been focused almost entirely on this area for two days now, trying to clear a path.

For that matter, he kept a wary eye out for any workforce he might unwittingly cross paths with.

Sloane's snort seemed to him to be a sign of laughter. She had so many, he often confused them. "Not yet, wise guy. That's what the work is for."

"Fair. As to the purpose of this call, I wonder if you might talk with Addison."

A beat. "About?"

"This may require a bit of discretion."

Even through the tinny speaker of the omni-tool, he could hear her laugh. "Please tell me you want me to slip her a note in class."

Tann considered this. Did not find sense in the offer. "There are no classes," he replied, frowning at his wrist as though he may find the answer there. Without Sloane's face to guide him, he couldn't be sure which conversational gambit to take. "But if you suppose a note would be helpful?"

"Oh, for—Never mind," she said, more clearly exasperated. "It's a joke. What am I talking to her about?"

Ah. Sloane's jokes were as mercurial as her cooperative spirit. He shrugged. "I have some concerns about her declining mood. I am no doctor or psychologist, but I believe she is suffering from depression."

This did not go over with the ah-ha moment he'd hoped. "Yeah, no kidding," she replied. "As it turns out, even an idiot like me can see that, Tann."

See? Mercurial. He sighed. "I didn't mean that you are an idiot, Sloane."

"Yeah? What *did* you mean?"

"I thought perhaps you, as a human female, might be at a stronger advantage for..." He paused. Considered the words. "For bonding? The kind between like, rather than commitment," he added, in case she misunderstood. Species interplay was only his forte in that he understood the politics.

Relationships within other species were utterly beyond his realm of understanding.

When she didn't answer right away, Tann hurriedly added, "Unless that is your predilection, in which case you have my full support to—"

Sloane laughed, then. Sharp, but not hard. "Relax," she said on the end of it. "I know what you meant. Sorry, I'm running on two hours sleep here. You want me—as a human female—to talk to her, try to get her out of her funk, is that it?"

Relief. "Precisely." After a second he added, "This type of thing is not one of my strengths." A little truth to salve the sting.

"You and me both," Sloane said. "I'm no counselor. Still, you're right. And it's pretty damn thoughtful of you."

Relief eased to a surprising note of… what was that? Pleasure? At her rare praise? Tann opened his mouth to thank her, but she didn't pause to let him.

"I guess—Yeah, sure, I can try."

Unexpectedly easy. And most assuredly surprising. "Thank you, Sloane."

"When things have settled here," she added quickly, with emphasis that said she expected a fight on it.

He did not deliver. "Of course."

"Anything else?"

Tann *did* have something else in mind, but decided that despite this little bit of team building, it would be better left unspoken.

"No. Please, by all means, return to your—"

"Out," Sloane said, cutting the link.

Classic Sloane Kelly, to the last. But perhaps, just

perhaps, this was who she was with everybody. That, at least, left him something to consider as he proceeded on his way.

Had this bit of effort been the right thing to do? Only time would tell, of course, but if his estimations were correct, not only might Foster Addison rise from her foul mood, but the impetus to do so would come from Sloane, rather than him. He wasn't sure how that might alter Addison's impression of—and allegiance to—Sloane, but it might serve to make Sloane a bit more sympathetic toward *him*.

A tiny push toward cohesion. If they could all just trust him, Tann felt sure the mission would be back on track in time to assist the Pathfinders and, ultimately, colonize Andromeda. "To paint their masterpiece," as Jien had so wonderfully put it.

Now for the next item on my agenda.

He steeled himself, for this was likely to go in a much different direction. No omni-tool this time. A personal visit would be better. An opportunity to make clear that *Acting* Director Jarun Tann was no longer acting.

He went in search of Nakmor Kesh.

CHAPTER TEN

The Nexus, he thought, could still be classified as a wreck. That would not change for some time. Still, as Jarun Tann strode through the labyrinth of halls and chambers, he could not help but feel a sense of hope. The progress made in just one week was remarkable, even with the extra damage provided by the Scourge.

Or perhaps, he reflected, *because of.* Little could be as motivating as immediate danger.

Just two days before, in order to walk from his co-opted Research Lab to Operations, Tann would have had to descend two levels, cross the Fabrication workshop, climb an unintended ramp made of a collapsed portion of ceiling, duck under a foul-smelling bundle of ruptured pipes, then finally climb back up the two levels he'd descended by using a ladder bolted to the wall of an unpowered lift tube.

While he still had to do most of that, the ruptured pipes were no longer leaking. Someone had welded a salvaged sheet of metal across the lot of them.

In so many cases, the little things made for a greater sense of optimism.

Although revenue had been his placement, Tann had not fallen so far into numbers that he did not maintain a healthy regimen of exercise, when applicable. This route appeased that need—and never so completely felt than when he hauled his own body weight up to the floor outside the unpowered lift tube.

Efficiently fit, perhaps, but a soldier he was not.

He lay back on the gritty floor, waited for his breathing to settle. This took longer than it should have, even on exhausted days. His lungs absolutely burned, and did he detect a bit of a wheeze? No doubt from all the toxins he'd been sucking in since the calamity.

Ventilation, as of yesterday, had yet to cross the 50% effectiveness threshold, despite all the progress by that team.

Once he felt he could breathe again without hitching, he rolled over and clambered to his feet. He saw nobody the rest of the journey. Operations was empty. The bodies of their unfortunate leadership had all been removed, placed in the improvised morgue until a proper memorial could be arranged. Someone had even cleaned up the blood, the rubble, and righted the overturned furniture. Other than its temporary wall, and the fact that nearly every screen was still dark, the room looked relatively normal.

Almost as it had before they'd left the Milky Way. *More ghosts, perhaps.* A reflection that caught him off guard. Salarians, and Tann especially, saw no use for the concept of specters.

"Why'd you leave?"

The voice boomed in the hollow chamber, slammed into his aural cavities and jerked him around. His wide eyes took in the empty—

No. The once-empty chamber.

Nakmor Kesh stood behind him, as if she'd followed in his footsteps. She pushed past him even before her voice had died.

"I beg your pardon?" he asked stiffly.

"You heard me." She didn't turn around to address him directly. He watched as she strode toward a dead bank of monitors on the opposite wall, lowered her large bulk to the floor. Without ceremony, she began to pull burnt system boards from an open access panel.

He had, of course, heard her. But the meaning escaped him. "Leave what?" He approached cautiously. Not because he *wanted* to be in reach of krogan fists, but because he felt it necessary to maintain a certain amount of ground in front of one.

"The Milky Way." She spoke to the cables and cords, the fried wires and burnt boards. Not to him. "Everyone has their reasons. What's yours, Jarun Tann?"

"Ah." A popular topic among the crew. He'd heard enough of them discussing it with friends or co-workers in the crowded common area. All reminding one another of what they'd sacrificed, as a sort of reminiscence-based motivational technique. A coping mechanism, no doubt.

This was the first time, however, anyone had asked Tann the question. He grew nervous. Anticipating questions and preparing natural-sounding-yet-carefully-rehearsed answers was something of a pastime for him. Improvisation wasn't a skill he had ever quite mastered, though this did not thwart his attempts to try.

The timing. It all came down to the timing.

Which he'd just blown, he realized, as the krogan heaved a long-suffering sigh and sat back on her haunches to glare at him. "You must have more reason than just salarian instinct to stick fingers in all things at the same time," she said heavily. What may have been a lighthearted joke from anyone else did not translate as such when a krogan said it.

"No need for that," he snapped, stiffening. "If you must know, I left because I've always wanted to explore. Yes," he added in irritation, "grin away, but it's the truth. I once wanted to roam the stars. Third-assistant to the deputy administrative director of revenue projections, *that* was the detour. I see the Initiative as a chance to choose again."

"Why?"

Why? He looked down at her. Or tried. Krogan were too big for easy disdain. "Although we are among the most intelligently advanced species in the gal—" He caught himself. "—in the Milky Way, we salarians don't have the longest of life spans."

Kesh snorted, turning back to her dysfunctional processors. "It's one of my favorite things about salarians."

Another would-be joke carried on sharp teeth from a krogan. Worse, a krogan he had no power to remove for her temerity in existing with such confidence on his station.

Nakmor Kesh held a position within her species that was not, in a word, desirable. Liaison to others, a sort of cultural interpreter and ambassador all rolled into one. This wasn't a role a krogan killed to achieve, it was a role they killed to get out of. The fact she seemed to enjoy the role only aggravated his sense of decency.

Unfortunately for both of them, it was her job to interface with the leadership of the Nexus. *Especially* Jarun Tann, Director of the Nexus.

Tread carefully, he reminded himself. Krogan or not, he needed something from Nakmor Kesh.

So he would play her game. "And you?" He phrased it as politely as he could. "Why did you join the Initiative, Nakmor Kesh?"

Kesh lay back and pushed herself under the desk beside the broken displays. She tore at scorched wires, tossing them into a pile by her knee. The display was not lost on Tann.

Look how strong krogan are.

Salarians did not roll their eyes. Well, not as a sign of disdain. Salarians could, and Tann had, but only in situations where the thin, protective membranes needed extra help in defending against dryness or irritants. Yet, in this moment, all he could imagine was what it might look like if he mirrored Sloane.

"They invited us."

The krogan's words, muffled somewhat by the desk, tore his focus entirely away from hybrid metaphors, pinned his gaze squarely on those bent krogan knees. Bulbous things, horrifyingly misshapen. Though densely packed with muscle.

Like krogan skulls.

Tann pasted on a pleasant look of interest. "Invited, you say?"

She grunted. "The Nakmor clan put muscle and bone into this place. When it neared completion, we received an invite."

Tann knew all this. However, he found it a reasonable avenue to social compromise. "I was given to understand," he said carefully, diplomatically as he could, "that the krogan were not the galaxy-hopping kind."

This time, her muffled grunt sounded like a laugh. "Who is?"

A valid point. They were, after all, the first to travel so far, and for so long.

"The Nakmor have a higher resistance to the genophage," Kesh continued, tone much more flat now.

Ah, the genophage. Tann took a wary step back. Conversations regarding the salarian-created, turian-delivered anti-reproductive disease afflicting the krogan species did not often end well.

Kesh did not, however, let loose with the usual flurry of muscleheaded posturing. "Jien Garson thought that might mean we're a hardier bunch."

"I see," Tann said. He hadn't known of the clan's genetic resistance—did the Dalatrasses, he wondered, or was it a closely guarded secret among the Milky Way Nakmor? How had Jien Garson found out? Save perhaps by genetic investigation. All of the pioneers had undergone rigorous testing. Perhaps she had stumbled upon something the salarians had not.

Perhaps the Nakmor clan had known all along.

If so, that would have made the krogan clan among the first to keep such an important fact away from the salarian matriarchs and their most skilled intelligence operatives.

Tann, of course, was neither. And even if he had been among the Dalatrasses' informants, there was little he could do about it now. So he filed that little bit of genetic information away.

It might, he reflected dourly, *be a matter to correct in the future.*

Krogan, after all, had the evolutionary capacity to breed like varren, if left unchecked.

A problem for another time. As Kesh appeared somewhat chatty, he thought to probe a bit more. "But that does not explain why you accepted. An invitation is not a reason."

This time, her laughter had a dark, graveled undertone to it. "That's not like you, Tann," she said, ripping an entire bundle of blackened gear from under the table and heaving it aside. "To miss the obvious."

He folded his arms, frowning at the krogan. Then

it hit him. It wasn't that he'd missed it. It was that he took the obvious path regarding the information. Not the path that credited the krogan with any agency at all.

A hedge against another genophage. Or perhaps against any attempt to control the species as a whole.

So they had thought themselves in a position to alter the course of the future. He could not fault her for that, nor the rest of her clan, who'd all joined with their clan leader. But he could remember it.

"I see," he replied, this time with a slow turn that revealed how much he truly did. Best to let her know that he had accepted the information, and allow her to believe it resolved.

Her grunt seemed to indicate she did.

Kesh dragged herself out from under the brutalized counter and lumbered to her feet. She walked in his direction, rubbed two sooty hands in great swaths along her uniform as she went. Each step taken with unwavering purpose.

Not to him. At the last instant, he realized she meant to walk *through* him if he didn't move. Tann stepped aside, sweeping an arm as if allowing her to exit.

Message received, all right.

She passed without a word, and he fell in just behind her. For lack of any further discussion on the topic, he volunteered his purpose. "I actually came up here looking for you."

"Oh? Well, here I am."

This, at least, Tann had rehearsed. "I am assembling a database. In case of further emergencies, I mean, seeing as the central systems are all still offline and their integrity is not yet known."

"A database of what?"

"Critical information. Things which, as of this

moment, only exist in some of our heads. Were there to be further, well, sudden departures from the 'living' portion of the crew, we risk considerable loss of knowledge."

"Are you asking for my life story or something?" Kesh asked. She ducked under a decorative tree that had been tossed nearly twenty meters across a greeting space and become embedded in the wall paneling. The large hump of her back nearly jostled it.

Tann ducked from habit, but as tall as salarians were by nature, krogan bulk dwarfed them in comparison. He jogged to catch up. "No, nothing like that. What I'm specifically looking to preserve is certain maintenance codes. The technique by which you and your subordinate—"

"Calix."

"Yes, Calix. The tech—"

"Corvannis," she added succinctly.

Tann bit off a sharp answer. "Calix Corvannis, yes. The turian. In specific, it seems prudent to record the technique by which you were able to manually draw crew members from cryostasis. If nothing else, for—"

"No." One word. A single syllable, delivered in Kesh's graveled voice.

Tann had anticipated this, and had already decided on an appeal to her sense of duty. "Nakmor Kesh, I'm *sure* you realize that if something were to happen to you and Calix Corvannis, we would have no method for reviving others. There are still several thousands of individuals in their pods. Our chances of success here would be doomed."

The krogan gave a heavy shrug. "The only other party that should have that is security, and Director Kelly already declined."

That surprised him. "On what grounds?"

"Ask her."

"I am asking you."

Kesh came to a door, which appeared to be her destination. She turned to Tann and looked him up and down. From the sweep of his, if Tann thought so himself, pleasantly shaped horns to the very tips of his Nexus standard, efficiently maintained boots.

She, however, did not appear impressed by either. "Sloane doesn't want the responsibility," she finally said. "You don't either."

Tann drew himself up, all the many and appropriately stern centimeters of him. "You have no right to assume such."

She was already shaking her head. She braced one hand against the drop frame and bent, so her face appeared very close in Tann's vision. "You misunderstand. Not thirty minutes go by without someone asking me, begging me, *ordering* me, to revive a friend, a loved one, or some other person they've decided is critical to the effort."

"I would be happy to manage—"

The krogan's wide mouth twisted. "Tch. Of course you would. A lot of power to place in someone's hands, letting them decide who lives and who doesn't."

"They all *live*," he countered, waving that away. "Nor is that my intent—"

"I'm sure it never crossed your mind."

Well, then. Tann's chin rose. This turn in the conversation he had also anticipated, but he'd rated the chances low that Kesh would leap to such conclusions so quickly. "I am beginning to feel," he said tactfully, "as if you and I have gotten off on the wrong foot."

Kesh's twisted grin showed teeth. "History is a bitch, isn't it?" She turned away. Paused, and then swung her shoulders back around to peer at Tann. "I'll ask Calix to place the maintenance overrides in a secure file, coded for Sloane Kelly. That's the best you'll get."

"But—"

"Excuse me." An avalanche would sound less final. She picked up her stride and the door slid open, revealing a room full of krogan workers, all being supervised by a handful of other crew. They were laboring over one of the Nexus's massive engines—critically important should they encounter the Scourge again.

He beat a hasty, politically appropriate retreat.

All in all, he considered the outcome of their chat a minor victory. All it really meant was, should the situation call for hard decisions to be made regarding the revived population, he would have one more person he could negotiate with. Sloane Kelly. She, so far, had proved something of a wildcard. It might be easier to predict her position on a given matter via a roll of the dice, and that he found most frustrating.

However, there was the third person in this equation, someone to whom he had not yet spoken beyond the briefest of introductions. Tann decided a small, diceless gamble was in order.

||||||||||||||||||

He settled on a more official approach. Tann found an unused but relatively tidy office near Operations, settled into a chair, and waited.

Thirty minutes passed before there came a knock at the door—the chime was broken. Tann called out, "Enter!"

He would have preferred to appear busy. Some papers to shuffle through, or a terminal screen to study intently. He had to settle for fiddling with his omni-tool, pointedly turning it off the moment the turian entered.

"Ah, Calix Corvannis. Please, sit."

The turian glanced around, as if expecting to see someone else. Kesh, probably. An unusual alliance, to say the least. Krogan and salarians did not, as a rule, mesh, but the krogan had not forgotten the turians' role in, as it were, the widespread emasculation of their clans.

Calix folded his arms, talons turned in. "I'd rather stand, if you don't mind."

"I understand, you're busy."

He shook his head, chitinous features reflecting a mild sheen as he did. Metals. Some blend of whatever environment his people had evolved in, to be somewhat less than precise. All turian exoskeletons displayed some version of it or another. A relic of the metal-poor core of their home planet.

"Busy, yes," the turian replied, "but also sick of sitting. I've just come off a long-term calibration and I could use a stretch."

"Oh, I see." Tann, like most, had not really mastered the art of turian facial tics. Calix seemed reasonable enough. He would have to assume it true, for now. "May I get you anything?"

"Not unless you have some Tupari stocked away somewhere." Before Tann could reply in any form, Calix added, "No, thank you. It would be nice if you could make this quick, however. There's more critical work to do." He paused. Glanced around again. "What is this, exactly?"

Tann allowed himself a few seconds to process this. He leaned back into his chair and studied the turian. Calix's uniform was stained, unkempt. Not unusual given the situation, but remarkably for it, he still seemed to hold an air of... not superiority, not exactly. Tann had dealt, at least on the fringe, with Primarchs. *That* was superiority.

Calix Corvallis displayed confidence. Everything about Calix's tone and posture implied a total sense of ease. *Very interesting.* Tann wondered if the turian always enjoyed such a comfortable air around people of importance, or if perhaps instead he didn't consider Tann to be important.

Perhaps both.

He'd also noticed the lack of Sloane and Addison. An astute observation from a simple life-support technician.

"It is a minor matter, actually, and yes, I will be brief. I do not," he added dryly, "have any Tupari on hand, and I believe it best for everyone this way."

Calix smiled—Tann thought he did, anyway. The mandibles moved. The... fringe-y teeth-like exoskeleton of his mouth seemed to shift. But mostly, he simply waited, hands clasped behind his back as if this were some kind of military meeting. When he shook his head, Tann felt it less a dismissal and more a gesture of boredom.

Jarun Tann began to feel an unease he did not care for. It was one thing to have entered into a conversation for which he had not truly prepared. To do so knowing little about the other participant made things considerably worse.

Well, it was time he gave it his best. Sparing little, he gave the same speech he'd given to Kesh. Entirely true, if not necessarily for the justifications given. Critical information, in the hands of so few, was dangerous under normal circumstances. With the Nexus in its current state, biometrics offline, the main database damaged and the state of its backups unknown, keeping the stasis maintenance overrides in the heads of just two people bordered on the criminally negligent.

"I hope," he finished tactfully, "to avoid consequences of either."

Calix watched him. "So you want me to give them to you?" the turian asked.

Tann leaned forward. A touch of the conspiratorial, a signal that they were, after all, on the same side. "I merely want to catalog this knowledge—"

"Why not ask Kesh?"

And there, the interruption. Tann was beginning to see it as a sign that others found him not worth hearing out. It grated. But he answered. "I did."

"And?" he asked.

Tann suspected the turian already knew the answer, and only wanted to hear him say it.

Fine. Let the turian score a point. "She declined."

Again, that sense of a smile. The mandibles, a bit of a crinkle at the less rigid skin around the eyes. He glanced around at the room again. "The very definition of backroom politics."

Perhaps, but he needed the turian to understand *why.* "Look, Calix, you must understand the natural mistrust Nakmor Kesh has for me. For all salarians."

"Your people earned that."

"So," he pointed out, "did yours."

That earned him a slow, thoughtful stare from the engineer.

Tann continued. "Neither point requires debate. The fact remains, however, that sometimes in such a, er, leadership dynamic, approaches must be taken that avoid bringing such prejudices into the equation."

Calix rubbed at his jaw. "And you think I'd be willing to risk going against my direct superior."

"As opposed to going against the Initiative director?" Tann delivered it as a counter, but a thoughtful one. Something for the engineer to chew on.

Did turians chew? Calix didn't seem to take the time. "You do realize I work *directly* for Kesh, right?"

"I am aware of that."

"And if I go to her, tell her about this meeting?"

Tann spread his hands. "You would merely reinforce what she already thinks of me. I would be no closer to my goal, but at least I would have tried. You, on the other hand, would no longer be the engineer I choose to confer with in station matters." He paused briefly. Put on a show of thought. "Perhaps the other turian engineer. What was his name?"

"Her." A short, curt correction, and then Calix put his hands on the desk. Positively loomed. "What is that goal of yours, really? Don't give me any more of that crap about cataloging critical knowledge."

Tann stared into the turian's intense eyes. Was it the mention of another turian? The loss of leadership? He weighed his words carefully. "It occurs to me that in the very near future, we may find ourselves in a situation where hard decisions must be made."

"Go on."

Jarun Tann leaned back, forcing an air of comfort rather than withdrawal. He kept one hand on the arm of the chair, the other on the desk. Open to attack. Not that he expected attack; he merely wanted the turian to see how little defenses Tann put between them. "I worry that other prominent figures aboard the Nexus are incapable of making such decisions."

Very slowly, Calix nodded. "I agree that time

may come," he said, also slowly. For a moment, Tann thought he'd won. Broken through.

And then the turian pushed away from the desk and took a step for the door. "Sorry, Director, can't help you. Not in the way you want."

Blast. Tann stood, one hand flat on the table. "Why?"

The turian shot him a look Tann would *swear* was almost pitying. His skin tightened, body tensing with the fury that roiled under Tann's careful veneer. "Because," the turian said simply, "I believe in that old Earth phrase: 'Absolute power corrupts absolutely.'"

That was it? Calix Corvannis refused to share information because of some *fear*? "You must understand that there are Dalatrasses, *Primarchs*," he added, to reflect the turian's own society, "who retain possession of so much more."

"Yeah. *That's* why." Calix's words were sharp, practically a slap across the face. "So here's what I'm prepared to do. I will keep this conversation between us, and take your altruistic motives at face value. If you require a stasis pod override, and the situation is too sensitive to gather consensus, go ahead and come to me."

Tann sat back into his chair, the springs creaking. "So you can tell me to go ask Kesh?" he asked bitterly.

The turian shook his head. "I won't. As much as I might want to, I actually do understand what you mean about the complex nature of inter-species dynamics. If your reasons are sound, I'll handle the override process myself. Good enough?"

That… was acceptable. Tann knew when to take a deal. "That will do."

"Good. Now, if there's nothing else, I've got a station to save." He did not wait for Tann to dismiss him.

Nobody ever did.

After the door closed, Jarun Tann sat for several long minutes behind the desk. Not moving, his gaze unfocused. A casual observer might think him in a trance, or just asleep. His mind was quite busy, though.

Certain assumptions and expectations had to be changed. Much else he had been able to predict with reasonable accuracy, and account for. But Calix Corvannis, a mere pawn on the chessboard, had just proven himself quite a bit more astute than that. A turian who made easy friends with a krogan. Who did not jump at the chance to rise.

An interesting wildcard. But yet another wildcard all the same.

Eventually Tann shook his head. He needed sleep, he decided. Almost as much, he needed a friendly conversation.

He found he rather disliked always being made to feel like the bad guy.

CHAPTER ELEVEN

Sloane slumped back in her desk chair, rubbing both hands down her face. Every bone in her body cried out for rest. Every strand of hair, every cell. How many days had it been since she'd had anything approaching a good night's sleep?

Her laugh sounded saltier than even she'd expected. "Not a chance," she told her open palms. Pressing them against her eyes didn't help, either.

At least now she had some downtime. Until the next meeting. Or emergency. Or whatever else. It'd come. Sloane didn't understand everything about the Nexus's many technical issues, but she knew a floating fixer-upper when she saw it. If nothing else, there'd be another glitch, another fire, more supplies growing legs, another thing breaking.

Another strand of that deadly Scourge thing to avoid.

And here they were—Sloane, Tann, Addison, even Kesh; playing house with thousands of lives. The refrain stuck in her head.

What matters is what we do when we arrive…

It was enough to drive a woman to drink.

She'd settle for a nap.

Sloane let her hands drop to her sides, tilting back until the chair supported the weight of her head. Her temporary quarters were guest accommodations in the Cultural Exchange, far enough from the chaos that she could take a breather away from the constant pressure. It beat the common room.

Foster Addison had assigned the place to Sloane without asking for input. Privately, she figured Addison wanted her to have somewhere she could go to swear when things got too much. A nice gesture, all things considered.

The past two weeks had thrown down progress and obstacles in equal measure. Some Sloane could handle without any oversight from the acting director—even if Tann always gave her the eye afterward.

Other things required dialogue. Debates.

She didn't get a lot of private time, either. She was always with her team, going over basic security, with groups of krogan engineers, or with Tann and Addison. And the addition of Addison's sleaze-bag assistant... *Ugh*, data pushers got on her nerves.

Sloane spent most of her time dealing with something or someone. Scores of people, each focused on a task, each task part of a net that wove through the Nexus.

Each success bolstered the odds of getting the station into shape, of becoming the central location the Pathfinders would need them to be. But every failure dragged down the net, too. Systems fried and took down others nearby, corridors crumbled and sealed the way to necessary installations. More and more it looked like they'd need the Pathfinders to support them, not the other way around.

People worked tirelessly. Anxiety pressed in on all of them from every direction. Those off-shift or in non-critical systems bunked down in the shuttles locked in at the Colonial Affairs hangars. CA had a whole fleet of shuttles, just waiting for something to do. Right now, acting as glorified bunks made the most sense.

In critical sectors, the workers racked out in temporary cots near the worksites. Nobody was ever where they were supposed to be.

Even the krogan hadn't started any fights. Not real ones. The usual dominance stuff krogan always pulled, yelling and headbutts—or maybe it was just their way of showing affection.

Sloane opened her eyes to blink away the tired spots that fuzzed there. Just in time for the comm tone to drill through her hard-earned silence.

"Director Sloane, are you available?"

She dug both index fingers into the bridge of her nose, rubbing the tired out. "I am now. What do you need, Spender?"

He caught the irritated note in her voice. "Hey, sorry to bother you during downtime," he said, "but I came across some information and I thought, 'Wow, Director Kelly should—'"

"Get your lips off my ass and get to the point."

"Of course," he replied, but with a conciliatory addition she recognized as learned from Tann. A bit of affronted dignity. Almost a sneer he couldn't quite hide. The man spent as much time at Tann's side as he did Addison's, juggling administrative tasks for both with—she could admit—a surprising amount of skill.

That didn't mean she trusted him. Not even close. To Sloane, he was just another bureaucratic voice arguing against the things she *needed* to be handling.

Of course, it might be her own bias talking.

"I was preparing the post-stasis report for the staff that was awakened early," he said, the comm crackling only once. Much better than it used to be. Tann had done good there. Kesh and her technicians were a marvel of ingenuity. "One in particular caught my attention."

"Go on."

As he spoke, she booted up her own terminal and logged into the security access. Much of it was still locked up behind firewalls. Only Garson had all the access privileges. Just in case.

With the original leadership now gone, Sloane and a few others had access to some of the data, but nobody alive had all of it. She wasn't sure Spender should have been among those with access, but as close as he was working with Tann and Addison, she couldn't be sure that he didn't need it, either.

"The name is Falarn," Spender told her. "Priote Falarn. I'm sending you the records now." It took no time at all. Within the space of her *mm-hm*, the records showed up in her mail terminal.

"A salarian," she said aloud. "One of our contracted Sur'Kesh specialists." Her whistle was low as she scanned the list of recommendations attached to his file. "Highly trained in communications and arrays. Your team, right? Colonial Affairs. What about him?"

"I'll be blunt. He stinks."

"You should call medical."

"What I mean is I have reason to suspect him."

Great. Now Spender was starting to *sound* like Tann. Sloane grimaced, reaching over to flick the video array on.

The advisor's haughty features filled the screen. His eyes briefly widened, as if he hadn't expected a face to face, but settled again with a half-apologetic smile and nod.

She nodded back out of habit. "Okay. Talk to me."

"Before we launched, a few of our staff were undergoing some last-minute checks. Most were officially cleared." Her eyes narrowed dangerously, and he continued hastily. "Including Falarn."

"So?"

"So I thought it was a mistake, and I wasn't the only one," he replied. "The classification division was on to something, started building a case. Before we could take it to Director Addison, though, something strange happened."

"*Short* version, Spender."

His eyebrows knitted. "Most of the digital evidence was gone. Not destroyed, just..." His fingers popped into the air like a firework. "Poof. Never existed. I tried to backtrack the lead, but—"

Sloane's patience wasn't made to hold up to this shit. Her elbows hit the table. "Hit the bottom line in the next thirty seconds," she growled.

"Someone on the inside destroyed the case, and Falarn was the most likely candidate."

"Spender," Sloane said slowly, drawing out his name as if he were a toddler, "has this salarian done something wrong, or not?"

He hesitated. "I've seen him in places he has no business being in. Records show him accessing terminals he has no need to access. Yeah, it's a hunch, I admit it. But given the concerns before departure, and the fact that supplies have been reported missing, I thought... call it 'suspicious activity.'"

Sloane didn't drop her forehead to the desk. She'd give herself that much of a victory.

"Fine," she sighed. "I'll check this guy out. Where's he stationed now?"

Spender tapped a few keys, eyes flicking side to side as he pulled up the data. "In and out of Operations, according to the logs. And down in Central Comms."

"Wonderful. Fucking perfect." To his credit, Spender didn't flinch. If anything, his smile got a little less conciliatory and a little more wry at her salt. "I'll go see what I can find."

"Thank you, Director Sloane." The title still annoyed her, but at least he used her first name, and actually thanked her when he sent her on a wild goose chase.

Sloane signed off and gave a long hard look at the wall. "I really," she said, at first slow and level, and graduating to a shout with every word, "*really* need some *fucking coffee!*"

The wall did not comply.

||||||||||||||||||||

Somebody had managed to salvage some... Sloane wouldn't call it *music*, per se, but it passed the time in the temporary workspace. If she had to guess, they'd ripped some mixed techno beat from the Citadel's Flux and brought it along for nostalgia.

Six centuries old nostalgia, to be sure, and of the sort best left behind. Why would anyone want to remember anything that had gone on inside the walls of Flux?

It's not like the techs were partying to it. Inside the still-gutted room, the heavy bass beat thudded in tandem to the focused silence of the Nexus crew working there. Only one looked up when she stepped inside. A human she didn't know. Sloane sliced through niceties with a brusque nod and a gesture.

"Hate to interrupt but I need a minute of your time."

The man hurried over, running a broad hand over the tired lines of his dusky features. "What can I help you with, Director?" He pitched his deep voice low. The music *oontz*'ed.

An unapologetic yawn followed his question, but

as a few techs looked up behind him, Sloane noted they seemed a touch more settled than they were even a week ago. They'd found a groove.

"Falarn," she said crisply. "He here?"

The tech shook his head. "He's off shift right now. Last I heard, he was going to sleep until the next emergency."

"Must be nice. Where?"

"Wherever he can find a space," the tech said with a shrug. "Like most of us."

Yeah, take a number. "In commons? Maybe one of the hangars?"

He thought about it. Glanced back at his team, who also shrugged. "Most of us just crash under one of the desks in HQ2."

"What's that?"

"Just a room across the hall." He became defensive when she raised an eyebrow. "No one else was using it, and we were sick of walking all the way back to our temp quarters in the hangar."

"Whoa, slow down. It's fine." Sloane jerked a thumb back to the hall. "And Falarn, that's where he sleeps? You've seen him?"

"Uh, I don't know. Sorry."

Figured. "Thanks. As you were."

"Ma'am," he replied, and returned to his team. She didn't miss the subtle shrug he gave one of the other techs.

Sloane left, already writing the script in her head. *Yes, I know you were sleeping, sorry for waking you, I just have a few questions about…*

About what, exactly? Suspicious activity. Sloane grimaced, trying to recall why she'd agreed to this.

Maybe to do some actual security work for once.

Not that it was going to amount to anything. People of all departments were accessing terminals. If anything she should investigate Spender for wasting her damned time.

The temporary quarters were indeed just across the corridor, in a room that had been earmarked for some other purpose. Sloane wasn't sure what—something more technical and undoubtedly more redundant than necessary.

She manually keyed in the access code. The sensors still flaked out from time to time, leaving the doors stuck wide open or stubbornly closed. Manual remained the most reliable method of entry without risking bruised pride and a nosebleed.

Sloane cursed her tired brain. How was she supposed to run an investigation like this? Not that it was entirely Spender's fault. She'd made it abundantly clear that she wanted to vet anything suspicious, anyone skirting that line. He'd been right to flag it.

But she didn't like running blind, either.

The converted room was dark, lights dimmed to a level acceptable to sleep in. It was also, she noted from inside the open frame of the door, empty. Cots had been set up in rows, blankets folded neatly, pillows in place for those species who wanted or needed them.

No sleeping salarian.

No one at all.

She tilted her head. All right. So, maybe he'd be at the residency hangar. With each shuttle having its own life-support system, they made for good emergency housing. Finding which one Farlarn had been assigned would be a hassle, but nothing she couldn't manage.

Except nobody she contacted could find him. His bunkmate thought he was back in Ops. The guy she spoke to there suggested he could be at the common area. Nobody had actually *seen* him.

Maybe he was having a tryst, and they were all covering for him. Did salarians tryst?

"I guess with an asari," she muttered, earning a sideways look from a human she passed on the way to the next locale. By the time Sloane's instincts had caught up with her, she'd walked several laps of the operational bits of the Nexus. Even her sec team hadn't located him.

Great.

When her comm crackled to life, she had just enough civility left in her to growl, "This better be good news."

"No promises." Calix's now-familiar voice drawled the words across the channel. "Did you authorize some info-sec goon to access my systems?"

"Access, as in…?"

"As in, did somebody in security drop a forged stasis authorization into my queue? Maybe someone was testing procedures and protocols?"

"Hell no—" She stopped herself short, pausing in the hallway to activate the display on her omni-tool. "Shit. Give me a sec."

"You don't know?"

"Shut up," she muttered, earning one of the turian's dry chuckles. Calix understood the mess caused by red tape, especially when it involved Addison and Tann. That didn't protect her from his good-natured bullshit, though.

She scrolled rapidly through the latest communications. "No," she said slowly. "Nothing even remotely like that. The fact that you're asking this isn't making my gut happy, Calix."

"Wonderful." Dry as Tuchanka dust. "Then you should know that I've had about nine pods unsealed under a false work order. Sending you the list now."

"Who unsealed them?"

"I did, because they had Director Addison's approval."

Sloane grit her teeth. "But she didn't actually approve them."

"No. A confirmation made its way back to her and, luckily, she caught it."

"And you checked with Kesh? Is it possible she—"

"She didn't."

She grimaced. "I had to make sure." She scanned the list Calix sent. "Commerce? Customs? None of these people are critical."

"My thinking exactly," Calix replied. "I've got log-time about two standard hours back."

"Just enough time to acclimate," she noted. "How convenient."

"Yeah." She could hear the turian's shrug in his voice. "And time enough to be anywhere by now. Whatever their purpose, I just thought you might like to know. I'm leaving this in your capable hands, Sloane."

"Yeah, thanks." She quickly turned around to half-jog through the corridor. The first things people needed coming out of stasis were food and warmth.

She dialed up Kandros. "Find me every recent access log from Priote Falarn and Foster Addison," she said before he even had a chance to greet her.

"Who the hell is Priote Falarn?"

"Just do it."

"Yes, ma'am," he replied smartly.

She signed off to contact Addison. The faces she jogged past followed her trail, but she ignored their idle curiosity in favor of dodging the occasional construction tangle.

The comm link connected. "I was just trying to reach you," Addison said. Hurried words, very tense.

"We have a problem," Sloane said.

"We have more than one," the woman replied, and for the first time in a long time, Sloane heard a bit of steel in her voice. But there was something else, too. Something focused. Worried.

Sloane frowned. "Let me guess. You know who falsified approval documents in your name to wake up some non-critical personnel."

"Salarian by name of Falarn."

Sloane nodded. "And?"

"And," Addison sighed, "the bastard and about ten of his friends just stormed the hangar and surrounded a shuttle. They're demanding that we let them board it and then clear the hangar, or they'll start shooting."

CHAPTER TWELVE

Kandros met her at the hangar door accompanied by four of the team, including Talini. Good. Her biotics would no doubt come in handy.

All of them had come prepared as she'd directed, wearing Initiative-certified Elanus Risk Control Services gear and carrying just enough firepower to put down the problem without risking casualties.

"Did you talk to info-sec?" Sloane asked Talini.

The asari saluted. "Yes ma'am."

"And?"

"They're on it."

Sloane nodded her thanks. What she was asking info-sec to do would probably seriously piss off Tann, to say nothing of Addison and all the others, but security was *her* job. For now, until everything settled, every access to secure networks would be recorded. Visuals and all. If nothing came of it, great. But if something did…

Something like this?

Next time, she'd catch it before it reached this point. The privacy implications were worth never having a hostage situation again.

Kandros eyed the door through a modified Kuwashii visor, which fed him enough data to keep his shots accurate and his intel sharp. "Info-sec has all ten arrayed outside the ship, with the hostages still holed up inside. Everyone else has been evac'd."

"That should save on time."

He nodded. "We move in on your order."

Her blood already surging into adrenaline-fueled clarity, Sloane primed her Avenger. "Shoot to take in," she ordered clearly, "but do what you have to in order to ensure the safety of the mission. I want all of you upright when we've taken these bastards down."

She couldn't care less how many of the would-be thieves remained upright at the end of this, but she couldn't say that out loud. If these traitors had intended to hurt the people of this facility—pioneers like them—then they deserved whatever was coming.

Various degrees of salutes and nods met her order. Kandros's mandibles tipped up in approval.

Turians. It's like they had a weakness for women in charge. She'd never met one who didn't get all... *turian*-eyed when she started calling the shots. Except maybe Kaetus, but he'd joined one of the arks. Sloane rolled her eyes, and glanced at Talini. "Shields up when we open the door. Find cover, then lay down hell."

"You got it," the commando replied. She rubbed her un-gloved hands together with glee. "Say the word, ma'am."

Sloane checked her team. They all faced the doors, weapons ready. Faces set behind visors.

"Save that ship. Bring in those hostages." With a last breath, she gave the word they waited for. "*Move*."

Manually overriding the door took only seconds. As the panels swooshed wide, a rippling field of blue biotic energy spread in front of them, absorbing the first bolts of firepower. Sloane never really got used to visuals through a biotic shield, all distorted and slightly off, but it got the job done, and that's what she needed most.

The crew split, finding cover behind crates and gear and the stockpiles of stuff hauled out of the ships to make room for personnel to bunk down. Sloane ducked behind a row of tarp-wrapped blocks. Kandros plastered his back against a tall stack of crates. The shield in front of them rippled as cries rang out.

"Get them!"

"Cover the ship!"

The reports of enemy assault rifles echoed through the hangar. A quick glance over her cover showed Falarn at the back rear, eyes wide and rifle spewing uneven bursts of fire. Obviously not trained to fight.

"Get down," she heard. One of hers, too late. She jerked as a stray bolt slammed into her shoulder, triggering her shields. Sloane ducked, unable to give the enemy a rebuttal.

Instead, she locked in on comms. "Talini, drop a surprise for that back row. Kandros, take Gonzalez and circle right. I want that back entry covered. Keep them away from the hostages inside that ship. Someone lay down cover fire!"

"I'll keep them pinned!"

Sloane acknowledged the volunteer with a short, "Do it," and waited until she heard the volley of cover fire. "Go, go," she called through the comms, leaping over her own cover.

Just as she did, the space behind the thieves distorted, bulging inward and then blooming out in a vivid purple-blue wound of space and time. Falarn's expression cracked into sheer panic as the vortex caused by Talini's biotics sucked him off his feet, stripping away his gravity.

Two more yelled as they collided with the spinning distortion, and Sloane couldn't help but grin as Talini yelled, "Eat that!" in the comms.

Sloane landed hard on her feet, Avenger aimed and finger squeezing the trigger. Short bursts, that was all this one needed. Anyone lucky enough to escape the asari's singularity scattered, many finding cover behind elements of the shuttle. Smart, really. They knew it was as much an asset as those inside it.

"Get the hostages!" someone yelled. In her peripheral, she saw a would-be thief in a Nexus uniform dart toward the ship. Kandros was too far away. Talini was busy. Sloane swung her weapon around and let loose a short burst of firepower. Blood spurted as the human went down—leg and side, probably not fatal. *Probably.* But at least he wouldn't be going near the hostages.

"I could have taken that," she heard in her comm.

"Too slow, Kandros."

She grinned at his snort, then ducked as the butt of a rifle arced over her head. A millisecond later, Gonzalez let loose a sharp yell. "I'm hit!"

"We got bogeys in back," Kandros added.

And one in front of her—the owner of that rifle.

"Busy," Sloane gritted as a big human woman, all muscle and thick neck, dropped a heavy hand onto Sloane's helmet. Before Sloane could wrench loose, strong fingers found purchase in the crevice around the neck, then shook. *Hard.*

Her Avenger went flying, her sense of balance shattered under a wash of vertigo as she was jerked bodily off her feet. Pain slammed into her back as the woman swung her into what had once been cover. The kinetic barriers didn't help physical damage. Not nearly as well.

The enemy heaved her back up into the air and

slammed her against the next closest object. She didn't know what the hell it was—just that her head rang like a gong, her neck strained from the pressure, and she'd bruise from knee to ribs tomorrow.

Swearing, out of control, she flailed at the fastenings of her helmet as the woman jerking her around grunted with effort. Just as the world spun at peak speed and momentum, Sloane's helmet gave way.

She went sailing ass over elbows, barely remembered to protect her now uncovered head, and slammed into the side of the ship. *That* rang like a gong, too. A big one.

Anything Sloane might have said was lost in a groan of effort as she collapsed to the floor in a tingling, throbbing mess of aches and battered limbs. Fortunately for her, the bruiser of a woman hadn't expected to suddenly lose Sloane's mass. By the time she got her balance back, Sloane surged to her feet and charged.

Armor met muscles—which, Sloane reflected as her entire body jarred, were thick enough to act like armor anyway. The woman grunted again. Sloane mirrored it, legs straining, arms clamped tight around her opponent's middle.

Sloane tried to lift her. Throw her. Nothing happened. Then the impossibly heavy thief just raised a fist and drove it down between Sloane's shoulder blades. Her shields took the hit but not the force. Sloane stumbled back before she kissed the hangar floor.

"Damn, you're big," she gasped. She swiped a hand over her sweaty chin. "The hell do you do?"

"Cargo." The woman rolled her wide shoulders, thick lips peeled back in a wide, toothy smile. "Seven years." The name on her uniform read Graves.

Sloane sighed. *Guess it isn't all hydraulic lifters and easy pay.*

"You need some help, boss?" Talini asked wryly.

She didn't need help *or* sass. Keeping a wary eye on her beef-bound opponent, she tipped her head slightly. "Get those hostages out and lock down the ship."

"Joining Kandros," Talini replied, but that thread of humor lingered.

"Got four holed up on the ramp," Kandros added.

"Roger."

"Now," Sloane said, her attention centered squarely back on Graves. "Your team's getting dismantled as we speak." If her words came out with a little bit more effort than menace, well, she'd ignore it and hope the woman didn't notice.

Her opponent didn't even glance around her. Instead she clenched her fists. "We're not staying on this death trap," Graves replied. "And you can't stop us from leaving."

"Got news for you, lady." Sloane jerked a thumb back toward the sound of more firepower, and more yelling. "We need these shuttles. We need people who know what they're doing, too, and *you* should have been one of them."

The woman set her not insubstantial jaw.

"But since you aren't going to help make this future…" Sloane tilted her head side to side, heard her neck pop. Easing up on her stance, she shifted just enough to gain the edge she needed.

"Up you go!" Talini cried from across the room. Graves flinched and stepped back as two screaming uniformed thieves sailed over her wide head in a tangle of flailing limbs.

Sloane lunged, throwing her shoulder into the

brute's exposed midsection. The two spilled onto a crate just as Sloane dropped and rolled into Graves's ankles. The woman had braced, but in the wrong place. She tried to twist out of the way, too late and off-balance.

The accidental knee Sloane received to her gut drove the breath out of her. The less accidental collision of Graves with the two tangled thieves did its job. She landed on both of Talini's victims, smashing them to the floor and pinning them there.

Sloane rolled to one side and lay on her back for a moment, her shoulder numb. The sound of the fight continued around her.

"Last one's down," Kandros announced in her comm. "Two bogeys dead," he added grimly. Over her head, something sparked.

More work for maintenance.

It could have been worse. Sloane lifted a hand to her face, squinting at her omni-tool display. "Sloane to Addison."

The woman responded instantly. "Did you get them?"

Taking a breath made Sloane want to expel it on a stream of curses. She deferred to a gritted, "Yup," instead.

"Any casualties?" Addison asked, her voice strained.

Sloane thought about it for a second.

"Nope," she said, and cut the connection.

She really could use a drink. At this point, caffeinated *or* alcoholic would do.

|||||||||||||||||||

"This is a disaster," Tann said, pacing the section of the common room reserved for officers. "A total disaster. How could you let this happen?"

"It wasn't Sloane's fault," Foster Addison cut in sharply. She stood by the bulkhead window, watching the salarian pace while Sloane leaned back in one of the padded chairs likely appropriated from a conference room.

The tough security director didn't look too much worse for wear, if you ignored the nasty bruise around her neck and a cold gelpack draped over one shoulder. Addison knew from watching the footage how those bruises had been earned. Not something she ever wanted to experience herself.

Security had resolved the crisis like the well-trained force they were. Addison couldn't find anything wrong with how they had handled it, which meant Tann was overreacting. *Again.*

For her part, Sloane said nothing, as if she needed the time to take in air rather than let fly with whatever she *wanted* to say to the salarian.

He turned his glower on Addison instead. "Two more bodies in cold storage. Eight more locked up in…" He hesitated. "Where did we put them?"

Sloane grunted behind her gelpack. "Up your—"

"A temporary cell," Addison cut in hastily. She shot Sloane a look that was meant to be hard, but probably came across more exasperated. The woman wrinkled her nose in silent acknowledgement. "It will suffice. They're well away from any communication terminals, sans omni-tools, and with plenty of room to rest until we decide what to do with them."

"Space 'em," Sloane muttered. "They're traitors."

Addison ignored that. The security director might

be joking, but there was a very real possibility the hotheaded woman wasn't. She didn't want to press anybody's luck.

"A trial, then," Tann said, returning to his pacing. "A proper one, in full view of everyone so they know—"

"This isn't a circus," Addison said, her eyes widening. She took a step away from the window, hands automatically going to her hips. "Handle it quietly. You're going to start stirring bad blood if you try to make a show of this. The people down there in that cell aren't the only ones to come to Andromeda fleeing checkered pasts."

"Bad blood," Tann repeated, rolling his large eyes. His thin nostrils flared as he gestured vaguely toward the door—and ultimately, the quarters where the would-be thieves waited. "They tried to steal our shuttles. Hold *hostages*! We cannot be seen to go lightly on them, it will only encourage the behavior."

Sloane said nothing. She held the gelpack to her injury.

Addison squared on Tann. "So will crashing down on them. The morale around here is piss poor already. I'm not saying that we pardon them or anything. Just that maybe a kangaroo court isn't how we need to deal with our first security breach."

Tann stared at her for a moment. Then his face cleared. "Ah, a nearly extinct Earth species. I wasn't aware they held courts."

Addison bit back a sigh. "It's an expression, Tann."

"A very odd one."

"Speak for yourself," Sloane muttered.

Tann glared at her. "Director Sloane, if you please—"

The woman threw down the gelpack, revealing

the livid bruise beneath the torn shoulder of her uniform. She sat forward, elbows on her knees, fingers laced ever so pointedly, and drilled them both with a painfully hard stare.

"Look. All I know is that we can't afford to pretend like everyone on this station is happy and shiny anymore. Innocent people could have died. Two of my team are in medical right now. Addison's right about one thing. There's a decent chunk of the Nexus crew that have, shall we say, colorful pasts. Garson believed in second chances."

"She also believed in a large and well-funded security team," Tann noted.

"Yes, a team which resolved the situation. We did our job. Now do yours. Space these criminals before—"

"Isn't it your job to *prevent* this sort of thing?" Tann asked coolly.

"If you'd get out of the way and let me lead—"

"That is not going to happen in my... in any lifetime," Tann shot back. Addison's heart rate spiked into something she didn't *want* to call anger, but she was running out of options.

Okay, fine. So she'd handled it badly—the whole loss of Jien, Tann's appointment to take her place, and destruction of the station. She hadn't even mourned, not yet. She couldn't. Not until the station, Jien's legacy and the hope of thousands, was operational again.

Not until the Pathfinders arrived.

So she clenched her hands and pitched her voice an octave into *shut up*. "The point here," she said loudly, "is that we have to decide what to do with the criminals and then how to proceed. *We are not spacing them,*" she added, glaring at Sloane.

The woman shrugged, saying nothing.

"So let's return them to cryostasis," Addison suggested.

Sloane shook her head in pure disbelief.

"Hmm," Tann breathed. "Defer judgment until a more appropriate time. Wise. That might work. It implies a lack of authority on our part, but perhaps refraining from executing people would be good for morale." This last he pointedly threw at Sloane Kelly.

"They attacked Nexus security," Sloane said, her tone thin. Practically a knife. "You'll only encourage more of that, put more of my people on the line."

"Isn't that your job, Security Director Sloane?"

Her teeth bared. "At least it *is* my job, *Acting* Director Tann."

"*Enough.*" Addison all but leapt between them, arms spread. "This isn't helping anything!"

Tann's eyes narrowed, but at least he withheld any comebacks. Addison had no doubt there'd be more to spare later. With patience and absolute finality he said, "I've made my decision. Make the arrangements to return the prisoners to stasis until such a time as a proper court can be established." He waited for Sloane to argue, but the security director finally, mercifully, backed down. Tann went on. "Document everything, as you would any case, so that it can be addressed fairly and properly when the time comes."

Sloane sneered. "If you think I'd do anything less—"

"I didn't say that," Tann said, "I just want to make sure we're all clear."

"Clear," Addison said. She glanced at Sloane.

"Yeah, okay," Sloane said. "Clear."

Addison took another breath. "The real question is how we prevent this from happening again."

Sloane, head hanging, nevertheless moved on from the conflict with surprising speed. "Re-code access, before someone else we haven't vetted finds their way into a mission-critical space."

"I agree," Addison said. "As for the hangar, set Kesh's team to repair and reinforce it."

Tann's long, spindly fingers began to tap together as he mentally worked out the calculations. "We can spare workers, but it's going to require time and equipment. Two things that remain in short supply."

"Equipment we can find," Addison pointed out. "Kesh will know where."

Sloane sat back in the chair, draping an arm over the back. "I'll have my people start stepping up patrols. We've been too complacent," she added, a thin thread away from accusation as she glanced at Tann. "We need to stop assuming everyone here is still a hundred percent on board with putting the mission before themselves. The assholes who tried to take our ships, for example." Her displeasure was obvious. Hard to tell, though, if it was directed at herself or the situation. "Their approach wasn't detected, not quick enough. It should have been."

The salarian frowned, but he didn't disagree.

"If there are any more..." Sloane paused, choosing the word carefully. "...*unsatisfied* people on this station, they'll need to be dealt with. The trick is spotting them."

"With tact, I hope," Tann said pointedly. "Should you lack the means—"

"Sounds great," Addison said, again too loud. When they both looked at her, she made sure there was steel in her smile. "We know what to do. Let's get on it."

Maybe that did it. Maybe, she figured, it was enough to remind them what was at stake.

"Meeting adjourned." Tann turned toward the door. "Let us not lose sight of the ultimate goal here."

"Yes," Sloane repeated, watching him walk out. "Let's not."

Addison barely managed to bite off a curse.

Or maybe she was just surrounded by people so thick-headed, they gave the krogan a run for the gold star.

CHAPTER THIRTEEN

Things were going as well as could possibly be expected. Life support hadn't failed yet, and people were learning to count on Calix's team to keep it that way.

The krogan had managed to clear out enough working space that bodies weren't bumping into each other every time they took a breath. Careful maintenance and hair-trigger calibrations ensured that the most basic of failsafes didn't go haywire when the power shorted out anywhere aboard the station.

As they battled the chaos of a heavily damaged systems array, Calix Corvannis surveyed his team with a steady, critical eye. They were exhausted, worn down to the bone, and the muttering between them had intensified. He'd seen this exact scenario play out before, with this very team.

Same situation. Different ship. A frigate called the *Warsaw*, where a string of bad decisions by a stubborn captain had led to the near total loss of the ship.

Calix had been ordered to work his team to the brink of exhaustion and beyond. Get the job done, whatever it took.

Eventually, they'd figured out that the goal was not to fix the ship, it was to put his team in a position to plausibly blame for its condition.

Calix had refused.

His action had bordered on mutiny, but he'd won.

In the face of losing his entire life-support team, the captain had backed down.

Calix had also won the undying loyalty of his team in the process. The whole affair had earned him "administrative reassignment" off the *Warsaw* the moment the ship made port, but that was fine. Calix had left without a second thought.

He just hadn't expected his team to follow. Off the *Warsaw*, and into the Andromeda Initiative. They could have stayed and let him take the fall. Could have done so much more with their independence. But they chose to follow him.

These were hardworking, knuckle-scraping, straightforward people who believed in one cause above all else: loyalty. They said they'd follow him anywhere. Truth was, who else would take them? They'd walked away from their posts in protest of his dismissal, a mark on their records few employers would overlook.

Except Kesh.

Of course, the fact that things were going as well as could be expected didn't mean the situation was *good*. It just meant they were all hanging on—barely. His team, the Nexus, the future.

"Ammonia reserves at thirty percent."

Calix glanced at the speaker, a human named Nnebron. Lawrence Nnebron. Alliance stock, Earth-born, trained and capable... but very young. Calix's fingers dug into the systems frame. Thirty percent. Not enough. Not nearly enough for his peace of mind.

"Can we shift to electrics?" he asked.

"We're already skirting dangerously close to shutting down portions of the grid. This kind of additional draw, we're liable to trigger a blackout."

"Well," Calix mused, "we wouldn't want to be the ones responsible for that."

Irida Fadeer looked up from her calculations. "No, we wouldn't," the purple-skinned asari muttered. "Lest Their Royal Highnesses come barging in."

Calix didn't look at her. He was afraid of seeing the irritation on her face, the simmering anger behind all the exhaustion, and echoing it. He was tired, too. Of the hours. Of the orders coming down the chain of laughable command, each circumventing the last.

Not that he could blame anyone for feeling angry. Waking up abruptly had been a shock, to say the least. He could only imagine how it had been for the first survivors, to have been expelled from their stasis pods without care or warning. It had to have left them shaken.

That's why it was Calix's job to ensure the next group to wake up got everything they deserved. Everything denied him—and his exhausted team.

A tic jumped in the center of his brow. Right at the crest. It wasn't supposed to move like that. Calix rubbed at it grimly, but no amount of that would make the stress go away.

"How steady are we?" he asked. Irida passed him a screen. It only took a glance. "Right. It'll hold for now. Take some R&R," he added, setting the tablet on the dash—out of the asari's hands.

She noticed. "But—"

"I'll handle any backlash," Calix said firmly. "You're all working as hard as you can, and you've performed miracles out here on your own. Take a well-deserved break."

Irida exchanged glances with Nnebron, who shrugged. "If you say so," the human said.

The rest of the team were too tired to do more than drag themselves away from their stations. "Cookout in the commons!" one said, a decree met with cheers of support.

Irida eyed them warily. "Cookout, huh?"

Calix grinned at the asari's wrinkled nose. "Hey, don't knock it. Nothing beats a good cookout in hard times."

"Mm." Not really a word, but her skepticism came through loud and clear. "Don't cookouts usually require meat and vegetables?"

"Yeah, well..."

"And aren't they held, you know, outside?"

"Well," Calix repeated with a laughing shrug, "you get rations, and if you're lucky, some club music. Just go with it. It's called improvising."

Her nose was still wrinkled as she walked away, following the others.

Calix's amusement faded. A wave of exhaustion rolled over him, and he took a moment to lean against the dash and rub the back of his neck. Even his fringe ached.

What in the galaxy did they expect Calix and his team to do here? They couldn't wake more people. The krogan were great at labor and terrible at the finesse work—Kesh excluded, Calix could admit. And if they slipped up even a little, thousands of people would suffer.

Pressure?

Try an entire station's worth of pressure. A *generation's* worth of pressure.

The headache between his eyes had become a constant companion the past few days. Every time he found himself thinking like this, Calix told himself it was better than the turians' meritocracy. That the Nexus had real thinkers, planners, and doers up there in Operations. Not just some lucky bastards who'd survived a calculated decision.

Except...

Except that's exactly what they were. Weren't they?

The comm signaled a connection. "You coming, boss?"

Nnebron again.

"Be there in five," Calix replied, and he signed off before the youth could hear his sigh.

The turian meritocracy might not be Calix's idea of qualified leadership, but neither was some half-assed algorithm based on a reporting structure. All that accomplished was allowing stooges to fill in for the real talent.

He frowned as he made his way out of the system's arrays. They'd been hardwired together in places, interrupted by glossy segments of neatness where his team had started putting them back together. The paneling gleamed.

Foster Addison was fine enough as the director of Colonial Affairs. She had a steady head. Mostly. But seemed more like an organizer than a solid leader. The kind of brain that set things into plans and gave them to more forceful or subtle personalities to execute. Colonial Affairs was a good fit for her. Running a station without Garson's guidance? Not so much.

On the other hand, Jarun Tann was neither forceful nor subtle. The salarian's snide habit of looking down his nose at Calix and his team still got under his skin. And of course, he was the one with the "acting director" title. In theory he could make decisions entirely on his own, though Calix wondered what would happen if the salarian tried. Nothing good, he suspected.

Calix grumbled to himself as he paced down the corridor, unzipping his uniform at the neck to let him at least *feel* like he had more breathing room. Few people traversed these particular halls. A couple krogan lumbered past, grunting acknowledgement of his presence. He nodded, but didn't say anything.

Too tired. Too past the point of exchanging niceties.

It was a trait he currently shared with Sloane, at least. He hadn't expected to enjoy the human's company, but her lack of ulterior motives and forthright personality appealed to the turian as the better of the three options. At least he could trust the security director to take care of problems the old-fashioned way. Hell, she'd probably have made a good turian, the way she liked to cut through the bullshit.

Sure turians politicked. Calix was all too familiar with that truth. But not the way salarians schemed and asari hovered.

Of course, humans could be just as bad. The First Contact War had proved it. But the way Calix saw it right now, Sloane was a leg up.

One out of three ain't bad.

Voices peppered the quiet corridor as Calix approached his destination. The lights were kept dim to save on resources, but that didn't stop the music. It threaded through the sound of merriment and shouting, with a techno beat somebody had decided was a good idea.

"All right, Corvannis," he muttered, his own voice cut with grim humor. "Face up." His crew would only be dragged down even more if they saw how defeated he was feeling. He'd buck up. *They'd* buck up.

They all had to.

He rubbed at a mandible as he worked on arranging his features into something much less brooding. It wasn't exactly a smile, not even by turian standards, but it'd do. He couldn't erase exhaustion.

Ready as he was for whatever version of a cookout the crew had managed, Calix didn't expect the voices he heard to translate into angry shouting. He rounded the corner and entered the commons with a greeting ready, only to draw up short.

Four of his team had gathered in a loose semi-circle around what appeared, to his ignorant eye, to be a still of some kind. They weren't looking at whatever chemicals dripped inside, though. They were staring at the other side of the room, where a row of brighter fixtures highlighted the faceoff between his young engineer Nnebron and Addison's twitchy assistant.

The shouting came from the peanut gallery, and the tension was like walking into a dust cloud. His facade of good humor snapped.

"What's going on here?"

The small crowd went abruptly silent. William Spender angled his body away from Nnebron, just enough to make it clear he considered the engineer of no consequence.

"Ah. Are you in charge of this motley crew?" the politician said. Calix's fingers twitched to zip up his uniform, but he refrained. They'd met before. Clearly, the man thought little of ground and tech crew.

"Calix Corvannis," he said calmly, striding past his crew, ignoring the still and planting himself between Spender and the rest. A nice, easygoing barrier. "Engineering."

Spender frowned. He shifted his tablet from one

hand to the other, waved it at him officiously. "I can see that from your uniform," he said. "Anyway it's not what I asked. Are you in charge here?"

"Yes." Clipped. Calix looked to Nnebron, bypassing Spender entirely. "What's going on?"

Nnebron straightened his shoulders. "We were setting up the cookout, sir, when this—" Behind him, Irida cleared her throat. Nnebron coughed whatever he'd intended to say and amended it. "When this guy comes sticking his face in where it don't belong."

Before Calix could ask anything else, Spender rounded on his engineer. "I am an advisor to the acting director, and Deputy Director of Colonial Affairs, and you will mind your manners when you speak to your superiors."

Calix saw Nnebron's mouth open, the flicker in his dark eyes. He headed off the man's response.

"Nnebron, go stand with the others."

One look. Just one, but to his credit, the engineer didn't argue. Instead he shook his head and retreated to join the rest of the crew.

Okay, Calix thought. *Good. One potential fuse out of the blasting cap.* He turned back to Spender. The look on his face pissed Calix off—smug victory, like he'd just won a hand of cards. "All right," Calix said calmly, "I'm going to ask a third time…"

He didn't have to. Irida spoke up when nobody else would. "It's like Nnebron said, sir. We were preparing the food when he—" she gestured, "—came in asking about permissions and requisitions."

"And then?"

Irida looked at her feet, confirming what he already suspected. They'd gotten rowdy. Her mouth twisted.

"He pulled the plug on the..." She paused. Frowned. "What do you call it again?"

"Barbecue," Nnebron supplied. A sullen mutter. He was still glaring daggers at the bureaucrat.

"Illegal use of Nexus materials," Spender interjected flatly. "Under no circumstances should rations and materials be used for this... *whatever* nonsense you call it."

Calix's eyes were still on Irida, and he didn't have to look. He just assumed the guy was waving his hand around. He seemed like the type.

Nnebron sneered. "We weren't doing anything wrong!"

Exhaustion warred with impatience. Calix turned to face the aide. "Spender, right?" A brisk nod. "Listen. This team has been working around the clock for days. They deserve some time to relax."

The man took a few steps forward, holding his tablet as if it provided some kind of backing. "It's not their time off I'm concerned with," he replied. "But dried supplies? Reconstituted rations? And *that*!" He pointed at the still. "That's not even covered under regulations!"

He tapped the screen, but didn't bring it close enough for Calix to read.

"This is a partial list of supplies," he continued, "as per current efforts to inventory. Since we don't know how long we'll be carrying out repairs, it's imperative that we keep a thumb on the amount and accessibility of rations."

The murmurs behind him mirrored Calix's sentiments neatly. "There's been no prohibition that we've been made aware of," he said. "Show me the authority to restrict?"

There wasn't one. He was sure of it.

Spender held Calix's stare, though. "I *am* the authority. Director Tann tapped me for the task. I decide what you can use—" he nodded toward the cooking gear, "—and what you can't."

Tough words, but Calix sensed little backbone behind them. His people knew a bootlicker when they saw one, though; it was something of a game for them.

One he needed to keep under wraps. Gossip was all well and good, but not in opposition.

A new tactic presented itself. "Look," Calix said, summoning all the conciliatory smoothness he could muster. He spread the three digits on each hand. "My team has been working hard keeping everyone alive. They deserve a cookout. Without some downtime, a little boost to their mood, mistakes might start to happen, and nobody wants that, believe me."

The assistant director's fingers tapped a tight rhythm on the readout. "I demand to speak to your supervisor. Head of your department."

Calix stared at him. "Are you serious?"

"*Very.*"

He sighed. "Irida."

The asari's voice came quick and remarkably poised. "Yes, Calix?"

Without looking away from Spender's narrow-eyed stare, Calix said, "Tell the boss a William Spender, Assistant Director of Colonial Affairs, wants to see him."

The first tic of discomfort began to distort the sides of the human's so-stern mouth.

"You got it," Irida said, her voice pleasant. "Hey, Nnebron!"

"What's up, Violet?"

"Tell the boss someone named Spender, Assistant Director to something or other, wants to see him."

Spender's fingers picked up rhythm.

"Sure thing." A pause, and then, desperately trying to hold in his amusement, Calix heard Nnebron half-turn. "Hey, Nacho!"

The salarian heaved a sigh. "It's Na'to."

"Whatever. Tell the boss some dude is—"

Spender made a disapproving grunt at that.

Never one to miss a cue, Na'to muttered, "I am not a secretary." But nevertheless, raised his voice and called out, "Corvannis, sir, there's a human to see you."

Calix put on a theatrical note of inquiry. "Oh, yeah?" He drawled every word. "What for?"

Na'to's shrug echoed in his tone. "Nnebron didn't say."

"Got it," Calix replied as Spender's skin began to turn red at the fringes. Or hairline. Whatever. Calix didn't so much as move a muscle. Not one twitch. He just paused long enough to make his point, then said cheerfully, "I'm Calix Corvannis, head of life support. What can I do for you?"

His team smothered laughter behind hands, coughs, clearing of throats.

Calix expected an explosion. Expected swearing, a fight, whatever this guy did when he blew his top.

What he did not expect was to be humored.

The glare, the tight lips, it all changed. The transformation was so abrupt Calix couldn't help but admire the savvy of it. He could almost see the political calculations going on behind those beady eyes, the effort of will that faded the apoplectic spots of anger. Spender's face practically lit up. "You know what? You're right. I'm being a hardass and that's unfair to you and your team. I'm terribly sorry for the misunderstanding, Officer Corvannis."

"Uh…" Some of the fight went out of Calix's spine. Even his team had stopped laughing.

Including Nnebron. And that said something, right there. The kid was attitude in a uniform.

Spender spread his hand wide. "I should be *thanking* you. Here you are, the folks keeping us all alive, and here's me, the guy who can get you what you need without all this needless posturing. Seems like we should be friends."

Calix didn't relax. But he did chuckle, a dry, knowing sound. "Got off on the wrong foot, that it?"

"Exactly," Spender said. "Exactly. The fatigue, the constant fear of the Scourge, it's making us all a bit screwy, isn't it? So forget what I said. Enjoy your party."

The gathering stirred behind him. He felt a nudge at his back plates. An elbow, probably.

Nnebron's, definitely.

Taking the cue, he folded his arms over his chest and said amicably, "We'd enjoy it more with something good to drink."

Just how much was the human willing to be the go-to guy?

Apparently, a drink wasn't over the line. Spender raised his hand and snapped his fingers, then pointed at Calix. "I've got just the thing. A case of something special I set aside. I'll have it brought down."

"Very kind of you." *And smart of you, setting things like that aside*. Calix filed a little note on that particular revelation. Spender, it seemed, wasn't quite as straight-laced as he pretended to be.

"See?" Spender said, clapping him on the shoulder. "No reason we can't help one another out from time to time."

His shoulder did not move as much as Spender's

hand rebounded. "No reason at all," Calix replied through what passed for a turian smile. Even he knew he'd done nothing to soften it.

Subtly shaking out his hand, the human backed away with a cheerful swagger. "Just remember me when things get tight," he called as he turned away. With that, Spender turned and left.

Irida stepped up beside him as Spender vanished around the corner. "Well, that was pleasant."

"That was... awkward," he corrected.

"Maybe. But telling."

No kidding. The abrupt turn around once he'd understood Calix's role as head of life support hadn't exactly been subtle. He looked down at the asari, shrugging his ignorance. "Well, whatever that was, thanks for not tossing him head-first out the door."

The asari grinned up at him. "Thanks for standing up for us. Again."

Two of the crew bent behind the array of wires and burners to restart the open flame. Three more poked at the still which, now that Calix thought about it, probably used other supplies to make its contents. Perhaps Spender's concerns weren't just power-mad gesticulations. The thought left Calix with a new worry.

Suppose Spender, all things considered, had a point? The man's obvious stock-exchange aside, the concern about rations would eventually crop up. What if it had already started?

He grimaced at the idea, but let it go. *For now.*

Nnebron rolled his shoulders as he glowered at the door. "Pencil-necked politician," he muttered. "Coming in here like he owns the place. Like he owns us."

"Relax," Irida said. She patted him on the shoulder. "Politicians are paid to be that way. All of 'em."

"Still not right."

"Maybe not," Calix said thoughtfully. He surveyed his team. His people. Hard workers, every one. Locked away with life-support systems day in and day out, conscious every moment of the hundred thousand lives that counted on them.

First, they lost Garson.

Then they lost the ability to work as a true team, divided instead into round-the-clock shifts. Now some middle-management politician wanted to ration supplies? *Save* them? For what?

Maybe the leadership knew something the rest of the crew hadn't been told yet. About the arks, or maybe this mysterious Scourge.

Across the room, one of his team shouted, "Yes!" as the gas flame flickered to life. The mood in the room lightened palpably.

Irida nudged him. "Something on your mind, boss?"

Calix rolled his shoulders, but it didn't ease his tension. "I'm just thinking," he said slowly, "what purpose it serves for Spender to start fretting over supplies before any sort of orders come down from Operations."

Nnebron folded his arms, his black eyebrows knitted. "You think something's up?"

He hesitated. Then, with a shrug, he admitted, "I'm not sure. But maybe it'd be a good idea if we keep tabs on maintaining our own supplies." *And keep Spender on our good side*, he added silently.

The asari tipped her head, just as thoughtful and cautious as he.

"You got it, sir." Nnebron dropped his arms. "Now let's get some grub before it runs out."

"Grubs?" Irida asked, appalled. "You've got to be kidding."

"Figure of speech," Calix told the horrified asari.

"Right." She grimaced again, nodded, then followed the kid through the crowd, all asari grace to his lanky gait. Calix watched them both and wondered if he should have said anything at all. He didn't want to stir up trouble. He just wanted to make sure his crew was taken care of.

He knew from experience how easy it was for untested leadership to forget about the crew in the unseen spaces—engineering, sanitation, all the things that just seemed to operate. Invisible to anyone who didn't make it past deck three.

The fact that Spender came all this way…

Calix didn't like it. Something *was* brewing up there in Operations. Something they knew, maybe, that the rest of the Nexus didn't.

Would Kesh know? Probably not. Tann wouldn't allow that.

Sloane, then? He'd have to ask. Find some excuse to talk to her without Spender or any of the others around. Until then, his first priority was the well-being of everyone in this room.

"Hero of the hour gets first dibs!"

With a firm shake of his head, Calix put his *everything's all right* face on again and joined Nnebron at the modified grill. "Okay, okay. What is this stuff, anyway?"

"No idea," one of his team said with glee. Andria lifted a plate filled with still-smoking things that looked like twists of some kind of meat-like substance, piled high with dark red sauce.

It smelled acrid and sharp, vinegary and…

amazing, Calix decided. But he knew immediately his gut would reject it. "Smells wonderful," he said tactfully. "But if it ain't dextro—"

They all paused.

Looked at each other.

Then rolled into a riot of laughter. "Gotcha," Nnebron shouted. Na'to, grinning, pulled out a plate of something that smelled *almost* as good, but didn't cause his gut to cramp in anticipation.

This was shoved into Calix's hands, leaving him laughing with his team. "Who won the bet?"

"Whether you'd be dumb enough to play nice and eat it?" Irida asked, snickering as she handed him another bottle. One labeled for turians, some kind of sauce.

"I bet you would," Nnebron added.

A red-haired human with her hair pulled high up her head raised a hand. "I bet you'd be too smart!"

Calix raised the bottle of sauce to her. "Thank you, Andria. At least someone has faith in me."

The team melted into relief, into relaxation and— what he most wanted for them—recreation. Most didn't even hear the clang from the door, but Calix turned in time to see Spender walking away, waving over his shoulder. He'd left a box just inside the room.

"Hey, go grab that, would you?" he said, tipping his head at Nnebron.

The young man crossed to the package and opened it. "Oh, shit! Barbecue sauce from Earth!" Well, now. "The suit wasn't kidding."

"I wonder where he got it," Calix mused, impressed despite himself.

"Don't ask," Nnebron warned him, already dragging the box to the gathering. "Don't jinx it. Don't even think about how many years it's been lying around. Just shut up and eat!"

Calix chuckled. "Have at it, team." He raised the plate in his other hand. "Don't let it go to waste."

While they still could.

CHAPTER FOURTEEN

The krogan didn't get rest. They kept working. They worked, and they worked, and even when some of the softer crew got days to rest, the Nakmor were still working. Why?

Because that is what Clan Nakmor *did*.

But did they get thanks for it?

No. Because that's what everyone else *didn't* do.

Same shit. Different galaxy.

Arvex picked up a curved panel of welded steel with one hand, tossed it up into the air to seize it at a better angle, and casually flung it at the farthest wall. It did not fly as fast or as hard as he'd hoped, but this was the problem with the area—*not* with Arvex's strength.

Gravity on this side of the station was set at minimal. Saved on power, apparently. Nevertheless, despite the almost graceful arc of the plate's trajectory, it hit the far wall with a strident *clang*.

His two krogan companions, huddled over a tangled nest of bent and mangled piping, jerked upright with mingled growls and grunts of surprise. The plate rebounded off the wall and caught the closest, Kaje, across the temple, earning a pained shout.

"What's the idea?" Wratch bellowed, stepping in front of the howling grunt.

Arvex growled right back, dropping one foot heavily to the deck plating as if digging in to charge. Arteries leading from every organ pounded and pulsed under his tough krogan hide. "I am sick of the wait," he roared, hands splayed in fist-crushing fury. "Nakmor did not sign onto this floating *wreck* to be *janitors*."

An old argument. A common one. Impatience and frustration and sheer centuries of fighting instinct. Another day in the structure mines. Another hour spent waiting for the technicians supposedly coming to fix the failing conduits outside.

Another brawl between clan brothers.

Kaje shouldered past Wratch to stomp, slowly and with effort in the low-grav environment, toward the sealed door. "Can we get back to welding or not?" he demanded.

He already knew the answer.

Arvex glared at him anyway. "Not until the life-support grunts get here. Now stop your whining and get back to peeling off those scored plates."

They were in one of the warehouses, sorting through the twisted mess of ground vehicles tossed like pyjaks in a box. Those that survived, anyway. Not three meters away, the warehouse—and the vehicles still on this side of it—abruptly vanished on a ragged edge of shorn-off metal, hanging wires, drifting junk.

Beyond the emergency bulkhead, only the endless black and blue and whatever other fancy colors other species liked to look at glittered.

Arvex didn't care. Space was space. He was Nakmor born, Tuchanka forged, and mercenary hardened. Whether in this galaxy or the Milky Way, he didn't give a varren's wet turd what it looked like.

What he cared about—what he wanted—was the same thing all of Nakmor wanted.

New territory, carved by strength and glory, and made worth protecting by the first of the krogan females to give birth to a new generation.

For all their posturing, Kaje and Wratch felt the same.

Arvex would stake his life on it.

No more losses. No more dead. The genophage had claimed enough krogan spirit. With the genetic prodding the clan leader had subjected them all to, there was a chance—a possibility—that any one of the krogan here could be fertile.

Could bypass the damned salarian-designed plague meant to cow them.

Arvex crouched at the verge of the sheared edge, glowering into the vast emptiness of space. Not even the ripped-off wreckage of the Nexus remained in view anymore. Whatever had torn it off, nothing had gotten in its way to halt its drift.

Except maybe the weird tangle of energy out there.

"Scourge, huh?" The words rumbled from his chest. As close to musing as Arvex ever bothered with.

Wratch heard. He dropped a large structural beam into a pile with others, each twisted as if superheated to some ungodly degree and bent beneath its own weight. It bounced a bit. Clanged every time. Before it even settled, he pitched his voice to carry. "Heard someone say it broke the sensors."

"That's what you get for listening to garbage," Kaje shot back, pushing away from the door. "Sensors can't see it. It's *different*."

"Yeah," Wratch grunted. "Like your ugly face."

"Suck on a hanar, Wratch."

"None around."

The krogan snapped his teeth in reply.

Arvex's lip curled with his grunt, but he didn't bother shouting them down. Whatever this ship-twisting, station-wrecking star-pocked web of destruction was, it wasn't something the krogan could shoot at, wrestle, or burn.

His eyes narrowed as spots of color gleamed from inside the tendrils.

The sounds of work continued behind him. Arvex held his position, trying to figure out if the damn stuff moved or if staring out into the dimensional cavern of space just made his eyes think it moved. It didn't help that enough junk floated around, debris and bits of once-functional station, to make the whole scene a bloody eye-boggler.

When the comm in his helmet pinged, he grunted into it. "Arvex."

A smooth voice filled the line. "Calix Corvannis here. I understand you need a few of my crew?"

Irritation had Arvex surging to his feet. But he didn't yell. Kesh had at least pounded that much into him. Into most of them, at this point.

Hardest bloody head this side of Nakmor Morda. Or maybe Drack.

Damned female earned her blood by way of one hell of a grandfather.

So, instead of risking another *meeting* with Kesh, Arvex growled, "You're late."

"I'm sorry about that," the male voice said. Flanged. *Turian.* Ugh. "Three of mine are available now. Have you prepared the site?"

Arvex looked down at the ragged ribbon of torn-off hull.

He didn't care if his laughter sounded like a challenge. "Oh, yeah," he said, folding his arms over his wide chest. "It's ready."

The turian hesitated. Then, with a directness

Arvex recognized, said, "My engineers are in your hands, Nakmor Arvex."

Yeah, yeah. He almost shut off the comm link without a reply, then thought better of it. A little respect from a turian seemed a decent way to keep Kesh off his back. "We'll make sure they keep their delicate feet on the deck plates."

Whatever Calix Corvannis might have said, Arvex didn't care to hear it. Promise made, link cut.

"Wratch!"

A huffed sound of acknowledgement.

"Kaje!"

"What?"

Arvex's wide, thick lips peeled back into a toothy grin. "Lay out the welcome mat, boys. We got squishies incoming."

<hr>

"Are you sure about this?" Na'to's nervousness translated easily over the comm link, and visibly in the set of his narrow salarian shoulders.

Reg laughed heartily, tinny through the faceplate of his helmet but nevertheless loud. "Relax, Nacho. What's a few krogan?"

"Intimidating," he muttered back. They approached the sealed dock doors in a wedge formation, and somehow, Na'to had ended up in front. *Not sure how that happened.* Reg, with his overdeveloped human physique and thick skull, should have been first to face the krogan on the other side.

To his right and behind him, he heard Andria muffle a laugh.

A nervous laugh, he noted. He wasn't the only one worried.

But they all seemed intent on behaving as if this were well within regular patterns. Whether it was for him, or for their own nerves, he didn't know. But he could play along. "And," he added in clipped tones, "it's Na'to."

"Whatever you say."

Na'to adjusted the tools strapped to his waist, firming his resolve. Nothing had quite unfolded as expected, but in many ways, this hadn't come as a surprise to the salarian. Things rarely did; or at least, people who planned would do best to plan for multiple contingencies.

Failing to do so, he reflected grimly as a heavy, wide silhouette passed in front of the viewport, was how they got *krogan*.

He paused outside the doors, keyed in comm frequencies and waited for them to acknowledge. They did. Well, one did. Mostly by a growled, "Yeah, yeah, hold your soft—" Whatever it was they were supposed to hold went unsaid, as the comm abruptly winked out again.

Na'to turned back to look at his other teammates, hoping the *I told you so* look on his face could be seen through the faceplate of his helmet.

All he got back were reflections. And a shrug.

"Well, this is off to an excellent start," he said dourly.

"Men," Andria muttered.

With a strained groan and lengthy creak, the doors opened. A quick survey inside showed much of what he had expected: stark, bare, broken, and—

"Good god." Andria's voice. Horrified.

"Yeah." The krogan manually operating the door sounded entirely too gleeful for the moment. He peered not at them, but at the sight spread before them. Space. So much space, millions and billions of stars and gases and black in between. "Ain't it something?"

It was something all right. It was a deathtrap. The debris alone would present something of a problem, if no shield was in place—which he knew was not.

"Mostly," Na'to said briskly as he strode into the room with exaggerated care, "it's something to deal with on task. I'm—"

"Unless the next words out of your mouth are 'here to do my job'," came the deep, guttural voice of another krogan, "we don't care." The big meathead gestured to the edge of the crevice, where space met the corner of the emergency bulkhead. "Arvex is waiting."

"Well, then." Na'to turned back to Reg and Andria, shrugging at them with exaggerated emphasis. "Guess we'd better get to it."

Andria, much smaller than Reg or the krogan, didn't stomp so much as stride with pointed effort toward that brink. The minimal gravity didn't allow for much by way of heavy tread. Her shoulder clipped one of the krogan's thick wrists, which didn't really move.

The krogan, his features much more visible in krogan-specific protective glass, leered at her as she passed. "Ooh, this one has *attitude*."

Reg and Na'to followed the piqued engineer, ignoring the toothy smile behind them. "A hull-walk," Reg grumbled. "Awesome."

"I don't know why you're complaining," Andria replied back, slinging her large pack to the metal flooring. "Na'to's taking the walk."

A fact he was well aware of. Na'to eyed the fascinating ribbons of unknown energy as his companions finalized last checks for the gear that would see him over this remarkable ledge and into all those stars and black. The energy hovered in bothersome layers of black and gray, shifts of yellow and orange. Not so close that he had to worry about brushing through the stuff. Not so far that it wasn't on his mind.

"You good, Nacho?"

"Mm," Na'to said, looking out again into the black. A word that wasn't one, he realized when he glanced back at his team. "It doesn't seem close enough, and barring any unforeseen alterations in trajectory or force, it should remain so."

The krogan looked at each other, then shrugged in unison. "It's weird," one said.

"Yeah," the other added. "Like a thresher maw pet."

"What?"

"I think," Na'to translated slowly, "they mean it's unpredictable."

"All right, then. Let's get this conduit scoped in record time."

Without further ado, Na'to coiled enough slack to keep Reg on his toes and made his way to the emergency hatch that had, miraculously, survived the devastation. "Well," he said, testing the comms with false cheer while the air hissed out around him and the small hatch pressurized, "it could be worse."

"Oh, yeah?" Andria's voice sounded younger in comms than it did in person. A fact he had pointed out once to unfortunate consequences. "How so?"

Once settled, the exterior hatch opened to reveal little but space. And the occasional projectile, albeit none so large as to block the breath-taking view. Na'to's smile tipped up behind his mask. "I could be stuck down there smelling krogan."

One of the krogan grunted something Na'to

thought might be a laugh. "Don't worry," he graveled through deep chuckles. "It could be worse in here, too."

"Yeah?" asked Reg, thoughtful but focused. Na'to knew the slack of his secure cord was in good hands. "How do you figure?"

A large, bulky shape blocked out the stars in Na'to's peripheral. "Because," came a voice deeper, meaner than the others. He turned slowly, grav boots locking with each step, to stare into the faceplate of a krogan whose hump towered well over Na'to's head. Despite the sizable mass, all he could catalog for sure was a row of ragged, sharp teeth. "They could be stuck with *me*."

"Ah." Na'to went still, swaying faintly as his coordination struggled to get used to zero gravity and the singularly difficult boots meant to counter it. Na'to nodded his head. "You must be Arvex."

"And you're the tech-head sent in to secure this piece of crap so I can get back to work." Arvex bent to peer at him. "Funny. I didn't think they'd send in a salarian."

Na'to sighed, sending up a small prayer to the Dalatrass that had birthed him. "Funny," he responded in kind. "I didn't expect a krogan to think."

The comms were dead silent. The only sound coming back to him was his own breath, and the illusionary hum of tension as it filled the vacuum between them.

Arvex rapped out a burst of laughter. "Come on."

He turned and led the slow, methodical way across the hull. Each step thunked in force felt more than heard, while the delicate sea of mysterious tendrils seemed to drift without form or reason. So close, he felt like all he had to do was stretch a hand to touch it.

A fallacy, of course. Distance between what his eyes could perceive and the depth of dimension provided by the Scourge, the space it occupied, the pattern of light refracted off of the quietly floating Nexus, and his own fascination provided inaccurate perceptions.

The hatch, though. Now that was something a salarian could dig his hands into. To start, anyway. Arvex stopped first, folded his arms and glared at the brightly lit interior. "Here's the thing. Do what you came to do and then let's get the hell off this hull."

Under the light, wires and connectors gleamed in pristine condition.

Well, nearly so.

"Ah," he muttered to himself, climbing the last steps up the station's hull with eyes fixed on the hardware. "Definite auxiliary," he reported, tenderly lifting a bundle of wires to the side. "Can't see the source of the problem, not yet. But this... and this..."

"What's *this*?" A question Reg asked, but not to him. To Andria.

She had visuals through his feed. "It feeds life support, all right. An auxiliary power source, and one that I would guess wasn't meant to provide as much power as it currently is."

A grunt from the krogan beside him. Na'to didn't pay much attention.

"Andria?" Reg asked.

"Yeah. I'm worried, too," Andria replied quietly. "Listen, Na'to, that Scourge is giving me the creeps out there. It's closer on this side than on the populated side."

Na'to made a thoughtful sound, but most of his mind was already entangled with power draw and mathematic values.

"He ain't hearing you," Arvex cut in. "Typical salarian."

"Typical Nacho, anyway," Reg replied with

a sigh. "Let's keep an eye on the stuff and see if it shifts. Mumbo! Jumbo! Go stand watch on either side of the bulkhead."

"Who do you think—"

A foot clanged against the edge of the hatch. "Do it," Arvex growled. Then he felt the weight of the krogan's stare, heard him shift to crouch down on his haunches. "You hear that, appetizer? Get this old shit running like new before it all goes sideways."

Old? No, no. New. Cutting edge. Failing, perhaps— fuses were beginning to show char. Overheating, maybe. Stress, decidedly. The salarian ignored the krogan, bent and thrust his face almost fully into the hatch. He wished he could take the helmet off, really use all his senses on the receptors and the connectors and just… just know what the tech was doing.

Why it struggled.

But that would be too easy. The sound of chatter faded into the background as Na'to focused on what was, ultimately, his one and only love.

"I don't get it," muttered Arvex.

"We don't either," replied Andria, "but we let him do his thing."

A pause.

Then, as the krogan's metal-shod feet clunked against the hull, he shifted stance to keep a stern watch over Na'to's head and said flatly, "His thing is weird."

The salarian smiled faintly to himself. They didn't have to understand. They just had to let him work his incredible intellect.

Emory got off the comm with a sigh of irritation, mingled with resignation. He'd known what it meant to marry an engineer, but it still wreaked havoc on every effort to create something like a normal schedule.

Not that there was anything normal about this.

The Nexus was a wreck, hydroponics wasn't responding, and he was *positive* that the next step would be some serious rations. Nothing else made sense.

Dr. Emory Wilde was, of course, a scientist. A botanist, to be precise, with awards in astrobiology, xenobotany, and, as it turned out, husband-wrangling.

Only two of those things would help the Nexus.

The third helped Reggie, but only when the stubborn mule allowed it.

Emory realized he'd been hunched over the microscope so long that his back was starting to curve naturally into it. Worthless, given he was currently sitting in one of the organized mess halls and not the lab he shared with the other hydroponics team.

There was nothing to stare at under a microscope here, unless one counted the porridge they'd taken to pulling together.

Given the look of the bland sludge, Emory didn't care to do so.

The chair across from him squeaked, announcing a table guest with no preamble. Emory lifted tired eyes, summoning a smile when he recognized William Spender, aide to the directors. "Good morning. Or…"

"Good evening," Spender replied good-naturedly. He was a thin man, with the look of one who never really settled into place. Like a cat, or even some kind of rodent, always checking the corners.

It was, Emory reflected gravely, not a singular affectation. He'd noticed that look on a few more of the Nexus's personnel lately. Uncertainty. Anxiety.

Borderline haunted.

He'd seen it on Reggie's face more times than not. At least when the team's supervisor allowed him to get some rest.

Emory's smile faded to something more empathetic. Xenobotanist he may be, but he was still human. He still understood the toll. "You look spent."

The man allowed his forearms to rest on the table, hands tucked wearily within. "I feel spent," he admitted. "It seems there is always some emergency or another."

Emory could only guess at the veracity of his statement. "In hydroponics," he replied with what he hoped was suitable sympathy, "we are kept busy on the singular task of growing food. I can understand that you must have so much more to manage."

Spender's eyes crinkled, but it wasn't so much a smile as it was weary resignation. "Put out one fire, and another starts."

"Metaphorically and otherwise."

"You aren't kidding, friend."

Emory nodded at that, then, with a rueful smile, pushed his porridge toward the man. "Here, if you'd like."

Spender looked at it as if he'd rather eat anything but the soppy beige stuff, but when he looked up, the look had faded to one of remorse. "No, I couldn't. You must know how the food situation is looking."

Ah. He did. Most certainly, he did. His husband spoke often of feeling the weight of the lives still in stasis upon him, but Emory felt the weight of the lives he saw every day. Good men and women of every species.

They all needed food.

And the irradiated remains of their stock was not cooperating.

Emory laced his hands together. Squeezed them until the knuckles turned white. "I do," he confirmed when Spender said nothing else. "I am worried, Assistant Director. The progress with the seeds—"

"Yes, the progress." Spender leaned forward, weight on his elbows. He lowered his voice to a conspiratorial whisper. "Tell me, do you think you'll see a breakthrough soon?"

Around them, the usual hub of diners trying to make the best of their third meal buzzed and hummed. Few enough seemed to take note of them, and even less seemed to care.

Emory thought about it. "If by 'soon,' you mean within the next two weeks? Unlikely. Samples need time to incubate, and we are investigating the genetic damage—"

Again, Spender interrupted him. "I see, I see. Good progress," he said with a smile, a reassuring nod. "How's the team?"

Another pause. Emory studied William Spender's face, searching for the motive in the questions. Admittedly, people were less his forte than plants. The man appeared little more than interested.

As assistant to Directors Tann and Addison, of course he would be.

Emory spread his hands, forcing his fingers to unlock before he hurt himself in his anxiousness. "They struggle," he admitted. "We are not so deep into the station that we aren't aware every moment of the Scourge." Spender nodded encouragingly. "We are all overworked, and rightfully so," he added, "but exhaustion and fear make for poor bedfellows."

"Of course, of course." Spender looked down again at the gruel offered him. With one finger, he slid it back up the table at Emory. "You better eat this," he said ruefully. "I have a suspicion that it's all we're going to get for a while."

"Rations?" A pause, then Emory clarified, "I mean, is our food to be fully rationed?"

"Rationed?" Spender shook his head, smiling dismissively as he rose to his feet. "Not yet, friend. Not yet." A pause, and then as if he thought better of it, he only reached over to shake Emory's hand and repeated, "Not yet."

With that, William Spender made his farewells and left the mess hall.

Emory watched him go, with doubt churning in an already knotted gut.

He missed home. He missed his old lab, to be sure, but he missed the comforts he and Reggie had carved for themselves. A home Reggie could return to between outposts. A place to let go of the weight of the worlds upon them.

Here, weight was all they seemed to have.

First, the weight of the thousands still in stasis.

Now the weight of men and women about to be very hungry.

Not yet, Spender had said. Rueful. As if it were inevitable.

Emory folded his hands together and rested his forehead against them.

Most of all? He missed his husband. More than ever, he wanted Reggie to take a break, come and see him so that he could share these new worries. Talk it over.

Face it together.

But for now, all he could do was gather himself, his courage and his failing strength, and shake off the miasma of fatigue for one more effort at hydroponics.

An effort that would turn into two. Then three. Then days.

One breakthrough. That was all they needed.

Because rumors were already starting to spread: *Supplies are running low.*

Spender knew. Emory had to trust that this meant the directors did too.

They'd all come up with something.

CHAPTER FIFTEEN

"Na'to's finally got it!"

"Well, sing a goddamn chorus of whatever," Arvex growled in comms. His voice had gotten surlier and surlier, and swapping out with his other two meatheads hadn't softened it any. Now he was back out on deck watch, one krogan—Wratch, Andria had learned—perched just by the hatch.

All of them had taken a turn for the irritated.

As the hours clocked in, and Na'to only occasionally muttered to himself, the krogan had run out of ways to taunt him, and Reggie, and even Andria. They'd also run out of ways to bait each other.

Now Arvex sounded like he was ready to wring salarian neck to get out of the warzone the Nexus's steady drift had placed them in.

The palp of the Scourge had spread. Somehow, as if pushed by an unseen force, the past few hours had seen it increase in length.

Worrisome.

"The good news," she said, tapping her comm feed, "is that we're just about done consolidating power through this auxiliary."

"What's the bad news?" Reg asked behind her.

She was very much aware of three krogan heads all focused on her. Even if two of them remained outside an airlock. "Well," she said slowly. "The bad news is that once we're done here, you, me and Na'to get to go have dinner."

A beat.

"Why is that bad?" Reg asked.

"You clearly don't pay attention to what you eat," Kaje said. He'd taken up position near Reg, taking a break between shifts playing Shoot the Trash.

Andria hid a smile. "Basically."

"Hey, if it means I can have dinner with Emory, I'm all for," Reg replied defensively.

"Oh, right. The sweet couple." Andria made a gagging sound.

"Don't be jealous."

"You know I am."

"What are you humans babbling about now?" Na'to's voice finally cracked the comm, sounding tired but triumphant. "I look away for just a minute and you're already engaging in verbal showdowns?"

"A minute?" This from Wratch. Sheer disbelief. "What kind of salarian loses track of time?"

"A brilliant one," Na'to said primly. Andria watched the camera feed bounce as he pulled himself out of the hatch. The wires, fuses and platelets attaching it all securely whizzed by in a streaming blur.

"Uh…"

"Shut it, Wratch. Like you never lost time in the varren pits," Kaje laughed.

"No, that—"

A clatter drew Andria's attention. Then another. She looked around, saw Reg doing the same.

Then Kaje surged to his feet. He pointed out over the emergency bulkhead. "It's moving!"

"Shit," Andria hissed, already reaching for the next frequency in her omni-tool. "Shit, shit—Engineering to bridge, I'm looking at a tangle of Scourge just outside Warehouse 7B."

"Copy that, engineering," someone said. She didn't know anyone in bridge, had no idea who was talking, what rank. "Approximate depth?"

"The hell if I know!" She scanned the black, trusting Reg to keep a close hand on their friend's gear. "It's all over the place up here, one wrong move and—"

A large shadow loomed slowly into view. Brilliant lines of gold and red energy laced across them, through them, as if something superheated had dragged through the plates.

Her mouth dropped open.

Kaje reached out, caught her by the arm and dragged it closer to his face. "Those explorers sucked out of Dock 11? Yeah," he growled into the mic, "they're coming back!"

||||||||||||||||||||

Addison met Sloane coming out of central commons, synthetic feathers in her hair and a puzzled sort of amusement twisting her usual broody expression.

"Hey," she said by way of greeting. Her eyebrows knotted. "Did you shoot a giant chicken?"

Sloane looked down at her Avenger, then up again with the same odd look. As if she'd stumbled into an alternate dimension and wasn't sure how to proceed. "Hey, Addison." A pause. She offered a hand. "Pinch me, would you?"

Addison blinked. Then, when Sloane didn't drop her hand, she took a fold of the security director's skin and pinched.

Hard.

"Son of a—*thank* you," she said sharply, jerking

her hand back. She looked back at the commons door, and for the first time, Addison heard what sounded like screaming.

Her eyes widened. "Sloane, you *didn't*."

Sloane, shaking out her hand, moved away from the door. "Please. One, there's no chickens to shoot here, unless you're counting turians—"

Addison cleared her throat.

"Two," Sloane added, "I didn't shoot anyway. They're…" A pause.

Addison splayed her hands, eyebrows raising even higher. "What? Because from here, it kind of sounds like someone's getting cannibalized. And *you* have a gun."

To her surprise, a half-smile curved Sloane's mouth. She gestured, with the hand she'd pinched and not the firearm. "You can look, but maybe you shouldn't."

"Why?"

"Because it's a mess."

"*Sloane.*"

This time, when the security director started laughing, Addison threw her hands up. She marched around the woman, waved frantically when the sound of screaming intensified. The door slid open and Addison saw…

Synthetic feathers. Specifically, feathers covering two people, and a round of drinks being poured for five more. A larger crowd surrounded them, fist-pumping and throwing bets.

"A drinking contest?" Where the losers were feathered by synthetic stuffing. And the winners just kept drinking.

And the bets just kept climbing.

Addison very slowly backed away, and let the door ease shut again.

Sloane's laughter bordered on the hysterical. "And you… you know what?" she gasped.

Addison turned, still trying to wrap her head around the sight. "There had to be at least fifty people in there."

Sloane's nod sent her off-balance. She fell back against the corridor wall, cradling the Avenger.

"Drinking."

Another nod. Tears began to leak out of her eyes, rolling down red cheeks as she struggled to breathe.

Addison's hands lifted to her face, covering her mouth as it dropped open in horror. "And you just rolled right in with your rifle, didn't you?"

This had Sloane howling with mirth, sitting down hard on one of the empty decorative tiers stationed at various intervals.

Unbidden, laughter began trickling up through Addison's mingled horror and exasperation. "Sloane," she said, trying for curt. But her humor betrayed her.

"I know," Sloane panted.

"An assault rifle!"

The woman held it up, barely able to hold onto it. "I know!"

"You could have used the cameras!"

But Addison had started laughing too, and as Sloane just shrugged in elaborate, breathless hysteria, she gave up all pretense and just let it all fly. Addison hadn't seen that much smiling or heard laughter like that since the drunken reverie of the departure celebration.

That had been months… make that years—make that *centuries*—ago. The last time she'd seen her fellow directors.

Inappropriate, yes. Untoward. Overreactionary. But as the doors slid wide and two humans stumbled out, a barrage of shouting, howls of the losing betters, and wild cheers followed them out.

Peals of laughter filled the corridor. "What, hey, Directors!" said a cheerful human.

Sloane could only wave them aside. "Let them drink," she told Addison, still chuckling. "Blow off steam. If it gets rowdy, I'll send in a few krogan to glare."

Addison winced. "Maybe less krogan, more coffee?"

"I sup—"

The comms crackled to life all around them. "Warning! Brace for impact," came the order, and all amusement abruptly died. Sloane caught Addison's arm, who swept another around the most unsteady of the humans staggering by.

Just in time. The station shuddered.

Then it rocked.

iiiiiiiiiiiiiiiiiiii

Na'to yelped as a large fist grasped him by the front of the suit, jerked him bodily out of the hatch. He felt the sole of his boot catch on something, heard it clatter. "Watch it," he exclaimed, already attempting to twist around to check for damage.

"No time!" Arvex's voice, never quiet, now practically buried him in its intensity. "Get back to the hatch, go, go!"

Na'to flailed as the krogan slammed him feet-first onto the deckplates. For a moment, he forgot that he'd switched the magnetization of his boots off to work within the delicate interior of the power conduit. When the hand in his suit let go, Na'to felt his feet lift again. "Emergency," he said, then louder, "Emergency!"

"Rock-dumb salarian, turn your boots on!" That

hand grabbed his faceplate this time, spun him around and slammed him back to the plate. Arvex waited until Na'to's boots sealed to the deck. Once assured Na'to wouldn't go careening off into space, he pushed him toward the other krogan—*Wratch*, he thought dumbly.

"Nacho, don't just stare!" Reg's voice, slack tight at the gear securing him to the station.

A spray of bullets erupted just behind him.

His brain, deeply invested in fuses and synaptic power cores and the unfortunate mess of wires he'd corrected along the way, struggled to catch up. At least until the first bit of debris clipped his shoulder.

It didn't hurt. Not really. It was too small for that. Na'to flapped a hand at it, forcing his magnetized boots to unlatch and make for the airlock. It spun away, a rotating disc of something or other. *Out of my field*, he thought. He didn't do structural.

"Na'to," Andria warned, her voice high and even younger in consequence. "Focus!"

He shook his head, pulling his attention back to the deck he walked across.

And to the virtual landmine of debris ahead.

Some small. Some medium.

Some very, very large.

All of it caught in ephemeral tendrils of black and orange and yellow and—

"It moved!" he exclaimed, so fascinated by the concept for a moment that he stopped trying to run.

Behind him, a loud clang jerked his attention back to the hatch. Nakmor Arvex knelt over it, grunting with effort as he secured the bolts back into place. Overhead, debris spun and gathered, whipped into frenzy. Whether it was the energy fringe turning large debris into smaller, the collisions of each as they magnified, or the bullets peppered by the krogan as they attempted to target debris out of their path, it only served to make it worse.

Action and reaction.

Calculating the rate of motion plus the additional force caused by the krogan's efforts at firepower control, eyeballing the distance to the airlock—

None of it mattered.

"Oh, shit," Andria whispered. "Ohshitohshit—"

"*Get your slimy carcass inside,*" roared Arvex.

Na'to tried. Panting, struggling to coordinate his slim build and the heavy magnetized grip of the boots, he struggled to take strides that would eat up the hull. Get him closer to the airlock. To safety.

Behind him, Arvex swore—or yelled or encouraged. Na'to couldn't be sure; it was all krogan to him.

What he did know is that at the rate of force between the remains of a spinning rover and his own feeble momentum, he wouldn't make it in time.

The comms filled with too many voices, yelling and shouting, pleading and encouraging.

Na'to looked up, saw nothing but somehow just *knew.* He jerked to the side, forcing his boots to unlatch. It threw him sideways, a floating kind of dodge, but it also pulled him free of the station hull.

Just as molten red furrows scored through the plate.

"Out," Wratch bellowed on comms. "Seal the warehouse!"

"But Na'to—"

"I got him," Reg said tightly.

Na'to's safety went taut. He flailed, caught in a free-float that sent him careening into a large portion of a broken wing, jarring every bone in his body and ones he'd feel later, too. Black flashes turned to white behind his eyes, and as he clung to the bit of metal, he managed, "Here! Pull!"

"Don't pull," Arvex shouted, but too late.

Reg yanked on the cord. Na'to's fingers ached around the rim of the torn wing, and the air jerked out of his chest with the force of it, but he felt himself move.

Felt the whole thing move with him.

"No," he muttered. Then, forcing the membranes over his eyes open, yelled it louder. "No, no! Let go—!"

Krogan curses filled the line as Na'to stared, horrified, at the surface of the station. From this vantage, the horizon spread wider, farther than any of them could see from the hull itself. The void of space, black and blue and red and white and every beautiful color stretched out in unfathomable eternity.

Captured, it seemed, as if in a perfect sphere of tangled nebula.

"Let go," Arvex ordered.

Numbly, Na'to obeyed. His hands spasmed, the sheared metal fragment peeled away as his whole body jerked to the side.

"Out, out!"

"Reg!"

Na'to couldn't see what was happening inside the warehouse. Couldn't place the edge of the hull or the deck he'd stood on. He spun, out of control, in a slow circle.

But the trajectory of the wing, that hadn't changed.

"Brace for impact," Arvex roared on the line.

Him? Heh. Na'to couldn't. Not out here. He watched helplessly as the disaster unfurled in unstoppable, achingly slow motion. The slack around his waist unfurled. The sound of his own breath in his helmet thundered.

And down below, mere meters from the likely impact of debris to hull, Arvex had both hands wrapped in Na'to's secure cord, feet braced and locked, every breath a growled echo of Na'to's own.

The salarian splayed his hands. "Let go," he said, calmer than he thought he'd be. His brain ran thousands of kilometers a second, no, a *nanosecond*. He knew what this looked like. What it'd end with.

That wing was going to do more damage than the already struggling structure could handle. The Scourge would tear through the rest. Somehow, miraculously, Na'to hadn't floated right into the thicket rising like a terrifying black sun just past the warehouse hull breach—*but no*, he thought.

Not miraculously.

A krogan.

And it would kill them both.

"Let go," he said again, louder. He wrapped the cord around his wrist, pulled. But his might was nothing compared to an angry krogan.

"Na'to," Andria cried.

"The hell I will," roared Arvex, yanking back with all his strength. "I said I'd keep your boots on deck *and Nakmor keep our word.*"

With nothing to brace against, no support, he had no way of stopping the thick-headed reptile-spawn from playing this through. Heroism, he reflected as everything drifted into one inexorable outcome. The heroism of krogan, of salarian. Of those who struggled to rebuild what was already lost.

The first sparks shot golden arcs across the hull as the giant mass of debris collided with the station.

The secure rope Arvex wrapped around his arm grew thicker, the stars and sparks reflected in his tempered faceplate.

Na'to smiled. "Andria... Reg... Seal the outer antechamber. The hull will buckle at approximately fourteen points."

"Damn it, no!"

Arvex hissed a long, hard sound as the hull cracked under his feet. Bent and rolled like metal shouldn't. The nest of harmless-looking threads rose in Na'to's field of vision. Tendrils brushed debris, sheared it through. Cast even more to scatter, to pepper the station.

He watched it come closer. "Krogan, unless you wish to join me, *let go*."

Far too late. Far too little. The hull snapped back against the collision force and threw the krogan hard off the plating, breaking the magnetic seal holding him on. His shout was buried in the sudden chatter on comm lines, the rush of too much breath. Gasping. Yelling.

And the thought that consumed Na'to.

Just one.

"Tell them," he said quietly as he careened away from the station. "Tell them the Scourge is aptly named."

Poetic. To be named by a salarian and fit so well.

Whatever else he might have said, whatever other feedback he could have given as the first tendrils scraped past, it died in the sudden system failure of his electronics. The comm. The air regulators.

New tech. Old tech. It didn't seem to matter.

The Scourge tore through it all.

CHAPTER SIXTEEN

Where one emergency ended, another took its place. The progress made before the loss of life was buried beneath the weight of the knowledge derived, and Kesh could offer nothing but the steadfast words of a krogan to Calix for them.

He stood in one of the few places Kesh preferred to have such meetings, an out-of-the-way office rarely found or sought after. He stared out over what should have been a courtyard of some kind, but remained dark and closed. Silent.

Kesh put a large, heavy hand on his shoulder. Squeezed. "He died well, Calix. With honor even my krogan salute."

"Yeah." The turian's voice fell flat. "I'm sure he did."

The lack of respect for her words didn't bother her. Kesh knew something of what he was feeling. Krogan were no stranger to loss, but to lose to something so vicious, so unpredictable as this Scourge...

She let out a gusty sigh. "At the very least," she said, letting him go, "he confirmed for us what we'd suspected. The energy that drifts around us is not harmless."

"Worse," he muttered. "It's hungry."

"Maybe." She turned away, lumbered for the door. "More like *we* are hungry, and in our haste to rebuild, we neglected the real priorities. Return to your unit, Calix." She paused at the door, braced one large hand on the frame, and looked back at the forlorn turian, his head bowed. "The power conduit they'd intended to fix held, Calix. The hull damage didn't rupture the core. There's something in that worth holding onto."

He didn't answer. Didn't say anything. He simply nodded, slowly. Wearily.

Sympathy and determination made for difficult friends. Lacking anything better, Kesh sharpened her voice. "Let's make sure we lose no one else."

Calix said nothing.

She left him in silence and shadow, hoping that he was as strong as he needed to be. That he'd gather up his sorrows and his grief and press on. His team needed him.

This station needed him.

And they all needed the lives he and his crew kept alive.

CHAPTER SEVENTEEN

Sloane expected something of a rollercoaster ride, but the highs and lows of the recent weeks were wearing on her.

On the upside, work got done. Progress was made, and quite a lot of it. Kesh's krogan were efficient and basically tireless. If they grumbled, it was indiscernible from the usual krogan surliness, and so didn't require security to monitor. Not even the loss of one of their grunts put a dent in their work ethic.

Cold, maybe. Sloane couldn't be sure it wasn't just the krogan way. Krogan died. That was kind of what they did, right? Lived big, full, bloody lives and invariably bit the big one.

So they kept working.

In the interim since the collision with the Scourge, no one had tried to steal another ship, or take more hostages, or go on a murderous rampage. Even if they had, the hidden cameras she'd ordered info-sec to install were in place and functional. *Had* they been needed, they existed.

And if they were never used? Even better.

Tann hadn't asked for specifics, and Sloane didn't offer them. Somehow, she didn't think the salarian would go for what he'd call spying, but which Sloane called common-freaking-sense.

On the downside…

Calix.

The set of his features when she'd sat through

a painful meeting about power draws and energy reserves made her chest hurt. She had seen turians pull through more than their fair share of pain and loss. Kaetus had once explained to her, in his usual surly way, that turians learned to process loss like factors in one's life. Every victory was achieved on the back of those who didn't make it.

It made the victory somehow better. Mean more.

Sloane understood. You didn't strive for success without losing something along the way. But it was her job to keep that to a minimum, dammit.

Not that she could do much against this Scourge. She'd had her hands full with the mass panic inside the commons, and more than a few injuries thanks to that. The Scourge hadn't rolled all the way through, thank whatever god still hung out on this floating wreck, but the aftershocks had left the whole populace looking panicked for days.

Calix, he didn't do panic. Weeks after he'd lost Rantan Na'to, his face still bore the sign of his mourning. His whole team felt it. Shock, mostly. Two of his crew had been given temporary leave—she didn't know where they'd gone off to, but if it was her, she'd guess somewhere the booze still flowed.

But he pressed on. So did she.

They all did. And according to Calix, life support was that much safer. Thanks to his salarian teammate.

And the krogan who'd tried to protect him. Nakmor Arvex.

A salarian and a krogan step out for repairs…

The joke wasn't supposed to end in death. How was anyone supposed to guess that they'd blindsided right into a Scourge patch? Without sensors, they were all blind.

But the damned things refused to work. And there was only so much she could do.

The only thing they had going for them was confirmation. The Scourge blew. Also, it blew things up. Namely, the Nexus. And anything that got in its path. How, why, was a mystery for scientists to unravel.

Her job was to make sure nobody panicked. This was getting to be something of a crapshoot.

With some semblance of routine came time to think, and with time to think came a sudden abundance of opinions. Everyone she talked to lately seemed to know exactly what the crew's priorities should be. Who just *had* to be woken.

They should abandon the station and set up a colony on one of the planets. All in or bust.

They should disperse everyone to the farthest corners of the station, in case the core experienced another catastrophe.

They should test weaponry on the Scourge.

They had to turn around and go back to the Milky Way.

They needed to put a billiards table in Commons 4.

Sloane agreed with that one. The rest, though… not so much.

She sat in one of the intended parks, borrowing a little peace and quiet while everyone else busied themselves with, well, *staying busy*. The days had proven one thing for sure: No matter the to-do list on everybody's plate, any effort at relaxation seemed to turn into panic. The Scourge, the lack of the Pathfinders, the loss of life, the next collision…

And when the opinions turned to panic, to fear, to anger, it seemed as if people sought her out specifically. To yell. To plead. To demand.

She'd wanted to lead. To make a difference. Here on the Nexus, people looked at her, spoke to her, with certain expectations. She could see fear in their faces if she had a scowl on her own, whether it might be due to a reactor failure, or gastrointestinal issues. One wrong twitch on her part and the effects rolled out like ripples.

She never thought being a politician would be such a hard job. It had always seemed to her like strutting around, smiling all the time, slinging bullshit and platitudes like rice at a wedding.

It was goddamn hard, though. She could admit that to herself now. No point in letting Tann know she'd reached that particular epiphany, however.

And yet, like a demon summoned by name, her omni-tool chimed.

Was it Tann? Of course it was. Luck wasn't her game. "To what do I owe the pleasure?" she asked.

"We need to meet," he said flatly. "If you can spare a few minutes." He knew she could. Knew exactly where she was, and what she was doing, thanks to the device on her wrist, which now functioned more or less as intended—albeit with limited range.

Sloane inhaled a long breath of recirculated air. "Is it important?"

Tann's irritation snapped with—and she could sympathize—fatigue. "It always is."

All right. Fine. She rolled her aching shoulders. "On my way."

░░░░░░░░░░░

The three of them gathered in a conference room just off Operations. Tann and Addison were already there when Sloane arrived, but that was normal. She seemed perpetually doomed to make them wait, and at this point neither of her fellow leaders even mentioned it.

"It's been a while," Addison said. "Tann and I thought this might be a good time to assess where we're at."

"Okay," Sloane said, flipping a chair around so she could straddle it. She rested her arms across the back and laced her fingers together. "Assess."

"Do you want to start?" Tann asked her.

"Nope."

"Are you ever in a good mood?"

Sloane barked a laugh. "Usually about twenty seconds before my omni-tool goes off."

"I'm sorry if I ruined your day," he said dourly.

"It's not you, Tann," Sloane said. "It's meetings." She stared at the center of the table. "I really hate meetings."

"Then think of this as more of a chat," Addison put in, not quite able to keep the annoyance out of her tone.

"The only thing worse than a meeting," Sloane said, "is a meeting with no agenda. AKA, a chat. But okay, I'll try. Promise. Let's chat."

Addison and Tann exchanged that look. It was a look that had been exchanged when the first meeting of the cave clan was held around a fire, to decide what to do about the spear tribe from the next valley over. The *do you want to start or shall I* look. Sloane forced herself to relax. It had been four weeks, after all. Maybe a little progress update couldn't hurt.

Tann went first.

"There is one thing I would like to discuss," he said in a vague, casual tone. "Supplies."

"Supplies," Sloane repeated. "I feel like that's all we ever talk about."

"Only in the immediate sense. The micro, not the

macro. We need to discuss the long-term prognosis."

This, Sloane reluctantly agreed, probably merited a *chat*. Maybe even an honest-to-God meeting. Supplies were a problem that loomed like an overdue planetquake, just distant enough that everyone knew it was coming, yet no one wanted to do anything about it. Except Tann, of course. Truthfully she found little fault in his thinking.

"Hydroponics," Tann said, taking their silence as permission to continue, "is behind schedule. It will be another four months, I'm now told, before we get our first edible crop, and meanwhile the effort is a massive drain on our available resources."

"Four months?" Sloane repeated. Last she'd checked they were claiming three to four weeks. A single month at most. "First I've heard that."

She regretted the words the moment she'd said them. It amounted to an admission that she hadn't been paying attention, which was largely true.

"I asked Spender to do some calculations," Tann said. "At our current burn rate, we will run out of our reserve caches in eight weeks or so."

"So soon?" Addison asked.

Well, at least I wasn't the only one tuned out, Sloane thought. That, or Addison's own advisor had left her out of the loop, which seemed equally likely.

"That isn't the worst of it," Tann went on, gaining steam. "Water will run out sooner. Reclamation and filtration are woefully behind schedule. There was far more damage down there than anyone realized. And this assumes we're out of the woods regarding the Scourge, which is so far wishful thinking."

Sloane looked at Addison, saw the same surprise she felt. "How is it you know all this and we don't?"

she asked Tann. She feared the answer, but had to know. Sloane braced herself, ready to learn that she'd been oblivious to reports or blowing off meetings. She expected some kind of condescending answer about how, as acting director, it was his job to know. The reply took her by surprise.

"I walk," Tann said.

"Huh?"

"I walk. I roam the halls. Well, usually I just pace in my lab, but sometimes a change of scenery helps me think, so I wander. And when I wander, I see things. I hear things. Later today," he added ruefully, "I have no doubt that we will be officially told by Nakmor Kesh that these two critical projects are not going well."

"It's not Kesh's fault," Addison quickly said.

"Did I imply as much?" he asked blandly. "I did not. But that you leap to it does make one wonder." Whatever Addison wanted to say—and all the swearing Sloane didn't have the heart to throw in— was halted by a dismissive wave of his hand. "This type of news tends to take its time filtering up to us, and occasionally as I walk, I catch on sooner. I gather hints. I connect the dots... but this is not the issue. The issue is supplies. We should focus on that."

"I really don't like where this is going," Sloane said.

"Oh?" Tann fixed his gaze on her.

Sloane inhaled, puffed herself up. "The solution to a supply problem isn't exactly a security officer's dream scenario. Fed people are content people. Showers are generally appreciated and really damn useful for morale."

"Understood," Tann said, but then he added, "We will begin by discussing rationing."

"Is there another alternative?"

"I believe there is, but let's start with this." He glanced at each of them. "We made a mistake by allowing free rations. At first, our shared sense of purpose led people to naturally be aware of their draw on our resources."

"Yeah," Sloane said. "Not so much now, though."

"Precisely," he agreed. "The crew has become accustomed to taking whatever they need, when they need it. Over time, as routine set in and our immediate dangers were mitigated, the lack of worry has led to... I won't call it gluttony, but certainly people are behaving like, what's the word?"

"Assholes?"

"No."

"Selfish pricks?"

"No."

"Inconsiderate cunts?"

"What is a—?"

Addison cut in hurriedly. "Short-sighted!"

Tann snapped his fingers. "Yes! That's what I was looking for, thank you. Also, thank you, Sloane for the colorful commentary. It is always, er, linguistically fascinating. I shall have to consult the database on some of these terms."

"Knock yourself out," she said. "But we got hit by the Scourge not that long ago, if you recall. Has there been a dip in ration use?"

Tann shook his head grimly. "The reverse, in fact. As if once aware that rations bore no restriction, desperate times seemed to create further draw."

"Well." Addison gestured, indicating all things outside the room. "If people are losing sight of the mission, what their duty is, then let's remind them."

Tann rested his chin in one hand and tapped at

his jaw with one long finger. "What do you have in mind?"

"A few ideas," she replied. "Maybe at meal time tonight we should put Jien Garson's departure speech on the vid screens. She can—pardon, could—motivate better than any of us, I think, and it could be passed off as a memorial. Since," she added pointedly, "we haven't actually stopped to mourn yet."

"Hmm." Tann continued tapping away at his jaw, his gaze unfocused. "That's not bad. Perhaps it is time."

"Yeah," Sloane said. "Then, the instant the video is over, we tell them dinner's off and that they should all stop gorging themselves."

Addison shot her a glare.

Sloane couldn't help herself. She went on. "I'll have my security team on hand to quell the riot you'll have started."

"It doesn't have to be like that," Tann said.

"Doesn't it?" Sloane's mouth twisted as she sat forward, elbows on her knees. "Look, like you said, we haven't been rationing—and yeah, that was stupid of us. But it means that when we start, people are going to be upset. Finger pointing, accusations of hoarding or unfair ratios, the full gamut. Trust me. I've seen it before."

"I know you have," Tann said.

"Really?"

"I read your dossier."

"No shit?"

"No sh—, er, correct." A beat. "This is a surprise? I've read almost everyone's by now. Those who are awake, I mean. Especially after the Falarn incident."

Sloane stared at him for a moment, then shook her head. "All I'm saying is, rationing is going to kill the mood around here, right as everyone's *just* starting to settle from the last Scourge hit. My team is going to have to start spending all their time defending what supplies we do have before things start magically disappearing."

"That," Addison said, "is already happening."

Tann and Sloane both turned to her.

"I was going to bring it up next. It's all in Spender's latest report. Certain items have been growing legs."

Tann went rigid, his eyes impossibly wide. "Some kind of biological agent? An alien meta-molecule infection?"

"No, no," Addison said hurriedly. "It's an expression. Things have been vanishing as if they'd walked away on their own."

"Oh," the salarian said. "I see." He sounded almost disappointed.

"No one thought to inform Security about this?" Sloane asked her.

"Like I said, I was going to bring it up next. Spender only mentioned it in his report this morning."

"I'd prefer to learn about criminal activity the moment it happens, not in a fucking report."

Addison waved off the terse rebuke. "It's not like that. He called it a vague concern. A 'rounding error,' perhaps, but he suspects there may be a problem."

Sloane forced herself to ease off. "Fair enough. I'll talk to him, get someone to investigate."

"Good," Addison said.

Sloane swung her focus back to Tann. "You said there was another option, other than rationing."

"Well, yes. I should think it's obvious." When neither woman took that bait, he went on. "The time has come, I believe, to have the majority of our workforce return to cryostasis."

Addison stared at him.

Sloane spent a good ten seconds laughing.

Jarun Tann endured this like the calm professional he clearly thought he was. When Sloane's amusement finally abated, he continued.

"They were woken to help us overcome the immediate danger, and that has been accomplished. We're all in agreement on that. It is perfectly reasonable to return them to stasis now, until we have our first crop from Hydroponics." He shot Sloane a look. "I fail to see what's so amusing about the idea."

"Last time we put people in stasis it was a punishment. For a severe crime."

"I fail to see the relevance to this situation."

"Tann," she said, "despite the relative calm, we're still in a world of shit here. Trust me, the last thing anyone's going to want to do is be ordered back into their pod, and hope they'll wake up again. They're awake *now*. They're going to want to stay that way. If we want to return them to stasis, it'll have to be by force."

"So we ask for volunteers."

"If you get ten out of the thousand currently awake, I'd be shocked."

This caused him to get up and pace. No easy feat in the small conference room.

"Perhaps Addison's suggestion applies here, too. Garson's speech may remind them of the sacrifice they made to come here. They've already been placed in stasis once and survived, I might add."

"Well, sure," Sloane said sarcastically. "A hundred percent of the survivors *survived*."

"You know what I mean."

A brief silence, broken by Addison.

"It can't hurt to ask, can it?"

Sloane stood. "Yes. *Hell* yes it can hurt. Trust me, it's not going to go well. And with the implied threat of rationing looming behind that request, the self-preservation instinct is going to kick in."

For a time no one spoke. Tann even stopped pacing and leaned against the wall.

"I guess," Sloane said with abundant reluctance, "the alternative is to go straight to rationing, and that's just not going to work." She rubbed her temple. "At least asking for volunteers eases us into it."

Tann nodded. "Agreed. I've made my decision. This evening we will let Jien Garson herself remind everyone of why we're here, and of the sacrifices we all made. Then I will put out the call for volunteers."

"Sounds like you're trying to convince yourself."

Tann blinked. "Perhaps we could all do with a little reminder of why we're here, don't you think?"

<hr />

Sloane made an appearance in one of the common areas, eating and drinking with a random group of crew, rather than her usual place with the security staff. Her dining companions were a lively bunch at first. Two members of the Nakmor work crew, a sanitation systems expert, and a soft-spoken asari who only poked at her food.

When pressed, the asari, a Dr. Aridana, admitted that she'd been trying to fix the main sensor array, and felt it wouldn't be resolved until one of the arks arrived with spare parts. "Assuming they are not in the same, or worse, shape as us."

Sloane finished eating and drifted toward the door, ready to leave and summon security at the first sign of trouble. As she walked, the few functional screens around the commons bloomed to life, displaying Jien Garson's face.

A hush fell across the crowd, and in that solemn quiet their fallen leader's words were heard by all. It was one of history's great speeches, Sloane mused. Inspiring, thoughtful, and yet somehow "blowing happy gas up yer ass," as her old station chief used to say. Regardless, every word in Garson's speech rang true.

And then came Tann's.

"Wise words from our fearless leader," he began awkwardly. "How about a round of applause?" And then he clapped. No one else joined, but Tann had no way of knowing that. The poor bastard clapped for a full minute, then resumed. "I'd ask Jien Garson to address you all now, but alas, she is dead."

Oh crap. An awkward silence followed.

"And if we are not careful, a lot more of us will die," Tann went on.

"Oh, Tann, what the hell..." Sloane muttered, burying her head in her hands.

"A lot more of us will be dead if we run out of supplies." Tann stared into the camera for a moment. "We have made some incredible progress these last few weeks, and I am happy to report the state of emergency has ended. In recognition of that, and because of our rapidly depleting reserves, your interim leadership is asking for volunteers to return to cryostasis." He paused, then added, "You deserve a little rest, don't you?"

That's it. I can't listen to any more of this. Even worded well, Sloane doubted many would take Tann up on his request. Delivered like this, though, he'd be ignored at best and ridiculed at worst. Already Sloane could hear snickering from a few places across the room. She grabbed a bottle of something from their "rapidly depleting reserves" and took the straightest path she could to her room.

||||||||||||||||||

Showered, meds kicking in, she slipped on a cleanish uniform and pulled the omni-tool onto her forearm. Sloane had checked out and checked out *hard* last night, drank until she thought she'd drowned the horrifyingly awkward moment she'd witnessed.

It had only sort of worked. Now, as sixteen messages lit up her screen, she could only imagine what she'd missed.

She ignored them all and tapped in a link request to Tann. *Might as well get this over with.* She wondered how many had spotted the island of logic hiding in his ocean of poorly chosen words.

"Good morning," Tann said, his voice telling her everything.

Sloane asked anyway. "That bad, huh?"

"That bad."

"How many volunteers?"

A second of silence. "None."

"*None*?"

"As you predicted, no one volunteered to return to stasis. None whatsoever."

"Damn."

"Well, there was one."

"Oh?"

"She claimed to have selected the option in error, and changed it."

Sloane could think of nothing to say.

"Go ahead and gloat," Tann said.

"No, no," Sloane replied. "Not going to do that. I had a feeling this would be the result, but I'm not going to hold your feet to the fire. Next time, though, you might want to get some help on your speech. That was... not great." She took her first sip of coffee.

"Spender wrote it."

Sloane spat out her first sip of coffee. "You're joking."

"Not at all. I thought it was fine."

"Tann, that speech was... I think the technical term is 'a turd sandwich.' Seriously, put Spender out the airlock for that one, and then follow him out for not realizing it yourself."

His eyes went wide. "I hardly think such a punishment—"

"I'm joking, Tann. But—*gah*, never mind. Next time let Addison give the speech, okay?"

"The crew seems to listen to you."

"Yeah but I have to buy into an idea before I go asking others to swallow it."

The salarian let out a frustrated sigh. "Well, we're right back to where we started."

"No," Sloane corrected, "we're worse than that. You've planted the seed now, the 'supplies are running out' seed."

"Yes. Well, about that," he said. "We need to draw up a plan for rationing."

"That we do."

"Are you available now?"

Sloane glanced at the clock, then felt the pang from her stomach. "Let me find breakfast first."

A big meal, she decided. As much as she could stomach, before the belt had to be tightened.

And then she'd crack some skulls, if needed, yell

some obscenities, if confronted, and all around wait for the station to explode.

Or maybe everyone would just cope.

Nah. She still didn't feel that lucky.

CHAPTER EIGHTEEN

Sloane had been right, Addison mused. They'd gotten lucky, at first. Perhaps that's why the security director volunteered to join Kesh's team on their mission to clear a path to the nearest ark docking bay. Once there, they hoped to locate a backup set of sensor interfaces—one that could be brought online.

Addison couldn't really blame her. Sloane had waited a day, to make sure there was no violence in the wake of the announcement, then left a competent team behind. She gave the security director that much credit. Had there been any backlash, Addison had no doubt Sloane would have stayed.

Really, things weren't so bad. Some harsh words and a half-hearted punch or two thrown in the commons, then everyone had taken the announcement with a sort of "what else can go wrong" sunken attitude.

With things in shape, Sloane had taken Kesh's offer of hard, manual labor and taken her version of a vacation.

That had been two days ago.

Maybe it had just taken a couple days to really sink in. A couple days of newly instated rations and the sudden realization that the rations they *did* have were already in the red.

The mood *had* changed in the Nexus. Drastically.

Addison walked the halls, as Tann had suggested, though it only made her feel more useless. She oversaw colonial affairs for a failed colony, an advisor to their "acting" leader. Soon, people would begin to ask what "acting" meant, exactly.

Seeing the Garson recording had an unintended consequence: It reminded them of what they'd signed up for versus what they'd actually got.

She avoided the sidelong glances people gave her as she walked. The growing hunger in their eyes, the thirst, and with those the accusation that it was her fault. It wasn't fair, but she supposed politicians were always the ones to take the blame when a natural disaster took the population by surprise.

In every pair of accusatory eyes, she heard their unvoiced anger. *How could you not have envisioned this? We trusted you. We sacrificed everything because we believed in your plan.*

Fair or not, that's what she heard in her head as they looked at her. In truth she hadn't been much involved in the disaster-scenario planning. She'd been laser-focused on her actual job, drawing up plans and contingencies for first-contact scenarios with the species they would meet.

Oh, how she'd dreamt of those moments! Alien races unlike any they'd experienced in the Milky Way. The possibilities, and challenges. She'd pictured herself seated at a formally set table, sipping asari wine, Jien on her left and some dignitary from a benevolent and wise new species on her right.

Instead she was sleeping on the floor, boiling water to purify it as if she were on some survivalist training course.

Addison stopped in a hallway bridging two sections, expansive windows on both sides with what should have been magnificent views of space. Days earlier she'd come through here by shouldering her way past the "watchers," a group who'd volunteered to act as lookouts until sensors were online, lest the Nexus be totally blind. They'd sat or stood, day and night for weeks now, watching for any signs that the Scourge was making a return appearance.

Or, more hopefully, scanning for the approach of a Pathfinder ship. So far they'd seen neither. Just unfamiliar stars, and with the rationing news, they'd evidently found better uses of their time. Today the hall was empty.

Addison sat in the middle of a bench and folded her hands in her lap. For a time she did not move, drinking in a whispering quiet marred only by the ever-present whir of life support, which she had to admit had been working flawlessly since that turian and his team had made emergency repairs.

They were working around the clock to keep it limping along, but still it was impressive. It must feel nice, she thought, to be useful.

Addison shook her head. That wasn't a healthy way of thinking, and she knew it.

Her omni-tool chimed. Couldn't be Sloane, her team was too far away for the meager comm network the crew had hobbled together. She answered and sat back as Tann's face appeared floating in the air before her.

"Any word from Sloane?" he asked.

"No," Addison replied. "A runner from their group came back this morning. He said he'd asked if she wanted any message delivered, and she'd just laughed."

"That sounds like her," Tann mused.

"The runner said they think they'll clear the passage by tonight, and then we'll know if we have sensors or not soon after."

"Hmm…" The Salarian tapped at his chin. "It's taking longer than I'd expected."

Addison could only shrug. Everything seemed to be taking longer than expected, since the food shortages became common knowledge.

"Well," Tann said, "as much as I value her advice, decisions still need to be made."

Addison paused, gauging his words. Wariness and excitement, but most of all? She'd grab anything to be busy. And in the end, things had to be done. No matter what.

"What did you have in mind?"

The salarian smiled. "As long as you've advised me, that still counts as being advised, yes?"

"True."

"And you know how Sloane gets annoyed when she's asked to weigh in on minor matters."

"Also true," Addison said, already seeing where this was leading.

Tann went on. "I think we should see how many such minor matters we can clear from the list before she returns. It's what you'd call a win-win I believe. Not only do decisions get made, but Sloane is spared from the monotony of the process."

"Minor matters," Addison repeated. "Like what?"

"I had an idea that perhaps we should repurpose one of the refrigerant tanks to serve as an additional water purifier. The team tells me it's possible with the materials we have at hand, and would only lead to a slight temperature increase within the livable areas. As a result, we would have enough extra fresh water to allow people showers once every two days."

"Oh," Addison replied. A hot shower sounded like extreme luxury. Her skin tingled just thinking about it.

"Define 'slight'?"

"Well within human tolerances."

"Tann…"

"Two degrees Celsius, on average."

"Better, thank you. Um, yes, I think that sounds like a good plan."

"There," he said, "you see? A decision made, and one less thing for our security director to worry about when she returns."

"What else have you got?" Addison asked. A bit too quickly perhaps, but she was beyond caring. Doing something that felt like actual accomplishment felt too good to care.

"Let's meet in Operations and go over the list?"

"Perfect," Addison replied. "On my way."

||||||||||||||||||||

She walked down a hallway where a team of krogan workers was welding a complex, if somewhat ramshackle, array of support beams into place. A temporary fix to a ceiling that could no longer support the weight of whatever lay above. None of them paid Addison any attention, so complete was their focus on the work.

And yet as she passed she thought she could feel something radiating off of them. Not hatred, or even resentment, feelings she often sensed from other races in the emergency population. No, this was something else. Their body language, so deliberately continuing to work despite her passage. Their lack of eye contact, as if by force of will they were allowing her a brief respite from the accusatory glances others cast her way.

They seemed to be saying, *"We'll handle this, now go solve the bigger problems."* Addison stopped at the end of the short hallway and turned back toward them.

"Thank you," she said.

This earned a few confused looks. They looked to each other as if trying to figure out who she'd spoken to.

"Thank you," Addison repeated, "for all the hard work."

"Well, sure," one of them replied. Then he went back to the task at hand.

Addison continued on, mind churning now. So many questions, concerns, and possibilities. Answers were still apparitions at the edge of that mental fog, always blurring away to nothing if she tried to grasp at them.

And then, one didn't. It stayed just visible, moving no closer or no farther as she worked toward it. This became a path, of sorts, and with each little step Addison found some of her old confidence. Her sense of purpose. This was the right thing. The idea she'd been waiting for.

So simple, she began to curse herself for not thinking it sooner. It was the price to pay, she supposed, for allowing herself to become so depressed, but she'd fix that now.

Over the last leg of her walk, Addison worked out the basics in her head. She resisted the urge to call Spender and task him with figuring out the details. That was something she'd done too often of late.

No, this was hers to begin.

Help could come later.

Foster Addison swept into Operations with her chin up and a focus she'd not felt since the Scourge first struck.

Two crew members sat at the main console, in a hopeless vigil that sensors might magically start to work, or a signal might get through. "Any sign of the arks?" she asked them as she passed.

"Negative," they both said in unison.

Always the same answer.

Tann stood just behind them, looking at a datapad.

"I have a proposal," she said before Tann could speak.

"Err, good!" the salarian said with more than a little dubiousness. He had his own list already displayed, but with a tap of his long finger it winked away.

"We can spare eight ships," Addison said firmly. "I've worked through the numbers, and with the rest we could still support an evacuation. It's time, Tann. We can't wait for the Pathfinders. We need to scout the closest worlds and find out if there's anything useful nearby. A suitable location for an off-Nexus colony, resources we can harvest or mine."

"Hmmmm," he replied.

If I can just convince him… Addison forged ahead. "We can't just keep huddled up in here, hoping our supply problem will magically go away. Hoping the Pathfinders will come and rescue us. They should have been here by now. We all know it. It's time we accepted it."

"Addison—"

"Let me finish." Tann drew back, clearly surprised. "As for rationing, it only delays the inevitable. It won't take another run-in with the Scourge to kill us all. One more little thing goes wrong in hydroponics and it's over. We're done."

"You're right," Tann said. "I agree."

"My plan will work if we staff—" she pressed. "Wait, what?"

"I agree with you."

"That was… easier than I expected."

He sensed her puzzlement and explained. "My attempt to persuade people to return to stasis failed," he said. "And now rationing has had a negative impact on morale, cutting into the progress of repairs. So, yes, I agree."

"Well," Addison said, "shit, Tann, I'm glad to hear that."

"Sloane won't like it," the salarian added. "But, go on. Staffing, you were saying?"

She'd almost lost her train of thought. Yesterday she might have, but the focus she'd gained had done wonders for her mental state. Addison felt like herself again.

"I thought at first a simple pilot and co-pilot arrangement would be best. Minimal, so as to not take able-bodied personnel away from the efforts here. Perhaps even letting the automated systems handle the flights, essentially using the ships as giant unmanned probes.

"But now I realize we not only can, but *should* fully staff the shuttles. Mount true exploratory missions. Not only will we get better results, but we'll reduce the drain on our supplies aboard the Nexus."

"Very interesting, indeed," Tann said. He stood and joined her by the table, bringing up a display showing the nearby star systems. The map had been created using old-fashioned measurement methods, based on visual observations. Rough to the point of being useless, but it was all they had.

Tann manipulated the interface. "These, perhaps?" He pointed.

"Yeah," Addison agreed. "That would work."

"Hypothetically, who would comprise the crews?"

Addison had already worked out the basics, but decided to allow Tann the feeling of participation. Besides, he might discern a better way.

"Pilots and co-pilots, those are easy, and in fact we already have capable pairs awake. Beyond that, a sensor tech for each."

"Don't we need them here, to fix our own sensors?"

"No," Addison said. "To calibrate them, yes, eventually, but right now they're all waiting on fabrication. They've taken to menial tasks in the meantime."

"I see. Okay, who else."

The list went on like that. Xenobiology, astrogeology, engineering, medical, and security.

"Security?" Tann asked dubiously.

"I think that would help ease Sloane's concerns. Just in case someone suffered a mental breakdown, or one crew decided to take their ship and forge their own path."

"Neither of those seem very likely," Tann observed.

"Still, Sloane worries about that kind of thing, and her team is… excessive in number," she said. "I think that's fair to say."

"Until food runs out," Tann responded. "Then they all will be needed."

"Well, yes, but that's the whole point of this. Preventing that day from arriving. Besides, these systems are close enough that all of these ships should return before our supplies reach critical levels."

Tann stared at the display, scanning the map and, Addison guessed, mentally juggling the pieces that would be in play.

"Unless any of them run into problems," he muttered, as if to himself. "A mechanical failure, the Scourge, or something unforeseen."

"It's a risk," Addison said, nodding, "but we're not going to get out of this without taking some chances."

"Hmm." Tann stood and began to pace. In that moment Addison knew she'd convinced him. The rest would be details.

Finally, her time had come.

She pinged Spender. "Get to Operations right away," she sent, hands shaking slightly as she typed the letters out. "Colonial Affairs is open for business."

Spender took on the task of creating preliminary crew manifests for the eight missions. While he did that, Addison went to the Colonial Affairs hangar and made a personal inspection of all the shuttles.

Many were already in use as temporary shelters. But not all of them, and moving the occupants around in order to fully empty eight craft wouldn't take more than a few hours.

The bigger issue, which she had anticipated but underestimated gravely, was supplies. The temporary occupants had been heavy-handed in raiding the stores, evidently thinking that because they'd made the ships their homes, that meant everything inside belonged to them.

Discussions turned heated, but Addison's quiet summoning of security to help "clear the air" soon took care of that.

"Thank you," she said to Kandros, the officer who'd arrived.

"It's my job. No thanks necessary."

Addison moved on toward the next craft.

"What's all this activity about, anyway?" he asked, lingering alongside her.

"We've decided to send some scouts out. Catalog the nearby worlds, hopefully find some resources we can use, or make contact with the arks."

"Security Director Kelly is on board with this?" he asked, sounding dubious.

Uh-oh, she thought. "Sloane didn't have any objections," she told him, watching carefully for his response.

He just nodded, studying the flanks of the nearest vessel. "You know I have some experience with that kind of thing."

Addison stopped and turned. "Do you?"

The turian shrugged. "It's sort of why I came here. Why I joined up, I mean. Somewhere along the line I wound up in security, but back home I was in counter-terrorism."

Addison didn't know this man, barely knew his name, but she could see a look in his eyes she'd seen in the mirror often enough.

"Spender's in charge of the rosters," she told him. "If you're interested, I mean."

He stared at the sleek ship for another long moment, then glanced at her and smiled. He quickly looked away, then walked off, saying nothing more.

Addison tapped a quick note to Spender on her omni-tool. *Kandros in sec ideal for scout mission, if you need one more.*

The reply came a minute later. *I'll talk to him. Thanks!*

Foster Addison smiled to herself. Good morale was a powerful thing, she thought.

By evening the first of the scouts slipped out from the Nexus's shadow and lit off into the vast emptiness beyond. Addison and Tann watched it from Operations, which still lacked a forward wall and thus provided one of the more impressive—if terrifying—views of their surroundings.

Provided, Addison mused, *you only want to look forward*. Which suited her just fine.

They toasted each departure, wishing the assigned captains good hunting as they neared the very meager range of the Nexus's transmission capability.

Kandros, commanding the shuttle *Boundless*, promised they'd be back soon, and added, "Tell Sloane to save my seat at the card table," seconds before powering past comms range.

Addison couldn't recall how many times she'd smiled that day, but this one felt best.

CHAPTER NINETEEN

Sloane Kelly hadn't worked so hard in years. She returned with the work team dead on her feet, hungry, bleary-eyed. She didn't know what time it was. She didn't know where her political counterparts were, and felt glad for that. She could sneak to her room and grab some sleep before anyone realized she'd returned.

Eight more hours of zero bullshit, that sounded beyond incredible, and she wasn't about to ruin it. Better still, she could delay reporting that the mission had only been a partial success. The great hallway had been cleared enough to allow passage, yes, but there had been no cache of backup sensor arrays to plunder at the far end. The Nexus would remain blind a while longer, and that wasn't going to make anyone happy.

She stuck to the plan. Avoided everyone. Ignored the messages waiting for her. The one from Kandros was tempting, but it didn't have any of the emergency flags on it, so it could wait. It *would* wait. Eight damned hours, they could give her that much more.

She'd earned it, hadn't she?

Sloane slept like a rock.

A rock then kicked loose by a careless boot to tumble down the mountain.

She woke eight hours later, sore and famished. It had been a long few days out in the "wasteland" with Kesh and her team. This was the term they'd adopted for the parts of the Nexus that hadn't yet been visited.

They only used it among themselves, Kesh explained, so as not to offend or worry any of the non-krogan crew. The fact that they'd let Sloane in on the slang was something of an honor. She'd learned a long time ago that when the krogan honored you, you don't take it lightly, no matter how inconsequential it might seem.

She'd worked alongside them, clearing debris and pulling cable with the no-nonsense attitude they maintained. They didn't need security at their side. She needed the work. To lose herself in it. To—

Suddenly the message from Kandros registered front and center in her mind. "See you soon," the subject had read.

A knot formed in her gut. He'd never seemed the suicidal type, but those words weren't like him, and this was just the kind of thing she kept dreading would happen.

Sloane fell off her borrowed couch and fumbled around looking for her omni. She found the thing and almost dropped it twice trying to get it activated. Nervous, she tapped with a shaking finger through the menus until she found it.

"Sorry I didn't get to say goodbye," she read aloud, though at a whisper. "Should be back in a few months. Thanks for the opportunity." That was it.

"What. The. Fuck," she added, without even noticing the growing anger loaded on each word. Sloane slumped back against the cushions and stared at the wall. Months for what? "What goddamn *opportunity*?"

Kandros had given no details. Which meant he assumed she already knew what he was talking about. Sloane pushed herself upright, turned and marched, fists balled, toward Operations.

Sloane stormed past the two techies at the console, in their fruitless vigil. "Any sign of the arks?" she asked, not waiting for their answer because they always replied with the same damn thing.

"Negative," they said to her back.

Sloane laughed, sardonically.

Tann was at the main navigation table, stooped over one of the maps, one hand at his chin, finger tapping away. He lifted his big eyes at her entrance and his face brightened considerably. "Welcome ba—"

"Where's Kandros?"

"I… errr…" Her tone, as she'd hoped, had him already backpedaling.

"Where. The *fuck*. Is Kandros?"

"Aboard the shuttle called *Boundless*," Tann said.

"So I would assume, then," she replied, "that if I were to stroll down to the Colonial Affairs hangar, I'd find him there?"

"Ah, well, of course not." Tann gestured to the table in front of him, and Sloane finally focused on what he'd been so intent on reviewing when she'd come in. A three-dimensional map of the space around them, crudely done, but the Nexus at the center gave it away. Tann pointed at a small glowing icon some distance away from the station.

"They're here, now. Roughly speaking, I mean. We have no way to be precisely sure."

Sloane came around the table, grabbed the salarian by his chin, and squeezed hard.

"Why is the ship gone, and why is my officer on

board?" He could barely mouth a reply. Sloane eased up, but only just.

"Spender—"

"Spender," she repeated. "Enough said." She patted Tann on the cheek and walked away.

William Spender. The name wormed through her mind as she stormed toward his quarters. He'd taken over a glorified closet near one of the empty hangars they'd converted into storage space. Her omni-tool said he was there, and she could have just ordered him to come to her, but somehow it felt like a personal visit was in order. Her omni-tool told her other things, as well. It wasn't just Kandros.

Eight of her officers were missing.

Sloane positioned herself in front of the door to his little cave and rapped hard on it.

"What now?" an annoyed voice asked from within.

"Open up," she shot back. "Or do I need to kick the door down?"

"Oh," the reply came. "Sloane. Thought it was that thug from life support again. Nnebron."

"Sorry to disappoint. Open up."

"Just a minute."

"No. Immediately." She heard rustling within. "I'm giving you five seconds, and then I'm going to see just how sturdy this door is." She'd barely uttered the last of that when the door pulled suddenly inward.

Spender squeezed himself out of the pitch-black room and yanked the door closed behind him. "Sorry. Room's a mess. We can talk in the commons, maybe?"

He took a step in that direction, avoiding her gaze. Sloane slammed her fist into the wall, a mere centimeter from his nose, and held it there. Spender slowly turned to face her.

"Okay, here's fine."

"I want you to explain to me why Kandros and seven other officers under my command are no longer aboard the Nexus."

"The scouting mission," Spender replied.

"What scouting mission?"

The man blinked, his brow furrowed slightly. "You don't know?"

"Obviously I don't know."

"Seems to me you need to speak with Tann and Addison."

"I'm here, now, speaking to you. Start talking."

He looked like he'd just swallowed a hunk of rancid meat. Sloane didn't budge, not even a little, and the man withered under her stare.

"It was decided that eight ships—"

"Decided by whom?"

"Well, Tann... with you and Addison in support, naturally."

Sloane filed that. She could guess the rest, but watching Spender squirm proved oddly satisfying. Sloane twirled a finger. *Go on.*

To her extreme annoyance, Spender grinned at her. "You weren't consulted," he said more to himself than to her. Then he glanced at her fist. "Can't say I'm surprised."

"Spender, I'm going to send you on a solo scouting mission, unsuited, if you don't tell me what I want to know."

The weaselly grin faltered only a little. "I was informed that you guys had decided it was time to send a few CA ships out to the nearest star systems. Look for supplies, you know?"

Sloane leaned in until her nose almost touched his.

"Stop assuming what I know or don't know. Just talk."

"Okay, okay, jeez." He licked his lips. "Addison informed me of all this. The decision, the plan."

"She said I was in agreement?"

"Er, I don't recall the exact words. She didn't say you weren't. I didn't ask. It was implied, I guess."

Sloane frowned. "Keep talking."

"Well," he said, "she said they—you—they wanted to send eight shuttles, with full crews, and that I was to draw up the lists of who would go." Before she could ask the question he raised his hands, palms out, pleading. "I thought you were aware. Okay?"

"Why Kandros? You know how much I rely on him."

"Addison," he started. "No, wait. Don't go blaming her."

"I'll blame whoever the fuck I want. Just give me the facts."

"Addison sent me this message, while I was prepping the rosters. About how Kandros was ideally suited to lead one of the ships."

Sloane couldn't argue, but that wasn't the point. Spender continued.

"I thought that meant she'd cleared it with you. I mean, you were gone with the krogan, how was I supposed to know? How'd that go, by the way?"

"What? How'd *what* go?"

"With the krogan."

"Don't change the subject. I'm the one asking questions." Sloane lowered her arm, though. Her anger had transformed. Blinding rage to the more thoughtful sort. Addison and Tann had done this. Spender was just a tool, in every sense of the word.

"Get the hell out of my sight."

He straightened his coat, looked her up and down, then walked off. Seconds later she stood alone in the hall, staring at the door to his quarters through which he'd emerged like a snake from its hidey hole.

Sloane stood there for a long time, fists clenching and unclenching. Half of her wanted to march back to Operations, throw Tann into the wall and swing him around by the feet until she could toss him into Addison and watch the bosom buddies tumble to the ground.

The other part of her wondered what the point was, though. They'd teamed up against her. It was easy to think that. Easy to assume, as Spender had. Assumptions were dangerous though, and Sloane could make other assumptions, too. Could hear Tann's reasoned, nonchalant excuses already.

You were the one who stepped away from your duties, Sloane. You said you knew I'd make decisions whether I had your advice or not, so what difference did it make? We were only doing what we're supposed to do. We thought you'd be pleased.

The Kandros bit, though, that made her fume. The rest of it? *Okay, fine, you sent some shuttles. Not the end of the universe.* But deliberately or not they'd taken one of her best people out from under her, for *months* the message had said, and she knew—hoped at least—that he wouldn't have agreed unless he believed she was on board with the idea.

He wouldn't have thought that, not with any kind of certainty, unless Spender had really sold him on it.

Weasel, she thought, sourly. She punched the wall again. Thought about kicking his door in after all, just to toss the room about a bit, like they used to do when they had a suspect they couldn't quite nail down, but wanted to send a message.

The problem was, until she could talk to Kandros, find out who told him what and when, there was no way to know exactly what had happened. For now, she decided, she'd have to swallow this. Pretend it didn't bother her, if only to make calling them on it later that much sweeter.

In the meantime, she'd keep a very close eye. To do otherwise was too dangerous.

CHAPTER TWENTY

"Hey, Reg? You better come quick, man."

Reg cracked open a crusted eyelid, expecting to see the bunk he shared with his husband empty. That was the usual. Most times, Emory was gone by the time Reg woke up, and Reg was often up too late for Emory.

This time, in the shadows lit by a faint blue glow, he was very much aware of the weight pressed in against his side, and Emory's breath on his shoulder.

That meant it was somewhere past his bedtime, and before Emory's wake-up.

His surly glare lifted to the culprit. A roommate. One of several who swapped in and out per shift. What was his name? Aldrin. Alder. Something. "What is it?" he grumbled, careful not to shake his sleeping botanist awake.

The guy lifted his light, the better to outline the path to the door. "It's your crew," he said, whispering. "The asari. She's tearing up the commons."

Ah, shit. Irida, not again.

Exhaustion clung to his muscles, gritted up his eyes. Reg wanted nothing more than to nestle back in, arm around his husband, and go back to sleep for the few hours they got.

Instead, knowing he had no other choice, he carefully eased his arm out from under Emory's motionless body. The cot creaked as he shifted over, then rolled off to land heavily on his feet.

Emory stirred. "Nn?"

Wincing, Reg reached up and smoothed back Emory's pale brown hair. "Go back to sleep, babe," he said, and dropped a kiss on his forehead. "I'll be back."

"Nn."

With any luck, Emory wouldn't even remember the exchange. The man was as ragged as Calix and his unit were. As Reg himself was.

And Irida, she'd taken Na'to's death hard.

Muttering under his breath, Reg pulled the crumpled uniform on over his boxers and T-shirt, aware that all of them could use a good washing. Rations meant less wash, more wear. A fact he found skin-crawling, but necessary.

By the time he joined the human—Alden, for sure—out of the quiet dorm, he was a little more awake.

A lot more resigned. "Let me guess," he said as he made his way to the commons. "She's throwing things again?"

"Shields, mostly."

Reg blinked at him. "What?"

Alden shook his head. "Just... man, you'll see."

And he did. It was hard to miss. A handful of people loitered outside the commons, in various stages of upset, while a few clustered around the door. From inside, Reg could hear shouting. Yelling. Swearing.

And crashes. Tables, he figured. Dishes. Hardy stuff, the things in commons, which made it easy to throw.

Heaving a sigh, he edged into the crowd, pushing them aside with a burly strength nobody wanted to contest. Reg had that going for him, at least. He was big. A brawny guy, with a head to keep it that way. It made for an unusual pairing, what with Emory's slim nerd-build, but it made him happy to think he could protect his husband if it came to it.

Much as he wanted to protect his team.

Especially, he thought as he pushed his way fully into commons, the ones still reeling after Na'to's loss.

Irida had, as Alden suggested, been playing with shields. Two people were held aloft in biotic balls of energy, both swearing up a storm, while another rolled across the floor. Irida sat on the table in the middle of a mess of them, many shoved aside or turned over, drinks pooling in a combined morass of sweet and sour and sharply alcoholic.

He cringed as he stepped over a brew that smelled krogan.

He ought to know. Wratch and Kaje had dragged him out to "celebrate" after Arvex and Na'to went up in Scourge smoke. He'd barely escaped with his intestines intact.

Two of the Nakmor grunts now sat in the corner, nursing their drinks without care. If they were at all bothered by the asari's display, they didn't seem to show it.

Irida glared at him. "Look! Pets." A wave of her hand sent one biotic shield slamming into the other.

Reg winced as they yelped. Shouted.

Slowly, he lifted a hand, inserted his body between her sight and her playthings. The bottle in her other hand tipped toward her mouth.

"Irida," he sighed. "Come on, you don't drink well."

"I drink," she said curtly, *"just fine."*

Crash! A table. One shield flickered, winked out. The human went rolling ass over elbows and lay stunned just in front of the door. "Call... Call security!"

"No, don't," Reg called over his shoulder. "She's

just…" Drunk. Hurting. *Grieving.* "She's working through it. I got this."

"Yeaaaaaah," the asari slurred, leaning forward. The bottle she cradled tipped its contents.

More krogan brew.

Damn.

Reg took a few steps closer. Reached out to encircle the bottle with gentle fingers. His hand engulfed most of it. "Come on, Violet. Let's go walk this off."

"No!" She jerked. A sharp scream and crash said the other shield had fizzled out, leaving its prisoner free to clamber unsteadily to freedom.

Reg's heart ached for the girl. However old she was, whatever years she had on Reg, he didn't need to be ancient to see how badly she was coping. The team had been together for years. Served together. Fought together.

He tried for logic. "Come on. You know we're getting rationed, let's not make it worse for the boozers, huh?"

"Rationed." She spat the word. "What good?" She tugged at the bottle. Seemed confused when it didn't so much as budge under Reg's grip. "Rations won't bring 'im back."

His gut kicked. Sorrow plucked at his voice as he murmured. "I know, Violet. I know. But Na'to, he wouldn't want you to wreck yourself—or the commons," he added, looking around, "like this."

"How'd you know?" She glared at him, with her pale purple eyes wide and wet. "How'd anyone know?"

"Shit," murmured someone behind him. "She's a mess."

He glanced over his shoulder, saw Nnebron as he edged his way in. His smile, Reg knew, was sad. "Yeah," he said quietly. "Come on, let's get her somewhere quiet."

Wordless now, Nnebron approached on Reg's left, popping out with a smile from behind the larger man. "Hey, Violet, you game to help me with something?"

She stared at him, bemused. Swaying. "Maybe." She didn't fight when Reg looped an arm around her shoulder. "Will I need my leathers?"

"Her what?"

"Commando leathers," Reg muttered to Nnebron. The kid stared at him.

"No," Reg added for Irida's sake. "Not tonight."

She nodded, allowed herself to be helped off the table. "'Kay. Next time?"

"Next time," Nnebron said firmly. "Right now, I got a powerful need for some help, uh…" A pause. "Uh, for…"

"Nnebron needs an escort," Reg said quickly. "He's struggling with some power conduits. You wanna help?"

Irida shrugged, and as they led her across the floor, her bleary, watery eyes focused on the crowd.

Her mouth twisted. "Cowards," she spat.

"Whoa!" Nnebron put his arm around her waist, helping her while Reg moved forward to guide— and ultimately shove—a path through the staring, muttering crowd.

"They jus'… they jus' sat… and watched…"

"Oh, girl." Nnebron's voice wavered. "Come on. Let's go drink this off."

"Gonna show them," she said as they half-pulled, half-led her down the corridor. She turned over her shoulder, her features set in acid lines. "Gonna show you! You don't understand… What happens when they start this!"

"Okay, Irida," Reg murmured, exchanging a look with Nnebron.

"First people die," she shouted, stumbling. Reg held her up. "Then rations! It won't end!"

Nnebron and Reg, they knew. They'd been there. Death. Starvation.

A leadership that would do anything to save their own asses.

"Not until we do something," Irida said miserably.

Nnebron and Reg both laced an arm around her waist, all but carrying her between them as they strode away from the silent, staring commons. "Okay," Nnebron said patiently. "Okay. But first, maybe we drink to the memory of the best damn salarian we've ever known."

Reg nodded in exaggerated agreement, until Irida noticed and tipped her head in mimicry. "Sounds good, right? Let's drink to Nacho."

"To Nacho," Irida repeated.

Nnebron's smile didn't reach his eyes. "To Nacho."

"They'll see," the asari whispered.

"We'll be okay."

||||||||||||||||

Weeks. Goddamned *weeks* of watching her compatriots like a hawk, reconfiguring her security patrols and duties to cover the eight officers stolen from her, and dealing with more and more outbursts among the rationed. The reasons didn't matter—they all varied, anyway. Tempers were short. Fears were high. Stomachs were empty. Water almost gone. One wrong word, a look, a gesture…

Hell, Sloane had been awake for less than fifteen minutes before she had to bust up a brawl between a krogan and some idiot who didn't understand lethal differences in weight categories.

Her head hurt.

All this because what? The slim hope that their scouts would find some nearby garden of bountiful delights? That the Pathfinders wouldn't run into the Scourge themselves and wind up torn to shreds before anyone even woke to know about it?

A grim thought, even for Sloane.

The tension in the Nexus was palpable, a sort of stretched hope and rising desperation. She felt it in the corridors, in the galley and mess hall, in the training rooms her sec forces used to release whatever stress they could.

Rations were getting tight. Tighter by the day. Even so, Addison's faith in the scout ships remained unwavering—a slim beacon of hope slowly bleeding those who held onto it. Faith, *determination*, was strained.

Along with everyone's tempers.

Definitely Sloane's.

She paced hydroponics because at least the budding green hope of future food felt more peaceful than the bare, stark metal and busted plating of the Nexus halls. The krogan were *everywhere*, handling emergencies, rebuilding hydropod frames, shoring up tattered bulkheads. Sloane hated to admit it—if only because of the prejudices they couldn't seem to shed— but Kesh's krogan workforce was a goddamn lifesaver.

Literally.

They were also big, and a unit, for all intents and purposes. So far willing to work under rationed sanctions, but for how long? They didn't eat light.

Yet another concern among the many Sloane had vying for top priority in her head. The krogan. Tann's increasing willingness to ignore her advice, if he even sought it in the first place. The near constant stream of scraps, arguments, and quibbles. Those could turn big, fast—and then what?

Sloane paused in front of one of the shattered hydroponic frames, staring blankly at it while she chewed on that question. Across from her, a krogan grunted as another brought him—her?—a panel to weld onto the frame.

The hiss of the seared metal and the wicked orange flare of the krogan's omni-tool lit them both to a wild hue, flickering in and out like a demented strobe light.

Sloane frowned. She imagined what would happen if Kesh's workforce decided enough was enough, that their labors weren't to be taken for granted, or that their bellies needed to be full if they were going to keep up this frenetic pace. She tried to picture her security force standing up to a horde of angry krogan, and shuddered. If things tipped too far, she'd have no choice but to turn her forces on them.

The very idea of it made her queasy.

She tucked a fist against her sternum. Heartburn that had been simmering there for the past week, and she made a face as it gurgled.

Addison said she stressed too much. That she needed a break. Maybe she did. Maybe she stressed just enough. Either way, it didn't matter. This was Sloane's job—and despite what snide data-pushers thought about her straightforward way of getting things done, Sloane Kelly didn't enjoy using her officers as a threat mechanism.

None of this could be blamed on the crew. They were hungry, scared people. That still couldn't be an excuse to let them go wild. Somehow, morale needed to be raised.

But, shit, how?

Sloane growled under her breath as she spun and paced the distance back to the farthest hydroponics bay. This one gave off a warm glow, nurtured by the light designed to stimulate ecologically sound plant growth. All the hopes in the galaxy rested on these fragile little green blots. Well, on them, and on the scouts Addison had sent out.

Prognosis? Not good—and for the first time in her life she couldn't blame the leadership, because she was the goddamn leadership.

"Shit," she hissed, reflexively clenching her fist. She wanted to punch something. Anything. *And how would that look?* Who knew how people would react. Sloane didn't want to be the flame that lit the damn fuse. No matter how good a brawl might feel right now.

Fortunately for her unraveling temper, Talini interrupted her brooding with a well-timed comm chime.

"What?" Sloane snapped, barely giving the asari time to register the visuals much less offer a greeting. Less fortunately for Sloane's unraveling temper, the asari didn't look like she had good news.

"We need you in maintenance, deck eight." Flat. Grim. "There's been an accident." Behind the digitized tension in Talini's voice, Sloane heard shouting. Pain. Anger.

The fucking fuse already?

"On my way," Sloane said abruptly as she spun on her heel. The krogan watched her go, only the briefest pause in the clanging accompaniment to their work.

||||||||||||||||||

The first indication of trouble met Sloane the moment the elevator doors hissed wide. Darkness hid half of the corridor, the other half illuminated in stuttering pulses by lights struggling to maintain connectivity to the grid. Emergency lights bloomed red where they worked, flickered weakly where they didn't.

Two medical personnel flanked a stretcher in the hallway. It held a salarian security tech. Green blood stained the emergency bandaging wrapped around his neck, shoulder, and chest. He gave her a weak grin and an even weaker salute, cringing with the effort.

"Be still, Jorgat," one of the medical crew said crisply. "Ma'am," he added to Sloane.

"How is he?"

"Lucky," he replied with a bluntness that told her more about her teammate's condition than anything else.

"I'll be fine," Jorgat wheezed. Behind the words came a gurgle Sloane didn't like. She put a hand on the stretcher to stop it, halfway onto the lift. The doors binged unhappily at the interference.

The medics frowned at her.

"Who did this?" she asked, ignoring them in favor of the watery-eyed salarian. She bent over the stretcher to keep him from having to speak up. "What happened?"

He coughed, and flecks of green speckled her uniform. He managed, at least, a brittle laugh, even if it bubbled.

"Was a fool," he wheezed. "Let myself get distracted."

"An accident?" Sloane asked, her voice low to keep the rumors from spreading. She needed to put a lid on this, whatever *this* was, and fast.

Jorgat shook his head weakly. She understood.
Sabotage.

One of the technicians tugged at her arm.
"Ma'am—"

"Go ahead." Sloane let the stretcher continue,
stepping entirely out of the way. The salarian's large
eyes closed in pain. "Take care of him," she added.

"We will," the woman at the front said.

The doors closed on Jorgat's coughing fit.

Did salarian lungs collapse like humans' did? If
so, it would explain the sounds. Nothing time and
care and proper medical technology couldn't fix, but
as a spike of anger jammed into the back of her brain,
Sloane's fists clenched. That didn't matter.

He shouldn't even have to be in this position.

Sabotage. Someone had hurt one of her crew.

Someone had hurt more than just Jorgat, Sloane
realized as she strode down the corridor. The hollow
feeling in her gut grew with each step. Bodies
hunkered against the plating in the uncertain light,
cradling various wounded limbs and digits. Burns,
mostly. Electrical? Chemical?

Talini waited by a large door, a datapad in her
hand. She used it to emphatically wave Sloane down.
A deep furrow creased her brow, but a once-over told
Sloane the asari hadn't been part of whatever had gone
down. No wounds, unbloodied uniform.

Sloane dragged a hand over her face, pushing
strands of hair from her eyes. "Speak to me," she said.
The asari gestured at the knot of uniformed technicians
filing in and out of the half-open doors.

"A pipe carrying coolant to one of the server rooms
burst. It burst about fifteen minutes ago."

Sloane looked back at the array of injured crew.

"That's a lot of damage for a busted pipe."

"High pressure," Talini replied. She flipped the datapad in her hands and pulled up the information she'd been busily recording. "This is one of the main processor hubs. Kept cooler than others for obvious reasons, but high-pressure conduits were used because they're—"

"Cost effective," Sloane finished dryly. "Yeah, I've heard the pitch." The asari handed her the data. It didn't mean much to her, but she got the gist—at the critical moment in the timeline, the pressure sensors went off the chart.

"There were some concerns about the amount of pressure it'd take to keep the coolant flowing, but eventually it was cleared."

"Except?"

"Except," Talini replied with a sigh, "in case of manual override."

Sloane's half-smile felt brittle. "Right. Jorgat says he was distracted?"

She nodded. "He says that the shift change for server maintenance had just begun. He knows almost all of them by face, at least, since he's been stationed down here for a while."

Sloane looked down the corridor, where lights peppered on and off in mimicry of the ones behind her. "Did he see an unfamiliar face then?"

"No." Talini gestured back, moved toward the server room, and beckoned Sloane to follow. "In the middle of the shift-change, while a few of the techs were swapping the usual greetings, Jorgat says he heard something strange from *inside*. He came in to look—"

Sloane gasped when she stepped inside. Her breath immediately fogged, and ice crystals shuddered precariously from panels, plating, and dashboards. Although the physical damage looked minimal, Sloane picked out immediately where the worst of it had occurred. A solid spread of scratched, bent, scarred material.

"As you can see," Talini continued grimly, "the paneling didn't stand a chance."

"Neither did that pipe." Sloane frowned, tracing the signs of damage back to the wall that had buckled under the coolant pressure. It had been shut off already, which she imagined would strain the servers for now, but that wasn't her immediate problem. The fact that ice still clung to every surface, and the number of coolant-burned limbs in the corridor behind them, made it obvious how cold it really had been.

She raised a hand to the hole in the wall, testing the edge of the metal. It was still bitterly cold. The edges of the rift peeled outward like a blooming flower. The busted pipe and various other innards had launched shrapnel out into the room.

Sloane looked back over her shoulder, mentally mapping the spread. Jorgat would have been standing right where Talini stood now. Dead on in that path.

Damn, the medic had been right. Jorgat had been *very* lucky. Sloane frowned, angry and frustrated in a tidy bundle called *pissed off*.

"What was the sound he heard?" she asked over her shoulder.

The asari tilted her head, then scanned her data again. "He said, and I quote, 'Something like a reverse explosion, a kind of *whoomp*, but backward.' End quote."

"Mm-hm." She leveled a look on the asari that she hoped didn't reveal the seething anger roiling up in her chest. "Do me a favor, Sergeant. Pop up one of those circular vortex things of yours." She gestured. "Toward the ceiling."

Talini wasn't anybody's idea of a dumb broad. Sloane's smile showed teeth as comprehension dawned on the asari's pale blue features.

"Yes, ma'am," she said, and gathered her biotic energy, however biotics did it. Sloane didn't know. She'd gratefully never been a biotic. The humans who were, in her experience, had some killer side effects—at least back in the day. Time and technology had apparently gotten better, but Sloane was old school.

Asari, on the other hand, all seemed naturally inclined. Talini pulled a singularity out from, well, wherever, forcing a rift in reality that sort of... reverse-popped.

Sloane nodded.

"That sound like a backward explosion to you?"

The purple and blue strains of biotic energy whirled, and even from this distance Sloane could feel strands of her hair lifting. They were too far away to succumb to the wonked-up gravity, but it disoriented her all the same.

"That could do it." Talini turned her frown on the rift. "Given the pressure and the chemicals inside, mixing it up via biotics could produce a bottleneck large enough to cause this."

"A biotic, then. Asari?"

"It could be an implanted human," Talini murmured.

"I don't remember anyone cleared on the wake-up roster, do you?"

"No. At least not anyone with that strong a grasp on the ability," she admitted.

"We should go over crew logs," Sloane said. "Just to be sure."

"But you think it was an asari."

"Any krogan throwing biotics around you know?" Sloane asked dryly.

Talini thought about it. Seriously. "No battlemasters around here. Only one I ever heard of was of the Urdnot clan."

She was serious. Sloane stared at her, then gave up the thread entirely and said instead, "Let's investigate the rosters anyway."

Talini nodded again, keying in a few items to her datapad. The screen glowed as she lowered it to study the large network room. "This begs the question—why here?"

Sloane wondered the same thing. The answer, unfortunately, wasn't too difficult to assume. "Server room, right? Information." She jerked a thumb at the hole in the wall as she strode back toward the doors. "That's a distraction. Like Jorgat said. Find some techs capable of going over entry logs. I want this place examined from every angle. You sit down with one of our info-sec crew and access the visual registries. *Quietly*, Talini. Rumors of espionage or sabotage are the last thing we need right now."

"Yes, Director," Talini responded smartly. She turned and followed Sloane out. The door hydraulics whirred, shuddered, but couldn't close. Jorgat's impact had jammed one side off its track.

Whoever did this, whoever put one of her own in the medical ward and put the lives of these techs in jeopardy... Sloane's hands clenched again. Her teeth locked down on a series of words Talini didn't deserve hearing.

She'd find them.

No more crew members would die on the Nexus. No more civilians, no more techs, *no more*. This was her station. She'd go down protecting the people in it.

Especially from themselves.

॥॥॥॥॥॥॥॥॥॥॥

Irida Fadeer might have swapped her commando leathers for an engineer's uniform, but that didn't mean she'd lost her touch. Breaking and entering wasn't the hard part. A few decades ago she might have relied on brute strength to get the job done, but technical expertise plus experience made it simpler than that.

Not without some casualties, she admitted silently as she left the engineering bunkroom. She'd done her best, but humans had this saying about breaking eggs to create meals, right? Fortunately, no one had died.

A big plus in her ledger.

The other plus being the database she'd acquired. Calix had told them to keep an eye on their supplies, but it wasn't enough. Between the rations and the rising tension that filled the station, Irida knew something would break soon. They all knew. Calix was ahead of the game, at least, but worst-case scenario? They'd have supplies, but no information. Information made all the difference in situations like this. Especially the kind she'd taken. The protected stuff. The things they didn't want anyone to have.

The contents were too much for her to fully digest. She skimmed enough to know it was a true prize, though. Patrol routes. Camera placements. Plenty more, no doubt. Calix could do a lot with that kind of knowledge. Protect themselves, their supplies, and the people still in stasis.

She couldn't help her smile. It felt good to do something to ensure the safety of her unit, her crew. Calix deserved that, and so much more. He'd stood up for her, for all of them, before. He'd do it again, and this time she'd have his back, too.

"Feeling proud of yourself?"

Irida froze as the security director's nonchalant voice rolled out from the corridor ahead of her. Sloane Kelly stepped around the corner, her hands empty, gaze sharp as a vorcha smile. Irida blinked. Her insides lurched, but she simply widened her grin and nodded respectfully.

"Director?" she said. Easily. A greeting, a little inquisitive. But behind her, she sensed as much as heard more security officers move into place. *Damn it all.* So she hadn't been as careful as she'd hoped. Had the salarian seen her after all?

Maybe she should have killed him when she had the chance. Just to be sure.

Too late now. Sloane prowled closer. There was no other word for it—not that Irida could summon. She understood Calix's respect for the woman, but this put both of them in a bad spot.

"Irida Fadeer," the director said. "You are under arrest for breaking and entering, destruction of Nexus property—"

"To say nothing of asari, salarian, and turian property," said a woman's voice from behind Irida. She was trapped.

Ugh, great. That meant Irida would have even less luck popping out of this one. She'd *seen* the sec-force asari at work.

"*Destruction of Nexus property*..." Sloane repeated loudly, with a twitch under her eye that did more to cause Irida concern than anything else. She frowned, taking a half step back.

"Wait a minute, Director, what am I supposed to have—"

Sloane didn't let her finish. With surprising speed and greater strength than Irida expected, the human pulled back a fist and rammed it hard, fast, and ugly into Irida's face. She grunted at the impact, hit the corridor wall and rebounded into a wobbling pile at the security team's feet. Stars swam in her eyes. Her cheek went from a strange tingle to sudden howling anguish.

Irida shook her head. No use.

She should have seen this coming. Hell, she should have planned on it, but for all Irida's mercenary experience, she never would have expected a human Alliance officer to break protocols.

"…and for assaulting one of my team and fourteen Nexus crew," Sloane snarled, panting. Irida didn't know much about the woman, but as the security team wrapped hard fingers around her upper arms and dragged her to her feet, she knew one thing for certain—no Alliance, not even Sloane Kelly, would attack someone without being absolutely certain of the facts.

She'd been caught. A quiet rage welled in her, at herself more than anything.

"Take her to the brig," Sloane snapped. "Prep her for questioning. And search her goddamn bunk," she added sharply as she turned on her heel and strode away. Irida sniffed hard. The blue splatter of her own blood left dark streaks down her shirt. Pain danced in her sinuses. Her cheek felt as if it were on fire.

This was it. The end for her.

"Got anything you want to say?" It was the human holding onto her. Irida's gaze slid to the asari gripping her other arm. Nothing. No help, no sympathy there.

Ah, well. Sisterhood only went so far.

"No," she said, and spit a wad of blue-tinged mucus to the floor. If nothing else, she'd be damned if she took anyone else down with her. That part at least she'd done right. Calix knew nothing of her actions, and could not—would not—be dragged into this.

Mentally, Irida dug in. The Initiative wouldn't execute her—they wouldn't dare. Worst case, she'd be put back in cryo, like that bunch that had tried to steal a shuttle. And who was it who could override stasis pods?

At least, she figured as her escort double-timed her to the lift, she'd get some much-needed sleep.

The doors closed on her smile.

CHAPTER TWENTY-ONE

Eos loomed dead ahead, an eerie crescent against the veins of the Scourge and the starry backdrop far beyond.

"Anything yet?" the captain asked, voice aimed at his science officer.

The turian shook his head, saying nothing.

"How is this possible? We're right on top of it, for fuck's sake."

The bridge of the tiny shuttle was crowded, even down two members who lay sedated in crash-bunks just aft. More victims of the Scourge, and not likely the last. Right now, though, it wasn't the injuries Captain Marco cared about, it was the goddamned sensors. The Scourge could make the tiny shuttle flop about like a fish on dry land, sure, but it absolutely annihilated any chance for a reliable sensor reading. Every scan came back different, or not at all. Despite Eos, the closest habitable world to the Nexus's current position, being right in front of them, the screens oscillated between empty space, several moons, an asteroid field, and even a sprawling fleet of quarian cruisers, depending on which second you happened to look.

His shuttle was as good as blind. The data couldn't be trusted. Yet they could all see the planet, growing ever larger.

He had to make a decision, and soon. It took only one glance at his haggard crew to know what they'd vote for: Head for home. Enough's enough.

Marco had no intention of doing that. Not yet. The Nexus couldn't afford for them to return empty-handed, and his crew knew it. They were just scared, and who could blame them?

"Captain?" his navigator called out. "In sixteen seconds we won't be able to escape the planet's gravity. If we burn now we can slingshot around and make for the Nexus. Let them know our—"

"Negative," he said. "We're not going back empty-handed."

No one spoke.

An eerie howling began somewhere at the nose of the ship and worked its way down her hull. Joints in the hull, grinding as the weird tendrils of the Scourge continued to toy with them.

"Nav, we're going to burn, but not to pass the planet by."

"You can't actually intend to land without sensors?"

"No," he admitted, "not land. But we're going to dip into that atmosphere and see what we can see."

Eos had a thick layer of high clouds, preventing a view of what bounty the surface might hold. Scans made, hell, centuries ago now, indicated plant life and plenty of water. A prime settlement candidate. Now, though, the sensors returned only gibberish. So they'd do it the old-fashioned way and take a look with their own eyes.

Again, no argument from his crew. They all knew what they were signing up for coming on this mission, but that didn't take the sting out of it. This was a hell of a dangerous maneuver, especially relying on visuals alone, and perhaps the anguished groans of the hull plating.

The engines roared, right on cue. Ahead, Eos

began to swivel as the small craft angled its thermally shielded side toward the green-gray clouds.

Marco didn't need to order everyone to strap in. They hadn't left their flight chairs since the first friendly love tap from the Scourge, about a million klicks out from the Nexus. By then the battered station had been too far behind them to hail, and the turbulence quieted down, as if daring them to go a little farther.

The planet blotted out the stars now, and the ropy blurred limbs of the Scourge. Sensors hadn't learned anything new about the phenomenon, either. Readings were garbage, totally useless, not to be trusted.

"Comms," Captain Marco said.

"Here," the engineer replied. Not a trained comms officer, but the woman had handled the task admirably.

"Keep trying to raise the Nexus, and the arks. All bands, all frequencies."

"I know," she said, not impatiently. He'd given the order before, twice, and she'd always been on top of the task.

"Transmit everything we see, understood? I don't care if it's scrambled. Maybe they'll figure out a way to decipher it. We have to try."

"Understood," she replied, a catch in her voice this time. There was more finality in his words than he'd intended, but nothing to be done about it now.

The shuttle began to rattle, and not from the Scourge this time. Eos's atmosphere had begun to scrape their hull.

His view became a maelstrom as flames began to lick and curl around the bottom of the craft. The hull shuddered under the stresses. The black of space began to transform into the high, dusty brown clouds.

In seconds they were enveloped, visibility

obliterated. Marco gripped the armrests until his knuckles went white.

All at once the violence ended. The clouds lifted. They were below it, and in danger now of dropping too far.

"Engines!" he shouted. "And roll us!"

The craft punched forward and, in the same instant, began to overturn.

Marco leaned forward, breath held tight in his chest.

Eos should have been a garden world. Lush, with long winding rivers and two shallow seas. So the scans had said, long before the Nexus even reached Andromeda.

He couldn't see well enough. Against his better judgment, Marco unlatched his harness and leaned as far as he could to press his face to the window.

The captain did not see gardens. Or forests. No jungles or vast canopies of giant trees.

He saw barren desert. Desolation. Dust.

And something else, too. A massive monolith that towered over all around, punching upward like a crystal shard. "What... is... that?" he asked aloud, each word a struggle.

"A wasteland," someone whispered, and Marco wondered if they meant Eos, or Andromeda itself.

Movement caught his eye, above. A snaking black tendril roiling with thousands of tiny explosions. It tore through the atmosphere, twisting and bending as if searching for something. As if—

The long finger of the Scourge bent and then slammed into the shuttle with the force of a hurricane. The ship heaved violently. Someone screamed. Marco thought maybe it was him. There came a smack as his skull slammed into the frame of the window, and everything went black.

Marco remembered falling, and pain, and words that sounded incredibly distant.

"Get us out of here," someone was saying. "Get us out!"

॥॥॥॥॥॥॥॥॥॥॥

"She's ready for questioning."

Sloane took the tablet Talini gave her, scanned it briefly. All the usual red tape was in order. After her brief and annoying conversation with Tann, she at least had that going for her.

Tann had demanded that she "handle it," which Sloane had every intention of doing, but she'd do it her way, not his. He thought throwing Fadeer into stasis would suffice. After all, it had made for a tidy end to the hostage-takers. A punishment that required no trial. Sloane had other ideas. Ones that included questions about Fadeer's motives. Her intentions. Her support.

The asari had a good record, she noted. Excellent references. Calix himself had vouched for her, including a sterling letter of reference for her service in his previous deployment on the *Warsaw*. Sloane pondered that. All of his team, at least the core group, had served with him there. And they'd all followed him here.

Interesting.

Whatever caused Irida to sabotage the Nexus and injure personnel along the way, it couldn't be anything as simple as Tann clearly hoped. Sloane needed to know for certain, though. She handed the datapad back.

"Has she said anything?"

"She asked for water. I got the sense it was meant to be ironic."

"How very clever." Sloane shook her head. "Anything else?"

"She says she'll be pressing charges for the assault."

Sloane snorted.

The asari took that as the answer it was. "I should also warn you that we're getting heat from the network techs injured in the sabotage."

"What do they want?"

"Answers, I'd suspect." She spread her long blue fingers in the universal gesture of *who knows*. "Retribution for some, compensation for others."

Sloane's lip curled. "Tough. We're not Omega." She rolled her shoulders, heard both of them pop from the tension. "Give them the usual line. If I hear of a *single* outburst, I'll lock them up, too."

"Yes, ma'am."

The asari would deal with the administrative bullshit, so Sloane's full focus was on Irida Fadeer. She'd walked the corridors until most of her anger burned off, yet plenty still simmered in her gut. The guard outside Fadeer's cell saw her coming, and opened it.

"Ma'am," he murmured.

The prisoner sat primly on the narrow bunk, her hands in her lap—and still in the biotic-proof full-hand shackles. Fadeer looked cool and calm. Blood was still smeared on her cheek, ruining the impression a touch. Just enough to make Sloane grimace. Okay, so maybe she'd get some censure for that one. Wouldn't be the first time.

"Director," Fadeer said in greeting. No fake smile this time. Just that mysterious air asari all seemed so fucking good at. Sloane stopped just inside the door. It closed behind her with a solid thump.

The asari didn't flinch.

That alone made Sloane want to start hitting things.

"Start. Talking."

"Without a lawyer? I think there's one in stasis," she added pointedly.

"This is an unofficial chat."

Fadeer's nose wrinkled. "Then maybe we can both get some answers. You seem sure I was the perpetrator. How do you know?"

"You tell me, smartass." Sloane tucked her hands behind her, military at ease—even if nothing in her body felt at ease. Not her muscles, not her gut, not her stewing anger.

The asari's nose unwrinkled into a faint smile. "I'm positive the salarian security guard didn't see me. None of the network technicians noticed me. So that leaves security footage." Her head tipped, the light glinting over her purple frill. "Except I avoided the cameras."

Sloane didn't like this tack, not at all. She took a step forward. "What were you looking for in the data core? What'd you take?"

Fadeer chewed on her lip for a moment, thoughtfully studying the security director. The urge to punch her—*again*—practically drilled a hole through Sloane's fraying temper, doubled when understanding dawned in the asari's gaze.

"You've tightened security, haven't you? What is it?" She smiled. "Hidden cameras? Automatic image capture when a network is accessed?"

Shit. Sloane said nothing, not aloud, but her scowl spoke volumes. It seemed to be all the answer Irida needed. A dark brow lifted.

"Director," the asari said coolly, "I don't believe the general populace agreed to secret surveillance, nor were we informed."

"Yeah, well, the *general populace* is what you assaulted with your stunt," Sloane snapped. She flung a hand out, her gesture taking in the entire Nexus beyond the small cell. "That extra security caught *you* in the act. The general populace can knock on my door and scream all day, as long as I'm putting criminals like you away."

"Tsk." The asari just spread her hands, wrist shackles clanking at the jointed center, and said musingly, "Well, that will be interesting to watch unfold." She turned her face forward, settling her hands back into her lap. "Good luck."

Sloane glared at the asari. An assault in the heat of the moment was one thing—it wasn't her first, and wouldn't be her last. She couldn't kick in Irida Fadeer's teeth, though, and get away without repercussions.

"The data, Fadeer. What did you access?"

Nothing.

"Is Calix Corvannis in on this? Does he know?"

There. A twitch. A bit of a frown.

"No."

"Then why? And who helped you?"

"I acted alone."

"Bullshit."

As if she had all the time in the world, the prisoner looked steadily ahead and said nothing else. That was that. She was done talking, which meant Sloane had two problems. She still didn't understand the motives of a saboteur, and the asari knew about the extra security.

She hadn't even told Tann or Addison.

Damn it.

Sloane turned and rapped on the door. The guard opened it and shut it hastily behind her. He even managed not to jump when Sloane turned and punched the door as it locked in place. Only the briefest flash of satisfaction crossed her features when the so-cool asari flinched on the other side.

"Orders, ma'am?" the guard asked. Sloane shot him a look that had him bracing for impact.

"Tell Talini I'm going to see a turian about a traitor."

"Er…"

"She'll figure it out," Sloane said curtly, and she strode away from the scene of her own bloody frustration. Maybe Fadeer's boss would have insight. Maybe he'd have the answers.

Maybe she'd have to arrest him, and the whole damn life-support crew.

Fucking great.

|||||||||||||||||

Calix preferred the comfort of his engineering surroundings first—obvious by how often she found him there—and the comfort of the Consort's chambers second. That one came by his own admission, and Sloane couldn't blame him. The asari Consort's chambers used to be a favorite of many Citadel visitors. Since there was no such thing here on the Nexus, and he wasn't to be found in engineering, she made her way to the commons.

It was late. Late enough that the only people in the area were quietly unwinding for sleep, using whatever was available. Books, some quieter music, dim lights, or in Calix's case, a glass of what was probably turian whiskey. He didn't seem the type to risk anything else. Dextro-amino acids had been carefully stocked and prepared for the turians on board, which provided an extra pinch to rations, yet they couldn't eat what the humans did.

He saw her enter, raised his glass in one hand. The dim light threw a sheen over his metallic carapace.

"Director Sloane. Come have a drink."

"I think I will, but not that stuff," she said as she approached. "I've got enough shit to deal with without adding literal—"

"I understand," he cut in dryly. His eyes gleamed. "You look like you've had a hell of a day." Calix watched her as she snagged a bottle of beer from behind the commons counter. His head tipped. It was faintly avian, she thought, which also made him seem harmless.

Sloane wondered just how true that was. She threw a leg over the closest chair and settled into a not quite easy comfort.

"Got a moment to talk shop?"

The turian blinked. "You want to… talk commerce? I don't mind, but it seems somewhat premature." It took Sloane a second to remember that turians, like salarians who didn't care to read up on human culture, tended to miss the metaphors.

"I *mean*," she stressed, a smile tugging at her lips despite her simmering frustration, "do you have time to talk about Nexus business?"

His expression cleared, mandibles moving as he chuckled. "Oh, that. Sure, Sloane. Or should I stick with director?"

She grimaced. "Sloane."

"Got it." He tipped his drink into his mouth in that unique way turians did, and Sloane took the opportunity to study him as she took a pull of her beer. There was a one-drink limit at the commons. Sloane had to make the best of it.

Calix didn't look like a turian managing a criminal enterprise. He was as relaxed as she'd ever seen him, though still as weary as ever. They all were. She watched him carefully as she, well, metaphorically ripped out the tooth.

"Irida Fadeer is in custody."

"Irida?" Another blink. "For what?"

"Sabotage, illegal access to secure networks, classified data theft." She ticked them off with raised fingers. "Causing a lot of collateral damage and casualties."

"Any deaths?"

"Not for the lack of trying," Sloane replied bitterly. "Half a shift is out of commission for a few days, and we've got a salarian in medical who's critical. Might be that by morning we'll be adding murder to the charges, instead of just attempted."

"Hell, I'm sorry." He rubbed at his crest with his free hand, looking up at the ceiling. "I don't know what to say."

"Were you involved?"

He went rigid at the accusation. She watched him, studied every line of his features. Some said turian faces were hard to read, but it wasn't so. Sloane spent enough time with them to get the gist. He was upset—though at the question, the casualties, or disappointment in Irida? She couldn't be sure. But he met her gaze with a forthrightness that somehow managed to reassure her.

"I had nothing to do with it. Nor," he added calmly, "did anyone else in my crew. I'll stake my job on it."

Sloane let out a relieved breath. She couldn't say *why* she believed him, but she did. He didn't prevaricate, didn't dodge the question or her stare. Her body relaxed a fraction more, and she took another swig from her bottle. The frothy beer fizzed going down.

"What did she take?" he asked. "You said classified."

Sloane tipped her beer, frowning down into the dark neck of it. Buying time, really. Deciding how much to say. Sloane decided to enfold him in her trust, get him on her side of this, lest his loyalty to Irida become a barrier.

"A database. Full of maintenance data, equipment placement, that sort of thing. I can't figure out why."

"Can't you?"

That got her attention. Sloane's gaze lifted to meet his. "Explain."

The turian let out a long, gusty sigh. He shifted in his chair, set the whiskey on his leg and cradled it there. "Think about it," he said slowly. "You've felt the tension in the air, right? People are worried."

"I know." She pulled a face. "It just adds to the real problems."

"It *is* a real problem," he corrected. "First we woke up in chaos, then we found our leadership dead." He gestured at her. "Suddenly, there were three people in charge nobody *really* knew. No offense to you or Addison, and okay, maybe a bit to Tann, but Garson was the heart and soul of this mission."

"Thanks for pointing out my lack of heart and soul," she cut in wryly. His eyes twinkled with returned humor, but he didn't stop to address it.

"You wake up a lot of people to get things back in order, they see the mess and lack of stores of food, not to mention this mysterious and downright dangerous Scourge looming all around us, and then you ask them to go back to cryo on faith that things will be okay. When they don't agree, they start getting rationed. Rations are inevitably cut, and people start getting hungry. They want answers. Hope. Will the scout ships return? Will the Pathfinders ever arrive? Will the Scourge finish us off? Patience dwindles by the day, Sloane."

The list annoyed her, mostly because he was right. She leaned forward, cradling her beer between both hands, braced her elbows on her knees, and scowled.

"Justification isn't what I'm interested in, it's motive."

"You humans have a saying for it," he said, unfazed by the irritation she didn't bother hiding. "Waiting for the shoe to fall?"

"Close enough."

"The pioneers aboard the Nexus have hit obstacle after obstacle." He gestured at the commons around them, which was deceptively quiet given the nature of their discussion. "Tensions are running high. Every emergency, accident, and failure leaves them feeling more exposed. Less safe. Leadership treats them like babies you can put down to bed—"

She couldn't help but snort. "You aren't a parent, are you?"

He laughed outright, shaking his head. "All right, perhaps that was a bad analogy. Point is, to them, leadership seems to want them to perform like VIs—on command, when necessary, power down when done. Like good little machines." He shrugged. "They're scared, Sloane. They think no one will protect them when that shoe falls. They don't want to be in cryo, helpless, when it happens."

She could see it now.

"By stealing that information," Sloane said slowly, thinking it through, "Irida could be ready when the shoe drops—she'd know where everything is, and perhaps how to get to it. But for what? A siege? A threat?"

"No," Calix said quietly. "Think about it the other way around. It's a ticket to some freedom. Maybe she just wants to make sure there's a place where she and others like her might feel *safe*."

"Great." Sloane rubbed at her forehead, then pinched the bridge of her nose between two tense fingers. "Meanwhile this presents a threat to everyone else on board. What are the odds she passed the data off to someone else?"

"Only she and whomever she may have talked to know for sure. The real question here, I think, is how do we stop the shoe?"

That was an excellent, *excellent* question. How did you reassure hungry, scared people that everything was going to be okay? Hold out hope for the Pathfinders? The scouts? Talk up hydroponics? Would an "everything is going to be okay" cover it?

Hell if Sloane knew.

Maybe Addison would. Maybe even Tann would have ideas that didn't involve forcing people back to sleep.

"If you don't mind me saying," Calix offered cautiously, "it may start with how you treat Irida." She scowled. "I know, I know, she's on my team and of *course* I want her treated well, but if she winds up out the airlock, if her punishment is perceived as a warning to others…"

She squinted at Calix, and thought of the way she'd carried herself during the arrest. The punch she'd thrown, and what she'd said. But more than that, the punishment Sloane herself had advocated back when those terrorists had tried to steal a shuttle.

"Do *you* think I'd space somebody over a dissenting opinion?"

His crack of laughter forced him to put a long hand over his drink to keep it from spilling.

"You? Nah. You're a hard woman, Sloane, but you're not completely heartless." At her grimace, he cocked his head again. "Why, is our 'acting director' spreading rumors?"

"If it helps his position." Now she grimaced. "Ugh, I shouldn't say that. I have no proof."

"Probably don't need any." He hummed a low note of wry humor. "He's a real piece of work, isn't he?"

Sloane's chuckle felt sharp in her chest. "And then some."

"Well, stands to reason."

"Because he's salarian?"

"Just an observation." Calix leaned forward, fingers curved around his glass so he could swirl its contents at her. "He's a numbers type. An 'at all costs' sort, right? It's important to him to keep the upper hand in a power play. After all, power is money."

It should have been *money is power*, but in this case, the turian was dead right. Tann, she admitted silently, would much rather have the power. "Whatever that'd net him on this floating wreck," she said aloud.

The turian's index finger uncurled from around the glass to point at her. "It'd net him plenty. Including full say over operations. I bet he wants a finger in everything."

Sloane grunted a laugh, uncomfortable at how cozy this conversation had become, but unwilling to draw a line. It felt good to talk to someone who understood the clusterfuck the council had become. Calix seemed to understand.

"Sorry I don't have better news, Sloane. Things are tough."

"Things are out of control," she replied.

"Why did you come here?"

"Fadeer. And the drink." She lifted her bottle in salute.

He studied her, slowly shaking his head. "I mean why did *you*, Sloane Kelly, security director, come to Andromeda?"

"A fresh start," she said automatically. Calix was too clever by far for this pat answer, though. And she didn't have any reason not to say. "Because I didn't have anything to leave behind. Because it was a chance to do things right, for once. To be better."

"You could have been better back home."

"This is home."

"You know what I mean."

Sloane looked away, gathering her thoughts. "It's hard to make things better," she said, "when you have so much momentum in a certain direction. Thousands of years of ingrained biases, time-tested laws that no one even remembers why they were written. Regs in place because that's the way it's always been done."

Calix inclined his head, agreeing, and also encouraging her to go on.

"That sort of cruft drives me insane," she continued, though she couldn't quite say why. "No, the problem with 'back home' is that even if you could be a catalyst for change, you can't hope to do more than get the process moving. And hope that, well after you're dead and gone, something works."

"You could have requested a post at some colony, far from the Citadel. Surely there's no shortage of out-of-the-way places where you'd have the rank needed to be in charge."

Sloane found herself nodding. "True. I thought about it, but that's a fresh start only for me. And eventually the colony would be drawn back into the fold, the day it's no longer considered irrelevant."

He chuckled dryly. "I'd say you're jaded, but that would be an understatement."

"Yeah, well," Sloane said, then trailed off. "Thanks for the drink, Calix."

"You got it."

Sloane downed the rest of her beer, then pitched it toward the receptacle. Calix watched it arc through the air. It clinked as it rebounded off the inner edge, then sank into the bin.

"A fraction to the left," he murmured, "and you'd be cleaning up glass."

"Story of my life, friend." Her smile showed teeth as she forced her weary body up from the chair. "Story of my fucking life."

The turian lifted his glass in solidarity—sympathy, acknowledgement, and good luck all in the tip of dark amber liquid.

She'd need it all before this ended.

⁞⁞⁞⁞⁞⁞⁞⁞⁞⁞⁞⁞⁞

Sloane went back to the security offices, dragging ass and she knew it. As she threw herself down into the nearest chair she wrestled with the truth—that Calix hadn't offered any answers. Just more questions, and the metaphorical shoe.

Had Irida Fadeer been working alone? Was she

after something specific? Rations, or other resources?

Were other Nexus personnel involved? If so, how many?

Talini looked up from her temporary desk, setting her tablet down gently. "Did you get anything from Corvannis?"

"Yes... and no."

The asari cupped her chin in her hand, elbow planted. "Let me guess. More questions?"

"How the hell do you do that?" Sloane muttered. "It's like you *know*."

"I just figured. There hasn't been much interaction on the feeds to indicate the existence of co-conspirators. Chatter between members of her team, of course, but we haven't found anything damning. They're just concerned for her, and angry with us. Typical. Judging from the surveillance, she acted alone, for what it's worth."

"Is it too much to hope that she's an independent?"

Talini shrugged. "There's a case for every scenario."

"Including the one that justifies sedition?" The asari's rueful smile told Sloane the answer. She cursed vividly. Cursed some more, and when Talini only shook her head, Sloane added a few in turian. For color.

When she finished Sloane leaned back in her chair and glowered at the ceiling, her mind furiously grinding on the facts. Calix had told her more than she'd asked. Made it clear and to her face that people were scared. It was one thing to feel it yourself, and something else entirely to hear it from someone else.

She rubbed at the back of her sore neck, wondering why she'd said as much as she had. An instinct, she supposed. An innate ability to spot the trustworthy, the loyal. The turian had shown her over and over that he'd work to the bone for this station. His team had, too.

So what set Irida Fadeer off?

A small cup of dark, steaming liquid clicked against the desk next to her elbow. Sloane glanced over, then sighed in unashamed ecstasy when the rich aroma of coffee filled her nose.

"I dipped into supplies," Talini confessed, nudging the cup closer. "You look like you need it."

Hell. Sloane wouldn't deny it. "Thanks." She picked up the cup and held it between her callused hands, absorbing its warmth, its fragrance. Talini rested a hand on Sloane's shoulder, in a brief moment of understanding.

"Hang in there."

"Best as we can." She glowered into the dark brew.

Six-hundred-year-old coffee. Fucking tragic, really. The coffee had aged better than all of them.

Sloane sighed. "All right. Let's get to work."

CHAPTER TWENTY-TWO

A pin drop would have boomed like thunder in the still room.

Foster Addison stood at the main console, behind two technicians seated in front of the only two monitoring stations that worked. Behind her, Tann paced. Sloane Kelly stood off to one side, leaning against the wall, arms folded across her chest. Addison could feel the pressure building inside the security director, like a balloon being flooded with air, flirting with that moment when the whole thing would burst.

Otherwise the modest control room within Colonial Affairs had been cleared of personnel. For security reasons. Addison studied the screen on the console, trying to temper her hopes as well as the growing ball of dread that lurked in her gut.

Six of the eight expeditions had returned, all empty-handed. The worlds they'd visited were in ruins, apparently ravaged by the same energy tendrils that had nearly destroyed the Nexus. What Tann had dubbed the Scourge.

Two of the returning ships had been heavily damaged, limping back to the station by the slimmest of margins. In one of those ships a reactor had failed as they rode the sudden wrath of a Scourge tendril. The entire crew remained in the infirmary, near death due to radiation poisoning.

The other ship had attempted to reach a promising

MASS EFFECT

moon in the local star system, Zheng He, only to find that one of the Scourge's larger tendril bands enveloped the entire rock, like a snake wrapped about its prey. Sensors were unable to penetrate the mysterious blanket, and the shuttle's captain had decided a landing would be too dangerous.

Four more vessels simply had met with similar results. Worlds seemingly once verdant were toxic wastelands, unable to provide anything useful.

Addison chewed on her lip. Not only had they failed to find a source for supplies or, barring that, a place to evacuate the Nexus, they'd also burned through a significant quantity of their rations in the process. Every returning ship was nearly empty, and their stores would have to be refilled if they were to fly again. Two of those were out of commission for repairs that might not even be possible to make with the parts on hand.

It had come to this—the last two. Addison couldn't look at Sloane Kelly. Her officer, Kandros, was on one of those ships. Addison had been partly responsible for sending him. Caught up in the excitement that her beloved idea was finally being taken seriously.

It wasn't her fault Sloane had been away, out of comm range, when the plan had been hatched. And few could argue Kandros's credentials. He was the perfect candidate to lead one of the missions.

Few could argue, yet it only took one. The security director hadn't taken the news well. In hindsight, Addison could see why.

"Hmm," one of the techs said. An older man named Sascha, human, gray at the temples with a calm way of going about his tasks. He hadn't been out of this room in more than a week—not since the reports started coming in—and he hadn't complained about it once. Same for the asari who was seated to his left. Both had been sworn to secrecy, an oath that would be taken very seriously since the arrest of Irida Fadeer.

Despite all the precautions, though, rumors had already begun to spread.

Doesn't much matter, Addison thought. *It's only a matter of time before we have to make an announcement.* The question was, would there be a celebration, or something decidedly less upbeat.

"Hrmm…"

"What is it, Sascha?" she asked.

"A blip."

"A blip?" Sloane repeated.

Sascha leaned in closer to his screen, pointing at an indicator. Addison had memorized these displays by now. Spent hours staring, hoping. The entire console had been rigged up from whatever parts people could scrounge, and part of her wished she didn't know the kind of kludges and scraps of code that were holding it all together.

In this case, a sensor used to inform the station's cleaning staff of a need for laundry service had been repurposed to listen for the transponder frequencies of the scout vessels. For a split second there, it had heard something. Then it had gone dark. Sascha leaned back, and let out the tiniest of sighs in impatient exhaustion.

"This is a waste of time," Sloane said. "Sensors can barely detect our own hull in this mess. We'd be better off with binoculars."

The light blinked again.

"There," Sascha said.

"I've got them now, too," the asari beside him said. Her name was Apriia, and while she lacked the calm demeanor of her counterpart, she more than made up for it in her attention to detail. The instant her screens noted the presence of the scout ship, the asari's hands began flying over the interface.

"Which one is it?" Sloane asked. "Get a reading before it vanishes."

Addison winced. She could see it already, but couldn't bring herself to answer. It felt like a betrayal, a weakness, to make Apriia say it, but she just couldn't.

"It's S7," the asari said. "Marco's ship. Mission target was a planet called... Eos."

Sloane gave no reaction. It wasn't Kandros, which meant they'd hear from him last.

"Try to establish a link," Addison said. "Quickly!"

"Already on it," Sascha replied.

Tann stopped his pacing and stood at Addison's side. They were in this together. He'd reminded her of this fact the first time an alert had gone out that one of the scouts had returned. Back then, though, Addison suspected his reminder had more to do with sharing in the glory. The fact that he still stood by her now—after six failures—said something about his character, at least. He could have distanced himself. Could have said she'd pressured him into allowing the scouts to go out, which wouldn't have been too far from the truth.

No, Tann had stood firm. They'd agreed to this, effectively cut Sloane out of the decision, and so its consequences were theirs to share, good or bad.

A loud pop sent Addison reeling, hands thrown up to protect her face as hot sparks showered her. Sascha went over in his chair. Apriia flew to her feet, backing away as flames began to flicker out from a gaping black hole that appeared on one of the borrowed bits of gear strewn about the workspace.

Addison blinked, turned to cry out in alarm, only to be elbowed aside by Sloane. The security director stepped in and sprayed the flame with an extinguisher she must have pulled from thin air. Fire out, she tossed the used-up device aside and was already kneeling beside Sascha when Addison's wits finally caught up.

With a shaking finger she tapped a message out on her omni-tool, sent directly to Nakmor Kesh with the highest of urgency. *Sec-cleared tech repair team needed in CA immediately. Most urgent.*

The reply came just seconds later. *Incoming.*

"Repair crew on the way," Addison announced to the others. "Will we need a med team?" This last directed at Sloane. The security director shook her head, and helped Sascha back into his chair.

Minutes later a team of four krogan arrived. Addison watched Sloane check each of them against a list Kesh had provided. Everything proved to be in order, and they filed in.

"Here," Sascha said, pointing. He needn't have bothered, though, since smoke still curled from the fried equipment. Two of the technicians laid heavy bags on the floor nearby and splayed them open, a pile of random parts and wires in one, various banged-up tools in the other. It all looked like so much junk.

This is never going to work. Her mind raced. There had to be another way to make contact—but of course there wasn't.

Tann sidled up to her. "Even without this latest… glitch, sensors aren't good enough. It's possible they'll arrive before we can make contact," he said. "We should prep a hangar, an empty one, and have a team waiting with food and water."

A burly krogan—burly by their standards—gently

but forcefully pushed Addison and Tann away from the console, making room. The tech crawled underneath and began yanking controller boards and who-knows-what-else from the bottom of the system.

"There was no damage down there," Tann snapped.

"It's all connected," the krogan shot right back.

Tann leaned forward. "Even so, this is an emergency. We only need it to work for ten minutes, not a lifetime."

"Let them do their job," Sloane said. She had moved back to her spot by the door, but her voice carried no less authority for it.

"Their job is what we say it is," Tann shot back. An uncharacteristic outburst. He smoothed the front of his uniform. "Forgive me," he said to Sloane. "We're all on edge here, so let's just try to remain calm."

Sloane looked at the ceiling and shook her head.

Tann pulled Addison aside. "We need to discuss what will happen if neither of these last two scouts return with good news." His voice was low, but Addison glanced toward Sloane nonetheless. She gave no indication of hearing.

"One of them will," Addison said. "They *have* to."

"Wishful thinking is not an effective way to govern."

"Well," she said, "I guess that's why you're in charge."

Tann stared at her, digesting her words. In that moment Foster Addison wanted nothing more than to be alone. In a sense she already was. She turned away from the salarian and moved to stand near the console again, ignoring the krogan's feet that almost touched her own. Tann was right, of course. They did need a backup plan. The problem was that every option Addison could think of ultimately led to the same result—abandoning the Nexus. Ending the mission. Walking away from all the sacrifice and hope.

Hell, we might as well turn around and go—

"Got it," the krogan said. He pushed himself out from under the desk and was standing in front of Addison by the time his words registered.

"Got it?" she asked, numbly. "It's fixed?"

"I think so. Try it out."

Before she could say anything Sascha and Apriia were back in their chairs, hands gliding over the interface screens. The group of krogan gathered a few meters away, their tools already packed, waiting to see if the fix had worked so they could get back to whatever they'd been doing.

A crackle erupted from the speakers, then a loud hiss of static masking urgent words.

"...injuries. Require... at docking..."

"Repeat, Scout 7," Sascha said. "The Scourge is effecting your transmission. Repeat."

"Good to hear your voice, Nexus," the ship's comm officer replied. Her words were still garbled, but clear enough to discern now.

"We need to know what you found out there," Addison said. "Please report."

"Nothing good I'm afraid," the woman replied. Addison had to strain to make out the words. "Marco's been badly injured. Hope the other... fared better."

"Please," Addison said, "the details."

"Copy that. Eos is a no go. Affected by Scourge. Atmosphere highly radiated... unsafe. No signs of life."

Addison stopped listening. She'd heard it before. Six times. The same damn thing. The comm officer relayed various statistics and readings, oblivious to the fact that every scout returning before her had met the same result.

There was only one left, now. Only one…

The krogan gathered their equipment and began to file out of the room, accompanied by Sloane.

"…permission to resupply and head back in search of the *Boundless*."

"Wait," she said, barely in control of her own voice. "Repeat?"

"*Boundless*," the woman repeated. "Scout 8. Requesting permission to go after them."

"What are you talking about?"

Sascha and Apriia were both staring at her, their faces pinched in dread or concern or both. Addison ignored them. She'd missed something, and there was no escaping it now.

"…were behind us," the woman replied impatiently. "Kandros reported… uninhabitable. And then they sent a distress call. We lost them a few seconds later."

Sloane was there. She shoved Addison aside. "Repeat that?"

"*Boundless* reported an anomaly and then… vanished. We'd like to return to look for them."

"Why the hell didn't you do that when it happened?" Sloane bellowed into the mic. Despite that, the voice on the speaker did not waver.

"We did," the woman said. "Circled back immediately, at great risk to everyone aboard. Searched for as long as we could. But Marco's… critical. We're out of food. We did everything possible. There was no trace. I'm sorry. We all agreed, though, we'd like to go back—"

"We understand, Scout 7," Tann said.

"Bullshit we do," Sloane hissed at him. Once again Addison felt trapped between them. This time as two unbearable truths registered at once.

She and Tann might have sent Sloane's best officer to his death, and every scout ship had failed.

There would be no resupply, no haven to colonize. Nowhere to go if the Nexus went critical.

Addison slumped back against the wall.

The mission was doomed.

CHAPTER TWENTY-THREE

Frustration burned inside Calix's gut.

It had been two weeks since Irida had been arrested. Two weeks of scrutiny as Sloane Kelly and her team scoured everything, physical and electronic, trying to discover if she had shared the bulkhead codes with anyone.

Of course, Calix felt responsible. In the note she left with the stolen database, Irida had justified it as "doing her part to mind the rations." She had gone too far, too fast, but as the days progressed...

Calix had yet to tell his team why Irida had been locked up. They asked, daily, but he just said he knew as much as they did. Claimed Sloane had told him only that the woman had been in the wrong place at the wrong time, and they were holding her for questioning. That wore thin each day this went on, but if he told them the truth they might get similar ideas of how to help.

Things were bad and getting worse by the moment. Everybody walked around like they expected to be jumped—by security, by the krogan, by their own friends and comrades. Fights had started breaking out between teammates. Things went missing constantly.

His own team had started hoarding. Turian rations, human rations. Tools. Sneaking whatever they could, whenever they could get it. Calix pretended not to see, and his team saw him pretending not to see. He realized that they took it as tacit approval.

Meanwhile, Irida waited in a cell. For his help? For rescue?

For… change.

Calix sat on the corner of an appropriated metal crate, watching the krogan work on a heavily damaged hydroponics bay. The finesse technicians had already come and gone, only to report an issue in the structural integrity of the space itself. The seedlings were too fragile to flourish in anything less than optimal conditions.

That left them with two mostly functional bays, and that wouldn't put a dent in ration concerns. Especially since—to his critical eye—one looked much less healthy than the other.

The krogan—Nakmor grunts Kaje and Wratch, respectively—worked in tandem. The curses they threw at each other seemed more like encouragement than anger, though rivalry was always a factor in krogan communications.

"You weld like a drunk vorcha," Kaje grunted.

The other krogan snorted long and loud. "At least I don't look like one."

"Said who? Your human buddy?"

"Said your mother," Wratch replied.

The bantering went back and forth like this with no regard for Calix's presence, and he chuckled softly. He appreciated that. Nice to sit in the gloom and just *be* for a while. Pockets like this were becoming exceedingly rare.

His chuckle caught Wratch's attention. The big krogan slammed a metal bar hard against the panel, holding it easily with one hand while he glowered across the gloomy distance.

"What's so funny?" he growled. They *always*

growled. He didn't take it personally.

"Just enjoying the company, fellas."

Kaje's omni-tool glowed as the welder activated, searing off any chance at conversation while the metal sizzled and fused. Once done, he glanced over, too.

"You're engineering, yeah?" His voice was no less grumbly—big krogan throats led to deep voices, even in the rare women Calix had known of—but of a sharper pitch. Like a supersized rotary drill. Embedded in granite.

"Life support and stasis pods," Calix said. He braced a hand on his thigh, elbow out, and strengthened his balance with a foot against the crate. It gave him a clearer view of both of the technicians.

"He makes sure the clan leader stays asleep," Wratch added to his partner. The other krogan grunted what Calix assumed to be thanks. Or just acknowledgement. Either way, not a threat. "Sent the appetiz—" The krogan paused. Then, grimly, "The salarian worked with him."

"Right." Another nod, this one, Calix felt, for Na'to. And Nakmor Arvex.

"You both seem to be in good spirits," Calix said thoughtfully. "Given everything."

"Scarce food and a barren environment, right?" Kaje chuckled, the sound like boulders grating. "Just like home." Another clang rang out over the large bay, echoing back from the gloom. He grinned a very, very wide and toothy grin over the paneling he worked to replace.

Wratch echoed the mirth, and Calix couldn't help joining in the laughter. They had a point. "At least we should hear from the scouts soon," he said.

The krogan exchanged heavy glances.

"Uh-oh," Kaje rumbled.

"Uh-oh," echoed the other. Wratch looked back at him, bracing his folded arms on the bar that had been welded in place. "You don't know, do you?"

Calix went very still on the crate. "Know? Know what?" The worry festering in his gut froze around the edges.

Kaje slugged Wratch in the arm. *Hard.*

"They're keeping it secret, idiot."

Wratch shrugged off the blow, snapping once in irritation, and looked back at Calix.

"Scouts already came back."

"What?! When?"

"Most, anyway," Kaje corrected.

"When?" Calix repeated. He could feel the muscles tightening in his mandibles.

Both krogan shrugged in mountainous tandem. "Few weeks."

For a moment, Calix couldn't even find the words. Couldn't settle on any one feeling. Shock. Anger. Betrayal.

The krogan didn't notice. "Heard it from Botcha," Kaje continued. He walked out from around the dark bay, stretching out his big, gnarled hands. His hide crinkled with every move. "Botcha was up in Operations repairing an inverter when the news came."

"*What* news?" Calix demanded. It took all he had to keep from launching off that crate and shaking— *trying* to shake—the krogan. Both of them.

"No planets," Wratch grunted as he punched the metal paneling lightly. It gonged. "No supplies."

"The Scourge destroyed 'em," Kaje added.

"Deader'n Tuchanka."

"Almost."

"Yeah. No turians."

"Yet."

The two exchanged another look and burst out laughing.

Calix couldn't join in on the joke—not this time. No supplies were coming. No scouts bringing good news.

"And the Pathfinders?"

Kaje gave a hefty shrug. "No sign of 'em."

No sign of the Pathfinders. They knew this, and yet the leadership was *sitting* on it. Toeing the same line they had since day one. *The scouts will return, the supplies will be restocked, the planets will be terraformed...*

Lies. All of it. Maybe not initially, but at least a couple of weeks' worth.

The krogan were still bantering when Calix, numb with betrayal, unfolded from the crate and left hydroponics.

Hydroponics, where two tanks of algae had taken root. One looked ready to fail. While that was worrisome enough, the leadership kept on telling them all that hydroponics would flourish once they had colonial resources to supplement it. That the scouts would bring back new seeds, new hope for fertile ground.

Without those resources, the Nexus was back to two functional hydroponic bays. Just two. That wasn't enough to feed a single *department*, much less the number of active people on the station. Priorities had to be re-shifted, information *had* to be disseminated. How else were they expected to survive?

None of this made any sense. *And how badly did I misjudge Sloane Kelly?*

Calix accessed his omni-tool and almost called her. Almost. He sent a short message instead. "Any news from the scouts?"

The reply came less than twenty seconds later.

"Nothing," was all it said.

He stared at the word for a long time, simmering anger building to rage. A blatant lie, assuming these two krogan could be trusted, but he saw no reason why they would make such a story up.

So the leadership was sitting on the news. Even Sloane, whom he'd imagined to be better than this. For weeks they'd known, and said nothing. Which meant…

His fury drove him back to engineering in record time. "Gather up," he said, stepping over his team's greetings. The lash in his voice had them jumping to obey. Not because they were afraid of him, he understood. Because they knew him.

Calix didn't rattle. Not easily.

The snap in his voice, tension in his demeanor, was all they needed to know something was up. In a matter of moments they'd put their work on hold and came to stand around their boss, each in a different stage of curiosity. As Calix surveyed the faces of his crew—many friends as well as subordinates—a pang of regret struck him at Irida's absence.

She'd been with him longer than most. Dedicated, skilled. Loyal. Had she seen this coming? Is that why she'd given him that data?

Irida had always been good at planning for this sort of stuff. She had been the first to smell the cover-up by the captain of the *Warsaw*. Maybe it came with asari intelligence. Maybe she just had a more realistic view of people than he did. Either way, Calix had what she'd given him.

And a crew ready to hear him speak.

Calix wouldn't let them down.

"You all know what kind of things we're dealing with," he began. "The situation here aboard the Nexus." His hands clasped behind his back, and in unconscious mimicry, much of his team did the same. Alliance and military training. Even contractors picked it up, if they stuck around long enough.

Nnebron's brow furrowed.

Smart one. Like Irida, but with less tact.

"Rations are tight," Calix continued. Nods peppered the team. "The station is in need of more repairs than it has crew to repair her." More nods, a few emphatic grunts. "Whenever we ask for updates, we get the same song and dance we always have." Calix met the eyes of his crew as he listed them off. "Scouts will return soon with planet coordinates. Rations will lift. The Pathfinders will find us. Just work a little harder, a little longer, and everything will turn out fine.

"New homes," he added as he turned and paced to the edge of the team. "New food and resources. A chance to create that new life we've all been promised. Away from the prejudices and the disasters of the old worlds from which we came."

The world they'd left behind. Six hundred years in the dust.

Calix had to take a moment, rest a hand on Nnebron's shoulder and swallow the pang of homesickness he didn't know he'd carried until he saw it in the faces of his team. His friends. His mandibles moved. He paused. Then said the words nobody had wanted to say.

"We all know what we left," he said quietly. "The kind of crap that happened on the *Warsaw*." Nnebron nodded at that, his mouth a thin line. "Leaders who order us to try and cover up their mistakes, or worse, withhold the truth from us and let us toil while they plan an escape."

Eyes widened. Calix nodded. "We thought Andromeda would be different. That we'd be leaving that kind of thing behind. And then we lost Na'to."

"Boss?" Nnebron took a step forward. His dark eyes spoke volumes, echoing the uncertainty in every face. "What's this about? Is it Irida?"

He closed his eyes. Took a deep breath.

"Secrets," he said, enunciating every syllable, "plague the Nexus leadership. Like a drug, a habit they can't break." He opened his eyes. Met the stares of his team, and made the call he knew he could never take back. "They told us we'd have new planets." His hands clenched. "It's false. They've known for weeks that the planets around us are dead."

Andria paled.

"Wait, dead?"

He nodded. Andria had been there when Na'to died. Reg and she both had taken time off to get it together.

Reg came back first.

Andria's tone earned an instant and total state of focus from the entire group. Her question echoed through them all.

"Dead," Calix confirmed. "Torn apart by the same Scourge that nearly took us."

She flinched, half-turning to hide the worry in her face. Nnebron put a hand on her shoulder.

"They lied," Nnebron said blankly, then he swore.

"Weeks?" Andria whispered, and she looked at Calix. Her freckles had almost paled out. "They've known for *weeks*?"

"So it seems."

She blew out a hard breath and jammed her hands in the pockets of her pants. "I don't—I can't believe it."

"Believe it," Nnebron said bitterly. He turned to the rest of the team, his slim back to Calix, and gestured expansively. "How long have we been working down here, eating every word they sent us? Like we were some kind of orphans begging for scraps." His voice rose, the anger growing. "We're part of the Nexus, too!"

"Nnebron, nobody is saying we don't exist." Calix tilted his head. "Only that—"

"Only that we're not important," Andria cut in, her pallor replaced by an angry flush. Calix knew then he couldn't let her down. Couldn't let any of them down.

"The planets aren't going to save us," he added, raising his own voice, "nor the Pathfinders. We need new plans, friends. New contingencies. New directions—"

"And new leaders!"

Who said it, he didn't see, but the words started a fire. Andria darted around Nnebron to grab Calix by the arm. Her grip bit.

"How long?" she demanded. "Until the supplies run out? Will they let us starve?"

Whoa. He hadn't expected this to move quite that fast. Calix covered her hand with his free one, pressing her fingers against his arm in what he hoped was a firm, comforting method. He had a hard time gauging human comfort, sometimes.

"Easy," he said, trying for soothing. "We aren't going to starve."

"No way the boss would let us starve," Nnebron added.

"Yeah… Hey, yeah!" The others started to nod. To

look Calix's way. To… to almost vibrate. The tension was palpable.

"Plans," one repeated. "Priorities… we need to lock down supplies."

"We need to spread the word!"

Andria stared, her gaze pleading. "We can't let everyone else starve. What about Reg? Emory? Some of us have friends out there…"

"We won't." He said the words before he could fully weigh them. Saw them take hold in her features, create a vortex of confidence he'd never known he could inspire. Suddenly his crew surrounded him, all reaching out to touch his shoulder, his arm. Pats of confidence, of pride.

Of support.

"Irida needs to be freed," he heard.

From someone else, "We need to secure the rations!"

"What about security?"

"Screw them," someone jeered.

It spun around and around him, a heady mix of anger and relief and confidence. All because of him. They looked at him as a leader. Calix's shoulders squared. He squeezed Andria's hand, then stepped back far enough that he could see them all in his field of view.

"First things first," he said, loudly enough to cut through the voices. They all went silent. Watching. Listening.

Really *listening*.

Heady stuff, that power.

He summoned every ounce of meritocratic confidence he never knew he possessed. But instead of laying down his orders and forcing them to obey, he met them as equals.

As friends.

He spread his hands. "We need a plan."

Nnebron's grin stretched ear-to-ear. "I think we can help you there, boss."

CHAPTER TWENTY-FOUR

"What a fucking mess," Sloane said. The words were directed not at Tann, who paced behind the desk in Operations, or Addison, who sat head-in-hands against the wall by the door. The farthest she could be from Sloane and still be in the room. No, her words were directed at the floor.

At the whole damned station.

Rage had got the better of her, weeks back. She'd stormed out of that crowded control room and kept on going, rampaging around like a petty tyrant, doing anything she could to get her mind off Kandros. The failure of the scouts was bad enough, but she couldn't get past the fact that those scout missions had cost her the best first officer she'd never had.

His ship had not been found, or heard from, since. Some had wanted to declare them lost, and to stop using critical resources to continue the search, but Sloane was having none of it.

Time had passed, which only made the situation worse, both in terms of Kandros and the fact that the general population had yet to be told of the scout's failure.

In fact, time had become a physical source of pain. Every day that passed without answers, without showing the guts to admit the truth to everyone, only made that inevitable moment all the worse.

"This cannot go on, my friends," Tann said. "We have only one option left."

This is it, Sloane thought, bile in her mouth. *The end of denial.* Jarun Tann, all business, as usual. The past, to him, was merely data. Sloane glared. "If you say that we turn around and go back to the Milky Way…"

"No," Tann said. The word cut like a knife. Unusual for him. Despite herself Sloane straightened her back. An involuntary reaction every soldier learned when they heard that tone. "I'm not ready to give up yet," he added, casting his gaze between Sloane and Addison. "None of us should be."

Slowly, like a marionette, Addison lifted her head and blinked.

"What option, then?"

"Cryostasis," Tann said.

Sloane laughed. Or would have. She wanted to, but nothing came out. Tann, she realized, was right.

The salarian went on. "Everyone goes back in, save a skeleton crew. We wait and hope the Pathfinders reach us. That we don't encounter the Scourge again. It's all we can do."

"Risky move," Addison said, though little conviction stood behind her words. She also knew he was right. Sloane could hear it.

"Absolutely," Tann agreed, "but then everything is these days."

The words settled. *Like a blanket over a corpse*, Sloane thought. For a long time no one said anything.

"I'll do it," Addison said. "I'll make the announcement."

"Are you sure?" Tann asked, thinking the same thing as Sloane—that Addison wasn't up for it. Her mood was… complicated, to say the least.

"Well, you can't do it," Addison said, almost laughing. "Remember your call for volunteers?"

"I'm still trying to forget." He frowned. "Why not Sloane?"

"Screw that," Sloane said. "You got us into this mess, *Acting Director*."

"That's unfair," Tann fired back. "I've done my best to consult the two of you in every decision—"

"You mean whichever of us was most likely to agree."

Addison hauled herself to her feet. "It's obvious, isn't it? No one's going to like this. It can't come from Sloane because while we make the announcement, she'll be getting security ready for the crew's reaction." She studied each of them. "It's why we've sat on our thumbs for two weeks and avoided this. People aren't going to go willingly."

"They must," Tann said.

"They won't," Addison replied. "Not unless they are… compelled."

Sloane Kelly clenched her jaw, shook her head. "What a fucking mess." Addison was right, though. No arguing that. "When do you want to announce it?"

"As soon as possible, I think," the woman replied.

"Okay. Okay." Sloane's mind raced through the preparations that would be required. Her team was already spread too thin, but that couldn't be helped. She'd pull them all in, brief them, and get ready for the party. Calix, she'd need to talk to Calix. Fuck, this was exactly what he'd warned her about.

They could at least drink to that.

His team would have to enter cryo last, so they could assist the rest. She wondered how willingly that bunch of hard-asses would help. They all looked at her now with one thing written across their faces.

You imprisoned Irida.

Sloane went to the door. "Give me an hour," she said as she left.

||||||||||||||||||

Exactly an hour later she had her entire team gathered at headquarters, a space little better than a ruin. Every time Kesh offered to send a team to fix it up Sloane waved her off. Too many other places were more important. Besides, other than the occasional arrest, her team hardly spent any time here.

Strange to see all their faces gathered. Stranger still not to see Kandros at the front of the group.

Her team had been briefed, and they were just waiting for the announcement. Sloane could have dispersed them ahead of Addison's speech, in order to have a security presence "in the streets," so to speak. An old tactic from the tyrant's playbook, that. In the end, though, she thought this might work better. A little reverse psychology. Let people think, hopefully subconsciously, that security wasn't even worried. That this was a perfectly acceptable step in the station's recovery.

Mostly, though, she wanted to be nimble. Dispatch her squads where the reactions—if any—were the most extreme. Calm things down before they got down to the business of shoving people back into their pods.

The public address system crackled and Addison's voice boomed out through the speakers, echoing in the hallways.

"This is Director Addison," she began. "As many of you know, ten weeks ago Colonial Affairs sent out a fleet of vessels to scout the nearest worlds—ones that might be suitable for habitats or, in some cases, offer resources from which to resupply our dwindling stores. Barring that, to find a place where we could move our population in the event that the station ceases to support the mission.

"I am sad to announce that those missions have failed. The worlds we identified from afar have all been struck by the same mysterious phenomenon that so damaged the Nexus—what most of us now refer to as 'the Scourge.'"

Not a bad start, all things considered, Sloane thought. She studied her team. Saw resolve and, more importantly, cool-headedness in each of their faces.

Addison continued. "One of our ships did not return, and search-and-rescue efforts are continuing as I speak. While we all hope for the safety of the members of that mission, we must now turn our focus to the survival of the Nexus and its inhabitants.

"You've all done an amazing job these last few months. Critical problems have been resolved. The station may still require an incredible amount of work before it is ready to perform its mission, but it is stable. You should all be extremely proud of this accomplishment!"

Another pause, waiting for the other shoe to drop.

"Our primary concern now is one of supplies," Addison said. "We simply do not have the resources needed to sustain our revived population. With the lack of habitable worlds near us, and the continued issues plaguing hydroponics, we have no choice but to wait until several crops can be harvested and stored. Alternatively, we will be contacted by the Pathfinders and a solution will come from them.

"Several weeks ago we asked for volunteers to return to stasis. None of you were willing to do that, and we understood your reasons. Unfortunately we have no alternative now. I must ask you to remember the words of Jien Garson. 'We make the greatest sacrifice any of us have ever, or will ever, make.' The time has come for a mandatory return to stasis for all non-essential personnel."

Another short silence, to let that sink in.

"Team leaders will be briefed shortly. Within the next twenty-four hours you will be contacted by security, who will escort you to your stasis pod and oversee the process. We look forward to your cooperation in salvaging the mission of the Nexus."

Twenty-four hours and this will be over, Sloane thought. And then she'd need to get her own team to go back under. To enter a coma aboard a station held together with tape and spit and foul language, surrounded by a mysterious phenomenon that seemed to destroy everything that came near.

Of course *she'd* get to remain awake. Of course. Wasn't that how leaders always did things? *Others have to make the sacrifice. But us? Oh no, we're much too fucking important.*

Sloane waited for more, but Addison appeared to be done. Odd that she didn't add a little thanks or godspeed or whatever. *Well, beggars can't be choosers.* At least it wasn't Tann making the speech, or Spender writing it. Sloane still cringed at that memory, and thought she would for the rest of her life.

"Listen up," she said. No need—her officers were already listening. "Stick the plan, okay? We have no idea how this is going to go, but we have to treat this situation like it's a group of colonists who don't want to evacuate their doomed planet. Some of us have been on duty like that before, and it's never fun. Just remember that we're saving their lives, even if they don't see it that way. They have their own best interests in mind. It's our job to remind them of the bigger picture. Understood?"

Nods all around.

"Alright then. Let's get this over with." Her omni-tool chimed. Kesh. Sloane raised a finger to her crew and stepped away to the wall. "Hey, what's the status? Are the krogan on board with all this?"

"I'm not worried about the clan," Kesh said, "but there is a problem."

"How can there be a problem already? It's been, like, thirty seconds."

"I'm unable to contact Calix."

Sloane's pulse jumped. Her mouth went dry. Calix was crucial to this effort—perhaps even more important than she was herself.

"Alright. Don't panic. Who's his second?"

"That's just it," Kesh said. "I can't seem to raise anyone on the life-support team. And without them—"

"—none of the pods can be prepped for activation."

"Exactly," Kesh said, then she added, "I could do it, but I'm not trained in monitoring the process."

"I hear you. Let's keep that option as plan B for the moment. I'll see if I can track down Calix. They might be in a rad-shielded area, making sure the infrastructure is ready for these pods to come back online." But Sloane didn't believe her own words. Something—some deep-seeded security officer's intuition—told her that something else was going on here.

Whatever it was, it wasn't good.

Because if someone out there, some group, wanted to avoid a return to stasis, taking out Calix and his team would be a damned good way to go about it.

"Right," she said, returning to her team. "I need four volunteers. We've got some people missing and—"

The PA crackled. Sloane stopped talking. Maybe Addison wasn't quite done after all. But it wasn't her voice that filled the halls of the Nexus. It was a turian voice. A familiar one.

"This is Calix Corvannis," the turian's voice boomed, "and I am here to tell you all to say no. Say *no*! Resist the order to return to stasis."

Oh, shit. No.

Sloane's omni chirped again. Spender calling.

"Not now," she barked as she answered, her mind reeling.

"No problem," Spender said. "I just thought you might want to dispatch a team to the armory."

"Who the hell do you think you are, telling me where to…" Then his words registered, and her wrath bled out. "Why the armory?"

"Well, I happened to be going past there and noticed the doors were open. Wide open. No guards."

"How the fuck…?"

Another alert erupted from her wrist. This one automated, a direct feed from the station's emergency systems.

"Fire in Hydroponics," Sloane read, unable to believe it.

She rushed from the room, sidearm drawn, the entire security staff on her heels.

CHAPTER TWENTY-FIVE

"Act casual," Calix said to Lawrence Nnebron.

The man acted anything but. Fidgeting, staring at the two guards for long seconds, not looking away when they returned the stare. He'd taken Irida's arrest worse than most, and was itching to get some payback. Not that he knew the true reason for her arrest, but this wasn't the time or place to get into that. Calix grabbed his upper arm gently but with enough force to turn him away from the hallway entrance.

"Our goal is what's inside," he said.

"It's not right what they did," Nnebron muttered. His eyes were downcast though. He recognized his own pettiness, and that was a start.

"I agree," Calix said, "but we don't need to draw attention to ourselves. We'll do so in ways that matter."

Nnebron kicked at an invisible pebble, scuffing the floor.

Calix glanced at the others around him. Just a bunch of friends, enjoying a few minutes of R&R before they went back to the repair work. Only Nnebron had fallen out of character, and perhaps that wasn't so bad, Calix thought. It gave him something to talk about with the two guards.

"The rest of you stay here, I'll be back." Before any of them could question him, Calix walked calmly over to the pair. He put on his best turian smile. "How are things, officers?"

"What's the matter with your friend?" one of them asked, jerking his chin toward Nnebron. The stained uniform identified him as White. An older human, squat and powerfully built, with a rather awful-looking pencil mustache incongruously framed by bushy eyebrows and overgrown sideburns.

"Yeah," the other guard said. "He doesn't seem too happy with us." Another human, her height and thin clean face an almost comical contrast to White. Her uniform read Blair.

"Don't mind him," Calix replied. "One of his friends was arrested, and he's still a little sore about it. I just wanted to apologize if his, er, attitude bothered you."

"If we bother him," White said, "maybe you should take your group elsewhere."

"We'll be getting back to work in a few minutes, don't worry. In the meantime, you both look like you're at the far end of a long shift. Need anything? Food, water?"

Blair turned her focus to him, now. Her eyes were sharp, narrowed. "Rations have already been distributed for the week. If you're suggesting that you can acquire—"

"No, no." Calix held up his hands, palms out. "I saved a bit is all, and I'm happy to share." He pulled a water bottle from his jacket and waved it in front of her. The clear fluid sloshed.

"I'm good, thanks."

White sized him up as well. "Why don't you rejoin your friends, sir. We're on duty here."

"Of course," he said. "Sorry to have troubled you."

Calix took one last glance at the bulkhead door behind the pair. Imprinted on the frame, in tiny lettering, a maintenance identifier had been stenciled.

He walked back to his team. Nnebron eyed him with curiosity, and perhaps a little bit of suspicion.

"Why are you offering water to those assholes?"

With his back to the guards, Calix poured the bottle of water into a planter. The plant was fake. The soil, too, no doubt scheduled to be replaced with something from hydroponics in that alternate reality where the Nexus wasn't a wreck.

"What the hell?" Nnebron asked. "I could have used that."

"I doubt that." He shook the last few drops out and returned the empty bottle to his jacket. "Unless you want to sleep for a week."

Nnebron blinked, looking at Calix with renewed admiration. An expression matched by the others from his team, who'd gathered around. In truth the water was just water. Calix had only meant to distract the two guards for a moment while he learned the ID code for the bulkhead. He hadn't anticipated what the gesture would look like to his own people.

They were already a little suspicious of him, ever since his lengthy talk with Sloane Kelly, and though that suspicion had remained unvoiced, he could tell they were looking for signs. From the looks on their faces, though, he'd not only dispelled the concern, but swung the pendulum in the other direction. Not only had he not offered the guards water, he'd tried to drug them.

If that was what they were made to believe, Calix saw no harm in it.

"We'll have to take a different approach," he said.

They all nodded. *Just tell us what to do*, their eager eyes said.

"They refused the water," he continued, already

feeling a bit trapped in the fiction he'd created, "so we'll need some other way to get them to leave the door."

"A diversion," one of his crew said.

"That's easy," Nnebron said. "I know just the thing." There was something in his voice Calix wasn't sure he liked. A malice, yet the enthusiasm couldn't be denied.

"Maybe another barbecue," he suggested thoughtfully. "Open flames are sure to draw a response."

"Count on it," Nnebron said. With a simple gesture he recruited two others from the group, and the trio strode away, talking in hushed tones as they went. Calix watched them go, and wondered how wise that assignment had been. Nnebron was a hothead, and the arrest of his friend Irida hadn't exactly helped matters.

Oh, well, he mused. *Nothing to be done about it now.* He could see it in the faces of the six who remained. They were looking to him to lead the way, but they were going to do *something*, whether or not he accepted the role. They needed a change. They needed to know that life wasn't going to be like this forever, working themselves to death on a station that should have been abandoned months ago, for an unqualified trio of leaders who made questionable decisions at every turn. Leaders still mired in the prejudices and politics the rest of the crew had wanted to leave behind.

They'd come here for a new beginning, not to prop up old, outdated bigotry.

The PA crackled, and the voice of Foster Addison began to fill the station. "As many of you know, ten weeks ago Colonial Affairs sent out a fleet of vessels to scout the nearest worlds…"

Calix and his little band of admirers listened without a word. The two guards, Calix noted, shifted uneasily, eyes scanning the few people in the common room. He wondered if they knew what this was about.

Activating his omni-tool, he dove into the endless menus and elaborate maze of files and folders he'd created to hide the thing he needed. The true prize in Irida's stolen data.

Addison's words continued to echo around the room and down the long hallways.

"I am sad to announce that these missions have failed," she said. Gasps from those who had gathered.

"I can't believe they sat on this for *weeks*," one of Calix's team said. It was Ulrich, a burly human whose gruff bruiser appearance often led others to underestimate him. The man was one of the finest engineers Calix had ever met. He'd been part of the team since the beginning—one of the first to join the Nexus mission.

"Stay calm, stay calm," Calix said, getting the tone just right. He'd had no idea Addison would announce this just as he and his team were going to act. It presented an opportunity, however, that he couldn't resist. Let them think he'd planned the timing.

Got it! Calix found the hidden file. The override codes Irida had stolen. He still couldn't quite say why he'd kept them, or why he'd lied about it to Sloane, the only member of the hierarchy "worth her salt," as the saying went.

"Here's the plan…" he said.

An alarm rang out.

Someone shouted, "Fire!"

It came from a connecting hallway. The same hall Nnebron and his friends had taken. Then another shout.

"Fire in Hydroponics!"

A message blipped on Calix's screen.

This should get their attention.

Oh hell, Nnebron—what did you do?

The two guards raced from the room, shouldering Calix aside as they abandoned their post in front of the bulkhead door. As diversions went, a fire in Hydroponics was about the best he could have wished for—only he hadn't wished for it. Not at all. If Nnebron damaged the food supply...

Calix didn't want to think about that. He had to act, now, while the guards were gone. They'd left the bulkhead unguarded, that much he had predicted. It was a bulkhead, after all, and only security could override those.

He scanned Irida's stolen list, found the ID code he'd spotted on the frame, and tapped in the override. A dull thud from inside the wall, and then the massive doors opened.

"Come on," Calix said to his team. "We won't have much time."

"What's in there?" Ulrich asked, suddenly dubious.

"The armory," Calix answered.

No further convincing required.

||||||||||||||||||

William Spender watched from afar as Calix and his little gang moved on the armory. He watched the door open for them as if it were welcoming old friends, too.

"Isn't that interesting," he said to himself, and glanced around to make sure he wasn't being watched.

He should report this to security. Probably be in a lot of trouble if he didn't.

But William Spender had little love for Sloane Kelly, and even less for a political landscape with only one side to play.

So, yes, he'd contact security. But first he'd give Calix a full minute inside the weapons vault.

Maybe even two.

iiiiiiiiiiiiiiii

Even deep in the weapons locker, Calix could hear Foster Addison's speech. She spoke of the mission, and the need to support its aims no matter the cost. That was her mistake, really. The continued and irrational belief in a dead dream. They were going to get everyone killed, except perhaps for themselves, and all because they couldn't see the truth.

Jien Garson was dead, and her vision died with her.

Calix found it slightly amusing, and more than a little frustrating, that their leaders just assumed the life-support team would go along with the plan. That he and his people would participate in this misguided effort. No one had asked him, of course.

He wondered if anyone had asked Kesh, but considering a salarian was in charge, probably not.

Around him, they were stealing every gun they could get their hands on.

"Bag it all," he said to them.

No one needed to hear it, though. They were on autopilot now. A veritable feeding frenzy of weaponry. His plan had been to take the weapons and relocate them to some hidden, out-of-the-way chamber. That would even the odds a bit, and give him a bargaining chip. Leverage to demand new leadership, and a more diverse security force. A new plan. And, of course, a full pardon for his team. Only then would he tell them where the weapons were.

Yet standing there, watching his angry crew stuff the tools of violence into tactical bags so heavy they could barely lift their prizes, he knew they'd never agree to return them. He'd been crazy to think it himself.

"That's enough," he said. "Security will be back soon, and we need to be gone."

"Where to next?" someone asked.

Calix had to think fast. He hadn't expected this to happen so quickly, or to go like this. For a moment he felt adrift on a swift current, the one person with a raft to which everyone else had decided, inexplicably, to cling.

"After what Addison just said," he replied, "I think we'd better get our hands on as many supplies as we can before the council barricades them."

If they haven't already, he amended silently.

"Even if they do, they won't be able to stop us," another said with a wolfish grin.

"Maybe so," Calix admitted, "but I'd rather be the ones defending it."

"Smart play."

Agreement all around. Again. Calix wished they'd think for themselves a bit, but this wasn't the time to encourage them. Far from it. No, he'd started something here, and there would be no walking away. In Andromeda, there was nowhere else to go, after all.

As they slipped out of the armory, each of them carrying two full bags and most with a third slung over their shoulders, Calix tried to picture this moment from the perspective of the bystanders. The few crew members milling about in the common room had backed up to the walls, hands outstretched, mouths agape as they watched this random group of techs walk out of security with so much gear.

Barrels of weapons poked out of the bags they strained to carry. Despite Addison's words that still echoed off the walls, they saw only theft. He needed to do something about that, and soon. The label of terrorism would be slapped on them, and quickly.

||||||||||||||||||

As they moved toward their destination, Calix's omni-tool squawked relentlessly. *Sloane, Sloane, Kesh, Sloane.* He wondered if they were trying to discover his location—he'd disabled that function an hour ago. Security might have a way around that, though, but he still needed the device to override the bulkheads.

Override the bulkheads.

Of course! Calix dropped the bags of weapons and knelt. His band of thieves silently gathered around, knowing something was up. He rushed through the menus again, from rote memory this time, and found the option he wanted.

"We're going to have to hurry after this," he said. With that he selected a command and entered it. Then he used his credentials to do one of the few things his chief's status would allow. He activated the station-wide public address.

"This is Calix Corvannis, and I am here to tell you all to say no." His words echoed where Addison's had just a few moments ago. "Say *no*. Resist the order to return to stasis."

The message was loud and clear. He thought he'd pulled it off, too. Stern and yet rational, collected. As he finished, the command he'd entered took effect.

Every sealed bulkhead door in the inhabited zone of the Nexus began to open.

Calix moved at a brisk walk, forcing a look of concerned focus onto his face, not meeting the eyes of any they passed.

Smoke billowed from Hydroponics. He walked on by without even glancing into the room. He didn't want security to see him, but more than that, he didn't want to know. Nnebron may have doomed them all by starting that fire, rendering all of this moot. They'd just have to hope the damage was superficial, or quickly contained.

A distraction, not abject sabotage.

He turned down a long hallway, his team following close behind like a gang of hired thugs. *What have I started?* he thought, then he pushed the question aside. All that really mattered was how it would end.

He turned on the PA again, before they removed his authority to access it. He spoke into it as he walked.

"Do not enter your pods," he said. "We are not robots who can just be switched off when our existence here becomes inconvenient. This station is ours, *all* of ours, and it's not going to be fixed by anyone but us.

"No one is coming to our rescue. No planets wait to harbor us. Addison got that part right. What she didn't tell you is that our leaders have known this for two weeks. Two weeks! The Nexus doesn't need all of you asleep. What it needs is all of you at your stations, doing what you came here to do. A great push to right this ship! A great—"

His access to the PA vanished.

His omni still worked, but the channel had been cut.

"Well," he said, "I guess someone didn't like what I was saying." That elicited laughs from his "gang." He looked at them over his shoulder. The *resistance*, they were. The *uprising*.

Calix couldn't quite pinpoint how he'd managed to be at the head of this, but he suspected it went all the way back to the Milky Way. The stand he'd taken against the captain of the *Warsaw*. Something anyone in his position would have done, as far as he was concerned. Yet the action had grown in that case, too, becoming an unstoppable thing that made him out to be some kind of legend. A role, evidently, that fate had found for him.

So be it.

He hoped Kesh would understand. He thought she might. After all, if a krogan couldn't understand rising up against oppressors, who could?

Calix stopped in an alcove one turn away from the hangar Spender had designated the station's temporary warehouse.

"Arm yourselves," he said to those around him. He dropped his bags and selected the first weapon his fist wrapped around. A Mattock assault rifle, at least he thought so. Not exactly his area of expertise. Whatever the specs, however, it would do.

"Once we secure the room," he said, "I'll need three of you to ferry these bags inside. Then we'll use the lev-carts to move everything toward the ark docking bays." The location just tumbled out, as if he'd worked it out weeks ago. In truth it had simply popped into his head, only because he'd heard a krogan say that they had cleared a path there recently. The space remained, as of yet, empty of any equipment, and Calix had a strong feeling that wasn't going to change anytime soon.

His team all nodded as if this were sage wisdom.

Only in that moment did he realize they were right. That he'd picked the perfect place. If only they could get there, and secure it…

"What lev-carts?" Andria asked.

Uh-oh…

"There's bound to be a whole bunch of them inside," Calix replied. He hoped it was true, otherwise this little rebellion would end in a very short siege.

Once everyone had selected a weapon, he nodded and took up the lead once again. He walked more slowly now, battling a voice in his head that kept shouting at him to stop here, to turn back. Rounding the next corner was the point of no return. Ahead lay a future as a traitor, an outlaw. Behind lay six heavily armed, overworked and underfed wrenchers with blood in their ears.

Right here, right now, he feared them more than what might lay ahead. With any luck, they'd take the supplies and be in a position to negotiate with the council. Find a way to keep the crew out of cryo. Scavenge the rest of the station if they had to. There had to be something. It just required a different way of thinking.

He rounded the corner.

Three guards were huddled in front of the open bulkhead, engaged in conversation with Spender.

"Going to need you to step aside," Calix said. "And keep your hands—"

One of the guards dove to the side, pistol drawn in a flash.

Gunfire erupted from Calix's group, ending any semblance of control he might have.

"Focus fire!" someone shouted.

The guard who'd dived, still airborne, began to

shudder as rounds slammed against his kinetic shield. Energies rippled across its surfaces and then, when it had taken all it could, the flaring stopped. The next round took him square in the forehead. His leap ended in a lifeless thud.

Spender made eye contact with Calix, then. A single glance. Then the bureaucrat broke and ran, arms clasped over his ears. He crossed in front of the two guards, elbowing one as he went, disrupting her aim. An accident? Calix wondered. Filed that. Soon enough the politician was clear and still running, out of the line of fire. Calix ignored him. He found he had his own weapon raised, his finger squeezed tight on the trigger. The weapon chattered, bursts of fire that nearly blinded him, the sound of it buffeting his ears and sending them ringing. On instinct he crouched and moved sideways, not that there was any cover.

One of his gang took a round to the gut and doubled over, howling in pain, rifle skittering across the floor. Armed maybe, but they lacked the armor Sloane's officers wore.

The two remaining guards backed up into the hangar, firing as they moved. One began to writhe under another salvo of concentrated fire. She shrieked and fell to the side as the shield gave out, her knee exploding. Calix had done that. Fired the round that wounded her. He only realized it a second later.

He'd shot someone. Ruined their leg. Ruined their—

Another shot hit the guard he'd felled, this one in the throat. The howling turned into a strained wet gurgle.

The lone remaining guard dove behind cover, a random crate, popping up a second later to spray bullets across the attacking force. Calix stood in the open, numb at what he'd just seen. He knew the danger, the bullets flying past him. One grazed his pant leg, a tug he barely felt. Then a member of his group tackled him.

He fell to the floor, a body landing heavily on top of him.

They've turned on me already, he thought. Then Calix felt a warmth at his side, reached down and saw the blood on his hand. The blood of the person who lay on top of him. He was dead.

A round pinged off the floor a hand's-width from his face. Sparks flew into his eyes. Calix had no time to mourn the body that lay over him, to honor the sacrifice this person had made. He couldn't even tell who it was yet. Instead he rolled toward the battle, causing the body to flop onto the floor in front of him, providing a barricade.

He saw then. It was Ulrich. He looked into the man's eyes and saw life still there. Ulrich blinked at him.

"I…" he said, blood in his mouth, and then bullets tore into his back. Three wet thuds, each leaving a little less life in those eyes until, finally, mercifully, they became glassy and still.

Calix felt the last warm breath on his face, and then nothing. Ulrich had saved his life, and in return Calix had just used the still-living man to further shield himself. That had been Ulrich's payment for years of loyalty and camaraderie.

"I'm sorry, friend," Calix said under his breath.

The corpse made no reply.

Anger welled up in him. The circumstances didn't matter. This death was a result of the poor decisions made by the Nexus's leadership. Not just those currently in command, but going all the way back to the planning days, when a fucking bureaucrat had decided on some asinine rules of succession that failed to take into account who might be put in charge. The system would pick whoever happened to be of highest seniority, as if that were all that mattered.

As a result, an inept moron bean counter and a depressed ambassador were making life-and-death decisions for thousands of souls. Sloane, at least, had her shit together, but as far as he was concerned her presence among that group could be attributed to luck, not design.

It culminated here, in the death of a hard-working innocent man, loyal both to the mission and to Calix Corvannis. He pushed himself to his feet and began to walk toward the hangar, his rifle raised. The security officer hadn't moved from behind the crate. Calix walked right around the side of the box and shot the surprised security officer point blank. A barrage that sapped her kinetic shield in seconds.

The woman convulsed under the onslaught, her mouth in an 'O' of surprise even as the life went out in her eyes.

"Grab everything," he said, to everyone and yet no one. "Carts are there." He pointed to a row of the levitating platforms all parked in a line along one wall.

Then he went after William Spender.

The man had made his home in a closet near the vast hangar, just a few meters down the hall. He'd locked himself inside. Calix tried his omni-tool, then remembered that his access had been yanked. So he knocked, hard. "Are you in there, Spender? It's Calix. Open the door."

A voice inside. Muffled. "I can't be seen talking to you."

"Why'd you help us back there?"

"Did I?"

Calix chewed on that, but only for a second. He wanted to hear the man's words, however calculated they might be. He needed to know if he had a leadership insider sympathetic to his cause. "If you're with us, just say so. I can protect you."

"I'm not with anyone," Spender snapped.

"Spender—"

"You might want to run along now, Calix. I have a duty to report this event."

Calix puffed out a breath. "We'll discuss this later."

A muffled, single laugh from inside. "Yeah. Who knows, maybe I'll see you on the other side."

And then Calix heard Spender's hushed voice, reporting the very attack he'd just helped Calix win.

Calix Corvannis could only shake his head, and hurry away.

CHAPTER TWENTY-SIX

She'd reached a full sprint when the armory came into view. Sloane stopped a dozen paces out, crouched behind a low railing, and surveyed the scene.

Bodies. The splatter of blood.

Her gut twisted into a knot. Those were her people in there. Her family. Cut down. *And by Calix, for fuck's sake.* She'd known he was clever. Politically savvy. But this? He'd kept this side hidden well.

"I've got at least two officers down," she said. "Who's armed?"

Several of her team chimed in, and without needing an order they came forward while the others moved to the back. Sloane pointed at two of them and gestured toward the right side of the armory entrance. The others would know to follow her to the left.

Pistol in hand, she was off, running again while bent at the waist, her eyes darting from the path ahead to the door off to her right. Her team moved like fluid, spilling through the sporadic cover and flowing across the open space before reaching the bulkhead like a wave against a seawall.

Sloane did not hesitate. She nodded once to the officer directly across the bulkhead from her, and the two of them rounded the corners and entered the room with barely a pause. She swept her weapon to the obvious hiding places, fist loose on the grip, finger resting on the trigger, all of it cupped in her off-hand palm.

"Calix!" she called out. "Surrender now and we'll show leniency. You have my word." Sloane wasn't quite sure if she meant that, but she knew her team wouldn't believe it. They'd see it as a tactic to get the enemy out in the open, and that was fine. Maybe that's what it was.

Nothing stirred. The room remained as quiet as the bodies that lay within it. Sloane moved to the nearest victim, felt for a pulse, and found none. A deep pain gripped her—and a fear as well. Whatever the reasoning for this, whatever Calix's motivation, blood had been shed. Security had been targeted.

Her team would be out for revenge.

Sloane debated giving the speech. One she'd had to give many times in her career. The need to maintain professionalism. Respect for the rule of law. Innocent until proven *blah blah blah*. In her experience security personnel always reacted the same way to that speech. Lots of nodding and agreement, and then it all went out the fucking window the moment they had their perp in sight.

Screw it then. This was more, so much more, than a simple altercation. They'd raided the armory. Stolen weapons. She glanced around and didn't need to take an inventory to know. Whole shelves had been emptied. This room had been stocked to handle whatever the Nexus might encounter in Andromeda, and for a security staff ten times what she'd been able to wake for the emergency.

Enough to supply a small army.

"Spread out," she said. "Search the room."

They were long gone already, but she needed a minute to think. Her team flooded in and began an aisle-to-aisle search. Sloane lifted her wrist and tapped into the omni-tool. She called for medics.

"Bring body bags." She reported the deaths of three security staff and one life-support tech in the armory.

"Sir?" She jumped involuntarily. One of her officers had approached from the direction of the weapons lockers. The ones with military training always called her "sir."

She let it slide. "Go ahead."

"They were smart," the woman said. "Only took the weapons that didn't have tracking gear. We won't be able to find them via sensors."

"Figures," Sloane replied, shaking her head. Calix knew his stuff, or someone with him did. She wondered what other surprises he had in store. She also wondered how long he'd been planning this. Bits of her interview with him after Irida's arrest replayed in her mind. She'd gone to get information from him, and somehow told him far more than someone of his rank needed to know.

He had that way about him. She shuddered at the memory of it, feeling like the victim of a con. Combined with the knowledge that his entire team had followed him from their previous posting, and phrases like "cult of personality" started to flitter through her mind.

Their search complete, the rest of her team gathered around. One look at their faces confirmed what she already knew. As she suspected, they'd gotten away.

"Tracking down these weapons is our top priority now," she said to them. "Arm up as best you can, with whatever's left. I'll need two of you to remain here with the door closed and locked. Minch, Kwan, you handle it. No one gets in unless you clear it with me first. Understood?"

They both nodded. Someone offered Sloane a rifle.

She took it, checked the load out, and deactivated the safety.

"Everyone else with me."

||||||||||||||||||||||

"We have to seal the room," Tann said.

He ignored the shocked intake of breath from Foster Addison. She'd reach the same conclusion soon enough. For now, there was no time to debate. He left her at the console and strode toward the doors.

Spender stood near the wall, casually reviewing who-knows-what on his omni-tool. More reports of looting or firefights, no doubt. Spender had been in the middle of just such a battle only minutes before, and barely escaped with his life from the way he told it.

Tann nodded to him as he passed. "Help me secure the room."

No guards were posted at the Operations door. Hadn't been since the Scourge had struck, in fact. Tann marveled at that, in hindsight. Despite everything, he'd never once thought to have security posted here. Whatever grumblings the crew might have, he had not truly believed anything like this could happen.

A miscalculation, one he intended not to make again.

Spender helped him with the doors. There were three entrances to Operations, two of which led to blocked passageways, but they sealed those all the same. The time for lax security, for taking chances, was over.

"In a strange way," Tann said as he rejoined Addison, "this altercation gives us the excuse we need to act with impunity. If the crew won't return to cryostasis of their own accord, they—"

"How can you even be talking about that?" Addison asked, naked disgust on her face. "Three people are dead in the armory. Who knows how many more in Hydroponics."

"That is exactly what I'm talking about," Tann said, confused at her resistance.

"The bodies are still warm and you're already trying to twist this into some kind of advantage."

He shrugged. "Of course. Any event must be factored into future decisions and directions. Naturally—"

"I can't listen to this right now," she said, and she walked away. Tann debated following her, explaining, but Spender caught his eye. The man held up one hand and made a face, a uniquely human expression that said, *I've got this.*

So be it. Tann went back to the console. Its capabilities were still limited, but one thing he could do was access cameras placed around the station. Not all of them, but some. Hopefully enough.

Every one of them showed nearly the same thing. People running about, or clustered in groups embroiled in heated conversation, some on the verge of violence. Panic and chaos. Exactly what Calix Corvannis wanted, no doubt. Tann stroked his chin, impressed despite himself. He'd underestimated the turian. Or rather, he'd had no reason to estimate him at all. Calix was middle-management. A capable life-support technician and a reasonably good leader of his team. Tann wondered what kind of background could lead someone like that to exhibit such political acuity.

He brought up Calix's personnel file and skimmed it. Nothing stood out. Assigned to various ships and space stations throughout his career, rising to a rank of chief only a year before the Andromeda Initiative put out its open call for volunteers. Interestingly, Calix's application had come in late, and it wasn't just him. He and his entire team had all applied simultaneously. In his application Calix had stated that they would join the Initiative together, or not at all.

Tann pondered this for a moment. He pulled a chair over and sat. Sipping water, he pulled up the dossiers on everyone that reported to Calix, skipping the summaries and analysis in favor of the detailed parts. He began to read.

⁣⁣⁣⁣⁣⁣⁣⁣⁣⁣⁣⁣⁣⁣⁣⁣⁣⁣⁣

Three levels below Operations, a group of armed civilians rushed into a common area frequented by the non-krogan members of the crew.

Calix had hoped it would be empty, that people would have decided it best to stay in their quarters until the situation settled down. He'd neglected to consider the fact that most didn't *have* quarters. They'd taken to sleeping in the commons, out of necessity and perhaps for the company.

And so there they were. Clustered in little groups, engaged in hushed, urgent conversations. The room went quiet at the sight of him and his... gang? Somewhere along the line he'd begun to think of them that way, and saw the truth of it in the eyes of those who were now staring, wide-eyed.

How we must look, he thought, barreling in with assault rifles in hand and the splatter of blood on their uniforms. For an instant Calix feared they might seek to block his path. Then came the odd sense that they might instead burst into applause. Congratulate him for standing up for their rights.

What actually happened was both.

Shouts of derision, exclamations of support, all mingled together into something else. The crowd split along ideological lines and chaos quickly ensued. Fights broke out. People shouted, falling to the floor, running for safer ground. Somehow he found himself at the center of it all, surrounded in a bubble of loaded weapons wielded by his almost perversely loyal team. His *gang*.

Yes, Calix thought, that really was the most apt description. No getting around it. Most of them had been with him for years. A bunch of misfits he'd somehow managed to tame, one at a time. They'd said—after the *Warsaw*—that they would follow him anywhere. He hadn't meant to put that to the test when he announced he was going to apply for Andromeda. In fact, he'd hoped to finally break from this life and start fresh. But they'd been good to their word, and before he even realized what was happening, they'd decided for him that the application would be for the entire team.

That had been born more of a desire to leave a horribly commanded ship *en masse* than anything else. He doubted back then, as he did now, that they'd really understood what they were getting into by joining the Initiative. They just wanted to be part of something.

Well, they got their wish, and then some, he thought.

Calix stopped halfway through the room. He held up his hands and called for silence as his armed escort maintained the circle around him, their guns pointed outward like spears. The crowd continued to jostle, arguments growing heated. Calix opened his mouth to appeal for quiet again, but before he could one of his techs fired off a few rounds into the ceiling.

The crowd went dead silent, all eyes on him.

Calix waited for the dust and debris to settle before addressing them.

"All of us were pulled from cryo for a reason," he said. "To fix the Nexus. This isn't just some ship we've been assigned to. It's not a temporary post. The Nexus is *our* home. Our shelter. We still don't know what damaged this place. Nobody does. Our leadership talks of the Scourge, but a name is about all they have."

He had their full attention. Decided not to squander it.

"Now we learn this Scourge has lain waste to every planet in our vicinity. One of our scouts didn't even return, probably another casualty. This unknown force could strike again at any time and we wouldn't know, because sensors are still broken with little hope of repair."

"Maybe the sensors team needs replacing!" someone shouted.

Another voice fired right back. "We can't fix anything without the parts. It's fabrications that can't cope with—"

Yet another voice interrupted. "Fab is doing everything it can to keep up. But every time we start manufacturing something, we're told to cancel it because a higher priority has come up."

Nods of agreement.

Calls of "bullshit."

Blame met with blame.

Calix raised his hands again. "We've all been working hard. If we blame anyone, it has to be our interim leadership. They were never chosen for this job, and they're clearly not capable of it."

A mixed response, but more in agreement than not. Good enough.

"Bad decisions," he continued. "Constantly shifting positions and priorities. Outright deception. And behind it all, the possibility we'll be hit again by this Scourge. Despite all that, their solution is for us to return to cryo. Just take a little nap and all our problems will go away." More were nodding now. He had momentum. "That's their plan? That we're supposed to go to sleep and place our trust in them?

"Well, I won't," he said, his voice rising. "My team won't participate. We've refused to operate the stasis pods. We want an election, leaders who can be fair and decisive. Most importantly, leaders who are willing to consider all possible solutions—including abandoning the mission for the sake of our survival."

A calculated risk, and Calix paused to see what would happen. His own team might turn on him, though that wasn't likely. The crowd might tear him limb from limb for opposing Garson's vision.

His team held their ground, and waited.

The crowd split like a cleaved log, and erupted into violence.

CHAPTER TWENTY-SEVEN

She heard the sounds of riot and raced toward it. Fifty officers at her back, their boots like thunder on the tiled passageway floor. Sloane clenched her jaw and ran scenarios through her mind. Surround the...

The what? What had Calix and his team become? This was no simple protest. His speech had implied as much. To resist the order to return to cryo-sleep, by definition it made these people a resistance. Some of them, anyway. That meant mutiny then, didn't it? A rebellion? Did the fucking semantics really matter?

She supposed they did, when it came to meting out punishment. Disobeying orders could be handled with as little as a warning, maybe some time in the brig. Mutiny, though, that meant death. That meant a short trip out the airlock and a long spiral into the nearest star.

The resistance, Sloane decided. For now. Some part of her still wanted to give Calix the benefit of the doubt. After all he'd said in that interview, and how much work he'd put into keeping them all alive, she owed him that much.

She reached the common area first. A few hundred people were jostling, arguing. Some were engaged in brawls. An asari chopped a human in the neck with the flat of her hand, sending the man to the floor in a choking gag. A turian threw punches at another of his species, who returned them blow for blow.

In the center of it all huddled a cluster that moved

as one. A circle, all the participants facing outward to protect whoever or whatever was in the center. Maybe someone was down, trampled, and those who'd managed to hold onto a sense of decency were trying to protect them from further damage.

No, Sloane knew better. She saw their uniforms—those of the life-support crew. But even without that, she could see their faces. Expressions she knew well, from a thousand sec-cam recordings and, less often, in person. Thugs and common criminals wore that expression while doing their deeds.

Then she saw Calix, right there in the center of them. They weren't protecting a fallen comrade. They were protecting their leader.

For a split second Sloane's eyes locked with the turian. She knew her gaze asked *why*? And his seemed to say, *Because you forced me to*. No remorse in that fleeting glimpse, nor any hint that this might end here, peacefully. He and his group weren't just going to lay down arms.

"Too many civvies around!" one of her officers shouted over the crowd. Sloane refocused on her immediate surroundings. Someone—a human male amped up on adrenaline—whirled toward her and threw a punch without realizing who faced him. He tried to pull the fist back, too late, and caught Sloane on the chin. The bastard was big, and even with his effort to stop himself there remained enough force behind that fist to send her staggering a step back.

She tasted warm rust in her mouth, and spat.

One of her officers, Martinez, stepped in and coiled to strike. Sloane tried to shout no, but only blood came out in an ugly cough. Martinez struck the man in his gut with the butt of an assault rifle. Sloane heard the air *woosh* from the man as he crumpled to the floor.

Not like this, she wanted to shout. Someone in the crowd saw the attack, hadn't seen Sloane get hit, and jumped to conclusions.

"Security's against us!" they shouted. "Resist!"

Sloane tried to grab Martinez by the arm, to hold him back, to appeal for cooler heads. But her fingers missed his bicep. She felt the brush of sleeve against her fingertips, and he barreled into the fray. Her officer slammed into the protester who'd shouted, leading with his shoulder, and the pair went down in a tangle of limbs. The crowd closed in around them, and just like that, Martinez was gone.

The melee changed, then. It took on a life of its own, transforming into an all-out brawl. Sloane knew this moment, too, from past experience. There would be no miraculous return to common sense. No, this would end only when one side was beaten into submission, or retreated. All they could do was push toward that moment, as fast as they could, and hope in the seconds between now and then that no weapons were discharged.

Calix and his circle were making their way toward a bulkhead opposite the one Sloane had entered. She kicked an asari out of her way and moved closer, ducking a punch in the process, returning it with one of her own that landed. A nose splintered under her fist. She didn't stop, dimly aware that she shouldn't get too far from her team. For the thousandth time she wished Kandros were here. He'd recognize this and know to stay at her side.

"They're going for the bulkhead!" a woman shouted. One of hers. Sloane realized the cry had been meant for her.

"I know," she called. "We've got to cut them off."

And then the woman stood next to her, with her, like Kandros would have. Another officer appeared to Sloane's left.

"Use your omni," she said. "Seal it."

Of course. Sloane knelt and tried to forget the combat swirling all around her now. A knee jostled her. Someone almost stepped on her hand as she struggled not to fall. Finally there was a precious second of calm. Sloane attacked her omni-tool, found the menu, accessed her location marker on the map. Then she found the door, and set it to closed.

She glanced up. The door didn't budge.

Calix and his group were almost to it.

"What the..." she said to herself. Her eyes narrowed. In her glimpse of Calix she'd seen the omni on his arm, and she remembered. The database Irida had stolen. Among the litany of items it contained, one was bulkhead maintenance codes. Calix had claimed ignorance of the stolen data, but he'd had it after all. *That's how he got into the weapons storage.* That was why all of the doors had opened. Everyone had unfettered access to everything—and she'd only left guards at the armory. She'd deliberately kept her forces out of sight, as a way to inspire calm.

"I'm such an idiot," she muttered. A list of all the vulnerable places ran through her mind. Operations. Security's offices. The Colonial Affairs hangar. The spare hangar appropriated for supply storage. The water tanks and reclimators. The still-sealed cryo pods.

The vast, unvisited, silent portions of the Nexus. Down a tunnel she herself had helped Kesh clear. Calix wasn't on the verge of being cornered. He was about to trap her and the rest of the waking crew in a tiny portion of the vast station.

Oh, fuck.

Sloane watched as Calix, his cohorts, and a small army of sudden converts to his cause all entered the access tunnel. She could see a whole fleet of lev-carts in there, and people waiting with them. Piled with rations and water and who-knows-what-else.

Now the door closed, at Calix's command via a wall panel.

Sloane Kelly called for a retreat.

iiiiiiiiiiiiiiiiii

She headed toward Operations, sending frantic messages to Kesh as she went. So far the krogan had not replied. Sloane wondered how the Nakmor clan was reacting to all this. They hadn't exactly jumped willingly back into their cryo pods either.

On the other hand, they were near the end of the list. And besides, Kesh could always threaten them with the wrath of Nakmor Morda, should they complain.

They should consider themselves lucky Morda's not awake, she mused. *Then again, we're all lucky Morda's not awake.*

Calix had betrayed Kesh, too. Technically he worked for her, one of the few non-krogan teams to report to Kesh. Had he discussed any of this with her? Were they collaborating? Sloane let out a worried sigh. She doubted it. *Refused* to believe it. Kesh was loyal to the mission, despite her differences with the leadership, Tann in particular.

But damn… if the krogan were part of this. If this turned out to be some kind of coup designed to re-cast the political landscape of Andromeda before old biases became entrenched once again…

"We'd be doomed," Sloane said to herself. Her

team, no matter how well trained, no matter how much help they received from civilians, were no match for an organized krogan opposition.

She glanced at her omni-tool again.

"C'mon, Kesh. Respond."

Her team passed clustered groups of the Nexus's crew. Some were gathered around wide-open doors, presumably defending what lay behind. Their work or their own possessions, Sloane hoped—though from what she saw in some of their eyes, their intentions might be decidedly less honorable.

"What's wrong with the doors?" someone shouted at her. "Why won't they close?"

"We're working on it," Sloane shouted back without stopping. She couldn't spare the staff to help defend the contents of those rooms. Calix knew this, too, the clever bastard.

She reached a promenade that ran parallel to one of the Nexus's long arms. The view should have been glorious. Verdant gardens. Personal vehicles streaking along, citizens strolling as they shopped or sought a meal and the company of their fellow crew.

But the wide space had been heavily damaged in the Scourge. Part of the deck above had collapsed along its edge, obstructing the exterior view. The net effect was a wide avenue lined with shops on one side, still packed with their wares, and a mess of debris on the other.

Shots rang out.

Sloane hit the ground even before the noise really registered. An instinct honed over years. She crawled forward to take cover behind a long low decorative planter as rapid bursts from an assault rifle hissed through the air and sparked against the walkway beside her.

There was a pause in the gunfire, and she chanced a look over the wall. All she saw were dark storefronts. Her team had become spread out as they'd made their way here. Only a few of them were with her, the rest still just silhouettes down the long hallway she'd just come through.

"Anyone see them?" she asked.

No one had.

"Spread out," Sloane ordered. She motioned toward the rest of her officers, now at the mouth of the tunnel, advising them to stay back. Of the four out here with her, three shuffled or crawled farther away from her, taking positions as best they could.

One hadn't moved since she'd given the order. Sloane felt an all-too-familiar knot of dread in her gut at the motionless, curled body.

A burst of fire clattered against the wall around the tunnel opening, sending her team there scrambling back into the shadows.

"In ten seconds I want covering fire," she said, just loud enough for the three near her to understand. "Disruptor rounds, for effect, understand? Overhead. Pin them."

On her belly she crawled to the other end of the planter and brought her own weapon around. Careful to keep her back low—the planter wall stood only a half-meter high or so—Sloane brought one foot up and under her, readying herself to spring.

Exactly ten seconds after her order the three officers began to fire on the row of storefronts. Sloane turned and shouted back at the hallway.

"Medic! Come now! One down, immobile!"

Without waiting for a reply, she pushed to her feet and ran, eyes on the ground to avoid the dazzling flashes that flickered all across the signage above the row of stores. She angled herself for the nearest shop and shouldered her way through the entrance, into shadow.

With any luck the enemy had not seen her cross. The gunplay continued, and it yielded one benefit— intel. She'd counted four of them. One in an adjacent business, three more farther down the row.

Moving through the empty aisles of the dark store, keeping her light off so her eyes could adjust, she swung her weapon at each corner. No one inside. No reason anyone would be, though. The place was empty.

No one at the back of the store, either. In fact the whole row was empty, as far as she knew.

So why were there armed thugs stationed there?

A maintenance door at the back let her into a labyrinthine tunnel system that allowed shop workers to come and go, deliveries to be made without bothering the flow of customers. Activity ahead gave her pause. Low voices and the sounds of gear being moved or assembled.

"You got too greedy," someone said.

"Shut up and help," another replied.

She glanced behind her, only to confirm what she already knew. She was alone here. Sloane crept forward in the darkness. The gunfire behind her dwindled into the background, sounding more like distant thunder. Ahead someone swore, then the sound of something crashing to the ground. Sensing her chance, Sloane rushed forward. She entered a small storeroom, empty save for a pair of human men in the uniforms of life support. Together they were trying to load a sack of something onto a lev-cart.

"Step away, hands where I can see them," Sloane said.

They dropped the bag. Tens of thousands of tiny pale objects skittered and bounced across the floor.

Seeds, Sloane realized.

Neither of the men surrendered. As their loot showered the floor, both turned and ran for the door opposite the one through which Sloane had entered. She stepped forward and let off a few rounds in their direction, aiming low in the hopes of hitting a thigh or knee, and ending their escape. But her foot landed on the carpet of small hard shells and she slipped. Not much, but enough.

Her aim went high and her first shot slapped into the back of the nearest of the two. The man went down, limp before he hit the ground. His companion rounded the next corner and vanished into the store beyond.

Sloane ignored the spilled seeds, aware of their value to the Nexus's survival but unable to do anything about it now. She paid them only enough attention to keep from losing her footing again. In seconds she crossed the room and stepped over the dead body.

More bloodshed. Sloane feared this was only the beginning.

The hallway split. She could go forward, or up a flight of narrow stairs, probably to some kind of office. Surprise no longer on her side, she flicked on her tactical light and studied the floor. There, on the steps, were the remnants of crushed seeds. She went up, two steps at a time, using only her toes to minimize sound.

When she was two steps from the top the space before her erupted in light and deafening sound. A flash round. She staggered back, blinded, deaf. Almost fell, somehow managed to keep her feet. She could see nothing, hear nothing, but the narrow space made the direction obvious.

Sloane fired blind toward the room at the top of the stairs, full auto now, her weapon set to alternate between armor-piercing and incendiary rounds. Her ears withered under the continued assault of noise, but her vision returned. Not much, but enough. She kept climbing, firing all the way, offering no gap through which the enemy could regain their footing and return fire.

At the top of the stairs she pushed on into the office, still shooting. Tables and chairs erupted into chunks of metal and splintered faux wood. A window at the far end, overlooking the promenade where her team had first come under fire, was suddenly riddled with a line of bullet holes, every other one ringed with black charring.

The window farthest to her right, though, was open, and Sloane just barely caught a glimpse of her prey's leg as he climbed out onto the signage and disappeared behind the wall.

She leaned into a full sprint, ready to pursue, but some instinct told her no, *danger*. She pulled up. Too late. A blow to her shins sent her sprawling. Her gun clattered away to vanish under one of the ruined tables. She twisted, ignoring the searing pain across her legs as she leapt back to her feet.

A fist. Sloane ducked, the blow grazing the top her head. She threw a punch of her own. Solid contact with the man's stomach. He grunted, doubled over in time to become acquainted with her knee to his jaw.

Her vision began to return in time to watch blood fountain from his mouth. He backpedaled. Sloane went after him, then paused when she saw his hand.

He'd been fumbling for a pistol, had it now. She turned and dove toward the table that had claimed her own weapon. Rolling over it, she landed hard on her back as his shots slammed into the metal surface.

"It's over for you," the man said, only somewhat intelligible with a mouth full of blood. "Calix has a plan, and he's ten steps ahead of you. Give up now and you can live—"

A terrible shriek cut his words short.

Sloane heard him crumple to the ground, and behind that, the low crackling of dissipating biotic power. She took a tentative glance over the top of the table. Talini stood there, her blue skin almost iridescent in the dim light.

"You okay?" the asari asked.

"Yeah," Sloane said. "Yeah, though if you'd been a second later... What did you do to him?"

"Reave," she answered.

"Not fooling around," Sloane observed.

Talini raised her chin slightly. "I think we're past that stage now, don't you?"

‖‖‖‖‖‖‖‖‖‖‖

Ten minutes later Sloane Kelly reached the door to Operations. It was sealed, a good sign. The one barrier that even Calix couldn't override. She pinged Tann and Addison on their private channel and announced herself. A few seconds later the door opened from within.

She almost collided with Spender coming through. He must have been waiting right inside.

"So?" he asked in an oddly hushed tone. "Did you catch them?"

"Afraid not," Sloane replied. It hurt to admit. She

almost launched into her story, but Spender gave a quick nod and stepped aside, letting her through as if he no longer cared.

"Well, well," Tann said, "the spymaster returns."

"Not now, Tann."

"You could have told us you were installing *hidden* cameras. We should have discussed the privacy implications—"

"I said I'd beef up security," she shot back.

"You neglected to specify!"

"*Look*," Sloane hissed, "this has to wait for later. We've got a mutiny to deal with, in case you hadn't noticed."

The judgmental glare did not waver, but he let her in all the same. By unspoken agreement the rest of Sloane's team remained outside. Talini gave Sloane a terse nod as the door sealed. A tiny incline of her head that somehow managed to say, *We may not be in there with you, but we're all with you.*

Emboldened, she turned back toward Tann. The slithery Spender loomed in the background, as if uninterested now.

"They hit the armory," she said, blunt and to the point. It seemed best. "At this point they might be better armed than we are."

"How could this have possibly happened?" Tann demanded. "The one room in this station that should have been impenetrable, and from what Spender tells me Calix and his criminal gang just waltzed right in."

"He had the overrides for the doors. It was in the data that asari stole. I don't know why I didn't think—"

"I thought the criminal you jailed had not passed that information on?"

"So Calix claimed."

"And you neglected to change these codes?" Tann asked, already pacing. "Despite the circumstances?"

"I…" she paused, allowed herself a steadying breath. "I think this is going to be a short fucking meeting if you try to pin the whole thing on me."

CHAPTER TWENTY-EIGHT

Tann paced, his steps so fierce Sloane thought it only a matter of minutes before he'd wear a visible path into the floor.

"Reports of looting are coming in from all over," he said. "Fighting in the common areas. Hydroponics is ruined, and may never recover." She let him rant, barely listening, her eyes cast upward to the ceiling.

"We need to get the doors closed," Spender said. "This station is wide open right now, enabling all this behavior."

"Agreed," Tann said. "In fact I don't understand why it hasn't been done yet." He aimed this at Sloane.

"Because Calix made sure it wouldn't happen, not without a full reset of the configuration."

"So do a full reset," Tann said. "What are you waiting for?"

"A full reset takes time, and while it's in progress a lot more than just open doors would be rendered insecure."

"Shut them manually then."

"A team would have to be sent to each door, and then it would need to be protected until the reset could be performed."

Tann only grumbled at this, because this at least he understood. Manually closing all the doors would require a large workforce, which meant the krogan. As of yet, no one had been able to locate them. Or Kesh.

Or Addison, for that matter. She hadn't been seen in hours. *Probably found a dark corner to hide in*, Sloane thought, but she didn't say it aloud.

"Spender," Tann said.

"Sir?"

"What assignment was the krogan workforce on when all this started? Where were they?"

Spender didn't need to look it up. "Replacing ruptured electrical conduit between decks nine and ten."

"And Kesh was with them?"

"Who knows. She's got her big snout in everything."

"Now, now," Tann said, though without any real force. Spender barely tolerated Kesh, and the feeling was mutual, which was probably why their paths so rarely crossed. Some history there, but Sloane had yet to ask either of them about it. "Answer the question."

"I have no idea if Kesh is with them," Spender said bluntly.

Sloane saw where this was going. "I'll head down there and find her."

"Send a team," Tann said. "A *small* team. I think you should remain here. You're the face of security. You need to be seen... securing."

Sloane glared at him. "With all due respect, I'll make decisions about how best to make use of myself and my officers."

Tann stopped, mid-step, and faced her. He said nothing.

Sloane went on. "Calix worked for Kesh. We don't know yet what Kesh's... attitude... toward this activity is."

"Are you saying she's in on it? That the krogan are part of it?"

"Do not go there," Sloane said quickly. The last thing she needed now was for Tann's natural distrust of the krogan to become a factor. A bigger factor than it already was, at least. "The krogan have been nothing but loyal from the moment they woke."

"So had our life-support team."

"I have no reason to believe they've turned on us. What I *do* fear is that Calix has already thought about this. That he chose his moment when he knew they would be far away, out of comms range."

Tann nodded thoughtfully. "He might have even done something to sabotage them."

"Well, I wouldn't go that far."

"I would."

Sloane sighed. "You know, no one has suggested the most obvious approach to this. I could try talking to Calix."

The salarian looked at her as if she'd spoken in an alien tongue.

"*You?*" Spender's eyebrows climbed halfway to his hairline. "That's a terrible idea."

"Got someone else in mind?"

Spender let out a smug laugh. "Someone with a bit more political finesse, perhaps. I'd be happy to deal with Calix—"

"Should we have a listen to the speech you wrote for Tann? As a masterclass in political finesse."

"This is an irrelevant conversation," Tann snapped. "We do not negotiate with terrorists."

Sloane stepped up to him, got right in his face. "Done listening to your advisors, are you?" To his credit, Tann held her gaze. He did not step away.

"Forgive me," he said carefully. "I assumed that you, of all people, would agree with such a policy."

"Oh, I do, I do," she replied. "I'm just not convinced yet that the term terrorist applies."

"You may need to reexamine your definition of the word then," Tann said, showing surprising backbone. "They assaulted the armory. Killed the guards you posted there! Burned hydroponics. I could go on, but really, isn't that sufficient?"

Sloane found she couldn't argue, yet didn't want to admit he was right, either. She clenched her jaw and stared him back.

Tann held up his hands. "Look," he said, "find Kesh. Maybe you could track down Addison while you're at it, but the bulk of your team needs to remain up here, visible. We need to restore order as much as we need to stop Calix, whatever method we end up choosing to stop him."

Sloane heard all this, agreed with it, even, but she shifted her gaze to Spender and glared wrathfully for a few seconds before speaking.

"When this is over," she said, staring at the weasel, "there's going to be some changes around here."

With that she turned, and left. In the hall outside her team waited, arrayed as if expecting an invading army to come at Operations. They all looked at her expectantly. Sloane steeled herself.

"Talini," she said.

The asari lifted her chin.

"Take three volunteers. You're to track down Foster Addison and bring her back here safely. Try the CA offices, or the hangar."

"Understood."

Sloane looked at the others. "I'll need three of you with me. Kesh and the krogan workforce are out of comms range, and we need them in order to secure the doors." There was no shortage of raised hands to pick from, so Sloane pointed at three randomly.

"Two stay here, the rest of you spread out," she said. "We can't defend Operations at the expense of the rest of the station. Start with the areas adjacent to here, make your presence known, restore order." She paused, then added, "Try not to shoot anyone, understand? These people are scared, they're on edge, and they have every right to be. If we're acting the same way, that only amplifies, understand? We need to be the reasonable ones."

Nods all around.

"Good," Sloane said. "Let's move."

She marched back through the common area outside of Operations, bolstered by the flow of her officer core around her. They spread outward to the left and right, the formation bringing a mixture of emotions to the faces in the crowd that had followed them here in the first place. Some looked soothed, others as if they were about to be beaten down.

"Stay in your rooms," Sloane said to them. "Or here in the commons. Anyone looting or causing a disturbance will be dealt with according to the laws of the Nexus." She said this loudly, for her own troops to hear more than anything. They needed to know the right things to say. Those exact words would be repeated as her officers spread from section to section.

With each area she entered, a few more soldiers peeled off to put down in-progress thefts or angry altercations. Sloane tried not to flinch when a bit of rotten food slapped against her neck, thrown by one of the malcontents. She ignored it, resolving to brush it away when they left the area.

But not before.

They passed back through the row of shops cleared earlier of Calix's left-behinds. Sloane saw shadows in those stores once again, only this time she knew they were citizens, taking anything they could find. She gestured for her last few extra officers to get in there.

"Careful," she said as they jogged away. "You're outnumbered." They nodded, fear obvious in some of their eyes, though they did not break stride.

People moved in the shadows, scurrying like rats as Sloane approached, hiding until she passed. At her back they shouted for new leadership, or simply the mantra that seemed to be catching.

"No Cryo! No Cryo!"

"Faster," Sloane said. They were only four, now, and still had seven levels to go before they'd find Kesh. "From here on we do not engage, we do not let ourselves be seen any more than we have to."

"Understood," her trio replied in unison.

Sloane avoided the next hall. Too many silhouettes lurking there. She led her group across the promenade fronting the shops and to the railing at the edge. There was a small gap in the section of ceiling that had collapsed across it. The space overlooked one of the Nexus's long arms, and the wall leading up to it was slanted. Sloane hopped over the railing, holding on as her body came to rest against the outer-sloped wall. She started to move along the length, looking for her spot, when a shout went up from the citizens in the shadowed hallway.

"Stop 'em before they freeze us!"

Cries of agreement, encouragement.

The crowds, Sloane realized, had already stratified. Those still loyal to the mission, and those who'd been broken by fear and encouraged by Calix's success. They rushed out. She watched them through the railing, considered lifting her other arm over it and firing off a few rounds to give them pause.

No, she thought. *Don't engage, it only delays us.* She let go of the railing and started to slide. Her team followed suit. As a group they slid, ran and sometimes tumbled their way down the incline to the next level, spilling over on to an unused balcony still coated in the residue of the fire suppression systems. No one had yet been here.

Sloane grunted as she landed, rolling with the impact to little effect. It hurt like hell. The rest of her group fared just as poorly, but within a few seconds they were up and, while in pain, ready to follow. The angry group above seemed content to celebrate the fact that they'd scared off some security officers, and did not pursue.

Enjoy your victory, bastards. She glanced at her team. "We keep moving, but not that way anymore. I can't take another landing like that."

The relief in their eyes matched her own. Sloane led them from balcony to balcony, hopping the low walls in between each, heading inward toward the main connected spoke of the Nexus. None of the lifts had yet been cleared for use, but thanks to Calix all their doors would be wide open, and the tubes had ladders built into the walls for maintenance and emergency access.

At the last apartment on the row Sloane slipped in through the open balcony door. Darkness waited within, along with the smell of dust. She flipped her weapon's lamp on and moved through the dim rooms at a jog, swinging her weapon before her as she went, finding no one.

Exiting through the font door, she peeled around

one corner, taking the left, trusting the officer behind her to peel right. The man did. The other two came out after him, crossing to the far side. Sloane motioned for them to follow her lead. Somewhere nearby a bark of laughter echoed through the halls. Then, more distant, the sound of someone crying out in pain.

"What a nightmare," the officer behind her whispered.

"Quiet," she snapped, as much as she agreed with the sentiment.

They bypassed the next common area. Sloane glanced toward it. This was where Calix and his core group had fled behind that bulkhead. The space languished in darkness now, lights turned off or perhaps deliberately destroyed. The beam from her weapon played across shapes in the darkness. Bodies strewn about the floor. Her gut twisted at the sight. Calix could never have wanted this. Advocated it. Ordered it. No way. That wasn't the turian she'd interviewed after Irida's arrest, or worked beside all these months.

The Irida interrogation, though... Sloane might not have seen any of this in Calix, but *Irida* had. Which meant Calix had completely and cleverly hidden a large part of his personality from her, or he'd underestimated the power he had over people. She wondered what had happened on that prior posting, that it had given rise to such loyalty among his team.

They reached the lift without incident. Sloane hesitated. Glanced back at the dark common-room-turned-graveyard.

"Kesh and her team are six levels below," she whispered. "You three meet up with her and explain what's happened."

"You're not coming?" one of them asked.

"Negative," Sloane said. "I've got something else I need to take care of."

Hesitation radiated off them.

"Look," she added. "I doubt anyone else went down there. Kesh is reasonable, and on our side." *I hope.* She left that unsaid, and went on. "Explain what's happened and bring her up here to within omni-tool range. Let her talk to Tann."

"Where are you going?"

"I have to find someone."

They glanced at each other, dubious.

"Need-to-know, understood?" She sharpened her tone. "I'm giving you three an order and I expect you to follow it."

"And if Kesh is being unreasonable? Or they've been... I don't know, sabotaged by the terrorists in some way?"

"Then don't engage, just come right back up here and report. I'll be in range." She didn't actually know if that last part was true, but it had to be said. She couldn't ask any of these three to go where she was going. "Move out, officers."

Grudgingly they complied, stepping onto the ladder and starting their descent into the depths of the Nexus. Sloane waited until they were three levels down before she boarded the ladder herself. She slid quickly, past ten steps, then sidled off onto the cool tile floor of the level below. There she took a knee and flicked on her rifle light. The beam found only empty corners in the shadows it chased away. Deserted, though some footprints had been made in the dusty surfaces.

She pressed into the darkness, ears pricked, every sense on high-alert. Sloane had been here a few months ago, scouting a possible way around the blocked tunnel she'd helped the Nakmor workers clear. An hour spent probing the ravaged, seemingly endless labyrinth and just when she'd found a promising route—though narrow as hell and almost inaccessible—Kesh had called her back, saying the way forward had been discovered already.

Sloane's inferior path was more convoluted and thus abandoned in favor of the other, but she remembered the way. At least she thought so. This lab seemed right, but there were so many. She recalled a dented door. Yes, there it was. And the pile of desks and counters that had formed a sort of odd pyramid in one corner, with a crack in the wall at the top that led where she needed to go.

Hmm, she thought, *not seeing them now*.

"Where the hell are you?" she asked the darkness.

To her surprise, the darkness answered.

"State your business here." A gruff voice, heavily accented. Sloane didn't recognize it. No surprise, she knew only a fraction of the people on the Nexus.

"I'd ask you the same."

"We'll be the one asking questions." Movement, to her left and her right. Shadows within shadows. Sloane forced herself to remain calm. It would hurt her cause to enter this place with the tip of her rifle.

"I'm not here to fight," she said.

"What are you here for?" the voice asked.

"I want to talk to Calix Corvannis."

"Never heard of him."

Sloane shook her head. "So the three of you just happen to be down here, in the dark, guarding an unused, yet-to-be-repaired lab that just *happens* to have a hole in the wall back there leading to the section of the Nexus where Calix Corvannis has set up the headquarters of his uprising. Pure coincidence, that it?"

A lot of guesses, but their silence made her grin.

"Now," she went on, "why don't we cut the macho guard-the-door bullshit and get on with this. Either you go let Calix know that Security Director Sloane Kelly is here, *alone*, to speak with him, or I repaint the walls of this room with your innards and go meet him in person. What's it going to be?"

The shadow in front of her materialized as the man stepped into the beam of her light. A tall, hulking figure that looked like he spent every off-hour he had lifting krogan for sport.

"I think we'll go for a third option," he said. "The one where you put down that rifle, and we haul you to see Calix in cuffs. Just so you can know what Irida felt like, *Director*."

Gambling time, she said to herself. Give in now to get close. She would just have to hope that these frontline grunts wouldn't act without their leader's okay. And she doubted Calix had given any specific instructions about her, as opposed to just anyone who showed up, which meant they'd have to ask before they could rough her up—or worse.

So she set her weapon on the floor, and placed her hands at the small of her back, and waited.

They weren't gentle, but despite the vengeance they unjustly wanted for their incarcerated friend, they didn't hurt her, either. Sloane soon found herself being marched, prodded, and pushed through the narrow twisted passage that led, after nearly twenty minutes of walking, to join the corridor she and the Nakmor clan had cleared months ago.

The hallway, one of the Nexus's main arteries, was

clear in only the loosest application of the word. Debris and jumbled equipment still littered its length, but it had all been piled to one side to allow reasonably easy passage. Sloane regretted that decision, now. It had been the easiest way to open the corridor, but now all that piled junk served as cover for Calix's makeshift army. Every discarded crate or torn-out hunk of air processor she passed had one or two rebels crouched behind it, all of them well-armed thanks to their score.

Any regrets she felt about coming here alone, however, vanished at the sight of them. If she'd come here by force with an entire squad at her back, it would have been a bloodbath no matter which side emerged victorious. These assholes might be untrained, but there were a surprising number of them, and they had the advantage that they could wait and remain behind cover as long as it took.

"Looks like you've made yourselves at home," Sloane said to the brute in front of her.

"No talking," he grunted back.

So original. Sloane sighed and went on counting the enemy, creating a little database in her mind of their positions, weapons, and any other details that might be of use. She hoped she'd never need it, but it beat trying to talk to the walking barricade.

He led her into a fabrication room where massive machines lay under protective coverings, dormant and cold. Surrounding these were untidy rows of shelving and workspaces, twisted and jumbled together by the Scourge. More cover, and plenty of room for the rabble. Beyond, if Sloane's memory served, lay one of the empty ark hangars.

From there Calix and his people would have access to nine tenths of the station's real estate, not to mention the access and expertise required to wake whomever they felt they needed—people they could tell any story they wanted. Sloane could no longer deny how brilliant this action was. Calix was no mild-mannered supervisor. Far from it.

"Director Kelly." His voice filtered in from the adjoining small office at the side of the factory floor. Sloane turned and saw him step out, to stand amid a core group of life-support techs. His trusted inner circle, no doubt. These things always took on the same characteristics.

She nodded to him. "Calix," she said. "Not sure what title to give you, actually. Sorry."

He jerked his chin at the brute, his wishes implied in the gesture. A few seconds later Sloane felt her wrists being freed. She immediately went to work flexing the numbness from her hands and rubbing the ache from her wrists.

"I don't need a title," he said. "I just need better decision making."

"Tann's doing the best he can. We all are."

He chuckled, dryly. His cronies picked up on it and echoed the reaction. *All a bit forced*, Sloane thought. *Typical*.

"Can we talk?" she asked him. "In private?"

"Depends," he said. "Is this just a diversion? Get me away from the front when the attack comes?"

"No one's coming to attack, Calix. We need you—all of you—back at your stations."

"You need us in stasis," he said. "And before that, you need us to put everyone else back in stasis. But that's not going to happen." He said this for his own gathered cronies, not her. A tactic she knew well.

"No one is coming to attack," she repeated. "I just

came to talk. I want to understand."

"Understand what?"

"All of it." She swept her arm across the room, indicating the band of wild-eyed miscreants this turian had somehow rallied to his cause, whatever it may be. "Why you did this. People are dead, Calix. Many more are injured. What little supplies remain to us have been looted or destroyed."

For several seconds he just stared at her, as if still trying to decide if he could trust her. If he felt any remorse over the loss of life, he managed to keep it off of his sharp features.

"Take her omni-tool, Reg," Calix said to the brute. He waited in silence while the device was removed, then took it when it was offered to him. Calix powered it off and tossed it aside. He cast an accusing glance at the brute, and Sloane understood that they'd made a mistake by not taking it from her in the first place. She filed that. She hadn't taken the time to have it auto-transmit her location back to anyone, but she could always *say* she had.

"All right," Calix said. "Let's talk." With that he turned and went back into the room.

The brute, Reg, nudged Sloane toward the door.

CHAPTER TWENTY-NINE

The hours ticked away with no word from Addison, Kesh *or* Sloane.

Tann waited, watching the feeds as rebels barreled through the hallways on looting sprees that left injured in their wake. The longer he did so, the more he began to suspect malfeasance from his would-be council partners. The more he suspected, the angrier he became, with one person as his focus.

He understood the urge to go against the grain— even if that grain represented the fundamental basics of law and order. Every being, whatever the species, eventually strayed. It was only natural. *Biological*, even. An imperative that appeared in every sentient lifeform.

Tann wasn't unfeeling. He did understand. With anything else—anything less weighty than the future of the Nexus mission at stake—he might have entertained Sloane's efforts at rebellion. After all, opportunity could be found in all things, even this.

But in that moment, as the Nexus crew rose up in mutiny around them, Tann couldn't take the chance. Too much was at stake. The timepiece on his omni-tool moved inexorably toward *too long*. He started making plans.

Contingencies, backups, failsafes.

Somebody had to take charge of this clusterfuck, as Sloane would so colorfully describe it.

"Spender."

"Yes, sir." The human unbent from his near-permanent hunch over the feeds he monitored, turning his full attention to Tann. Smart man. Easy to get along with, Tann felt, especially when it came to getting things done—and right now, Tann needed something done.

"Leave us," he said over his shoulder to the few other people who occupied Operations. The pair, assigned to watch the erratic sensors for any signs of the missing arks, looked at one another. "But what if a signal—"

"Have there been any signals at all?"

"Negative."

"Then you can afford a break. Now, go."

"Uh… where, sir?"

Tann's large eyes squinted across the room at them. "Find somewhere," he said tersely. "You are intelligent beings, by all accounts."

They retreated without further argument, murmuring as they went. *Good.* At least somebody around besides Spender would do as he asked. Once they had moved far enough away that he could expect some semblance of privacy, Tann turned back to his assistant and braced both long hands against the dash. For emphasis, not because he needed to lean.

"This has gone on long enough. First Addison and Kesh, now Sloane, all incommunicado. We're on our own. We need to act before everything is lost."

"Act, as in what, exactly?" Spender asked. Then, as realization dawned, he added knowingly, "Arms."

Tann nodded. "If nothing else, the feeds have shown us that these *rebels* are only going to respond to one thing. The time has come to nip this in the bud."

"Not without us."

The voice came from behind. Spender's eyebrows

furrowed, his glance darting so quickly over Tann's shoulder that the salarian had no problems guessing what he saw. He turned to stare at both Addison and Kesh as they strode into Operations. The faces of the crew that had let them in projected a conflicted apology.

"Where have you been?" Tann snapped. The best defense, after all.

Addison's eyes glinted dangerously from between narrowed lashes, but it was Kesh's pronounced limp that had his attention.

"Ran into a bottleneck," the krogan said simply, and left it at that. Given the state of the station, Tann didn't bother to pursue. More fighting. More bloodshed.

Enough was enough.

"I'm glad you are safe," he said. Kesh inclined her head, content to take his sentiment at face value, apparently. Good.

Addison regarded Tann coolly. "Making decisions alone again?"

"I thought I *was* alone," he returned mildly. A pulse thumped high on Addison's forehead. She *had* walked out, after all. "Speaking of which, where's Sloane? She left specifically to find you and Kesh."

"We haven't seen her. Some of her people found us, said Sloane left them to take care of something else."

"If you people would just remain in Operations we would not have these problems," Tann interrupted, too pointedly for it to be anything other than a cut. "Let's review our failings later. Right now, it's time to act. Primarily, we need to put down this uprising."

"They aren't *dogs*, Tann." Addison planted both hands on the console, glaring at him and Spender in equal measure. "They're people. *Our* people, and they're scared."

"That might have worked a few weeks ago," he replied, "but you heard Corvannis. We are no longer dealing with scared protesters. Blood has been spilled, and we keep underestimating them. We can no longer afford to give these people the benefit of the doubt."

"I simply meant—"

"The way I see it," Tann said over her frustrated protest, "we have two options."

Kesh leaned against the console next to Addison, favoring her side. The blackened edges of battle scarred her uniform, and hasty bandages peeked out from the torn fabric. Tann paused, surprised. To make a krogan bleed, that implied some serious weight.

Even more reason for him to push.

He met Addison's eyes first. "Either we send our entire security force into a battle to crush every last mutineer, in a bloody foray that will cost us hundreds of lives—"

"Unacceptable," Addison said sharply, her eyes still narrow.

Exactly. He let his gaze turn to Kesh. "—or we wake up Nakmor Morda."

For a long, long second nobody said a word. He waited.

"Morda," Kesh repeated slowly. Her broad face, always so serious to his eyes, didn't so much as shift. He couldn't read her. Never could with krogan. Damned big-headed, thick-skinned floaters.

Yet it was those big heads and that thick skin that would end this once and for all. Tann nodded with all the gravitas the situation warranted.

"We send Morda against Calix Corvannis," he acknowledged. "We end this quickly and decisively. Overwhelmingly so."

"Then what?" the krogan asked shrewdly. She didn't fill in any options, though—that fell to Tann.

He smiled. "Then we hold a meeting—"

"Great," Addison muttered. "That's been working so well."

"—where we include everyone, and hear their grievances," Tann continued firmly, earning a startled look from the human woman.

Spender nodded enthusiastically. "And we pitch to them our plan for the future, knowing what we know about the state of the galaxy."

"Precisely," Tann said.

"What plan?" Kesh asked.

"The plan," Tann replied, "that we will formulate when we are not spilling each other's blood in the corridors." He raised his brows at them all. "I believe there is a great deal of room in which to maneuver, don't you?" Then he waited.

When all three nodded with various degrees of enthusiasm and belief, Tann knew he'd made the right choice. The key was the future. There would *be* no future if they didn't get this handled. Tann turned back to Spender.

"And that's why I would like you to go wake up Nakmor Morda, and request her help with Corvannis."

"Him?!" Practically a salted snort, Kesh thought so little of the choice.

Spender blinked. Opened his mouth. Closed it. Glanced at Kesh.

"Not that I'm unwilling, but why me?"

Tread carefully, Tann told himself. This must be played just right, because the true best option was Kesh, but the last thing he wanted to do was give Morda the impression of a krogan power position here.

He gestured at himself ruefully.

"I am inclined to believe that direct negotiations between a salarian of my standing and a krogan of—such as it is—*hers* would not go well. No offense intended, Kesh."

"None taken," Kesh replied seriously. "It makes far more sense to send me, though."

"All due respect, Kesh, but I gather that a powerful clan leader such as Nakmor Morda will not react well to the fact she's been left asleep when the labor force was revived."

Kesh's mouth sealed into a grim line.

Got her. He continued. "By sending my aide—"

"*My* aide," Addison said sharply. She frowned at Spender. "For all he seems to have forgotten it."

"I've only been trying to help," Spender shot back, equally sharp. "Wherever my help is needed."

Tann inclined his head. "Mr. Spender has been incredibly helpful and, more importantly, extremely flexible with his time. For this reason, he has earned something of a reputation for speaking on my behalf."

Addison's face pulled into something Tann couldn't distinguish between a grimace and a flinch. Both, maybe? Human faces, so malleable.

~~~~~~~~~~~~~

"Is Sloane on board with this Morda plan?" Addison asked.

"If she hadn't vanished I would have consulted her."

Addison squinted at him. "Maybe we should wait for her. Whatever she went off to do, it must be important."

Tann wondered what that could have been, but

decided it did not matter. "We must hope she is safe," he said, "but there is no time to wait." Privately, he wasn't convinced that Sloane would approve of his current plan. She rarely approved of any of them.

Besides, this really could not wait.

Tann cleared his throat delicately. "As I was saying, by sending Mr. Spender, we are showing Morda the respect that she is due."

"By sending a puppet?" Kesh asked bluntly. Then, to Spender, with zero feeling, "No offense."

"None taken," he replied, echoing Kesh's earlier words, but Tann saw his mouth twist.

Kesh made a deep grunt. "Only I can initiate the stasis override."

Tann felt as if he were suddenly at the edge of a cliff. He'd forgotten this little detail, and now, for the first time since she'd entered the room, he really *looked* at Kesh. "Will you do it?" he asked. "For Spender? I realize there's little love between the two of you, but you must see that I'm right, Kesh."

"I... reluctantly agree it is a good plan."

"And Morda? Will she listen to Spender?"

Spender opened his mouth to say something, but Tann waved him quickly to remain silent. *Let this be Kesh's idea*, he tried to say with his eyes.

Kesh shifted her weight from one foot to the other, thinking. She said, "By sending a representative that is *far* beneath her in standing but above *me* in the political hierarchy, you will show her the importance of the request." She flattened a hand over the blackened tears in the clothing at her side, as if it pained her. "Morda will be pleased by this, and also enjoy the opportunity to intimidate a puppet." Her smile showed a lot of fang, and she aimed it squarely at Spender. "Treat her like *just any krogan*, little man, and she'll be picking your bones out of her teeth."

Spender smiled back. It was strained. No love lost between these two.

"Good," Tann said loudly, and he clapped his hands. "It's decided. Spender will go negotiate with the Nakmor leader for krogan assistance in this unpleasant matter. The mutiny's ringleader will soon be taken care of, and *we*," he stressed, gesturing at Addison and Kesh, "can begin working on ways to address the people's concerns."

Spender was already nodding.

"What of Sloane?" Kesh studied Tann in that slow way she had.

Easily decided. "We tell the krogan to look out for her," Tann replied readily. "And if possible, escort her safely back to Operations so we can include her in the discussions."

"All right." Addison's brow was a red tangle of eyebrows and frown lines, but she nodded in a slow, uncertain rhythm. "I'd rather this get solved before anyone else dies on our watch." She rested her fingertips on the edge of the console, pinning Spender with a hard stare. "Don't aggravate the krogan, Spender. Morda is… well, you know."

"Believe me," Spender said as he straightened his uniform jacket. As earnest as Tann had ever seen the man. "Pissing off a krogan war band is the *last* thing I want to do."

Tann gave him a pat on the back and guided him to the door. "Listen," he said under his breath. "I realize we're asking a lot of you here. I appreciate—"

"Chief of Staff," Spender said.

"What?"

"Make me Chief of Staff. If Morda agrees, I want to work directly for you, and not as a damned gopher."

Tann looked him square in the eye and saw a hunger not present in Addison's gaze, or Sloane's. "I believe that can be arranged," Tann replied. "*If* Morda agrees…"

CHAPTER THIRTY

Spender's hands were damp with nervous sweat by the time he received word that Morda had unfrozen. Kesh had initiated the process ten minutes before, and left once the vitals all showed green. She'd chuckled as she passed him, a sound that still echoed in his ears.

Standard stasis pods weren't huge, by necessity. Big enough to comfortably fit the species their design called for. The outlier to the design came when they'd suddenly had to deal with a complement of Nakmor krogan. Such pods were understandably larger.

Much, *much* larger.

While Spender had no illusions about the objective size of krogan warriors, Nakmor Morda's reputation cast a long shadow. As he waited for the only available technicians to get her through medical, he found his leg bouncing in uncontrollable nerves.

Nakmor Morda.

The profile he'd devoured on the way to the guarded communications room painted a bleak picture. A female clan leader, which said a *lot* about her capabilities. The Tuchanka Urdnot leader, Wrex, hadn't been a krogan who suffered fools, and Spender knew from diplomatic association that anyone who could impress *him* was bound to scare anyone else.

By all accounts, Nakmor wasn't a soft clan—they were brutish, impatient, and aggressive. All traits the krogan valued, all reasons William Spender wanted to get this over with as soon as possible.

It was pretty much a given that she would be angry. She'd probably also stink like a—

Abruptly voices were raised in warning. They echoed the heavy, dangerous tread of a krogan on the warpath. Spender braced himself as much as he could before the door flung wide. It cracked into the back paneling and boomed out a metallic, dissonant *gong*. Just what the Nakmor clan leader needed to mark her entrance.

As if Morda wasn't imposing enough.

Maybe more so than rumor suggested, and rumor had suggested quite a damn lot. Her eyes burned with a righteous fury as her gaze landed on Spender.

"Where the *hell* is my clan?" she boomed in a voice shredded by glass and granite.

"Safe," Spender said hastily, before remembering *safe* wasn't exactly in krogan vernacular. "Er, waiting for your orders!"

Morda moved like a tank. Strength and muscle forged a piledriver that pushed everything in its path out of her way. Spender's spine went rigid as she strode up to him without slowing, barely keeping from mowing him down.

He couldn't help himself. He flinched.

Half a second later he still found himself breathing, and cracked open an eye to find Morda's broad, flat krogan face mere millimeters from his. She filled his vision.

Dominated it.

"Who are you?" she growled. "Where is Kesh? Or Garson? If I am not talking to Kesh, the only other I should have to suffer is Jien Garson."

All the rigidity in Spender's spine threatened to

wilt. He forced his legs straight, made himself look her in the eye.

"My name is William Spender, chief of staff to the Nexus leadership." Well, he would be, if she agreed. And if she didn't agree it wouldn't matter anyway. "Jien Garson is dead. Long story," he added when her broad nostrils flared.

She inched that much closer. "There is only one human in this universe I consider a friend, and that is Jien Garson. So tell it. *Now*."

He did. He told a shortened, much faster version. She simply stared at him, unblinking. Saying nothing. When he wound down…

She still said nothing. The silence stretched, filling the minimal space between them until Spender was positive he heard it ringing in his eardrums.

"Kesh and the council decided to awaken certain individuals," he said, breaking the silence, "setting priority to those who could rebuild."

The krogan's gaze narrowed dangerously. Then, on an inhaled breath, she took one step back to give her large body room to break into graveled, guttural laughter. She thumped her uniformed chest with a knobby hand.

"*Rebuild*," she snorted, the laughter fading. "Rebuild! And now look at you." She half-turned, flinging that hand back toward the busted doors and the obvious signs of battle visible beyond.

Spender saw her point.

"How goes your *rebuilding* now, human?"

Rhetorical, Spender supposed. He sighed. "Yes, mistakes were made—"

More raucous laughter cut him off, and he took another deep breath before he did something he'd regret.

Like get himself killed.

When her gusty guffaws eased, he tried again.

"Clan leader, we're asking for your help in putting down the mutiny before it gets any more out of hand."

Her laughter, all trace of humor, abruptly vanished.

"Why isn't your security taking them in?" she asked bluntly.

He didn't want to tell her that even Sloane's force was too small. That no alternative existed. Then again, he didn't know how else to put it.

She read the truth on his face.

"So," she said slowly, "your pitiful forces can't handle it." He opened his mouth to protest, but she cut him off with a shrewd stare and a pointed question. "Or is it that you won't send them against your own?"

A valid, incredibly insightful question.

Spender thought fast. "We want to end this as quickly as possible. The fact is, by sending krogan forces—*your* krogan force," he amended hastily, "we're more likely to avoid a prolonged conflict, not to mention massive loss of life."

"So you want to throw tough krogan meat at these rebels, frightening them into submission without a fight? Do you mean to forbid combat?"

"No," he said quickly. "Not at all. Bloodshed is, of course, to be avoided if at all possible, but should the situation warrant it, you would be given full leave to do as you see fit. Whatever it takes to secure the mission."

Morda folded her arms over her broad chest, looking down at Spender from a distance that suddenly didn't seem all that much better than her close proximity earlier.

She'd crush his head in a heartbeat.

Or rather, that's what he was *meant* to think.

It was working.

Clearing his throat, Spender backed away under pretense of organizing the data he'd collected for this diplomatic mission. Putting a conference table between him and Nakmor Morda might not actually help, but it made him feel better.

"In short," he finished, "this uprising is a major threat to the well-being of this station and the mission—*including*," he added when she looked less than impressed, "the continued flourishing of the Nakmor clan." That earned him a gritted-teeth growl and her full attention.

"To be clear," she said in that bullish way he didn't think she knew how to change, "you kept me ignorant and asleep so you could use *my* people as you would, and now that *your* people are misbehaving, you want my help? *My clan's blood?*"

Spender felt himself pale. She hadn't moved, not a step, but the imminent fury carved into her tough krogan hide wasn't difficult to translate.

"We… we are, ah…" He wiped his sweaty hands on his thighs, hoping no one would notice. "We are prepared to compensate the Nakmor clan."

She leaned forward. "How."

It wasn't so much a question as a demand.

"I—that is, we," he corrected quickly, "are willing to formally recognize the Nakmor clan's services in public acknowledgement, up to and including the addition of krogan statuary—"

"*Screw* your statues," Morda snarled. Her fist came down on the table, causing the neat pile of his data to fan like a deck of cards. He barely kept from jumping, but his stomach didn't get the memo. It sloshed all the way up into his throat. Then down into a petrified pit.

"Every krogan knows this story," she continued

angrily. "You so-called civilized species get in over your head and beg us for help. We shed our blood, you thank us with one hand and sanction us with the other. Do you think we *do not learn*?"

Spender's mouth dropped open. "I… W-Well that was—"

"A pile of *shit*." Morda leaned in so close, all he could think was that her large mouth—and larger teeth—loomed close enough to take his face off, if the krogan clan leader wanted to. And she looked very much like she wanted to. "The Rachni Wars taught us a lesson we will never forget," she snarled, low and menacing. "You raise us up when you're all dying and when we save your collective asses, you respond by mutilating our people. Murdering our children! And give us what? *A fucking statue*." She braced enough of her weight on the table that it creaked. Alarmingly. "Different times, different wars. But we *learn*." Her teeth gleamed as she stressed the words. "Do. *Better*."

Spencer skipped the preambles. He'd way overstepped what little authority Tann had granted him, but results were what mattered. Results were what led to power, to recognition. He'd rolled the dice a bit with Calix, he could certainly double-down now.

"We are prepared to offer the Nakmor clan a seat at the council." The words came out with surprising ease, and Jien Garson's legendary confidence. He couldn't have said it better had he practiced it a hundred times.

"The krogan have been denied a seat at the council for generations," she said slowly. Suspiciously. She looked down at him from dangerously slitted eyes. "Don't mess with the Nakmor, little man. We will eat you."

It was so close to what Kesh had said that Spender almost laughed. Almost. The mood in the room changed palpably, then. He breathed out deliberately.

"The offer is legitimate." Or, anyway, it *would* be once he talked Tann into it.

Once the krogan stomped this bloody mutiny to dust, Spender had little doubt in his ability to convince the salarian to allow it.

Morda glowered at him. "Is the entire clan awake?"

"Only the workers," Spender said.

"I shall have my warriors at my side for this, to share in the glory. Wake them."

"Naturally. I'll see to it."

"As for your offer," she said, steamy breath in his face, "there must be witnesses."

"Of course."

"Yours and mine."

"Certainly," he said amicably. He pulled up his omni-tool communications, connected the short-range frequency to his nearest staff.

━━━━━━━━━

As an uneasy silence settled over the room, the stomp of boots once more preceded entry of five more bodies. Two krogan, two humans plucked from wherever they'd been found, and a third krogan trailing up the back.

Spender didn't recognize any of them. Not by face—at least in the case of the humans—and not by designation as Morda met the first krogan by grabbing him by the front of his armor.

"Wratch," she growled.

Whatever he may have said was lost as Morda yanked the krogan forward and delivered a solid headbutt. The sound of bone cracking bone ricocheted through the room, freezing all the non-krogan in place.

Wratch cursed as he clapped both hands to his head.

"I am your clan leader," Morda all but roared.

Spender flinched inwardly, but held still.

The krogan didn't let a little reeling stop him. "Yes, clan leader," he bellowed back. The others joined in. She rounded on them, with eyes wide and lips twisted into a feral snarl.

"*I* lead the clan in all battles."

"Yes, clan leader!"

"Remember that," she growled. "We stride into a bloody field, Nakmor. Let's remember why we are here." She made a fist in front of her face, tightened until the sound of popping knuckles peppered the silence. "And what we have come to do."

Spender watched, both repulsed and fascinated as Nakmor Morda cowed her krogan into unfailing obedience. All without *lessening* them in any way. They all beat on their chests in some kind of primitive salute—hell if Spender knew—before falling silent behind Morda. She rounded on the human witnesses.

He was aware of one, a bookish-looking man, taking a solid two steps back.

"We will fight your battle," Morda declared. "We will end this mutiny by tearing off its head. And when we are victorious," she added, her voice dangerously level, "*you* will make good on your promise." She prodded him with one thick finger.

Spender nodded. "Then it's agreed—"

Morda's fist pounded into her other hand. It cracked like bone. "*Say it.*"

Spender tried to find that Garson-esque confidence again, and only managed some. "If you end this mutiny, you will land your species a seat on the council, Nakmor Morda."

One of the staff behind him gasped.

Spender didn't turn. Morda pinned her gaze on his, holding it until the ache in his tight spine became a screaming pinch and his eyes were watering.

Behind their leader, the krogan grumbled what probably passed for victory cheers and bumped knuckles. Even the one who was nursing a squint under the dent Morda put in his forehead.

Finally, *finally*, Morda nodded. Once. Short. Sharp. "Consider it done." She turned, and the krogan parted like thunderous water to let her out first. As one, they left to prepare for battle.

As the last krogan boot cleared the doorway, Spender turned to face the two workers who'd been brought in to act as witnesses. "Get back to work," he snapped.

They glanced at one another, then quickly left the room, smartly using the other door.

William Spender watched them leave, and then stood alone for a long, steadying breath. "Nothing left to do," he said to the empty chamber, "but see which way the wind blows."

CHAPTER THIRTY-ONE

Sloane was thrust into a chair across a narrow table from where Calix stood. Her wrists were bound behind her back, the nylon strap looped through the seat's metal slats. The brute pulled the cord so tight she felt a warm trickle of blood down her wrists.

"That's really not necessary," she said, careful to keep the pain from her voice.

Reg only grunted. He moved to stand behind her, as if to grab her head and twist at the tiniest sign of trouble.

Calix took the seat across from her. He glanced up at his enforcer and jerked his chin toward the door. Reg left, and Calix tapped something on his screen. A few seconds later, Sloane heard the door click shut.

"Sorry about him," the turian said. "I'm afraid the leadership's favorability ratings aren't too high at the moment." With that he leaned forward. "You shouldn't have come, Sloane. It's not going to change anything."

"Your people are very loyal to you, aren't they."

"Just figuring that out now?"

Sloane shook her head. "I learned that from Irida. What she did, it was all for you, wasn't it? But this…" She would have swept her arm to indicate the small army outside the door, if she wasn't bound at the wrists. "I never thought they'd go this far. Never thought you would, either."

"To be honest, neither did I." He looked away,

lost in the past. "It started back home, on the *Warsaw*. I never expected to become their leader, or their hero. I think maybe I was even trying to get away from them when I decided to join the Initiative."

"So what happened?"

"They insisted, and I couldn't bring myself to decline."

The words trailed off. Outside, Sloane heard the busy sounds of barricades being erected, and the nervous idle chatter of people waiting for fate.

"It was the same with Irida," Calix said conversationally. "Believe it or not, but she went after that data cache entirely on her own, because she thought we might need it in the coming storm."

"You lied to me about that." Sloane lifted her chin a little.

"I suppose I did," he said, unapologetic and yet clearly not proud. "But then, you lied to me, too."

"Irida was treated—"

"I'm talking about the scouts," Calix said. He fixed a disappointed gaze on her.

Sloane went quiet at that.

"I asked you directly, Sloane. Remember the message I sent? Any news from the scouts? And your reply? You said nothing. That was the spark, you know."

"You're blaming this all on me?"

"The spark," Calix repeated. "Blame is impossible. This is the culmination of a hundred events and decisions—good and bad—which can't be pinned on any one person." He leaned in even closer now. "What matters is what we do now, Sloane. Not what we did."

The whole mess flashed through her mind. The Scourge, Garson, the waking of Tann. All of it. One common trait in all the bad presented itself to her, focused by Calix's words. The fulcrum that made every big decision fall on the side of the mission, rather than the crew.

She could see it now. And unlike her moments of exhausted weakness before, this time Sloane found she did not want to ignore it, or walk away.

"I lost my temper, I admit," Calix was saying. "Went back to my team and told them all about the scouts, and the lies. I guess I should have known they'd amplify and hone the whole thing into a call for action." Calix studied her, tapping one finger on the desk idly. "I can't help but wonder how things might have been different, if an announcement had been made the moment the news came back. It was the weeks, Sloane. The weeks of hiding it that got me. That made us all realize you—our leadership—were planning something that would not be in our best interests."

"Tann and Addison, they wanted to wait until there was a new plan," Sloane said automatically. "Until we could be ready to handle the crew's reaction."

"You went along with this," he said. Not a question. "I thought you were better than that, Sloane. I thought you were one of those who would stand up against that kind of thing."

"I am…" she said. "I was. Fuck, what the hell was I thinking."

"You agree with me, then."

Sloane looked into his eyes. "Yeah. Yeah I fucking do." Then, "But what's happened since, Calix. It's too far. Theft of weapons. Killing my people."

"The bloodshed couldn't be avoided. I wish that had gone differently, but… well, what can I say? Your people are loyal, too. They fought well."

She battled down an instinctual rage, born of the

loss and guilt as well as the desire to defend her people. Rage wasn't going to put an end to this, though. Nor would it fix the Nexus. "We have to find a way out of this, Calix. A solution that doesn't destroy us all. As soon as they decide I'm missing, they'll send the entire security team here—"

"Hence the raid on the armory," he replied. "There was one armed group on the Nexus, now there's two, and evenly matched. If history has told us anything, it's that the real talking can't begin until the odds are even."

"So let's talk. Come up with something and I'll take it to Tann."

He was shaking his head before she'd even spoken the name. "That's the problem now."

"Tann will listen to me. He trusts me." *Maybe*.

Calix drummed one finger on the table, staring at her. "Did you know Tann came to me, and tried to get me to give him life-support override privileges?"

She blinked. "*What?*"

"True story," he said. "This was months ago. Well before Irida's arrest. Not due to the recent… concerns. He just wanted it. No reason given. Just in case he needed to do whatever Tann thought needed doing. To make things 'better,' no doubt." The word better dripped from his mouth like a poisonous slug.

Sloane remembered Tann raising this idea in one of their meetings. He claimed to be concerned that the information might disappear if something were to happen to Calix, or Kesh.

"Why didn't he go to Kesh?"

"He did," Calix replied. "Kesh said no."

And that hadn't been enough to stop him. *Fuck*. Try as she might, Sloane couldn't chalk that up to the usual salarian–krogan tensions. This was something different.

This was straight-up deceit. She looked at Calix.

"I said no, too." She processed all this, or tried to. "I didn't know he'd come directly to you."

"Makes me wonder what else you don't know."

That made both of them.

"Sometimes I think I should have stuck to my first instinct," she said.

"What do you mean?"

"Leadership," she said, and felt a weight lift from her shoulders for the admission. "When we learned Tann was, what, eighth in line to stand in for Garson? Maybe I should have declared a state of emergency right then and there. I almost did."

He said nothing. Just looked sad; not an expression she often saw on a turian face, she realized.

"I should have refused to wake him," Sloane went on. "Protocol be damned. I never imagined anyone but Garson in charge. Never dreamed it could happen."

"Who could have?"

"Hell, we should have given the job to Kesh. She would have been perfect. At least made her an advisor. She would have held Tann in check, that's for sure. Hell, I should have put you in charge."

"Me?"

He seemed genuinely surprised by the suggestion. Sloane had made it without really thinking it through, but the more it hung there between them, the more it seemed right.

"Yeah," Sloane said. "Why not. Look at the way your people have flocked to you. Look, there's still time. I'll talk to Addison and Kesh if Tann won't listen. Maybe that's the path out of this. You become an advisor. Represent your crew."

"And Kesh? She deserves that more than I do."

"Tann would never allow that."

Calix shook his head, borderline angry. "You think he'd consider me, a turian who has committed treason and caused death and damage, but not a loyal and competent krogan? That's exactly the kind of thing we should have left behind, Sloane, and you know it. There's no place for it here. No point."

"I agree with you." The vehemence in the words surprised her as much as him.

He sat there for a long moment, thinking.

A knock at the door. Three hard pounding beats. Calix opened it with his omni-tool.

"They've come," Reg said.

Sloane stood, not caring that the chair came with her. "I'll talk to them. They're security, they'll listen to me. I'll explain—"

"Not security. Too many for that."

"Who then?" Calix asked.

"No idea, but they ain't here to talk."

Sloane Kelly's thoughts went from the possibility of peace to a dark, dark place in an instant. "Calix. You said there are two armed groups on the Nexus now. Equals. But that's not true, is it?"

"Meaning?"

"There's a third, Calix."

And she saw the understanding dawn in his eyes, an expression quickly replaced with... not fear, but stubborn resignation. "Nakmor," he said, in a low, terrible tone.

Sloane, her back to the giant, thrust out her hands, the chair dangling painfully. "Cut me loose and get me my omni-tool. Kesh will listen to me."

"Kesh ain't with them," Reg said.

Sloane turned slowly toward him. "Who then?"

"No idea."

"Get everyone on the barricades," Calix said, already moving toward the door.

"Cut me loose!" Sloane shouted at his back.

One foot out the door, Calix paused. He slipped a tool from his belt and tossed it in her direction. A compact foldable blade. She couldn't catch it, of course, so she let it bounce off her midsection and clatter to the floor. "Wait," she said urgently. "Wait! What are you going to do?"

Calix met her eyes. "I'm going to defend my crew. That's all I've ever done." A hard statement, for all the passion around it.

"Don't. Don't fight. The moment you do—"

"They sent the *krogan*, Sloane." He shook his head. "You don't get much more direct than that. The time for talking is over."

"It's not the right way," she argued. "Calix, if you surrender now…"

The turian's laugh was bitter. "What, you think Tann will just accept our apologies—and clean up his act, too?" Another shake of his head, hard. "We tried, Sloane. It's time to do what's right." A shrug, half-hearted at best. "Whatever the cost."

She stared at him, stunned.

He left without another word.

The door remained open behind him.

Hell.

Sloane dropped to her knees, rolled over to get her hands on the tool, then rolled again onto her side. She fumbled with the handle, worked her numb fingers around the sides of it, and pulled until the short, sharp blade clicked into the open position.

Outside an eruption of gunfire. Hundreds of

voices shouting to take cover, to return fire, to flee. The very definition of a disorganized rabble.

Biotic force shook the walls.

"No, no!" Sloane shouted. She'd been so close. A solution could have been found. No one else needed to die.

She slipped and cut her own arm, ignored the pain and kept sawing at the stupid little nylon strap. She sawed and sawed. Damn the little thing was *tough*. Sloane roared in frustrated anger and a growing pain as she slid the blade back and forth across the strap.

A tiny sound, barely audible with all the thunder pouring in through the doorway, signaled success. The strap fell away. Sloane came to her feet at a dead run, pushed out the door. Blood from the cut flowed into her palm. With each step she squeezed her hands into fists and then let them open. It hurt like hell, but the pain meant sensation returning and she welcomed it. It focused her thoughts.

In the space outside she skidded to a stop. Sloane had seen a lot of combat in her days. She'd put an end to brawls, started even more. She'd defended a research station until no one remained but herself when the dropship took her from the roof. She'd seen massacres, and been party to some of them. Those were doors in her mind she didn't open anymore.

She'd never seen anything like this.

Calix's rebels were entrenched, well-armed, and they had idealism on their side. They had numbers, they had ammo, and they'd already crossed that Rubicon known as violence.

They had a powerful desire to win.

But they weren't krogan. The krogan didn't have idealism. Didn't need it.

They had *joy*. The joy of combat.

The assembly plant had exploded into the ugliest, meanest, largest brawl Sloane Kelly had ever seen.

"Tann, you shit, what have you unleashed?" she whispered. Not really a question, for the answer was painfully obvious.

The krogan had powered in like a battering ram, and they hadn't come to talk. Some of Calix's rebels lay strewn around the barricade they'd erected, and not all of them were whole.

Sloane's brain kicked into tactical mode. The big picture was out of control, but here, in front of her…

A krogan warrior kicked a severed arm across the floor, then rushed into the shuddering barrel of an assault rifle. One meaty fist knocked the weapon aside, while the other took the asari rebel on the chin and sent her sprawling backward to slam against a dormant machine.

The krogan stepped forward again, ready to crush her under his massive foot. Sloane rushed in with her knife—her crappy little utility knife—and drove it into the eye of the krogan before she'd even realized what she'd done.

This only made him angry.

She knew better than to stop, to apologize, to plead for calm. The situation had gone well beyond that point. There would be no jogging up to them and appealing to reason. No, this was a battle now, and the krogan had the taste of sport in their mouths. Soon they would reach a state of blood rage. If that happened the massacre would be ruthless and utterly complete.

She watched herself, as if from a distance, as that punched-aside-rifle found its way into her hands and swiveled around to bark its magnificent bark at the krogan she'd wounded. The hulking worker, mad with rage, walked in even as the bullets tore through him.

Finally he fell at Sloane's feet, and behind him she saw the faces of a dozen more. The one in the middle caught her eye. Their leader.

Not Kesh.

A moment of disbelief settled like the blood that seeped into the crevices of the floor.

"Morda," Sloane whispered.

Tann had woken Morda. It had to have been him. Kesh would have known better, would have come here and tried to salvage the situation herself.

Morda.

Fuck. This wasn't going to end well, and Sloane— without thinking, acting on her first instinct—had sided with the enemy.

Nakmor Morda stood at the center of this fresh line of combatants, coming in from the breach they'd made in the barricade. If she recognized Sloane Kelly, or cared, she made no sign.

It wasn't just Morda, either. Her elite soldiers had been woken, too, and surged in beside her. Morda flicked her arm toward the battle and her guard surged into the fray without a second thought. Didn't matter who was involved, or why. The game was afoot.

"Nakmor Morda!" Sloane shouted over the fray.

The clan leader glanced in her direction.

"Stop this now! There's no reason to—"

But Morda only shook her head. "You're on the wrong side of the barricade, Kelly!"

"There is no right side," Sloane growled, and did not move.

Morda glared at her and there came the strange sort of quiet that can occasionally fall over a crowded place. Despite all the combat, the chatter of gunfire and the roar of the krogan flood, a silence stretched, if only for a second. And nothing was said. Morda's eyes did the talking; they said, *Time to choose, Sloane. With us, or with them*.

Sloane Kelly could feel the eyes of the rebels on her. Some of them, anyway. And half the krogan force, too. Waiting, if only for that fraction of a second, to know her decision.

She shook her head at Morda and raised her weapon.

The leader of the Nakmor clan grinned.

All at once the cacophony of violence folded back in and with it the chaos. Hundreds of combatants on both sides, all killing or dying.

"Fall back!" someone shouted. Calix, maybe. The cry was quickly taken up by the other rebels, though, and Sloane would never know who'd given the original order. Someone who didn't know the krogan, that's for sure.

She danced backward, shooting, never turning to flee. That would only further incite them into a truly cataclysmic bloodlust. But her effort made no difference. The rest of the rebels had broken and run. If she didn't do the same she'd be out here all alone, in no-man's-land, against several hundred of them. They'd tear her limb from limb, and she knew it.

So Sloane ran, soon overtaking some of the slower of Calix's rabble. The wave of krogan hit the stragglers from behind. She heard the screams, the crunching of bones, and the orgasmic howls of delight only meters behind her. A symphony of violence.

Vaulting a long shelving unit, she rolled over the top just a split second before a krogan slammed into the thing and sent it smashing into her back. She rolled to get out from under it, and the krogan loomed over her, fists raised.

An incendiary round took it in the head. Blood and gore splattered across her face. She turned to one side and tried to blink it away as the body above her shuddered, twisted, and finally came apart under the explosive hail of gunfire.

All across the vast room the rebels shifted to this new plan. Whatever concerns had kept them from it before, they were no longer relevant. Explosive rounds washed over the krogan front line. That entire side of the room became one long, roiling, thunderously loud wall of death and destruction. Krogan and rebel alike were consumed in shockwaves and diced by the sprays of shrapnel.

The tactic worked, at least. It kept the enemy back.

Keeping low, Sloane staggered back to the rebel line and heaved herself over a blood-smeared crate. No one batted an eye at this. She was one of them now. They might not be able to say how they knew that, or when it had happened, but they knew. Morda had demanded she choose. The side of rebels fighting for the right to be equals? To make their own choices?

Or the side of the machinations that unleashed a krogan clan on its own people.

Fine. She fucking well chose.

In the temporary reprieve Sloane cast about for a weapon. She'd lost the rifle at some point, and the knife. She thought of all those dead behind her, and the weapons they'd dropped. The krogan hadn't come armed—not all of them, at least. Perhaps because there hadn't been the supply, or the time, or maybe just because they wanted a challenge. She wondered if Tann knew what he'd ordered here, and whether Addison had been party to it. Kesh would never have agreed to this, though it would be just like Tann to go around her. Straight to the clan leader, waking her from her slumber and telling her just enough to get the desired result.

Salarian or not, it had worked.

There was a shoulder against hers. Calix. Their eyes met.

"Why'd you give me the knife?" she asked.

"To see what you'd do." He forced a smile on to his face. "Enlightening how we act when we have no time to think, isn't it? I guessed right, Sloane. I thought you might—"

A sharp report thundered across the barricades. Calix's brains left his body in a small gray eruption to the left. His eyes went unnaturally wide. He dropped to his knees and slumped against her.

Sloane turned, dumbstruck. The krogan were coming again. A wave of them, bearing down on the exhausted rebel line. But they did not carry rifles. She saw others, then, at the smashed barricade where it had all begun. Newcomers in uniforms like hers. One of them was lowering a sniper rifle from her shoulder, having seen Sloane in her sight, the target she would have shot next after Calix. One of her officers. Their eyes met, for an instant, and then the woman was gone, rushing back to report what she'd seen.

Sloane is with them, she'd say. *Gone over. Or maybe she's been working against us all along.*

As the enraged horde of krogan fell upon the rebels Sloane sank to her knees. She turned Calix over and looked into his clever eyes one last time. It was all she could take. The last straw.

This wasn't what she came here for.

This wasn't how it was supposed to be.

"What do we do?" someone asked.

After a second Sloane realized that the question had been directed at her. She glanced up and saw the brute, Reg. The one who'd savagely bound her wrists, the one whose "approval rating" of her had been rock bottom, according to Calix.

"What?" she asked, numbly.

"What do we do?" he repeated. He was asking her. Just like that. With Calix gone, this rabble was leaderless, and they knew it.

"We die," Sloane said, simply. "They won't stop until we're all dead."

The brute offered her a hand. "Then we die fighting," he said.

Sloane took his hand. A rifle was thrust toward her. She looked at it as if it was a foreign thing, despite the fact she could take it apart and reassemble it while blindfolded. She took it.

"Some other time," Sloane said. "Let's die on our terms. For now I say we retreat, deeper into the Nexus. Go underground."

He puffed up. A wall of a person. "I'm willing to die here."

"Are you willing to let your cause die here, as well?"

That gave him pause.

"What about family?" she demanded. "Friends? What about making a fucking choice that *matters*?"

Reg looked up. His eyes closed. Then, with a grunt, he nodded. "Emory'd never forgive me if I lost my head here."

The battle closed in around them. Sloane clapped

him on the shoulder. "Good. Then let's make this one matter, okay? For Calix."

A single, grudging nod.

"Retreat!" Sloane shouted, and she was off, moving away from Morda, deeper into the idle machines of the assembly floor. She repeated the call over and over, and Reg did the same. They joined up with a group of rebels near the back, armed with longer-range rifles, led by someone named Nnebron. He took aim at Sloane as she rushed up, but Reg stepped between.

"She's with us now," Reg said. Something in his voice convinced the others. Trust. In him, not her.

They backed across the room, covering one another, firing indiscriminately into the horde that followed. Sloane tried to ignore the screams, those who hadn't managed to back out fast enough and found themselves inside the storm of krogan wrath.

Sloane let Reg take point. He seemed to know the way. Perhaps he'd scouted this room for Calix, helped map its secrets and exits. Or maybe he was just as blind as the rest of them.

A thunderous explosion came from somewhere across the way. For an instant the far wall became lit with the silhouette of battle.

Ahead lay a door. Reg turned and leaned toward it and knocked a shelving unit full of spare parts out of his path. Sloane skirted sideways around the mess and heard someone behind her slip and go down. Or maybe the sniper had got them. Too hard to tell now.

Reg was five meters from the door when it exploded inward. Shrapnel splattered across his body. He dropped, a lifeless sack, and skidded across the final few meters into a cloud of smoke and debris.

Sloane tried to stop, but those behind her pressed.

They'd rather face the unknown than the krogan at their backs. She saw Nnebron at her side now, others behind him. All eyes were on the door as they continued to rush toward it, rifles coming back around to the front.

"Enough!" a voice shouted.

The one voice in the entire station that could make everyone in the room stop and take notice. Nakmor Kesh pushed through the smoke. Behind her, Sloane saw familiar faces. Her security team, or some of them at least. And she saw the accusation in their eyes, the disbelief, the growing hatred.

"*Enough,*" Kesh repeated, this time for Sloane specifically, all bile and disappointment. In response she held up her hands, letting her rifle clatter to the floor. Those around her were less willing, but somehow she'd become their leader and, after a tense few seconds, they did as she did.

Nnebron was last, and he stared at her as he let his weapon slip from his fingers. His gaze held equal parts accusation and resentment, as if to say, *This is all your fault.*

Sloane Kelly laughed, then, though no one else seemed to get the joke. Somehow she'd become both the reason for their rebellion, and its de facto leader. A failed one.

Isn't that just perfect.

CHAPTER THIRTY-TWO

All the fire drained out of their hundreds the moment their leader fell. Even if they hadn't stopped fighting, even if they'd pushed harder, desperate to the end, it wouldn't matter. Calix was the heart of them. And the opponent, well, few could be more terrifying.

Hope had turned to fear, and that fear had fueled a revolution they thought they couldn't lose. Sloane recognized that. She understood it. Felt the twist in her chest when Calix's brain and blood had sprayed.

That didn't mean she was going to be anyone's punching bag.

Lawrence Nnebron was a man on the edge—wiry, angry, and unwilling to let anything go. The moment Sloane entered the crowded cell, he came at her like a man with nothing left to lose, his lips peeled back in a twisted snarl and murder in his eyes.

As she sidestepped his swing, caught his wrist and spun him around, that look turned to something much younger. Much less sure.

Soul-deep loss. Of friends. Of self.

Of his place in the universe.

The paneling clanged loudly as she rammed him against it, pinning his head to the wall and tucking his wrist high enough up his back that he'd regret moving. He cried out, echoed by the other seven rebels in the cell. Just one cell of many, and all down the hall Sloane heard the arguments, the blame, and the anguish of loss.

"Stay put," Sloane demanded.

Talini watched from the door, one hand hovering. "Will you be okay?"

As long as the sergeant was there, the others probably wouldn't attack—but they wouldn't talk, either. Never mind that Talini wasn't there to help Sloane at all. She was there to lock her supervisor up for mutiny.

Ironic as hell, isn't it?

Still, the fact she waited long enough to watch Sloane's back meant something. Sloane shot her a grim smile, intended as thanks, and a silent acknowledgement of everything she couldn't say.

The asari didn't smile back. With a hard set to her mouth, she turned around and shut the cell door behind her.

For a long moment, the only sounds in the crowded room were Nnebron's labored breathing and the shuffling of people who couldn't figure out what the next step would be. They were tired, bruised, bleeding where the hasty bandages hadn't held. Like Sloane, they were hurt.

Unlike her, they didn't have the sheer pride that kept them from showing it. Sloane let out a short sigh.

"Let's get this over with. I'm not here to fight."

Nnebron jerked, but his arm strained and he froze again.

"Then get off me," he snarled.

"Not until you settle down."

"Fuck you," he gritted out. "Pig!"

Quaint. Sloane kept a wary eye on the indistinct shapes just in her peripheral, but they seemed content to hover. Without a strong leader, they'd lost their direction.

Without Calix, they'd lost their heart.

She was careful not to push the engineer's arm any farther, not wanting to break it, but she didn't let up, either.

"I'm not here as security," she said tightly. "I'm in trouble just like you. Just like all of you," she added, turning her head to nod at the others. At the flurry of suspicion and disbelief sent her way, she turned one way, then the other, so that they could see her sides. "Here for the same reasons you are. Calix believed in you. Will you let that go to waste?"

Sweat beaded her captive's brow. His eyes screwed shut and he tugged at her grip, only to groan in mingled pain and anger when she didn't ease up on his arm.

"Come on, Nnebron." She spoke to them all. "You guys took up arms against an injustice and your side lost. There's no getting out of that, for any of us."

"But —"

"I helped as best I could to save your lives from the krogan," Sloane cut in quietly. A knife's edge. "I couldn't save Calix, and for that I'm sorry. I really am. But he's gone now, and you're alive. I want to make sure you stay that way, you get me?"

"What about the rest of our crew?" For a man at a disadvantage, Nnebron managed fierce and determined admirably well. Sloane admired that much, at least. "What about Reg? He died. Ulrich, *Calix*…" He visibly flailed. "Reg's husband is still out there, we can't—"

"*These are the choices we made.*" Anger lifted her voice. Dragged audible claws through the crowd, and a grunt of surprise from Nnebron. "Get this through your head! I can't do much for anyone else while locked

433

in here, does this make fucking sense to you? We *have* to play the system now. *Any* opportunity out of this cell will be an opportunity to make new choices."

Sloane had done nothing but trust the system since the moment the Scourge caused her crash-wake. She'd done her duty, followed the Initiative's protocols. Tried to do right by everyone. And this is what it had gotten her.

Locked up and out of options. Even her fellow captives saw her as the enemy.

No more.

"Those who were too injured to be locked up here are under surveillance in the med-lab. Where they *will* get the care they need," she added firmly. She had Talini's promise on that. "Right now, what we have is us. You and me, Nnebron. The people in these cells. *That is it.* So what are you going to do?"

His wrist flexed in her hand, as if he intended to make a break for it, but when she braced, he didn't move. He just scowled.

Maybe he got it. Time to find out. Taking a gamble, she eased her grip. Drew away just enough that he could peel himself off the wall, but she held onto his wrist. Pointedly.

"I'm not above kicking your ass until you drop," she said flatly, "but I don't want to. It'd defeat the point."

The kid snatched his arm away, but only rolled his strained shoulder and glared at her feet. Sheepish, maybe. Or embarrassed.

Or just... lost.

Sloane backed away to give him space, but there wasn't much room to go. She settled for leaving her back against the door, where she could watch the kid and the others. All of them looked anywhere but at her. Most at the ground.

The tension in the air wasn't tight so much as it was heavy—a deeply rooted sense of despair. They'd given up. All of them, even scrappy Nnebron with his last flail for *something* that felt like victory.

Shit.

Sloane wanted to turn around and punch the door. Wanted to yell at the people who'd made the decisions that led them here. Waking Morda, that had been the worst of them all. The nuclear option when the opponent had only sticks. She wanted to wrap her hands around Tann's skinny little pencil-neck and squeeze until he *felt* all the pain the krogan and her warriors had caused in that goddamned room.

Mostly, she wanted to stop replaying Calix's death, the way his eyes widened, life abruptly snuffed out behind them.

She wanted a lot of things. What she had was the remains of a ragtag crew and the certainty, the bitter knowledge, that the leadership she'd worked for, advised, had betrayed her. Betrayed them all. She needed to make inroads somewhere. Calix had believed in this group.

Now Sloane needed them to believe in her. Like it or not.

She started from a footing she understood. "Here's how it works. Contrary to popular rumor, there is *no* way that anyone will be okay with spacing us." She regretted the time she had suggested exactly that. A moment of pure frustration, and the desire to actually solve one of the Nexus's problems rather than kick it down the road. Now *they* were the problem. "At worst, they'll want to make examples of us through some kind of public circus."

A woman wrapped her singed arms around her

waist, hugging herself with rounded shoulders. "Will we be executed?"

"*No*." The woman flinched. Sloane gritted her teeth. "No," she said again, firm but with less bite. She forced herself to remember who these people were. Technicians, engineers, laborers. Hard working and tough as nails, but not fighters. Seen combat, sure, of the worst possible kind. But they weren't trained soldiers, not as far as she knew. Sloane wondered briefly how many of them were of the sort that left behind checkered pasts. Secrets left back home, scrubbed from official records. And then there were the sympathizers. Last-minute converts she knew next to nothing about. She set that aside for another time. "This mission is too precious for us to lose more lives. Even they know that. But there will be consequences. The question is, are you willing to deal with them?"

Feet shuffled. Eyes shifted.

Nnebron lifted his chin. "Are you?" he asked, a challenge in his stare. Accusation flickering somewhere behind. Just like before. *You aren't one of us.*

Maybe that was true. Once. Sloane clasped her hands behind her back, met his gaze with unflinching resolve. "What do you want to hear, engineer? That nobody'll care that you and yours sparked a mutiny that killed dozens of Nexus citizens and crew?" The kid grimaced. "That you'll get off with a slap on the wrist and a wag of the finger? What about Reg's husband?"

That one earned a full-on flinch.

She drove it home. "You want to assume he'll just pat you on the back and say you tried your best?"

When he blinked rapidly, she took it as a win.

She shook her head once. "Won't happen. There *will* be consequences, and if you want to have any sort of life in this galaxy, you're going to have to grit your teeth and *deal with them*. Starting now."

"What about the krogan?" somebody asked.

Nnebron's eyes sparked with renewed fury. "Yeah, what about them?" he demanded. "They didn't even stop to negotiate, they just started killing!"

Sloane had no answer. It was true—they'd done just that. Ordered or not, it was a perfect example of just how much a "workforce" could stand in for an army. Especially a krogan workforce. To admit they'd been deliberately unleashed felt like a perfect way to get these people back on the mutiny train.

She knew exactly what Tann had hoped to accomplish by releasing Morda. The fact any of them were still alive was a fucking miracle. Surrender or no. But he'd failed at killing them off. Now he had to deal with them.

Another shake of her head drew Nnebron's heavy eyebrows together. "The krogan put down an insurgency," Sloane said. No salt. Just candor. It was all she had. "They won't be reprimanded. They'll be praised. Like it or not," she continued while the rest shuffled and muttered, "the mutiny failed."

He didn't answer right away. Others threw out thoughts, suggestions, but it didn't matter. Without Calix, they didn't have a singular goal. An end point for which to strive. They'd stormed the barricade, and got brutalized for their efforts.

She was all that stood between them and Tann's twisted sense of logic.

The decision was made. She read it in the slump of Nnebron's shoulders. The hang of his head.

"Fine," he muttered.

On that word, the others went still. Slowly,

painfully, Sloane watched them try to come to grips with the universe they hadn't expected. The one where they'd lost. No caring leadership. No fair shake. Just consequences and shame.

Sloane nodded. "Fine," she repeated.

It was all they had.

In the end, it was all she had, too.

CHAPTER THIRTY-THREE

"This is a nightmare," Addison declared. It was her opening salvo within seconds of striding through the office door. Caught mid-sentence with a small group of aides, Tann looked up from his informal briefing and frowned.

"I believe I specifically requested not to be distu—"

"I know what you requested." She glared at the aides and jerked her thumb at the door in silent demand. They didn't even look to Tann to confirm—an oversight he'd have to address sooner rather than later. They hurried out, avoiding her eyes entirely as they went.

Tann sat back in his chair—a salvaged thing from a conference room, for now—and studied the obviously ruffled director.

"What seems to be the problem?"

"Don't give me that bullshit," she replied flatly. Rather than sit, she grabbed the back of a chair and leaned over it. It was a typical Sloane move, but Foster Addison seemed to have adapted it well. He could appreciate a fine fury when it wasn't lobbing punches at him or aides. "We have wounded in the medi-labs, dead to tend to, a few hundred insurgents to deal with in rooms never meant to be jail cells," she continued, more loudly with each word, "and our fucking security director—one of *us*, Tann—is among them!"

Tann's eyelids tightened. He laced his fingers

delicately, elbows resting on the arms of the chair. "There is nothing to get worked up about," he said coolly. "The dead will wait until we can handle them properly, and the medics are doing all they can for those who still live."

He'd swear one of her flared nostrils twitched. *Fascinating.*

"That is an extremely cavalier view of our own dead," she said, a hiss somewhere under the tightness of her words.

He shrugged. He was right and he knew it.

"Of everything we need to address, the dead can wait," he pointed out. "They are hardly going to come knocking on anybody's door, unlike the very much alive men and women we must take care of immediately."

"What are we going to do about the insurgents?" she demanded.

"An easy solution."

"The hell—"

"Director, please." Tann held up one hand, as placating as he could. "At least hear me out." He gestured at the seat on which she leaned. "Sit."

Addison frowned. "I'm good," she said, "and I'm listening."

Well, it was better than Sloane, most days. The salarian allowed the woman her small rebellion, saying nothing more about it.

"Let's discuss this like rational creatures," he said instead. "What has been our primary consideration since waking?"

"Survival."

"True enough. And what else?"

Addison considered this. "The mission."

"Exactly." He smiled at her, pleased that despite

the horrors of the last few hours, her wits remained. Of course, he'd expect nothing less from the director of colonial affairs. In a strange way, it was nice to see her standing up to him, finally. Showing a little passion and intensity, a trait her file noted but he feared the Scourge had knocked out of her.

"The moment those people refused to go back into stasis, we started losing ground. With too many mouths to feed, too few resources, and the time and energy of balancing everything, they cost us more than we could afford."

"*Those people* are still part of the Nexus ecosystem."

"Exactly," Tann said. "Exactly."

"So?" Addison folded her arms on the back of the chair, leaning in a way that looked less menacing.

"So," he repeated, drawing the word out, "to handle the insurgents, all we must do is offer them two choices."

"Two?"

"For the sake of simplification."

"Fine." She raised her eyebrows. "Please don't say we're going to space them."

Tann chuckled. He couldn't help it. "Actually space them, as our erstwhile security director had suggested? That would be especially ironic, now that she is one of them, but no, of course not. However, it may be worth pulling a page from Sloane's own peculiar way of handling situations."

"What, like, give them a terrible choice and then a reasonable one?"

"Exactly," he said, nodding approvingly. "Option one, we offer them shuttles—"

"We can't afford—"

"Director, please. Allow me?"

Addison sighed. "Fine, go on."

"We offer them shuttles," he repeated firmly, "and supplies to last a reasonable—but not *unreasonably* reasonable—amount of time. Wish them well on their journey to find a world more to their liking."

"Exile."

"Precisely."

"In a corner of Andromeda plagued by a death nebula from hell, where all our scouts either failed to find anything useful or disappeared trying? Shit, Tann, just space them, it would be less cruel."

"Yes." Tann's smile just widened. "And they know it. Sloane does, at least. Which is why option two will sound so much more appealing."

"And that is?"

"Cryostasis. Which was all we were asking in the first place. Of course, a punishment hearing would await them at the other end of that, but at least it would occur under less pressing circumstances. Cooler heads, as it were."

She caught on immediately. "We can get everything settled, an infrastructure in place, and resources steadied." Her gaze sharpened on him. "In short, put this whole mess in a drawer for now and come back to it later."

"Crudely put, but apt enough," he acknowledged. "We have neither the time nor the capability to devote resources to a bunch of criminals who have proven they cannot be trusted to maintain order." He gestured in a vague way. "They can either leave, or sleep. Nobody in their right mind would leave, not with the Scourge out there. Not after what happened to the others."

"And after prison time, what, we reintegrate them?"

"Did you miss the part where they attempted to

seize control of the Nexus?" Tann asked. He tapped on the desk. "No, once they have had a taste of mutiny, there is no returning. Not," he added, "without more resources than we currently have."

She chewed on that for a bit. He could see the thoughts working past her eyes—she was probably weighing the pros and cons of his plan. *Good.* Tann knew she would reach the same conclusion, because it was the correct one. He'd thought this through to the last contingency. Nobody was suicidal enough to launch themselves into the Scourge-ridden void of exile.

Getting the populace back into stasis was the best option the Nexus had to offer. Had they listened the first time—no thanks to Sloane's polarizing arguments—none of this would have happened in the first place.

It was ironic, it was right, and it should have been done long ago.

Finally, Addison nodded. "All right. Let me contact Kesh and—"

"I'm sorry, but no. We don't need any additional krogan involvement," Tann interrupted smoothly. "They've done their jobs. Now it's time for *us*," he said, emphasizing the word, "to do *our* jobs, don't you agree?"

She didn't argue this time. Not, Tann knew, that there was anything with which she could argue. This was a sound plan. He liked to think even Sloane would have gotten behind it, even if she'd likely pepper it with more scare tactics. Threaten to throw them to the Scourge or something sufficiently brutal.

Tann relished the fact that this time, Sloane was on the opposite end of the decision-making process—where, he felt, she belonged.

And *he* wasn't a brute.

CHAPTER THIRTY-FOUR

"One wrong move or angry outburst," Sloane told the group as the guards approached the cell door, "and I'll feed you your teeth myself, am I clear?" Her voice was quiet enough, but there was nothing joking in her tone.

They all nodded grimly. Even Nnebron, whose dark skin looked sallow around the edges. Nerves, she figured. They all felt it—that crushing realization that nothing stood between them and whatever punishments the council would levy.

Nothing except her, Sloane reminded herself, and she would fight like hell to keep these people alive and striving for the future. Anything less would be worse than abandoning them. It'd be adding to the council's belief that these people had no cause to act, had no reason to fight.

Sloane knew they did.

If nothing else, Calix had let them fly too far off the handle. For them to make it through the next few moments, they'd need to shut up and let her do the talking.

They had all discussed it already. Sloane would go to bat for them, but only if they did what she said. Anything else was a waste, and Sloane didn't have the patience to arm-wrestle people into doing what was best.

The door opened. Talini stepped inside, flanked by two of Sloane's officers—her *ex*-officers. The prisoners shuffled in discomfort, unwilling to look at their captors, or at Sloane herself.

"Exit one at a time," Talini ordered. "Hands on your heads. No talking, not one step out of line."

Sloane nodded at the crew. "Go on."

Grim-faced, tight-lipped, they each stepped through the door, hands on their heads. The security team, assault rifles gripped tightly, lined them up two by two. When it was just Sloane left in the room, she paused just inside the door. Talini looked at her silently, a world of unspoken concern in her features.

"How bad?" Sloane asked quietly.

"I don't know," the asari replied, shaking her head. "They've been very close-mouthed."

"Probably afraid you're loyal to me," Sloane said with bitter humor. "I guess I get that much."

Talini's mouth twisted. "I'm sorry, Sloane."

"Yeah." She rolled her shoulders, then laced her hands behind her head, looking straight ahead. "So am I."

Sloane exited the cell. In the hall, the other prisoners stood in two long, erratic lines, and hardly anyone spoke. Well over a hundred rebels, she guessed, the fight in them tempered by the knowledge that next would be their punishment.

"March," Talini said, and took the lead.

That was the last anybody said during the long, tense walk to Operations. Along the way they were joined by more prisoners—ones whose wounds hadn't been severe enough to keep them under medical care. Upon arrival they were shown through the doors, and Sloane was utterly unsurprised to find the area ringed with her own security forces. At the center sat Addison and Tann.

Kesh stood a little farther away, engaged in a low,

tense conversation with Morda, Wratch, and another krogan—one paler than the rest, gray where the others showed more color in thick krogan hides. His was scarred, brutalized by wefts and ridges, and he very clearly looked older than the others. Ancient, given krogan lifespans.

Morda barely spared her a glance, save to acknowledge Sloane's presence with a grunt and lift of her broad head.

Kesh looked up, her gaze earnestly serious. Morda thumped her on the shoulder with a hard fist and said something low and rumbly. Sloane didn't know what passed between them, but Kesh's sigh rolled through Operations like a warning of distant thunder.

Tann slanted the krogan a startled, wary glance, which let Addison speak first.

"Thank you, you may all put your hands down."

Tann's mouth dropped open. "Didn't we—"

"We can at least afford them some respect," Addison said, an aside everyone heard.

"Respect? These people—"

"Cut the bullshit," Sloane interrupted, dropping her hands and pushing her way to the front of the group. "We all know what we're doing here."

Tann's gaze narrowed on her. "That's far enough."

"Yeah, like I'm going to risk getting shot just to wring your scrawny neck," Sloane responded, but she didn't push it. These two had unleashed Morda and her krogan warriors on Nexus civilians, and given the order for a sniper to take Calix out. One of Sloane's own officers had pulled the trigger. That stung, almost more than any of it.

"What's your stunningly brilliant plan this time, Tann?" she finished flatly.

Addison's glare sharpened. "How about you shut up for once and listen?"

"How about you look at the facts here?" Sloane shot back. She jerked a thumb at the group behind her. "You think they deserve everything *he* thinks they should get?"

Voices murmured behind her. Nnebron muttered, "It's his fault we were hungry anyway." Not quiet enough to go unheard. Not loud enough to grab center stage. But she saw the rims tighten on Tann's wide, round eyes.

"You're all here because you took part in a rebellion that put the future of the Nexus in jeopardy," he said firmly, clearing his throat in a bid for authority.

"Please," Nnebron snapped. Sloane shot him a fulminating glance over her shoulder, but he didn't look at her. His eyes pinned on Tann, hatred simmering under all that fury. "*You* made the choice to hide the truth from us! You were going to let us *starve* because of your indecision."

Anger and agreement rippled through Calix's crew. Sloane held out an arm, as if that single barrier would hold them back.

"As you can see, Tann," she said over the gathering noise, "you aren't exactly off the blame train either. *None* of us are," she added tersely, and if her stare pinned too long on Morda, the clan leader knew why. The Nakmor's toothy smile wasn't exactly friendly, but at the same time, Sloane didn't think the krogan held grudges. After all, they'd won.

Thanks to Sloane's surrender.

Tann bristled. "That is entirely unfair."

"She's right," Kesh said abruptly. She folded her arms over her chest, frowning at Tann and Addison where they stood by the central dash.

The salarian rounded on Kesh. "That is quite enough out of the third parties, if you please. The krogan have done more than enough, and—"

"They *killed* Calix," someone in the back shouted. Irida. *Shit*. Sloane hadn't considered the asari's habit of sticking a finger in metaphorically infected wounds. She reached back, grabbed the closest person—a turian with a blackened eye swollen shut and new scars appearing across her cheek—and jerked her close.

"Get her to shut up," she muttered.

The engineer nodded and pushed her way back through the prisoners.

"All sides in this," Kesh continued, utterly unfazed by the minor scuffle, "tasted death. Made mistakes. If we're holding them to theirs—and we should," she added sternly, "—then we should admit to our own."

Beside her, Morda snorted. It sounded almost as if she'd spoken. Said something like *"soft"*. Then the larger krogan added, clearly and sourly, "You have your own missteps to account for, Kesh."

Sloane raised an eyebrow as Kesh turned toward her clan leader. The pair started to square on one another, but then the ancient krogan, a male, stepped between them. "One target at a time," he said, every word rolling from his mouth like rusted railway spikes. A simple step, a casual comment, and both krogan paused.

Abruptly Addison raised a hand, frowning. "Sloane Kelly, as the security director, what do you have to say for yourself?" A hush fell over the rebels. Even Irida quit muttering.

Oh hell. Sloane didn't even need to think this one through. Ignoring the security—*her* security—she took three steps forward to stand squarely between the Operations council and Calix's crew. She wasn't stupid, though. She knew as well as anyone that several members of her team had a line on her as she moved. Would they shoot if she forced the situation?

They'd damn well better. She didn't train them to hesitate.

"I have a *lot* to say for myself," Sloane answered. She clasped her hands behind her back, settled her stance, and looked Tann dead in the eye. "Unlike some people here, I have a lot to say for others, as well."

"Now, you—"

"I speak for the people behind me," she continued, cutting him off. "They were hungry and terrified *already*, before learning their leadership had lied to them." Loud. Deliberate. "I speak for Calix Corvannis, who saw a bad situation getting worse, and did what he thought was best to bring hope to this failing station."

Tann's eyes narrowed to vicious slits.

"I speak for Jien Garson and the *real* leadership this station expected."

Addison's lips whitened.

Kesh's brief exhale mirrored the tension her words sent lancing through Operations.

"But most of all?" Sloane thumped herself on the chest. "I speak for the common fucking sense that said we *don't* lie to our people, we *don't* play the ruthless game of 'who can live and who can die,' just because we're too chickenshit to own up to our mistakes when we make them." She shot a glare not at Morda—who had earned her share of Sloane's fury—but at Tann. "We *don't*," she said, stressing every level word, "send our own *against* our own."

The salarian straightened, hand flattening on the panel beside him. "What would *you* have done?" he snapped. His voice trembled. "What could you, oh great security director, have done different that would have brought back order?"

Sloane shook her head. "I was already there, Tann. Talking it through, trying to bring Calix to... who knows. We'll never know, will we?" The finger she jabbed at Tann could have been a razor blade for the way he flinched. "*Somebody* sicced the krogan army on us before we'd gotten that far."

Addison shook her head. "They weren't supposed to go in shooting."

"Untrue," Morda cut in, a sudden surge of danger in her growled interruption. "We were told to go, and I quote the skinny sand-rat, 'whatever it takes to secure the mission.' Do not dare to cast the blame for this on us."

Tann sighed loudly. "Of course a krogan would assume that means 'kill everyone.'"

Kesh threw out a hand so fast that it collided with Morda's armored chest and sent an echoed *thud* through the rest of the crowd. Sloane tensed. While every security person reached quickly for his or her weapon, the clan leader let Kesh's hand stop her knee-jerk forward momentum.

"We *will* have words," she promised. "Rest assured on that." But Tann just shook his head in that way that suggested he had better things to think about. *Smug bastard.* The full force of his attention shifted once again to Sloane.

"Regardless, you broke all the regulations of your office," he said. "You *killed* members of the Nakmor clan—"

"They came at us guns blazing!"

"That you were there to witness it speaks volumes

concerning your own loyalties, does it not?"

Sloane's fists clenched. "I was *trying* to negotiate, you puffed-up fish-bait."

"Against orders," Tann reminded her, and Sloane didn't have a counter for that. She had gone against his request to wait. But then, had she waited, would the krogan have murdered them all?

Her lip curled. "I regret none of my choices."

"And you *will* be held accountable for them," he assured her. "Consequences."

Sloane didn't expect anything less. The real question was, what did he have planned?

"First, however," he continued, shifting his attention to the rest, "we handle Calix Corvannis's accomplices."

Nnebron's jaw tightened. "You can—"

"Shut it," Sloane snapped.

The man's fists clenched, but he jerked his chin and amended whatever he was going to say. "We fought. We lost. What now?"

Well, he wouldn't win any diplomatic awards, but Sloane appreciated the brevity.

Tann and Addison exchanged a glance.

Never good.

"You have two options," Addison said.

Tann nodded. "Option one grants you something of your initial desire. The urge to do things your way," he continued. Nnebron's dark eyebrows lifted.

One of Sloane's did the same.

"We are prepared to offer you a fleet of shuttles." Addison folded her arms, studying the crew. "Fueled and stocked with supplies. You can take your unsatisfied crew and set out on your own."

"Are you serious?" Nnebron asked.

"Yes."

"Exile?" Irida said, forcing her way to the front. Sloane bit back a sharp curse as more weapons primed, focused now on the asari.

"Fadeer, don't be so quick to get killed." She turned to Tann, eyeing him warily. "It's a non-offer."

Irida shot her a sneer. "Meaning what?"

Sloane could see it in Tann's face. The game he was playing. "Meaning he knows we won't agree," she said, never taking her eyes off his. "It makes him look generous and fair, all the while knowing we won't go."

"Why not?" Irida asked, still too consumed with anger to see it.

"Because it will be no small thing," Kesh interjected, "to be exiled to the wastes of the Scourge. You heard it already. The nearest planets are inhospitable."

That quieted things.

"There is a second option," Tann added.

"Spit it out." Sloane was losing patience. Fast. Tann, for all his smug superiority, seemed to know his time was limited. He clapped his long, knobbly hands and spoke with a bit of a flourish.

"Return to cryostasis," he said, "until the Nexus is repaired and fully operational."

"What?"

"No way..."

Some of the rebels stirred, forcing firearms to lift with renewed aim in the hands of the security team. Sloane shot Talini a hard look. The asari's reassuring nod was so slight, she wasn't sure it meant anything at all. But nobody opened fire, and that was something.

"There's no way," Nnebron said, his voice rising an octave. He took a step forward that put him within reach of Sloane. She braced, just in case. "You've been trying to get us to sleep since you first decided we were too much trouble!"

"How do we know you'd even let us out," Irida added hotly. "We're easier to handle cold, right?"

"He won't," a woman said. "They'll never let us out."

"No way."

Sloane let out a long, slow breath. It didn't do anything to ease the thunder of her heartbeat in her chest.

Tann studied them all. "So," he said slowly, drawing the word out. "You're choosing exile?"

"Hell, yes!" Nnebron shouted, fist in the air.

Sloane closed her eyes.

"It's better than a frozen eternity, forgotten in the Nexus's logs," Irida added.

"We can take care of ourselves!"

"At least we can trust *each other*."

Addison's gaze sought Sloane. She couldn't avoid the other woman's stare when she opened her eyes, and in that stare, she found apology. Worry.

Anger.

Yeah, well… Sloane only had to deal with one of those.

The salarian shrugged, and turned his attention to her. "Amazing," he said, sounding genuinely bemused. "You're going to lose everything for a bunch of exiles."

"Tann!" Addison's shocked cry of warning came just a hair too late.

Sloane's smile was as toothy as Morda's. Ignoring her team, ignoring Talini's sudden hiss of her name, Sloane closed the gap and let loose a right hook that she'd been *dying* to deliver for weeks.

Salarian bones were fine, but tough. The impact jarred her arm to the shoulder, but only because it caused Tann to spin with the momentum. The salarian squawked in a mixed-up bag of pain and alarm, and lost his breath when his ribs collided with the edge of the console.

Kesh's broad palm slapped her own face. It was almost as loud as the cheers and jeers from the rebels.

Miraculously, not one security member opened fire.

Addison swore fluently—an act that earned a bit of Sloane's grudging respect—and bent to keep Tann from falling over entirely.

"Fuck you," Sloane growled from between gritted teeth. She shook out her hand. "And fuck this station and *fuck* your classist bullshit. *You* get the grim little hell you've turned this into. *We* choose exile."

There was a moment of silence. A breath held.

Tann's fingers cradled his jaw, eyes wide and furious and—yes, Sloane noted, a little afraid. *Good.* But it was Addison who made the final call.

"Fine." She glared up at Sloane. "You'll have your shuttles. Spender will see to the supplies." The briefest pause. A beat. "I wish you the best. I really do."

"Yeah. Well…" Sloane turned, caught Talini's eye and tipped her head in thanks. "Bet we'll find somewhere to shack up long before you all get your heads out of *somebody's* cloaca."

Nobody had anything to say as she stormed for the door, the rebels—no, the *exiles*—following without hesitation. Enough was enough. She'd take her chances with the ones who believed in this new galaxy. Believed enough to shed blood for it.

When she met Calix in hell one day, she'd be damned if she'd tell him she'd abandoned them all.

Talini and her security flanked them on the way out.

CHAPTER THIRTY-FIVE

Things had barely settled when trouble sought Tann out in hydroponics. The salarian wanted someplace warm and isolated to sit and nurse his wounded pride without *something* requiring his attention. Watching the determined seeds, struggling to grow, was soothing in a way.

Four krogan, led by the clan leader, thundered their way into the chamber. Tann stood, unwilling to be caught sitting by the much taller grunt force. Morda's stare fixed on him with such intensity that Tann knew something was brewing. It didn't help when his omni-tool flashed, porting Spender's image.

"Sir, the Nakmor leader is searching for you."

"She found me," Tann said, keeping his gaze on the oncoming storm. "Send Kesh to hydroponics. Do it quickly."

The comm went dark. Tann's head tilted when the crusty-hided brutes came to a wedge standstill in front of him. He decided diplomacy wouldn't hurt.

Or at least it will hurt less than another punch.

"Clan leader. If you wish to discuss something we can convene in—"

Morda glared down at him. "Now that you have laid judgment on the exiles, are things proceeding to whatever passes for normal on this station?" Her thick, heavily muscled arms folded across her chest.

Blinking, he managed a surprised, "Why, yes.

Yes, they are. The shuttles are being outfitted as we speak, and the exiles and sympathizers are gathered for departure. We expect them to leave in a few hours."

"And Kesh?"

Tann hesitated. "And Kesh what?"

"Is she serving her function as expected of her experience?"

This seemed oddly formal for a krogan. Doubly so coming from Morda. Tann felt a queer sense of unbalance. Something wasn't right here.

"Yes," he said carefully. "She and her crew have been serving capably, save the recent betrayal by one of her teams."

Morda's eyes narrowed. "That's between you and her. I have no sway in the discipline of your officers. But," she added dourly, "Kesh should have not been so trusting."

"I agree," Tann said, surprised again. Still. Where was this going? "However, what is done is done, and—" He glanced beyond the formation of krogan as Kesh strode through the same doors. An ancient krogan followed behind her. Nakmor Drack, Tann recalled. Kesh's grandfather, woken with Morda. The old one seemed entirely unimpressed with the state of things, but as of yet had spoken little.

Relieved to have backup, he continued more confidently, "—and we are looking forward to putting this behind us. Forging the Nexus into a brilliant symbol of cross-species friendship and cooperation."

"Good to hear," Morda grunted. "Kesh." A greeting. "Stand witness as the Nakmor Clan's Nexus representative."

Kesh shot Tann a quizzical glance, but nodded once. "As you say."

Wherever this was leading, it was starting to churn acid in the back of Tann's throat. Before he could say anything more, however, Morda took a step forward and bent.

She *bent*. At the waist.

Like a bow.

Tann's eyes widened so far, the secondary eyelids strained.

"Then the Nakmor Clan has acted as agreed, and now officially accepts the offer of a seat on the leadership council of the Nexus."

For a long moment, not a sound filled the hydroponics chamber. Morda, perhaps uncomfortable in so uncharacteristic a position, looked up.

"What is she doing?" Tann demanded.

Kesh's frown deepened. "I don't know." She looked at Morda. "What *are* you doing?"

The clan leader growled, rolling her shoulders. Humility didn't sit well on her. "I'm claiming the council seat offered in return for our service in putting down the rebellion."

Kesh's eyes turned to Tann.

He blinked again. "The… what?"

Morda's frustration mounted, evident in her toothy sneer. "The council seat!" she repeated loudly, as if he were dimwitted. "Your sand-rat ambassador offered us—on your behalf—a seat at the official Nexus leadership council, in exchange for our loyalty and service and for ending the uprising."

"Spender." It was the only word Tann could form through the chaos of his thoughts. William Spender had gone to the krogan, and Tann had assumed the terms were clear. Taken aback, he shook his head and moved closer—hoping it wasn't *too* close. "This is impossible," he managed. "I did not authorize him to offer that. It was never even mentioned."

Behind her, one of the meaty-faced brutes slammed his fist into a hand.

"Wrong," he roared.

Kesh looked back and forth between them. "Spender said you'd get a seat at the council if you put down the rebellion?"

"Did I not just say that?" Morda growled. "There were witnesses." She jerked a gesture toward the krogan behind her. "And some humans, as well. I made certain of it."

Tann continued to shake his head. "I'm afraid there's been some sort of mistake," he said firmly. "No one species should be arbitrarily guaranteed a place on the council, much less by an unauthorized individual. It's ridiculous, and goes against everything the Initiative set out to achieve."

Morda became as still as a statue, glaring at him. Utterly intimidating. All the more reason the krogan would never occupy a council seat. Too much of a penchant for conflict. Despite the fear in his gut, Tann had to break the silence. He raised his hands slightly, appealing for calm.

"That offer should never have been made," he said. "I'm sorry, Morda, but there is nothing we can do. Spender will be reprimanded for this error." Error, his hydrodynamic head. "Now, if you'll excuse me, I'll speak with my aides and see if we can't draft plans for a more appropriate reward for your service."

Before the clan leader could reply Kesh stepped between them, and Tann made good his escape. Slipping through the door, he could still hear Morda shouting, her followers echoing her fury, and Kesh's loud efforts to get them to settle down. The sounds followed him all the way to the lift.

A fury unlike any Tann had harbored before roiled within him, aimed at William Spender and made all the more intense by his fear of Nakmor Morda. The intensity of the emotion left him barely able to think, his rationalizations spinning.

He paced in a tight square as the lift descended. Spender... how to deal with Spender. The man got results, but his methods were unscrupulous and, honestly, quite insane. Offering a council seat to Nakmor Morda, what the hell had he been thinking?

Tann supposed a little of the blame for that fell on him. He'd sent the human to handle that task, after all, and instructed him to win the clan's support at all costs. Tann should have chosen his words more carefully, but there was nothing to be done about it now.

He could not honor Spender's offer. That, above all else, was clear. The question was, how to avoid Morda's wrath at a faithless deal broken. Security certainly wasn't up to the task if the krogan became... uncooperative.

"Hmm," Tann muttered, still pacing his tight squares as the lift hummed along.

Morda was *entirely* unfit to sit on the Nexus leadership council. Kesh, perhaps, after an extensive trial period and a majority vote, but Morda? Impossible. She couldn't handle the troubles, the tough decisions, even—yes, even the boredom. Rulings upon rulings, the mind-numbing maze of regulations.

No, what the council needed were cool, calm heads and councilors ready—even eager—to handle the day-to-day minutiae of station control. It had nothing to do with prejudices. This was just common sense.

By the time he made it to Operations, he'd almost convinced himself.

᠁᠁᠁᠁᠁

Morda hadn't become clan leader by being *soft*. She pushed against Kesh with a roar, forcing the krogan to stumble back a few steps.

"You can't attack just anyone," Kesh shouted, nose to Morda's nose.

Morda's snarl drowned Kesh out. "I demand satisfaction," she growled. "I demand that they treat us with the respect we have earned here!"

"I understand, clan leader." Kesh glared at her, arms spread. Engineer though she was, that didn't make her any less of a krogan. Morda respected her enough to know that any conflict would end in blood and bruises, and both would lose teeth. And Kesh wouldn't back down. She turned her glare on them all.

"The human aide made a mistake," Kesh pressed. "He is an idiot—he overstepped!"

"An aide," Morda spat. "He presented himself as… what was it, chief of staff?"

Behind her, Kaje snorted his agreement.

"He played too hard," Kesh said flatly, "but that is not a reason to tear the salarian apart. Would you war with all of the Nexus now?"

Morda drew herself up. "I am Nakmor Morda, leader of the Nakmor krogan, I do *not* bend at the threat of war."

"But it will destroy us all nonetheless," Kesh replied. She fisted both hands, held them wide. "We are in a new galaxy, surrounded by a Scourge that tears our ships apart. Like it or not, we must work together. Will we drown this dream—this *masterpiece*—in the blood of our own?"

"They deserve blood," Wratch shouted.

Kaje huffed. "After all our work."

"We should just wreck the Nexus," Wratch added, nodding fiercely. "After all, *we* built it. Rebuilt it, too."

Drack reached out a casual, enormous fist and punched Wratch in the chest. "Watch your tongue, runt." With his craggy, scarred stare he forced the other to look away. "To destroy this station is a waste."

"Better to take it over," Kaje added, "and claim it for all krogan."

"*My* krogan," Morda corrected, her gaze pinned on Kesh. "Does that or does it not include you, Kesh?"

Kesh blew out a hard breath. "Clan leader, if we take over this station, we will enjoy the victory of a single battle, yes, but also doom our species to the same hatreds as those left in Tuchanka. We need allies. We need the other species."

Morda stared at her. The engineer had nerve. She'd always been smart—*too* smart—and Morda wasn't pleased about her divided loyalties. Kesh belonged to the Nakmor.

Even so. She wasn't wrong.

Morda stared down the shadowed corridor that had swallowed the salarian. He'd sent some lowly rat to speak for him, to promise things—no, to outright lie—in order to win her support. The clan had been used as a weapon. That's how they were seen and treated. They'd shed blood for this farce.

But to shed more…

Morda's head turned. The krogan that flanked her met her stare. Even Wratch, the dumb pyjak, had stopped grinning his bloodthirsty grin.

Kesh pressed her hands together. "Clan leader,"

she said, her voice low. "Are you willing to let this go?"

Morda looked back, teeth gritted. "*No*," she said. "It is one too many, more of the same when we had been promised a *new* life."

Kesh nodded solemnly. "Then I have an alternative, if you'll hear me."

Morda hesitated, but then the wizened Drack spoke, all the gravitas his thousand-some-odd years had earned him resonant in his voice. "Listen to her, Morda. She's more familiar with these two-faced councilors."

Fair enough an observation. She nodded once.

"Krogan are not new to tough environments," Kesh said. She gestured toward one of the large viewports—and the caustic, vaporous tendrils of death that tangled beyond. "We tamed Tuchanka and we will tame Andromeda, but perhaps..." She shrugged expansively. "Perhaps, clan leader, the krogan must find their own way, beholden to no one. Maybe," she said, drawing it out, "the krogan deserve to find what suits *us* on this so-called other side."

Clever, Morda mused. *Clever and bold*. She may not have always agreed with Kesh when it came to matters regarding the krogan and the Nexus together, but separately...

Kaje rumbled a thoughtful noise. "Sounds interesting."

Wratch's grin came right back. "Sounds fun." A beat. "Less turians." They both snorted.

Morda ignored them all. "And you?"

Kesh held her gaze. "I will stay."

Morda kept her gaze on Kesh. "Why?"

"I don't support what was done to the Nakmor clan," Kesh said flatly, "but I have put the blood of both hearts into this station. *Someone* from the clan must stay and ensure the krogan are not entirely without allies. I choose to be that someone."

Morda rolled her shoulder, even as she rolled the ideas in her mind. She wouldn't lie—the thought of taming this deadly galaxy, that so frightened the salarian and his council, pleased her perversely. And Kesh, for all her refusal to take sides, had a point.

Morda took a step forward, seizing Kesh by the collar. She jerked the krogan forward, but rather than the spike of foreheads that might have followed, Morda *stopped* and stared at her, eye to eye.

"You will not forget your allegiances, Nakmor Kesh."

"Never," Kesh replied.

Morda held that stare for another moment longer. Then, with a grunt, she pushed the engineer away, turning her back. On Kesh. On that prejudiced, stuffed-head salarian.

On the Nexus.

"Make the necessary preparations," she roared as she strode away, footsteps pounding like a batarian war beast on the hunt. "We leave when the exiles do."

Behind her, she heard Kesh exhale a hard, stilted breath. Morda decided to end the conversation there, to let Kesh stew no matter how cold it made her seem. Kesh knew what her suggestion had cost the krogan, and what it cost Morda to accept.

The Nakmor Clan would be victorious, with or without the Nexus.

It seemed that some things on this so-called "other side" would not be so different after all.

iiiiiiiiiiiiiiiiii

Generations to produce a dream.

Hours to shatter it.

Tann leaned against the solid metal frame of the viewport. The long hangar spread out before him, bustling with activity. Ranks of krogan filing into the small armada of shuttles being provided them, Nakmor Morda at the head of the group, arms folded in defiance and resolve, overseeing the exodus. Now and then she would lift her gaze toward him, and her stare would bore into him before he'd look away.

The krogan were matched in the distance by the exiles. Sloane Kelly and her band of criminals, and the sympathizers that had chosen a slow death in Scourge space than life on the station. Hard to think of them that way, but Tann couldn't get around the truth.

They were less organized, but just as fearless. Surrounded by security, their groups formed, and soon enough they began to head for their assigned ships, too. Bags slung over their shoulders, pushing lev-carts of bundled supplies. Two weeks of food and water, Spender had said.

Tann lowered his head.

Easy to see all this as misfits and malcontents taking their leave, and good riddance. Harder to admit the truth. The people out there represented a sizable number of the Nexus's population. His construction crew, and the better part of the life-support team, chief among them.

Tann might have won against the mutiny, but the cost was truly terrible. No getting around that.

A mess, he thought, and shook his head as Sloane boarded her shuttle without so much as a glance back toward him.

So many had given their knowledge, their time,

their bodies, and various forms of exertion to make the Nexus happen. So many had pinned their hopes and their dreams on this, their foray into Andromeda.

He looked up, farther than the docks and the folded hubs of sectors waiting for repair, saw the eerie colors of the Scourge, floating beyond. Waiting. Drifting. Somewhere in there drifted devastated planets.

The bones of dead civilizations, too, according to some of the scouts.

He folded his arms over his chest, trying not to notice that it felt more like trying to protect his aching insides, and less like casual posturing. A soft knock behind him alerted him to another guest, but it was too late to pull on his usual mask of logical calm now. At least it would be Addison. Something about her way of moving. She had a distinctive tread.

"Hey," she said.

Tann didn't look behind him. He didn't need to, and she didn't need him to. Foster Addison was a perceptive human. And he didn't know how to hide his uncertainties now.

"All that time," he said, not an answer or a greeting, but it was all he had. "All those plans and dreams and hopes. A masterpiece, and it was ours to create." In his peripheral, Addison climbed the steps to the large window and took up a similar position a short distance away.

"Jien Garson had a way of making it sound like an adventure."

"An adventure," Tann repeated sourly. "A grand new galaxy with innumerable fertile landscapes to provide us with all that we needed." He closed his eyes, let his head fall forward until his brow thumped against the solid pane. His breath fogged it on a shaky exhale. "I don't know, Foster. I don't know that I made the right choice."

"Which one?"

"Any," he admitted, his voice very small. "All I wanted was for the Nexus to blossom, to fulfill its role from the start. I swear to you, I made every choice with this in mind…"

Addison, in perhaps the most damning reaction, said nothing.

Tann laughed, and it felt weak, even to him. "Sacrifice," he said bitterly. "Jien Garson spoke of sacrifice. She said that by undertaking the journey, we made the greatest sacrifice we would ever make."

"Something tells me," Addison said quietly, "that was optimistic at best."

"At worst, a lie." Tann opened his eyes, lifted his head as a ship's exhaust flared at the docks. Wavering spots of color. He rested the tips of his spindly fingers on the pane. "Did she know, do you think?"

"Know what?"

"That what she said was probably a lie? Or, at best, marketing?"

Addison's chuckle was little more than a short exhale. "I think Jien Garson felt what we all felt." She straightened, made her way to Tann's side to watch the ships prepare. "Hope is a powerful thing, Tann. For a brilliant, ambitious woman like Jien, for governments willing to fund them. For normal everyday people." A faint trace of humor edged into her voice. "Even for logical salarians."

"Perhaps." Tann couldn't bring himself to smile, not even when Addison's hand curved over his shoulder. Sympathy or support, he didn't know. He'd take both, maybe just this once. "May I ask you something?"

The lines of her features were very pale in the cool light streaming in through the viewport. It made it easier to watch her eyebrows raise, her chin drop in a nod.

Tann didn't know why it felt as if his heart had taken up residence in his throat. Or why his insides felt so hollow. All he could say for certain was that for once, doubt consumed him. He looked away, back to the busy docks.

"Do you think she would have made the same decisions?" he asked. "Jien, I mean?"

Addison took a slow breath. "I don't know," she said on an equally as slow exhale. Tann nodded, expecting that.

"I think," she continued quietly, staring out over the cold and pitted station, "that Jien Garson would never have allowed us to get into this situation in the first place. I hate to admit it, Tann, but we—all of us—we were out of our element from the start. Hopelessly so."

Tann couldn't disagree.

"We did our best," she added. "Even Sloane. I believe that."

"Perhaps."

But they would never know. The mission had claimed the founder of this dream before she could leave any mark at all in the galaxy that was to be their masterpiece.

Sacrifice, she'd said. Tann had thought that he'd been prepared.

Perhaps Jien Garson had been wrong, after all.

"I think," he said again, much quieter than before, "the greatest sacrifice we will ever make wasn't coming here."

"No?"

He shook his head, but didn't give his thoughts any more words. He couldn't. To admit he'd probably been wrong was hard enough.

Addison squeezed his shoulder. In silence, she left him to the sparkling lights of the operations consoles, the busy preparation of the docks, and the lurid, hovering threat of the Scourge beyond.

To know, somehow just *know,* that none of this would have happened with Garson in charge... It stung. And it proved to him what he'd subconsciously been dreading since the moment he'd woken up to fire and fear.

See you on the other side.

The greatest sacrifice wasn't in leaving, he thought. It was *her.*

CHAPTER THIRTY-SIX

In the cold vacuum of space, ships drifted through the web of the Scourge, toward unfamiliar stars. Like a pack, they traveled together at first. Then, as if saying goodbye in silent harmony, they split into two groups.

Blue and white engine plumes flared as the exiles and the krogan truly set off, out of comms and sensor range now. They had officially departed the Nexus, perhaps never to return.

Kesh hadn't realized that she'd pressed a callused hand to the window until it fisted against the smooth pane. Knuckles aching, she watched the exhaust of her people's ships. Already, she missed the heavy, abrasive sound of krogan footfalls in the empty corridors. She missed the loud, often savage laughter.

The fights, the jeers.

The camaraderie.

Family. Above all things, krogan clans meant *family*—perhaps more so than any other of the species. After all, for so long, the krogan had only each other.

The other side, Kesh thought sadly, seemed to be one of loneliness. Of prejudices only half-forgotten, and conflicts given open ground to run free.

Had Garson expected that?

Kesh was not idealistic. She'd worked to the bone for this station, this Initiative, and she would die for it if she had to.

Or, as it turned out, leave her clan for the betterment of it.

With the resolution of conflicts, this mission had promised a new beginning, a chance at peace... yet the cost had been blood. Fire. Loss. What ground they'd all gained, what bonds they'd forged between disparate species as settlers of Andromeda, had begun to erode the moment Garson and her council died.

Maybe the krogan would find a new path on this side, maybe they'd survive—even *thrive*. Kesh believed in her clan leader. She believed in the genuine efforts of the Nexus leadership to guide and guide well. In the spirit of that hope, she remained behind as the seeds of the Initiative, watered by blood and toughened by flame, scattered through Andromeda.

What they became, what they chose to take from this, would be up to them. Kesh would remain here, with the station she'd helped engineer, waiting for the day they came back.

But first, there were so many to mourn. Survivors, bereaved and angry, to comfort. The work of a gentler touch than her own. Hers was to rebuild.

Preparing the Nexus, she thought as she turned away from the last glimmers of her only people, *for the eventuality of peace.*

|||||||||||||||||||||

Sloane watched the pitted lines of the scarred station as they drifted away. When—no, *if*—the Nexus finally came together, when all the damage was fixed and the elements were in place, it would be a remarkable place.

A place she would never get to see.

That was her one regret. Staring out into the eerie glow cast by the distant filaments of the Scourge,

Sloane studied the way the curves of the station distorted everything around it.

Nnebron, his back to the window, huddled over his knees in exhaustion. And fear, Sloane figured. There was a lot of that going around. They all knew what was out here—or rather, what wasn't. No planets. No food.

No hope.

Well, Garson be damned. This *was* the other side, and the idealistic woman's masterpiece turned out to be painted in blood. In old hatreds.

In the stupid pride of a few.

Sloane touched the viewing pane in silent goodbye. Then turned her back on the Nexus once and for all.

"Okay," she said briskly, clapping her hands hard. More than a few of the exiles jumped. Nnebron muttered something she didn't bother asking him to repeat. Ignoring him, she strode away from the last vestiges of hope and cranked her compass to where it should have been from the start—survival. Hers, and the people who had been relying on her since the moment they'd woken.

She should have done that, just that, from the start.

"Maybe we don't have a station," she said, her tone firm. Her gaze level as she studied her new crew. "Maybe we don't have a mission, but what we *do* have," she continued as she made her way across the floor, "is one another. And the strength and determination to survive this."

Irida, leaning against a panel, shrugged around her folded arms. "It's a death trap out there. What do you think we can do?"

"Starve to death," Nnebron said grimly.

"Come on—"

He cut the red-haired woman off, shrugged out

from under her reassuring hand. "It's true, Andria. Two weeks of rations, and we're expected to find somewhere when seasoned scouts didn't?" He laughed bitterly. "May as well just shoot ourselves now."

The fear in the ship ramped up a notch.

Sloane eyed Irida. Then Nnebron. Even the one called Andria curled up on herself. She saw only gloom there.

So it was going to be like that, was it? She weighed her options. A good security director would crouch down. Sit eye to eye with her subordinates and hear them out. Reassure them.

Play the game.

Well. Fuck that. The game had landed them all here.

Sloane went for Irida. The asari raised her chin, but she wasn't expecting the hand that went for her throat. Sloane spun, Irida's collar in one fist, and slammed the asari hard enough into the ship wall that crewmates down the length of it yelped when it vibrated.

"What the hell are you—!"

"Shut up," Sloane said tightly, shoving her face close enough to Irida's that she could see herself in the asari's irises. "You think that because everyone signed up for the Initiative all formal-like, that you're safe to say whatever you want. *Do* whatever you want."

Irida grabbed at her wrist, and Sloane responded by shoving her harder against the wall. Fist in her throat.

Nnebron leapt to his feet. "Hey—!"

"Be quiet," Sloane snapped, turning her head to glare at him. At all of them. "This isn't the Nexus anymore, and your inability to control your shit is why every one of you is out here."

Why Calix is dead.

Irida managed bared teeth and a strained, "What are you going to do? Space us?"

"If I have to."

Her even answer had Irida scoffing at first. And then, as Sloane's fingers tightened, she choked on her own realization—Sloane Kelly meant every fucking word.

"We get one shot at this," Sloane said flatly. *Screw reassurance.* "One life. We mess this up, we die. Now I don't know about the rest of you, but I *will* survive. I will make this work." Sloane's grip eased. "With," she finished in the same level tone, "or without you."

Irida sucked in air, her purple skin pale around the edges. She rubbed at the back of her head, eyeing Sloane cautiously.

"Goddess, fine," she rasped.

It was as good a concession as she was going to get.

Nnebron backed up a step when Sloane turned the full force of her impatience on him. Throwing up both hands, he spoke quickly.

"Relax. I'm with you."

"So am I," Andria said quietly. She closed her eyes, head hanging. "For Na'to, and Reg. For, hell, I don't know. Because I want to live."

It was a good enough reason for Sloane. As she turned, studying each of her newfound crew and gaining nods, shrugs, or even an occasional smile and thumbs-up, she nodded back.

"Good." Then, louder, "*Good.* They think we'll die out here? Let them." She left Irida still leaning against the wall, aware of the woman's venomous glare boring into the back of her head. Ignored it. If Irida ever made her move, she'd become an example. "This is a new life, now. New rules. We're not the idealistic adventurers they said we were." Not any more. Maybe, she thought as she made for the cockpit, they never were.

"Exiles, get some rest."

"What's the plan, boss?"

She paused, bracing a hand on the wall, and looked back over her shoulder. Nnebron gestured at the others—tired, scared. Some still wounded.

All of them hungry.

"Treat the injured," she said. "Catalogue the supplies. I'll meet with you in an hour to discuss logistics."

"Yes, ma'am."

Sloane wanted to laugh. Instead, as she turned back to the cockpit, she said casually, "Oh, and anyone caught stealing supplies is going to wish they'd died on the Nexus."

In her peripheral, she saw mostly nods. Agreement. No more idealists. *Good.*

Making her way to the cockpit seating, she slid in beside the only exile with piloting experience. A salarian, in fact. He gave her a nod, and said nothing.

A thousand times better than Tann already.

"All right," she said as she leaned back into the seat. The open vastness of space, the alien stars and eerily pretty ribbons of the Scourge stretched out before the ship. New galaxy. New rules.

New lives. Their own.

She watched the vaporous glimmer and smiled, wide and toothy.

"Let's see about taming this other side."

ACKNOWLEDGMENTS

We'd like to thank Nick Landau, Vivian Cheung, Laura Price, Becky Peacock, Julia Lloyd, Sara Marchington, Steve Saffel, and everyone on the team at Titan Books for all their hard work in bringing this book to life. Huge thanks also to the Mass Effect gang at Bioware, especially Chris Bain, Joanna Berry, John Dombrow, Ben Gelinas, Amanda Klesko, Mac Walters, and Courtney Woods. Their help and collaboration was extremely welcome. Thanks to our literary agents Sara Megibow and Lisa Rodgers for their constant support. Lastly, thanks to all the readers, and the Mass Effect player community!

||||||||||||||||||

Jason wishes to thank, in no particular order: Nancy Hough, Jerry Kalajian, Wayne Alexander, Jake "Odd Job" Gillen, Teddy Lindsey, Felicia Day, the Seattle Mass Effect Cosplay group, and my co-author Kace who rocked this party.

||||||||||||||||||

K. C. sends thanks to Ali O'Brien, Stephen Blackmoore, Jason M. Hough (shhh, don't tell him), and to Jordan Neuhauser, the best filthy assistant there is. To everyone who made *Mass Effect* a living, breathing entity: you rock.

Jason M. Hough (pronounced 'Huff') is the *New York Times* bestselling author of the *The Darwin Elevator* and the near-future spy thriller *Zero World*. In a former life he was a 3D artist, animator, and game designer (*Metal Fatigue, Aliens vs. Predator: Extinction*, and many others). He has worked in the fields of high-performance cluster computing and machine learning, and is a patent-awarded inventor. Find him online at **jasonhough.com**.

||||||||||||||||||

K. C. Alexander is the author of *Necrotech*—a transhumanist sci-fi called "a speed freak rush" by *New York Times* bestseller Richard Kadrey and "a violent thrillride" by award-nominated Stephen Blackmoore. She writes sci-fi, epic fantasy, and speculative fiction of all kinds, including short stories and personal essays about mental health and equality. Specialties include voice-driven prose and imperfect characters. Also, profanity. More at **kcalexander.com**.